Capers Dickson

John Ashton

A story of the war between the states

Capers Dickson

John Ashton
A story of the war between the states

ISBN/EAN: 9783744748445

Printed in Europe, USA, Canada, Australia, Japan

Cover: Foto ©Andreas Hilbeck / pixelio.de

More available books at **www.hansebooks.com**

JOHN ASHTON:

A STORY

OF

THE WAR BETWEEN THE STATES.

BY

CAPERS DICKSON,

An **Ex-Member** *of Cobb's Legion, Georgia Volunteers.*

ATLANTA, GA.:
THE FOOTE & DAVIES COMPANY,
Printers and Binders.
1896.

To

THE HEROES WHO WORE THE GRAY

AND BRAVELY BORE THE STARRY CROSS INTO FIERCE

BATTLE'S FOCAL FIRES, ACHIEVING SIGNAL VICTORIES OVER A WORLD IN

ARMS UNTIL CRUSHED BY OVERWHELMING NUMBERS,

THIS VOLUME IS AFFECTIONATELY DEDICATED

BY

THE AUTHOR.

PREFACE.

The fictional framework of the following story will be found to contain accurate pictures of some of the military incidents of The War Between The States. Some of those incidents came under the author's personal observation and a knowledge of the others was obtained from the official records of the Union and Confederate armies, as published by authority of Congress, and from other historical sources. Principally for the purpose of portraying these incidents in a manner that will render their perusal more interesting to the general reader than if a recital of them were embodied in an unvarnished and isolated historical statement, this volume has been written.

CAPERS DICKSON.

Oxford, Ga., 1896.

JOHN ASHTON.

CHAPTER I.

"Well, Ruth, what do you think of him?" asked Bertha Gray of her cousin, Ruth Middleton.

"I hardly know how to answer your question," said the latter. "He is handsome, as one can see at a glance, and has a *distingue* look and bearing that are quite impressive. His face indicates intellectuality and force of character but has an expression of sadness and reserve which suggests the idea that he has experienced great sorrow; and, either from choice or lack of friendly sympathy, borne his grief in silence, and thus acquired a habit of seclusion that tends to make him isolate himself from his fellows."

"If your ideas concerning him are correct," said Bertha, "he is not likely to prove a very attractive person, and, notwithstanding his handsome appearance and evident intellectuality, will be no acquisition to society."

"I cannot agree with you in the conclusion you have reached," said Ruth, "for I am confident that by nature and cultivation he is well fitted both to adorn and benefit society, if he can be drawn out of himself and induced to mingle with his fellow-creatures and participate in the social affairs of life in which most young men find recreation and pleasure."

"You may be right," said Bertha, "and we can only wait and see."

The subject of the foregoing conversation was John Ashton, a young lawyer who had recently located in B——, a small town in Middle Georgia. He was a native of Virginia and had graduated with distinction at the University of that State in the law class of 1860. Shortly after he returned home from college, his father, Colonel Aubrey Ashton, met a tragic death by being thrown from his horse. His mother was in very feeble health, and the shock which she experienced in consequence of her husband's death was so great that she never recovered from its effect and died about a week thereafter. John, being an only child, was thus left alone in the world with neither brother nor sister to sympathize with and comfort him in his sad bereavement. His grief was agonizing and grew in intensity as the days passed by, as everything about his once happy home vividly reminded him of his lost loved ones and kept constantly before his mind the heartrending misfortune that had befallen him. Having no near relatives to whom he could go for sympathy and consolation, he had to bear the burden of his grief alone, and at last determined to get away from the scenes and surroundings which daily reminded him of his bereavement and made it more difficult to endure. In consequence of this determination, he sold the family residence, together with its furniture, and went to B——, where he had begun the practice of his profession a short time before Ruth Middleton and Bertha Gray had the conversation with which this story opens. The occasion of this conversation was a casual sight which they had of Ashton at the village church on the preceding day. The interest which they had manifested in him was to some extent that which they would have felt in any newcomer who happened to be a handsome and eligible young man, and it had been enhanced by reason of the story of sadness and suffering that was so plainly written on his face.

The parties to this conversation resided in B——, and, as their parents were dead, had with them, as a companion and housekeeper, Mrs. Martha Foster, a distant relative of theirs. They were two of the most charming and interesting young ladies in the place. Bertha Gray was a bright and joyous creature whose presence brought sunshine and gladness to those with whom she came in contact. Ruth Middleton was not so lively and demonstrative as her cousin, but was equally as agreeable in her manners. She was quite intellectual, had great strength of character, an equable disposition and a calm dignity of manner that was suggestive of reserved force, and yet possessed a warm heart, and was quite animated when the occasion called for vivacity or joyousness. Indeed, there was nothing in her calm and dignified mien indicative of coldness or indifference, as it was so easy and natural, and her bearing was so frank and affable, that one was at once impressed with the idea that it was merely the accompaniment of a noble disposition. She was an excellent judge of human nature and her estimates of character were rarely incorrect. Her remarks concerning John Ashton indicated that she had formed a correct idea of his character merely from having seen him for a few moments.

The days passed by, and outside of the members of the bar and a few young men who had called on him, Ashton formed no acquaintances except such as he met in the course of his business. He felt an aversion for the company of comparative strangers and, of course, would not go into society with his great grief so fresh in his memory and bearing so heavily upon his heart. He devoted himself to the study and practice of his profession and, in the course of a few months, secured such a clientage as indicated that he had won the confidence of the people among whom he had cast his lot and was in a fair way of acquiring both wealth and fame. He persistently refused to enter society, although often invited by his male acquaintances to join them in their social gatherings. Hence months passed by without his meeting Ruth Middleton and Bertha Gray, and he might not have met them at all had not an accident brought about an acquaintance between them.

Leading a sedentary life it was necessary that he should have some exercise, and he was accustomed to taking a ride of several miles nearly every afternoon.

One afternoon he had taken a ride into the country and was returning by way of an unfrequented road that intersected the main thoroughfare leading to B——. When within a short distance of this thoroughfare he heard the sound of a horse's feet upon it, and, glancing in the direction of B——, saw a horse running at full speed toward the place where the two roads met, and on the horse a lady who appeared to have lost all control of the animal and was merely endeavoring to keep her seat in the saddle. Realizing the great danger that threatened the lady, Ashton at once put spurs to his horse and rode forward at rapid speed with a view to intercepting the runaway horse. He was superbly mounted and felt confident of succeeding in his purpose; but the other horse was nearer than his own to the intersection of the roads when the race began, and before he could be intercepted, had reached the place and dashed by with the speed of the wind. Ashton's only hope now was to overtake the animal by sheer rapidity of speed on the part of his own horse, and without a moment's hesitation he began the race. The runaway horse had about thirty yards the start of Ashton's horse and for a few moments gained on the latter. Ashton was not discouraged by this and had really anticipated it, as he knew that it would take a little time to get his own horse up to his full speed. Giving his horse free rein and touching him sharply with the spur, Ashton urged him on to greater speed. The animal readily responded to his rider's wishes and, rapidly increasing his gait, was soon perceptibly gaining on the other horse.

About three-quarters of a mile ahead, the road crossed a stream which ordinarily was quite shallow, but after every heavy rain became for a time impassable. In consequence of this fact, a bridge had been built over the stream a short distance above the ford, and the road leading to and across this bridge left the main road about three hundred yards from the stream. Only a few days before, this bridge had been washed away by reason of an extraordinary rise in the waters of the stream, and it had not yet been replaced. The result of this was that at this time there was a wide and deep chasm where the bridge had been, and Ashton knew that if the runaway horse should happen to take the road leading to this chasm and attempt to leap across the same, certain death awaited its rider. Fearing that this might be done, he redoubled his efforts to overtake the animal by urging on his own horse to yet greater speed. Believing that the former had reached his full speed, as he was running in consequence of fright, and perceiving that his own horse was gradually gaining on him, Ashton naturally concluded that his animal was the faster of the two and felt confident of overtaking and rescuing the lady if her horse should keep in the main road. But, alas! to his disappointment and horror, the lady's horse, on reaching the road leading to where the bridge had been, turned into it and dashed ahead without slackening his speed. For a moment Ashton's mind was almost paralyzed with horror at the thought of the **danger that** threatened **the** lady; but recovering from this temporary shock, he struck his spurs deeply into his horse's sides and with quick and vehement cries urged him on. At this time he was about forty yards behind the fleeing animal, and his own horse, smarting under the pain of the cruel spurs and seeming **to understand** from the tones of his master's voice that his utmost speed was required of him, sprang forward with long, panther-like leaps that rapidly lessened the space between him and the frightened fugitive. Faster and faster he sped, gaining each moment on the fleeing animal, and soon he had over-taken him and the two horses were running side by side.

Glancing ahead, Ashton saw that they were within fifty **yards of** the stream, and realized the impossibility of check-ing the lady's horse in that distance by any degree of force that he could exert by means of her bridle reins. **He** instantly conceived the idea of lifting the lady from her horse, and quickly but **calmly said**:

"Loosen your foot from the stirrup, **free your skirt from** the horn of your saddle, and be prepared to drop your **reins** and lean toward me when I give the word."

The lady having promptly done as he directed, Ashton bent over toward her **and** said, "Now!" and, as she leaned toward him, he clasped her form with his right arm and lifted her out of the saddle. Instinctively she clasped his **horse's** mane with her right hand and his saddle-bow with her left, and thus greatly lessened the weight that had **at first** been thrown upon him and relieved the strain **which he had** thereby experienced. Pulling hard upon the reins and speaking gently to his horse, Ashton succeeded in stopping the animal within a few paces of the chasm where the bridge had been, and safely lowered the lady to the ground. Quickly dismounting, he supported her to a spot near the roadside where there was an accumulation of fallen leaves, and there she sank down, completely exhausted from the effects of the terrible ordeal through which she had passed. She had not yet spoken to Ashton, but as soon as she had sufficiently recovered from her fright and state of exhaustion to speak, she said:

"I believe that it is to Mr. Ashton that I am indebted for the timely and inestimable service that has been rendered me and, as this service has evidently saved my life, I cannot find words to express my deep gratitude for the same, and can only say that with all my heart I thank you for what you have done."

"Now, that it is over," said Ashton, "I will not underestimate the danger which threatened you or the service that I was enabled to render you; but you must not waste your breath in thanks. The intense gratification which I experience in having rescued you from danger is more than sufficient compensation for what I have done. Had I failed in my effort to rescue you, the failure would have almost crazed me, although you are to me an entire stranger. And this reminds me to answer your interrogative supposition as to who I am, by stating that it is correct, and that my name is John Ashton. You, I know, are Miss Middleton of B——. Now, that our informal introduction is over, if you will excuse my absence for a few moments I will ascertain what has become of your horse. I fear that he is seriously and perhaps fatally injured; for when I last saw him he was disappearing in the chasm ahead of us."

Ashton then proceeded to the edge of the chasm and, on looking over, saw, at its bottom and near the middle of the stream, the lifeless body of Miss Middleton's horse. He was lying in such a position as indicated that his neck had been broken. Evidently he had endeavored to stop on reaching the edge of the chasm, and, being unable to do so, the momentum given to his body by the speed at which he was running had caused him to fall instead of leaping into the chasm, and he had thus lost his equilibrium and fallen on his head, thereby meeting instant death.

Ashton immediately returned to Miss Middleton and, as she appeared to have regained her composure, informed her that her horse was dead.

For a moment her face was pale with horror at the thought of the fate that she had so narrowly escaped; but almost instantly the color returned to her cheeks and her countenance was radiant with the joy that filled her heart in consequence of the fact that she had indeed escaped such a terrible fate. Ashton now began to wonder how he would manage to get Miss Middleton home, as he knew that it would be very inconvenient and fatiguing for her to ride on his saddle, and her own was lying in the middle of the stream and unfit for use even if it were accessible.

About this time two negro boys, accompanied by several dogs and evidently engaged in a rabbit hunt, came into the road a short distance from where Ashton was standing. Calling them to him, Ashton soon induced one of the negroes to temporarily suspend his contemplated chase of "the cotton-tails" for a less exciting and pleasant but more profitable employment, and bargained with him to go to B——, for a carriage. Mounting Ashton's horse the negro started on his errand in a sharp trot and was soon out of sigth.

Ashton then turned to Miss Middleton and asked her to tell him how her horse came to run away with her.

She informed him that she and her cousin, Miss Bertha Gray, were riding out from B——, and when they were within about three-quarters of a mile of where he first saw her, a ferocious dog ran out from a farmhouse near the road, and began to bark furiously at their horses. Her horse was greatly startled by the noise and at once started to run. Seeing this, the dog ran after him and kept up a loud barking at his heels. This thoroughly frightened the horse and, clamping the bit with his teeth, he plunged forward at full speed and soon became entirely unmanageable. Discovering that she could not control her horse, she had merely endeavored to keep her seat in the saddle. Not knowing that the bridge had been washed away, she had made no effort to keep her horse in the main road at the time that he turned into the other, and hence had not realized the full danger that threatened her until just before Ashton lifted her from the saddle, when she caught a glimpse of the chasm ahead of them.

"And now," she concluded, "let me again thank you for the timely service which you rendered me, and assure you of my lasting gratitude for the same. Permit me also, to express my admiration for the wonderful forethought, coolness, and dexterity manifested by you in your method

of rescuing me. **The calm tone of your voice,** when telling
me **what to do, was so reassuring that my** fears were
greatly relieved and my self-possession to some extent
restored, and I did not hesitate a moment in following your
directions. Indeed, I was **so** impressed by your **calmness**
that I would have done anything that you might have
directed."

"**Yes,**" said Ashton, "I noticed the promptness **with**
which you followed my directions and was thereby satisfied
that I would succeed in safely lifting you from your horse.
Had you hesitated or become nervously agitated, it **is**
probable that some accident would have happened and
that both of us would have fallen to the ground. Hence
you see that your promptness and calmness in following
my instructions contributed greatly to your rescue, and
indeed **were essential to the success of my effort** in your
behalf. Allow me to say that you are an exceedingly skillful rider. Although I came from Virginia where, one might
say, the ladies are almost reared in the saddle, **yet I have**
never seen a lady who excelled you in riding."

At this moment a lady was seen approaching **them on**
horseback, and Miss Middleton said:

"That is my cousin, Bertha Gray, who was with me **when**
my horse became frightened, and she is doubtless surprised
to see me alive."

On reaching them, Bertha quickly sprang from her horse,
without waiting to receive the assistance which Ashton
started to offer, and rushing forward clasped her cousin in
an affectionate and convulsive embrace, and, in broken sen-
tences interspersed with tears and laughter, said:

"Oh, Ruth, it was terrible! I was almost paralyzed with
horror—and you really are unhurt? How glad and happy I
am! I expected to find you dead, and can now see again **the**
horrible vision that arose in my mind of your bruised and
bleeding form lying **on the roadside.** How inexpressibly
thankful I am that it was only a vision, **and that** my dear
cousin is unharmed and with me again."

All this time Bertha had taken no **notice** of **Ashton, and**
would have continued yet longer to ignore his presence in
her engrossing manifestations **of joy** at her cousin's escape

from danger, but the latter, gently unclasping Bertha's
arms from her neck, said:

"Your manifestations of joy at my escape are very sweet
and dear to me, Bertha, but I must ask you to suspend
them for at least a little while in order that I may make
you acquainted with the gentleman to whom I am indebted
for my rescue from danger."

She then introduced Ashton to Bertha, who, both from lively
gratitude and warm-hearted impulsiveness, was exceedingly
profuse in her thanks to him for the service that he had
rendered Ruth. After thus overwhelming him with thanks
for what he had done, she insisted that he should tell her
all about the rescue and how he had effected it.

Ashton complied with her request, and in a simple and
modest manner gave an account of the occurrence.

While he was talking to Bertha, Ruth had, for the first
time, an opportunity for closely observing him without
attracting his attention, and this was the result of her
observation: She saw that his form was slightly above
medium height, perfectly erect and well-proportioned, that
his eyes were dark grey, his hair almost black, his forehead
broad and massive, his nose straight and small and his
mouth rather broad and firmly set, indicating firmness
and strength of character. Although his face was animated and bright while he was talking to Bertha, yet Ruth
could still detect strong traces of the sadness that marked
it when first she saw him; and her heart was touched with
sympathy for him in the misfortune which she inferred had
befallen him and the grief that he was still enduring in consequence of it.

Shortly after Ashton had finished telling Bertha of Ruth's
adventure, the carriage for which he had sent arrived.

Having placed Ruth in the carriage and assisted Bertha
to mount her horse Ashton mounted his own horse and the
party returned to B——.

On their arrival at the home of the young ladies, Ruth
and Bertha renewed their thanks to Ashton and gave him
a cordial invitation to visit them.

He stated that he would be pleased to do so, and bade
them adieu.

CHAPTER II.

When Ruth and Bertha retired to their room that night and had an opportunity for confidential conversation, Bertha said:

"Ruth, what do you think of him now? I guess that you have by this time learned how to answer my question?"

"Yes, to some extent I have," replied Ruth, "and I am fully confirmed in the opinion expressed in our former conversation. Moreover, I am satisfied that he possesses not only the intellectuality and force of character which I ascribed to him, but also a warmth of heart and nobility of soul that constitute him one of nature's noblemen."

"Whether he be that or not," said Bertha, "he is certainly a fortunate man to have won such praise from the lips of my fastidious and undemonstrative cousin. And she is also fortunate to have had such a man as her rescuer from danger, and the hero of to-day's adventure. How romantic it is! Of course, he will feel that he has met his fate, fall desperately in love with you, become your devoted slave, seek and win your love, and then, as the story-books express it, you and he will be married and live happily ever after."

Ruth slightly blushed in consequence of the picture which Bertha had thus glibly drawn, but promptly negatived the idea of its realization by saying:

"You are decidedly premature in your predictions, and show that you have but little knowledge of Mr. Ashton's character. He is not a person to yield to the supposed influences of what you consider a romantic adventure, or to fall desperately in love with any woman; and, moreover, his heart is so fully preoccupied by the sorrow which his face portrays that there is in it no place for the gladsome emotion of love. He will, of course, visit us in compliance with the invitation we gave him, and it is probable that his visits may be occasionally repeated and he and I may become warm friends; but, unless he experiences a great change, it will be a long time before he thinks of loving any woman."

"I can't believe that you are correct in your views," said Bertha, "and as to your denial of my supposition that he will fall in love with you, I am sure that it is simply the result of your well-known modesty. Nobody can help loving you when they know you; and for a man not to love you after saving your life, as Mr. Ashton has done, would be contrary to nature and simply preposterous."

"Thanks, dear cousin," said Ruth, "for your very flattering opinion of me; but I feel that it is merely the outgrowth of your great affection for me, and hence it does not shake my confidence in the views which I have expressed. Your surmises might be correct in regard to an ordinary man under ordinary circumstances; but, as I have intimated, Mr. Ashton is no ordinary man, and his heart and life are at present under the domination of an absorbing emotion that will probably for a long time control both his conduct and his feelings. For his sake, I earnestly hope that the occasional visits which, as a matter of courtesy, he may now make us will awaken him to a sense of the isolation that he has practiced and tend to make him take some interest in society, and thereby counteract the depressing effects of the burden of sorrow that he is evidently bearing in secret and alone."

"I heartily join you in this hope," said Bertha, "for I am sure that he fully deserves all the happiness that could come to a true and noble man under the most favorable circumstances. I shall certainly do all I can to contribute to his pleasure, and will be greatly gratified if I succeed in bringing the least bit of sunshine into his life."

At the time that this conversation was in progress, the subject of it was sitting in his room apparently engaged in reflection on some subject of absorbing interest. A short time before he had been reading on a branch of law involved in an important case in which he had recently been retained as counsel; but the book had been laid aside and its contents for the time dismissed from his mind. The subject of his meditations was one of personal interest, for he was thinking of the day's adventure, the unexpected and radical change that it had effected in his relations to at least two of the ladies of B——, and of how its results would probably lead to a complete revolution in his social life; for he realized that, in view of what had occurred, common courtesy required that he should occasionally visit Misses Middleton and Gray, and that if he visited them he would be expected to visit other ladies in the place, and perhaps would eventually be drawn into society. The thought was by no means pleasant to him, as he disliked the idea of relinquishing the life of seclusion which he had been leading, and felt that he could not endure to come in contact with the gay and thoughtless persons whom he would meet in society, when his heart was filled with a sorrow that knew no abatement. In contrast with the unpleasant feeling awakened by this train of thought, was a desire to become better acquainted with Miss Middleton, for he had been impressed with the idea that she was an exceptional woman as to her moral attributes and mental attainments, and felt that he would find her interesting and companionable. He felt also that her nature was such that she could and would sympathize with him in his sorrow should their acquaintance become such as to warrant him in revealing it to her. As a final result of his meditations, he reached the conclusion that the occurrence of the afternoon was perhaps providential, and intended to break up the depressing monotony of his sad and secluded life and open the way to such experiences as would, eventually, counteract the effects of his then absorbing sorrow; and he determined to let matters take their natural course and accept whatever consequences might result therefrom.

In accordance with this determination he called on Ruth and Bertha the next evening. He met with a cordial reception and both of the girls showed by their manner that they were really glad to see him, and at once made him feel perfectly at ease and as if he were with friends instead of comparative strangers.

The evening was pleasantly spent in conversation on topics of general interest, interspersed with vocal and instrumental music by Ruth and Bertha, who were excellent musicians. Ruth had an exceedingly sweet voice which had been highly cultivated, and sang with marked expression, throwing her whole soul into every song that breathed of

tender sentiment. Ashton was very fond of vocal music
and Ruth's singing gave him intense pleasure. She displayed great tact and consideration in the selection of the
songs that she sang; for while she avoided singing anything light and gay that would have been entirely out of
harmony with the settled sadness of his feelings, she also
refrained from singing songs that told of suffering and sorrow, which would naturally have reminded Ashton of his
own grief, and sang only such simple lyrics as told of quiet
joys and sweet contentment and seemed to be the natural
outgushings of hearts at peace with all the world.

On taking leave of the ladies, Ashton expressed his appreciation of the pleasure that his visit had given him, and
heartily accepted the invitation which they gave him to
visit them often.

While returning to his room, and after arriving there, he
allowed his mind to dwell on the incidents of the evening,
the marked friendliness of Ruth and Bertha, and the almost
homelike atmosphere which seemed to surround him when
with them, and realized that there had been effected a complete change, not only in his social relations but also in his
feelings. He almost reproached himself for allowing
this change in his feelings to occur, for he had cherished
his sorrow for the death of his parents so long and absorbingly that it seemed like disloyalty to their memory to let it
be even temporarily displaced by any pleasant emotion. He
knew, however, that he was not disloyal to the memory of
his parents, and began to think that, perhaps, the manner
in which he had previously manifested his loyalty to their
memory was a mistaken one and the result of morbid ideas
on the subject. And yet, he did not regret what he had
done, but was really gratified that he had thus acted, as
his conduct had been entirely in keeping with the promptings of his heart and the result of his deep and all-absorbing love for his lost ones. Reaching no satisfactory solu-
tion of the matter that was troubling him, he fell asleep
pondering on it and speculating as to what would probably
be the consequences of his changed social relations.

About a week later he again visited Ruth and Bertha and
experienced a repetition of the quiet enjoyment that had

2

rendered his first visit so agreeable. Their conversation took a wider range than the one in which they engaged on his former visit had taken, and he was surprised and gratified at the high degree of culture which Ruth had attained, as evinced by her familiarity with nearly all of the best poets and standard prose authors, an accurate knowledge of history, and a thorough understanding of the political questions that were then agitating the country and threatening to disrupt the Union. He was also impressed by the clearness and precision with which she expressed her views on every subject that was discussed, and naturally inferred that she had received exceptionally good mental training to have acquired such perspicuity and force of expression.

Although well-informed, and thoroughly capable of giving expression to her knowledge, she was not in the slightest degree pedantic, and invariably gave utterance to her thoughts in a modest, matter-of-fact manner, as if she were stating a simple truth with which every one was supposed to be familiar. This mental modesty and absence of display was very pleasing to Ashton, and greatly enhanced the interest that he felt in conversing with Ruth, and also increased his admiration for her character. Hence, when he left that evening there was in his mind a well-settled purpose to cultivate her acquaintance.

Ashton's next visit to Ruth and Bertha was made just after South Carolina's secession from the Union on December 20th, 1860, and their conversation naturally turned to that event and drifted into a discussion of the right of secession, the causes which had led to the exercise of this right by South Carolina and would doubtless induce the other Southern States to follow her example, and also the probable results that would ensue in consequence thereof.

Ashton, of course, took the leading part in this discussion, but Ruth's familiarity with the political history of the United States and her intensely Southern sentiments made her an appreciative and interested listener to the views expressed by him, and of which we will give an outline.

His theory of the American Government was, that the Union was a union of States, as such, in their sovereign capacities, under the appropriate name of the "United States of America," and not a union of the American people; that the Constitution adopted by these States in forming this union was a solemn compact between them whereby the General Government was created and made a common agent for all of the parties to the compact, and by which the powers delegated to this agent were distinctly defined and limited, and that in entering the Union the States had not surrendered their original sovereignty, but had merely intrusted to their common agent certain specified rights and powers to be exercised for their benefit and the general welfare, in acccordance with their joint will as expressed in the instrument creating this agent. In support of his theory of the sovereignty and reserved rights of the States, he spoke of the formation of the American Government, and mentioned the fact that the Articles of Confederation under which the original thirteen States were united, declared that "each State retains its sovereignty, freedom, and independence, and every power, jurisdiction and right which is not by this Confederation expressly delegated to the United States in congress assembled," and also that the Constitution of the United States provided that "the powers not delegated to the United States by the Constitution, nor prohibited by it to the States, are reserved to the States respectively, or to the people." Thus believing in the sovereignty and reserved powers of the States, Ashton maintained that a State had the indisputable right to withdraw from the Union when it failed to accomplish the objects of its formation, or became subversive of the rights, or injurious to the interests of such State, and claimed that this right was virtually recognized in the formation of the government, by the fact that New York, Rhode Island and Virginia entered the Union on the express condition that they should be free to retire therefrom and resume their separate independence whenever they found the Union inconvenient.

In further support of the right of secession, he referred to its exercise by the colonies in severing their connection with Great Britain, and its subsequent unquestioned and unmolested exercise by each of the States in withdrawing from the old Confederation, notwithstanding the declaration contained in the Articles thereof that "the Union shall be perpetual," and also the fact that the Constitution adopted by these seceding States in forming the new Confederation or Union, neither expressly nor impliedly prohibited to such States the right of withdrawing therefrom, nor gave to the General Government the power to forcibly prevent such withdrawal.

As conclusive evidence of the fact that the convention which framed the Constitution was unalterably opposed to investing the General Government with power in any form to control or coerce a State, Ashton referred to the emphatic rejection by that convention of each and all of the various measures offered for that purpose, and quoted the declaration of Alexander Hamilton, one of the leading advocates of a consolidated government, that "to coerce a State would be one of the maddest projects ever devised," and also that of John Quincy Adams that "the indissoluble link of union between the people of the several States of this confederated nation is, after all, not in the *right* but in the *heart*."

As later authority of other eminent Northern men on the subject under consideration, Ashton quoted the statement of William Rawle, of Pennsylvania, a profound lawyer and an able expounder of the Constitution, that the right of secession "must be considered an ingredient in the original composition of the General Government, which, though not expressed, was mutually understood," and read from a copy of *The New York Tribune*, published December 17th, 1860, and just received by him, an editorial in which Mr. Horace Greeley, referring to the Declaration of Independence, said: "If it justifies the secession of three millions of colonists in 1776, *we do not see why it would not justify the secession of five millions of Southerners from the Federal Union in 1861*."

As the legitimate result of his reasoning on the subject, as we have outlined it, Ashton deduced the conclusion that to each State belonged the right of peaceable secession for just and reasonable cause, and that such State was the sole judge as to the sufficiency of the cause, and the time for the exercise of this right. Hence, in speaking of the with-

drawal of South Carolina from the Union, he claimed that
she had thereby simply exercised an unquestionable right,
as there were **just** and reasonable **causes** for such **withdrawal**, and proceeded to enumerate them. Some of the
causes enumerated by him were as **follows: The unjust**
discriminations which the General Government had made
against the Southern States by providing bounties on fish-
eries for the benefit of the New England States, and estab-
lishing protective tariffs for the benefit of the Northern and
Middle States; **the** passage by **Congress** in 1821 of **an**
unconstitutional law, known **as "The** Missouri Compromise," **whereby slavery was** thereafter prohibited in
all **territory** lying **north** of latitude 36° 30′ from the
southern boundary line of Missouri to the Pacific Ocean,
except that included in that State, **this** legislation
being another unjust discrimination against **the** South, and
indicating a purpose on the part of **the North to** appropriate the greater part of the territory belonging **to** the United
States; the continued agitation throughout **the Northern
States of a desire and purpose to abolish slavery in the**
South; the passage by most of these States of anti-fugitive
slave laws in defiance of the constitutional provisions protecting the right of **property** of slaveholders in their slaves,
and the consequently frequent and unrestrained stealing of
slaves by Northern adventurers; the rapid **growth** and
menacing attitude **of the Free-soil** party **in** the Northern
States; the unjust and false construction given **by** leading
politicians of the North **to the** Kansas-Nebraska bill of
1854, whereby, under the theory of so-called "squatter
sovereignty," it was claimed that this bill authorized the
settlers, as such, in a Territory to determine whether **or not**
slavery should exist therein, even before the legal require-
ments and prerequisites for its organization as a State had
been met, whereas, under a just and constitutional construction of the bill, such Territory could not prohibit slavery
therein until it had become a State; the generally accepted
theory of Northern men that the United States did not constitute a Federal Republic, a union of States in which each
State had the right to regulate its own institutions, but
that they formed a consolidated national Democracy in

which the will of a numerical majority was the supreme law; the persistent, bitter and fanatical denunciation of the South by Northern men through the press and from the pulpit on account of its institution of slavery; the John Brown raid in the fall of 1859, in which that infamous ruffian and his associate assassins, invading Virginia, attempted to incite insurrection among the slaves of the State and precipitate a civil war, and especially the fanatical hostility manifested toward the South by Northern people in attempting to justify this treasonable and murderous outrage, and commending the conduct of its villainous perpetrators and apotheosizing their still more villainous leader; and finally, the triumph of a purely *sectional* party, of which Wendell Phillips, one of the ablest and most prominent of the abolitionists, had said: "It is the first sectional party ever organized in this country. It does not know its own face, and calls itself national; but it is not national—it is sectional. The Republican party is a party of the North pledged against the South"; and the election to the presidency of Abraham Lincoln, another noted abolitionist, on a platform of principles inimical to the South, and who, in common with W. H. Seward, held that "The United States could not exist part free and part slave; that there was an irrepressible conflict between the two systems; and that slavery in the States must be put under a process of extinction."

Ashton stated that he was confident that the other Southern States would follow the example of South Carolina and withdraw from the Union, especially in view of the indications that the Republican majority in Congress (then in session) would reject all measures providing for a pacific settlement of the pending national difficulties. One of these measures, known as "The Crittenden Compromise," was then pending in the Senate, and had been referred to a special committee composed of five Republican senators, five Southern senators and three Northern Democratic senators. This measure was intended to provide for the adoption of amendments to the Constitution of the United States, prohibiting slavery in all Territories north of latitude 36° 30′ and protecting it south of that lati-

tude; denying the power of Congress to abolish slavery
in the District of Columbia, or in ports, arsenals, dock-
yards or any other place where the General Government exercised jurisdiction; and providing for remuneration
to the owners of escaped slaves by communities in which
the Federal laws that provided for the restitution of such
slaves might be violently obstructed. The acceptance of
the proposed measure by the South would really have
been a surrender of her position on the slavery question,
and a renunciation of her rights under the Constitution, as
affirmed by the Supreme Court, for that tribunal had, in the
case of Dred Scott, *vs.* J. F. A. Stanford, already decided
that a slaveowner had the right to take such property into
any of the Territories, while this measure prohibited such
right in the larger part of the common territory of the
United States, and merely permitted its exercise in the
remainder thereof. And yet, so anxious were the Southern
senators and the people of the South to effect a final settlement of the slavery question, and avert a disruption of the
Union, that they would have willingly accepted the proposed settlement if an opportunity for so doing had been
offered them. But this was not done, for the committee
having the measure under consideration, took action at its
first meeting, on December 21st, whereby it was "resolved
that no proposition shall be reported as adopted, unless
sustained by a majority of each of the classes of the committee; senators of the Republican party to constitute one
class, and senators of the other parties to constitute the
other class"; and when the measure was finally voted on
by the committee it was defeated, as every one of the
Republican senators voted against it.

It was subsequently defeated in the House of Representatives by a solid Republican vote, and thus, by the leaders
and representatives of that "sectional party," was all hope
of preserving the Union destroyed. The responsibility of
this result and, consequently, of the subsequent disruption
of the Union, was at the time ascribed to the Republican
party by a prominent Northern man; for Senator Stephen
A. Douglas, in addressing the Senate a few days after the
committee of thirteen had reported their inability to "agree

upon any general plan **of adjustment**," said: "If you **of** the Republican side are not willing to **accept** this (a proposition of his own), nor the proposition of the senator *from* Kentucky (Mr. Crittenden), pray tell us what you are willing to **do**? I address the inquiry to the Republicans alone, **for the reason,** that in the committee of thirteen, **a few days ago, every member** from the South, including **those from the Cotton States** (Messrs. Toombs and Davis), **expressed their** readiness to accept the proposition of **my venerable friend** from Kentucky (Mr. Crittenden), as a final settlement **of the** controversy, if tendered and sustained by **the** Republican members. Hence, the sole responsibility of our disagreement, **and the only** difficulty in the way of an **amicable adjustment, is with the Republican** party."

Although Ashton believed that the Southern States could lawfully withdraw from the Union, and had just cause for so doing, he thought that it would be impolitic for them to do so at that time, or before some flagrant violation of their constitutional rights should be attempted by the party in power, and expressed the opinion that the Western States would doubtless espouse their cause if any such invasion of their rights should be attempted while they remained in the Union, as such invasion would be not only an act of oppression to the South, but also a menace to the rights of every State in the Union.

However, neither he nor his listeners hoped that this waiting policy would be pursued by the Southern States, and they confidently anticipated the disruption of the Union, and greatly deplored the disastrous consequences that would doubtless result therefrom, as they believed that it would be followed by a civil war with all of its attendant horrors.

Ashton informed Ruth and Bertha that, in the event of a war between the States, he would return to Virginia and enlist in some home regiment, as he preferred this to enlistment in a Georgia regiment where he would be among almost entire strangers.

As the weeks passed by, Ashton's visits to Ruth Middleton became more frequent. His visits are represented as being made to Ruth, because Bertha generally managed to

excuse herself shortly after his arrival, and thus left him
and Ruth alone as much as possible. Her reason for this
was the fact that she had noticed his increasing interest in
Ruth's society and, moreover, had her heart set on the realization of her prediction as to the consequences of their
romantic meeting.

And now let us see what were the prospects for its realization as indicated by the relations existing between the
subjects of it. Ashton's interest in and admiration for
Ruth had constantly increased, but thus far had developed
no warmer sentiment than that of pure and confiding
friendship, based on the superior mental qualities, womanly
virtues and sympathetic nature that characterized her, and
rendered her exceedingly interesting and companionable.
He had often thought of how thoroughly qualified she was
to fill and adorn woman's true and highest sphere—the
home circle—but in so doing considered her objectively, and
as the wife of some ideal man who would understand and
appreciate her exalted worth and also be worthy of her,
and did not think of himself as that highly favored person.
This may have partly resulted from his modesty, but it
was principally caused by the fact that he had not yet
recovered from the effects of his great bereavement, and as
his heart was filled with the sorrow which his affliction had
brought him, there was in it no place for the joyousness that
springs from love, and he still felt that in a measure he
would be disloyal to his love of the dead if he should allow
love for the living to take possession of his heart.

Ruth fully understood his feelings, and never for a
moment misconstrued his attentions to her. She knew
that they were purely of a friendly character, and was
fully confirmed in the opinion expressed to Bertha, that
until Ashton was freed from the domination of his great
sorrow he was not likely to love any woman, and she
knew that this time had not yet arrived. Hence, while she
felt a deep interest in him and admired him more than she
had ever admired any other man, she had not allowed herself to think of him in the light of a lover and, of course,
had not given him her love. Even if she had not felt sure
that his attentions resulted entirely from his friendship for

her, and that his mind had not even turned to thoughts of
love, her womanly modesty would have kept her own heart
whole, and she would not have assumed that he loved her;
for her theory in matters of this kind was, that a woman
had no right to believe that a man loved her until he had
declared his love.

Hence it would seem that there was no immediate pros-
pect for the realization of Bertha's prediction as to the
happy *finale* of the romantic beginning of Ruth's acquaintance with Ashton.

Several months had passed since this acquaintance began,
and they marked an important epoch in Ashton's life.
Through the medium of Ruth's enlivening and yet soothing
influence, he had been drawn out of himself, and led to
think less absorbingly of his sad bereavement and take an
interest in other persons and things beside his clients and
his professional duties. At her solicitation he had several
times appeared in society, and every one who met him was
favorably impressed by the easy dignity and winning
affability of his manners, and the brilliancy and force of
his conversation. He had continued to visit Ruth frequently, and during his visits often had her to sing for him,
and, as on the evening of his first visit, she tried to adapt
her songs to the condition of his feelings at the time. He
was most pleased with simple lyrics that told of homely
experiences and portrayed scenes of rural life, as they
brought, as it were, on the wings of harmony, the sight of
green fields and babbling brooks, the scent of wild flowers
and the songs of birds which cheered and soothed his heart.
Among these were several Scotch songs which Ruth sang
with great expression and tenderness, and Ashton always
experienced a feeling of sweet contentment while listening
to them. Indeed, the cheering and soothing effect of her
singing was more than momentary, and its influence on
Ashton was such as to greatly aid in relieving his mind
from the gloom of grief which enwrapped it when Ruth
first met him. Thus, since that time, the enlivening and
soothing influences growing out of Ruth's companionship
had gradually lessened Ashton's sorrow and partially
restored his cheerfulness.

CHAPTER III.

It was now the middle of April, 1861. Fort Sumter had surrendered to the Confederate forces under General Beauregard at Charleston. The efforts of conservative men North and South to prevent a war between the sections **had** failed, and hostilities had actually begun. Ashton's own State, Virginia, had exhausted **all** honorable means to effect a reconciliation between the General Government and her Southern sisters, South Carolina, Mississippi, Alabama **Florida, Georgia, Louisiana and Texas,** who had seceded in the order named; but her efforts had been fruitless and on the day before (April 17th), a convention of delegates chosen by the people of Virginia had passed an ordinance resuming the separate independence of the State, and this act of secession needed only the ratification of the people to effectually sever her connection with the United States.

On learning that Virginia had seceded, Ashton determined to immediately carry out his previously expressed purpose of enlisting in **some one of** her regiments, and that day repaired to the home of **Ruth** Middleton to inform her of his contemplated action. He told her that as soon as he could arrange for his departure he would leave for Virginia, and on his arrival there cast his lot among the soldiers of his own State, **for** the reasons which he had previously expressed.

She approved the decision that he had made, and fully appreciated the reasons why he had not already connected himself with a Georgia regiment. After conversing with **her a short** while and expressing his appreciation of the **pleasures and** benefits which he had derived from her **society, and** thanking her for the friendly interest which she had manifested in him, he left her with the expressed hope that he would be enabled to see her several times before his departure.

During the ensuing week, Ashton arranged his affairs with reference to an indefinite absence, disposing of his library and turning over all of his law business to an elderly member of the bar, who was physically unfitted for

military service, and hence did not expect to enter the army.
In the meantime he had frequently visited Ruth, and the
satisfying pleasures incident to these visits, combined with
the constantly recurring thought that he would so soon
lose the elevating and cheering influence of her companionship, greatly increased his interest in and admiration for
her. This was perfectly natural according to the principle
embodied in the old saying that "blessings brighten as they
take their flight."

Ashton fully realized its truth in the experience through
which he was passing, and was thereby led to indulge in
such introspection as caused a more thorough analysis of
his feelings for Ruth than any he had previously made.
Indeed, up to this time he had made no especial analysis of
his feelings for her, as he had thought of her only as a dear
and valued friend and a true and noble woman whose life
had incidentally touched his own and made him a broader,
better and happier man. While the recollection of the influence which she had thus exerted over him was a good reason for the great regret which he experienced in having so
soon to leave her, he began to question himself as to
whether it sufficiently explained the feeling of intense sadness and the depressing sense of approaching loneliness that
had taken possession of his heart in view of his coming
separation from her. He could not believe that it did, and
the more thoroughly he analyzed his feelings, the more
clearly it appeared to him that his interest in Ruth Middleton was more than a friendly one, that the wants of his
nature, which had been so fully met by her companionship,
could not have been thus satisfied by the society of even
the most sympathetic friend, and that the warm and
increasing admiration for her which her many charms had
awakened and nourished in his heart, was warmer and ten-
derer than the most devoted friendship and must be nothing
less than love. This conclusion startled and perplexed him,
for he had never anticipated the situation in which it
placed him, and was in doubt as to how he should act in
the light of the revelation which he had thus experienced.
His first inclination was to follow the promptings of self-
interest and immediately declare his love for Ruth, and seek

to win hers in return, especially as he was about to leave her for an indefinite period, and hence would not be present to compete with any rival who might appear as a suitor for her heart and hand; but the very thought of his early departure for the army awakened the nobler impulses of his nature and led him to the conclusion that it would be better, less selfish, and more in harmony with real love to defer the declaration of his affection for her, as he could now offer her only his love, and in a few days would have to leave her for scenes of strife and danger, the thought of which would naturally distress her, and among which there might be awaiting him a speedy death that would sadden and becloud her life if she reciprocated his love.

The conclusion thus reached by Ashton was strengthened by the thought that possibly his love for Ruth was not all that it should be in warmth, depth and strength to constitute a sure basis for a perfectly happy marriage, and that the stress upon his feelings occasioned by the circumstances of his approaching separation from her, and his depressed condition, might have caused him to misunderstand and exaggerate his regard for her. Having formed the resolution that he would not, at this time, declare his love, he strictly adhered to it, although he often found great difficulty in so doing. However, he did not fully succeed in concealing his love, for at times the inner nature broke through the restraints put upon it by the outer man, and Ruth caught occasional glimpses in his tell-tale eyes of a softer and more magnetic light than any she had ever before seen there.

Without the slightest conceit or lack of modesty, and simply by means of her womanly instincts and that indefinable agency that communicates thought and feeling without the aid of speech, she realized that Ashton loved her. Although the thought was pleasant to her, she gave no sign of gratification or embarrassment; for she felt confident that he was endeavoring to conceal his love, and believed that she understood his motives for so doing and, considering them from his point of view, approved them. The realization of the fact that Ashton loved her was seemingly inconsistent with her theory that a woman had no right to believe that a man loved her until he had declared his love; but she reconciled the apparent inconsistency between her theory and her experience in this instance, by the reflection that so far as her feelings and conduct were concerned, there would be no real difference as to results, as she determined to control the former and regulate the latter in such manner that she would not be sensibly affected by the discovery of Ashton's love, and he would not know that she had discovered it. This purpose was all the more readily formed in consequence of the fact that she was confident that Ashton was endeavoring to conceal his love for reasons which, as before stated, she approved.

Matters between them were in this condition when he made his final visit on the evening before his departure for Virginia. The occasion was to both of them a sad one and their parting was especially trying to Ashton, as he found great difficulty in overcoming an almost irresistible impulse to declare his love. By a strong effort he restrained his feelings and overcame this impulse, and at last with a forced calmness, which had almost the appearance of coldness or indifference, he bade Ruth good-bye.

On the following morning he left for Virginia, and in due time arrived at the town of T——, near which was his former home. He found that the citizens of the place and of the surrounding country were thoroughly aroused to a sense of the danger that threatened Virginia as one of the border States, and therefore liable to be first invaded by the Federal army; and in consequence thereof they were taking prompt action to furnish their quota of troops to repel the anticipated invasion.

On the day after Ashton's arrival at T——, he learned that a meeting of the citizens of the county had been called for that day at the court-house, for the purpose of organizing a cavalry company which would immediately offer its services to Governor Letcher with a view to joining the Virginia forces that he was then raising for the defense of the State. At the hour appointed for the meeting, Ashton repaired to the court-house, and finding that several prominent men of his acquaintance were leading spirits in the enterprise, he promptly responded when the call for volunteers was made, and later in the day took an active part in the organization of the company, which, in honor of one of Virginia's greatest men, was called "The Jefferson Hussars." Owing to the prominent position which his father had occupied in the county, and the fact that Ashton was known to be a brave and intelligent man, he would have been elected first lieutenant of the company if he had not declined any office, stating that he preferred to serve as a private soldier. Soon after its organization, the company reported for service and became a part of the State forces under General R. E. Lee.

During the following month the State became a member of the Confederacy and these troops were transferred to the new government. It might be interesting, but it is unnecessary, to give an account of the movements of the company which Ashton had joined, and of his own personal experience during the next fifteen months of the war. Suffice it to say that the company took part in General Lee's campaign in Western Virginia, was with Ashby under General Jackson in "The Valley" and came with the latter in his forced march to join General Beauregard at Centreville and took part in the first battle of Manassas, was subsequently transferred to General J. E B. Stuart's command and from that time rendered efficient service as part of the Ninth Virginia Cavalry.

This regiment was one of the three Virginia regiments, which, in conjunction with two squadrons of the Jeff. Davis Legion and a part of the Stuart Horse Artillery, constituted the force with which General Stuart made his famous "ride around McClellan" on the 13th, 14th, and 15th of June, 1862, while the Federal army was preparing for an attack on Richmond from the direction of the Chickahominy river, and the Jefferson Hussars did their full duty in this daring and unprecedented exploit. The expedition was one that afforded opportunities for exhibitions of individual courage and prowess, and in several instances Ashton's gallantry was so conspicuous that it attracted the attention and received the commendation of the commanding general.

After the seven days' fighting around Richmond, the retreat of General McClellan, and the defeat of General Pope at Cedar Run on August 9th, 1862, the Federal army under the latter general was concentrated in Culpeper county between the Rapidan and Rappahannock rivers. As General Lee had reason to believe that General Pope's army was being increased and there was no indication of an attack on Richmond from the direction of the Peninsula, he decided to advance on Pope, and about the middle of August arranged the plan of the contemplated movement. General Longstreet's corps was to cross the Rapidan at Raccoon Ford, General Jackson's corps was to cross at Somerville Ford and both commands, together with the artillery, were to move toward Culpeper Court-house, while the cavalry, under General Stuart, was to cross the Rapidan at Morton's Ford, proceed to Rappahannock Station, destroy the railroad bridge and cut the telegraph wire at that place, and operate toward Culpeper Court-house, taking position on General Longstreet's right. This movement was appointed for August 18th, but, owing to a failure to complete the necessary preparations, it had to be postponed until the 20th and the order directing it was not issued until the 19th. General Stuart had previously received secret instructions as to the part he was to take in the movement, and in accordance therewith, on August 16th, directed General Fitzhugh Lee to proceed with his brigade to the vicinity of Raccoon Ford, where he promised to meet him on the 17th.

General Stuart reached Verdierville, near Raccoon Ford, on the evening of August 17th, but General Fitzhugh Lee's brigade had not arrived. He remained at Verdierville that night, awaiting the arrival of Lee's brigade, and as a result thereof narrowly escaped capture. The weather being warm, he slept that night on the floor of a porch near the roadside, with his cloak for his bed. About dawn he was aroused by the sound of approaching horses and wagons, and walked out bareheaded to the fence near by and discovered that they were coming from the direction from which he expected General Fitzhugh Lee. Although he believed that the noise was made by the approach of Lee's brigade, he took the precaution to send Captain John S. Mosby and Lieutenant Gibson to ascertain the truth of the matter and was soon undeceived by the speedy return of these officers, who were fired at and rapidly pursued by a force of Federal cavalry. Hastily mounting his horse, General Stuart, together with Major Van Borke and Lieutenant Dabney, of his staff, succeeded in escaping by leaping a high fence, but his hat and cloak fell into the hands of the enemy General Fitzhugh Lee's brigade did not arrive until the night of August 18th, and was not in a condition to make a forced march on the 19th. Moreover, in accordance with instructions received by General Stuart from General R. E. Lee, the 19th was devoted to rest and preparation for the movement which was to begin on the 20th. This movement had been admirably planned, and if it could have been commenced on August 18th, as originally contemplated, would have placed the Confederate army between the Federal army and its reinforcements then coming up from Fredericksburg and Acquia Creek, and also from Alexandria by way of Manassas Junction, and the result would have been the certain defeat and probable destruction of Pope's army. But on the morning of August 18th, one of Pope's spies, who had been with the Confederate army, reported to him General Lee's contemplated movement; and its unavoidable postponement, for the reason before mentioned, gave Pope time to withdraw his army behind the Rappahannock. This he did and had made a successful retreat to the north bank of that stream before the movement began on the morning of August 20th.

General Stuart had with him Generals B. H. Robertson's and Fitzhugh Lee's brigades (Ashton's regiment being at this time a part of the latter brigade), and after crossing the Rapidan the former, accompanied by General Stuart, pushed forward to Brandy Station, while the latter moved rapidly to Kelly's and Ellis Fords on the Rappahannock, and had a successful skirmish with the rear of the retreating Federal cavalry near Kelly's Ford. General Stuart with Robertson's brigade attacked the Federal cavalry near Brandy Station and drove them back to the Rappahannock, where they were protected by their artillery on the other side of the river.

3

On August 22d, while a portion of the Stuart Horse Artillery, under Captain John Pelham, was engaged with the Federal artillery at Freeman's Ford on the Rappahannock, General Stuart received a note from General Lee approving a proposition that he had made to strike the enemy's rear with cavalry and endeavor to cut his communication with Washington, and he at once began the execution of the plan. With about fifteen hundred men, consisting of Fitzhugh Lee's brigade, part of Robertson's brigade and two pieces of artillery, he proceeded through Jeffersonton and crossed the Rappahannock at Waterloo Bridge and Hart's Mills, and reached Warrenton. From this point he began his march to the rear of Cedar Run for the purpose of destroying the railroad bridge over that stream near Catlett's Station and the telegraph wire there, thus cutting the enemy's line of communication with Washington. Riding for hours through a terrific storm, the command arrived in the vicinity of Catlett's Station after dark, captured the Federal picket and soon thereafter unexpectedly rode into the midst of the enemy's encampment.

As the storm was still in progress and the night intensely dark, General Stuart could not distinguish his surroundings, and his position was exceedingly critical. At this moment a negro who had previously known General Stuart was captured and brought before him. On recognizing Stuart, the negro informed him of the location of General Pope's staff, baggage, horses, etc., and offered to guide him to where they were. Accepting the offer, General Stuart promptly decided to send forward a regiment to capture Pope's staff, and the Ninth Virginia, under Colonel W. H. F. Lee, was selected for the purpose. Following their guide, Colonel Lee and his gallant regiment marched boldly forward through the drenching rain and dismal darkness until within a few paces of the tents occupied by Pope's staff, and then dashing forward at a gallop, charged the Federal camp and in a few moments were in complete possession of the same, having captured several hundred prisoners (many of whom were officers), General Pope's baggage, horses and equipments, and a large quantity of other property.

Ashton was among the first to reach Pope's headquarters and, in addition to securing several prisoners, captured some of General Pope's private papers, among which was his dispatch-book, containing copies of his official correspondence with the Federal Government. General Stuart promptly forwarded these papers to General Lee, and the dispatch-book proved to be of the greatest value to the latter. It contained information of the strength and movements of Pope's army, confirmed the information previously received by General Lee as to Pope's expected reinforcements, and disclosed the fact that a part of General McClellan's army had marched to join Pope, that the remainder would soon follow, and that the greater part of General Cox's army had been withdrawn from the Kanawha Valley for the same purpose. This information enabled General Lee to act promptly and efficiently in the disposition of his troops in such manner as to prevent the arrival of these expected reinforcements in time for them to aid Pope in the second battle of Manassas, which Lee forced on him a few days thereafter; and the first step taken by General Lee in the matter was the sending of General Jackson on his famous flank movement by means of which he got in Pope's rear, cut his communications with Washington and captured his principal depot of supplies at Manassas Junction, as will hereinafter more fully appear.

Immediately after the capture of the Federal camp where Pope's headquarters had been located, Colonels L. T. Brien and T. L. Rosser, with the First and Fifth Virginia cavalry, attacked another camp beyond the Orange and Alexandria railroad, but the Federals extinguished the lights in the camp at the first shot of the Confederates and took refuge in and behind their wagons, and the attack was not prosecuted on account of the intense darkness which prevailed and rendered a charge by mounted men impracticable. An attempt was then made to destroy the railroad bridge over Cedar Run, but this failed on account of the fact that the bridge was so wet that it would not burn, and the stream was swollen to such an extent that the axemen could not get to the trestles for the purpose of cutting them. Finding it impossible to **destroy** the bridge, General Stuart retired that night by the route **he had** come and rejoined the army the next day at Warrenton Springs.

On August 25th, General Jackson began the flank movement before mentioned, and in accordance with instructions received from General Lee that night, General Stuart, with Fitzhugh Lee's and Robertson's brigades, overtook **General Jackson** the next day near Gainesville and joined him **in the** movement. That night, by direction of General Jackson, General Stuart, with a part **of** Robertson's brigade, **and General I. R. Trimble,** with the Twenty-first Georgia and **the** Twenty-first North Carolina regiments, proceeded to Manassas Junction and captured the place together with over three hundred prisoners, eight pieces of artillery, seventy-two artillery horses, an immense quantity of commissary **and** quartermaster's stores, a long **train of cars** filled with **army supplies that had just arrived from** Alexandria, and about two hundred horses beside those **belonging to** the artillery, and also recaptured more than **two** hundred negroes.

The next morning General Jackson arrived at **Manassas Junction** with Hill's and Taliaferro's divisions and **soon thereafter General G.** W. Taylor, of New Jersey, **with a considerable force of Federal infantry** made a bold **attempt to recapture the place and lost his life in his daring effort. During the day General** Fitzhugh Lee, **with three of his** regiments, **including the** Ninth **Virginia, was** detached and **sent in the rear of** Fairfax Court-house to damage the com**munications of** the Federals as much as possible and try **to cut off the force that had been** led by General Taylor.

Unfortunately for Ashton, as the sequel shows, **he had** that morning **been detailed as** a special courier for General **Stuart** and did not accompany **his** regiment in **this expedition.** That night all of the captured property **that could not be** used or carried away from **Manassas Junction** was **destroyed, and** General Jackson moved **his command** to the **vicinity of Groveton and** halted near where **the first** battle **of Manassas was fought** the year before.

Early **in the morning of** August 28th, a dispatch had **been intercepted which gave the order of** march of the Federal army from Warrenton and directed a part of the cavalry to **report** to General Bayard at Haymarket. Having obtained General Jackson's permission for the movement, General Stuart proceeded to Haymarket with what cavalry he then had with him, and on approaching the place discovered the presence of a large force of Federals. About this time he saw the fighting in progress at Thoroughfare Gap, where General Longstreet was engaged with the Federals, who were attempting to prevent his junction with General Jackson.

Wishing to establish communication with General Longstreet and give him accurate information as to the location of General Jackson, General Stuart decided to send a dispatch to the former and Ashton was selected as the bearer of the same. The position of a courier is always a very responsible one and it is often fraught with much danger. If the reader has ever been intrusted with an important dispatch, on the safe delivery of which perhaps **depended** the issue of an impending battle, and **in order to deliver** the same it was necessary to either pass through or around the enemy's lines, he will understand the sense of responsibility and grave concern with which Ashton started on his mission. As the Federals were between him and Thoroughfare Gap, he knew that he must make a considerable circuit to avoid them in his effort to reach General Longstreet, and **that** even then he would run the risk of coming in contact with some of their scouting parties or pickets above Haymarket.

While he fully appreciated the difficulties and dangers incident to the errand on which he was sent, he felt no physical **fear in** consequence thereof, and was concerned about his personal safety only in so far as it was necessary to the success of his mission. Passing around to the right of Haymarket and avoiding the open roads, he proceeded for several miles in the direction of Aldie. After going as far as he supposed was necessary to flank any Federal outposts in that direction, he turned to the left and gradually approached the road between Haymarket and Aldie, intending to cross this road and make his way down to Hopewell Gap in Bull Run Mountain and there cross the

mountain, if the Federals were still in front of Thoroughfare Gap. He approached the road through a skirt of
woods alongside it, and hence could not obtain a view of it
until he entered it. Just as he rode out of the woods he saw
a Federal vedette on horseback about twenty paces from
him.

The Federal soldier was watching the road in the direction of Aldie, and Ashton had entered it behind him; but,
on hearing the sound made by Ashton's horse in entering the
road, he quickly wheeled his own horse and confronted
Ashton. The latter had drawn his pistol and at once ordered the Federal to surrender. Instead of doing this he
quickly raised his carbine and fired. The bullet passed un-
pleasantly near Ashton's head, but did not touch him.

On discovering that he had missed his mark the Federal
endeavored to draw his pistol; but before he could do so
Ashton had taken deliberate aim at him and fired. He
dropped his bridle-rein and pressed his left hand to his
breast, made one more effort to draw his pistol and then
reeled and fell from his horse.

At this moment Ashton heard the whiz of bullets above
his head and the almost simultaneous reports of several
guns behind him, and on glancing back saw a squad of
Federal cavalry mounting their horses about six hundred
yards in his rear. Without waiting to see whether he had
killed his late antagonist, but with mingled feelings of admiration and sorrow for the brave fellow, Ashton put
spurs to his horse and dashed off at full speed along the
road toward Aldie. Having so much the start of the Federals, he believed that he could escape them in a straight
race, but this he knew would take him too far out of his
intended route and unnecessarily tax his horse's strength;
and hence he determined to leave the road and dodge his
pursuers at the first opportunity. This opportunity soon
presented itself, for on passing the edge of a large body of
woods through which the road ran, he discovered that the
road made a considerable bend to the right, and immediately after he had passed this bend he was entirely out of
sight of his pursuers. Bringing his horse to a walk he rode
him into the woods on the left and, having dismounted,

quickly returned to the road and obliterated the tracks made by his horse in leaving the same, and **then** hastily remounting his horse rode off through the woods as rapidly as possible. Fortunately, the woods extended some distance in the direction in which he was going, and he soon felt secure from further pursuit; for he was satisfied that the Federals, in their rapid pursuit of him, would pass by the place where he left the road before discovering that he had left it, and that **the tracks there made** by their horses would render its location quite difficult and perhaps impossible. On emerging from **the** woods Ashton pressed rapidly on toward Hopewell Gap, reached his destination without any further adventure and delivered General **Stuart's dispatch** to General Longstreet shortly after dark.

Just before Ashton's arrival, the Federal force in front **of** Thoroughfare Gap had been repulsed by General D. R. Jones and retreated toward Manassas, and a successful passage of Bull Run Mountain at this point was thus effected by the part of Longstreet's corps which had come through that gap. At that time General Hood with two brigades was crossing the mountain **by a** footpath, and General Wilcox with three brigades was crossing it through Hopewell Gap, and that night the entire corps bivouacked east of the mountain.

In answer to General Stuart's dispatch, General Longstreet wrote General Jackson **that he** had successfully passed Bull Run Mountain and would promptly march to join him the next morning. Ashton was instructed to deliver the dispatch that night, and as soon as he had refreshed himself and his horse he started on this mission. It was after midnight when he reached General Jackson's headquarters and delivered the dispatch, and he decided to wait until morning to join General Stuart, who, as he **was** informed, was near Sudley Church.

The next morning, August 29th, Ashton started off to join General Stuart and proceeded parallel with and in the rear of Jackson's corps, which, as he discovered, had changed its position since he saw it the day before, and was now formed in line of battle along the unfinished railroad stretching from the Warrenton turnpike across the road from Sudley's Ford to Manassas Junction, the left of the line being near this road.

As Ashton was in the rear of General Jackson's line of battle and at times in sight of the same, he did not for a moment anticipate an encounter with the enemy and rode carelessly along, perfectly unconscious of danger. When he had nearly reached the extreme left of the line and was almost in sight of Sudley Church, a small party of Federals suddenly appeared a short distance in front of him and at once began to fire at him. He quickly drew his pistol and returned their fire, but had only fired twice when he was struck in the right breast by a pistol ball and fell from his horse. The fall from his horse rendered him unconscious for a few moments, and on recovering his consciousness he found himself surrounded by Federal soldiers. There happened to be a surgeon among them, and, true to the instincts of his fraternity and, doubtless, the impulses of humanity, he promptly sought to ascertain whether he could relieve Ashton, notwithstanding the fact that he was an enemy.

An examination of Ashton's wound showed that it was a severe one, but not likely to prove fatal, as the ball on entering his breast had struck a rib and, being thereby deflected from its course, had passed out at his side. The surgeon at once dressed Ashton's wound and directed that he be taken to Centreville, where the Federals had established a temporary hospital to which they were sending their own wounded and those of the Confederates whom they had captured.

In accordance with the instruction thus given, Ashton was carried off toward Centreville. The party of Federals then retired to the woods bordering the Sudley Ford road, and rejoined the force of which they were a part, and which had by some means succeeded in reaching the rear of Jackson's line at this point.

If Ashton's removal had been delayed for even a few minutes, he would probably have been recaptured, for shortly afterward the presence of this Federal force in Jackson's rear was discovered, and the brave and peerless Captain Pelham with his Horse Artillery routed them and recaptured several other wounded Confederates whom they had just captured.

Ashton was kept at Centreville only one night, for on the morning of August 30th, in anticipation of the desperate effort which General Pope was to make that afternoon to retrieve the disasters his army had suffered during the two preceding days, all of the wounded at Centreville who could be moved were sent to Washington, and Ashton was among the number. Thus again was his evil star in the ascendant, as but for this precautionary measure he would have been recaptured, for, in the general engagement which occurred that afternoon, General Pope was first successfully repulsed and afterward completely routed, and his entire army was driven back across Bull Run and did not halt in its wild retreat until it reached the heights of Centreville, and being flanked out of this position by General Jackson the next day, hastily retreated toward Fairfax Court-house, had a brief but bloody engagement with Jackson at Ox Hill near nightfall and continued the retreat in the darkness, reaching the breastworks before Washington the following day.

In the meantime Ashton had been carried to Washington and placed in a hospital, where he was receiving all necessary care and attention. His trip to Washington had been quite fatiguing to him and this result, combined with the harassing thought of a probably lengthy imprisonment, had so affected him that he had been thrown into a high fever which was likely to prove troublesome and perhaps dangerous. Indeed, on the day after his arrival at the hospital, his fever was such as to render him at times unconscious.

Thus far we have given an outline of Ashton's career as a soldier without even alluding to his experience as a lover since he left Ruth Middleton about sixteen months before. Leaving him for the present in the hands of the hospital surgeon and nurses, we will relate some of the incidents growing out of his relation to Ruth.

CHAPTER IV.

Before leaving Ruth, Ashton had obtained her consent
to a correspondence between them, and they had kept up
the correspondence as regularly as they could in view of
his surroundings, the frequency with which his regiment
changed its location, and the consequent delays in his reception of Ruth's letters. During the first twelve months
of the correspondence, Ashton's letters, whilst evincing the
highest regard for Ruth and a deep interest in all that concerned her, were purely friendly in their character, as he
had scrupulously kept his resolution to refrain from declaring his love for her. But for several months before he was
wounded, his letters had become decidedly warmer in their
tenor, and running through all of them there was an un-
dercurrent of tenderness the unmistakable source of
which was manifestly the fountain of love.

Just before General Lee began the movement against
General Pope which culminated in the second battle of
Manassas, Ashton wrote Ruth a letter in which he made
known his deep, absorbing and constantly increasing love
for her, explained why he had thus long refrained from
revealing it, and told her that he could no longer delay an
expression of his feelings. As this delay, as he explained to
her, had been caused by the fact that he had devoted himself to his country's service, was leading a life of hardship
and danger and could offer her nothing but his love, he
excused himself for having now seemingly ignored what had
previously prevented a declaration of his love, by telling
Ruth that he hoped and believed that these restraining
causes would soon be removed, as the recent signal victories of the Confederate armies gave promise of an early
termination of the war. He told her of the great struggle
which he experienced in restraining himself from a declaration of his love before leaving her, and how this struggle
had almost daily recurred in his life since then, and that at
times he was tortured by the agonizing thought that even
if there was a hope of winning her love, should his own
be revealed, this hope might be destroyed by the successful

suit of some other man while she was ignorant of his deep and deathless devotion to her. After telling her how anxiously and impatiently he would await an answer to his letter, he requested that she would direct her reply as follows: "John Ashton, Ninth Virginia Cavalry, Fitzhugh Lee's Brigade, Army of Northern Virginia," stating that as the army was about to begin an aggressive campaign he did not know where he would be during the next two weeks, but if the letter were thus directed it would be sent to his regiment and eventually reach him.

Ruth received Ashton's letter a few days after it was mailed, and the reader can readily imagine its effect upon her. She had long known that Ashton loved her, felt satisfied that it was only a question of time as to the declaration of his love, and in the meanwhile, despite the efforts which she had made to control her feelings, her heart had responded to his love and he had become very dear to her. Hence it was with an emotion of exhilarating gladness that she read the revelation of his deep and ardent love for her, and her soul was filled with happiness at the thought that she was "all the world" to such a true and noble man, and had it in her power to bless and brighten his future life, and also her own, by giving a full response to his love. If she had consulted her feelings alone and yielded to the impulse of the moment, she would have given Ashton's letter an immediate reply; but maidenly modesty and a regard for conventional propriety restrained her from writing for several days. She then answered Ashton's letter, telling him that his love was reciprocated and that she was very happy in the thought of its possession. With feminine inconsistency she playfully chided him for having so long refrained from revealing his love and thus delaying their mutual happiness. The letter was duly posted, but did not reach Ashton's regiment until a day or two after he was wounded and captured, and hence was not received by him.

On the morning of August 29th, and shortly after Ashton was captured, General Stuart with a part of his command met General Longstreet between Haymarket and Gainesville, and there learned from the latter that he had the night before **received the dispatch** which Stuart **had sent** him by Ashton, **and that he had intrusted** Ashton **with the** delivery of a dispatch to General Jackson. As Ashton did not report to General Stuart during the further progress of the battle, when it was over General Stuart sent a messenger to Ashton's captain to ascertain whether he was with **the** company and, on learning that **he** was not, inquiry was made at General Jackson's headquarters as to whether he had delivered General Longstreet's **dispatch** on the night of August 28th. The result of this **inquiry** showed that Ashton had delivered the dispatch that night, remained near General Jackson's headquarters until the next morning and then started off **in** the rear of Jackson's line of battle for the purpose of joining General Stuart near Sudley Church. No further information of his movements could be obtained at the time, and it was supposed that he was probably killed by the Federal force that reached the rear of General Jackson's lines on the morning of August 29th. This supposition was strengthened and, in the minds of some, confirmed by the statement of one of the wounded Confederates who had been recaptured from this Federal force that just before the recapture he saw a cavalryman shot from his horse near Sudley Church **by a** small party of Federals, that they rejoined the main **force a few** minutes thereafter, but had no prisoners with them, and hence he supposed that the cavalryman had been killed.

In view of the facts which we have stated, it was generally supposed that Ashton had been killed during the battle of Manassas, and he was so reported in the list of casualties occurring in his regiment. As Ashton was supposed to have been killed, Ruth's letter was forwarded to Richmond to be returned to its writer through the Dead Letter Office, but for some cause it never reached its destination.

Several months before, Ashton had ordered **the** *Richmond Examiner* sent to Ruth's address, and she had **been** reading it with much interest. Shortly after the battle of Manassas she received a copy of the paper containing an account of the part taken in the engagement by the Virginia troops and also a list of their killed and wounded. Among the former she found the name of John **Ashton, of** the Ninth Virginia Cavalry, and the shock caused by the unexpected and painful discovery was almost paralyzing in its effect upon her.

For a moment she was dazed, as if she had suddenly received a physical blow; her mind was in a whirl and she was hardly conscious of her surroundings, and could not realize the full meaning of this heartrending news. When its full significance found lodgment in her reeling brain and she realized that Ashton was indeed **dead,** her whole being was convulsed with agony and in tones of anguish she cried out: "Oh, John, John, my love, my lost darling, let me **come to you; my heart is broken;" and** fell to the floor in a **deathlike swoon.**

Bertha Gray was in an adjoining room and, on hearing **the** noise occasioned by Ruth's fall, hastily sought to ascertain its cause, and was horrified to find Ruth lying on the floor in an apparently lifeless condition. She at **once** aroused the household, dispatched a servant for a physician, and proceeded to do what she could to revive her cousin. Seating herself **on the floor, she placed Ruth's head in her lap and with the assistance of a waiting-maid** began to chafe her hands, **and bathe her** face with cold water. In a few moments she was rejoiced to see signs of animation in her cousin, and shortly thereafter Ruth returned to full consciousness.

When the physician arrived, **he** found that there was no **especial** need for his services, but he directed that Ruth **should** lie down and take several hours of uninterrupted **repose.** Ruth gave no information as to the cause of her **swoon, and** Bertha would not ask her about it in the presence **of the** physician and the servants. Even after she had conducted Ruth to her room, Bertha still refrained from **questioning her in** regard to the matter, especially as the physician had prescribed perfect quiet for her; and after she had made all necessary arrangements for **Ruth's comfort,** she left her.

On re-entering the room where Ruth had fainted, Bertha saw a paper lying on the floor and, having picked it up, was attracted by the prominent head-lines of a column of war news. Glancing down the column she soon saw the name of

John Ashton in the list of Virginia soldiers who had been killed in the recent battle of Manassas, and at once concluded that the sight of this had caused Ruth's swoon, for the latter had told her of Ashton's declaration of his love for her and of her own love for him. She was deeply grieved at the thought of Ashton's death, as she felt the warmest friendship for him, and her sorrow was greatly intensified in consequence of the agonizing effect which his death had produced on Ruth, and her heart was filled with tenderest sympathy for her cousin in her sad bereavement. Believing that Ruth would prefer to be alone during the first hours of her grief, Bertha did not go to her cousin's room until the next day. After gently rapping at the door and receiving no response from within, she entered the room expecting to find Ruth asleep. Instead of this, she found her sitting by a window gazing out-of-doors with a far-away look in her eyes and an indescribably sad expression on her face, which bore traces of recent tears. Without any previous salutation Bertha approached her and, placing her arms around her, drew her to her bosom and simply said:

"My darling, I have seen the paper and understand it all. I suffer with you and wish that I could thereby render your suffering less."

Ruth returned her cousin's embrace and said: "He was so good and true, and I loved him with all my soul. It is so hard to bear."

Nothing more was said, but for a long time the cousins remained locked in a close embrace, and from the devoted love and tender sympathy which it indicated on Bertha's part, Ruth received as much of soothing consolation as living loved ones can impart to one whose grief-stricken heart is sorrowing for the dead.

Leaving them locked in each other's arms, we will return to Ashton, whom we left in a partially delirious condition at the hospital in Washington. Instead of improving, his condition daily grew worse, and at the expiration of a week his fever was so high that he entirely lost consciousness of his surroundings and had no lucid moments. He was perfectly delirious and in an incoherent manner repeatedly gave expression to the thoughts that crowded his disordered mind. As is usual in such cases, these thoughts took a wide range and were constantly changing. At times he thought that he was in the midst of battle and would shout "the wild Confederate yell" as if he were charging the enemy with Ashby or Stuart. At other times he would imagine himself in his old home, surrounded by the loneliness and air of desolation that marked it just after his parents died, and he would give vent to his grief in bitter sobs and bewail the mysterious fate which had so suddenly darkened his young life. Then he would think of his adopted home in the Sunny South, run over again in imagination his rapid and thrilling race to rescue Ruth Middleton from the impending fate to which she was being borne by her frightened horse, and immediately afterward burst forth in hearty praise of some sweet song as if it had just been sung by Ruth with the utmost harmony and expression of which it was susceptible; and then he would rave about his love for her and the letter in which he had revealed it, and wonder why he had received no answer to his letter.

He continued in this condition for several days, and at times the hospital physicians thought that his chance to recover was but slight, and stated that the utmost care and attention were necessary to preserve his life. In the ward in which he had been placed there was a volunteer nurse named Annie R——. She resided in New Castle, Delaware, and was the daughter of a wealthy merchant of that place who sympathized with the South in the struggle then in progress, and as she shared her father's feelings in this matter, she had offered her services at this hospital for the purpose of nursing the sick and wounded Confederate prisoners who were its inmates. She had been at once impressed by Ashton's intellectual face and manly and distinguished appearance, and when she caught glimpses of his past life and experience as revealed in his delirious talks she became deeply interested in his case and did all in her power to secure his recovery. She was a young lady of refinement and culture, had a sweet and noble face and slightly resembled Ruth Middleton in personal appearance. It may have been owing to this resemblance, or, perhaps, to Miss R——'s deftness as a nurse and magnetic power, that she had better

control than others over Ashton and could often quiet his
ravings when every one else had failed to do so. The very
touch of her hand on his burning brow appeared to act
with magical effect upon his excited brain, and, in the midst
of his wildest ravings, calm the tempest of thought that
was raging in his mind. But nothing could entirely allay
the raging fever which was daily exhausting his physical
frame, and each recurring paroxysm made such drafts on
his strength as to lessen the chances of his recovery.

At last the crisis came, and the surgeon told Miss R——
that if Ashton could successfully withstand the ravages of
the fever through that night, he would probably recover.
She determined that she would do everything in her power
to aid him in the approaching struggle and, after obtaining
from the surgeon full directions as to what should be done
in every conceivable emergency, she arranged to spend the
entire night by Ashton's bedside. All through the night she
watched by his couch, keeping constantly informed as to
the state of his pulse and the degree of his temperature, and
faithfully administered the remedies thereby respectively
indicated as necessary to be used. Toward morning she
was rejoiced to discover that his temperature was falling
and, as there was a corresponding decrease in the beat of
his pulse, she was satisfied that his fever was abating and
that the crisis had been successfully passed. In this supposition she was correct, and about dawn Ashton sank into a
quiet sleep and was soon breathing as regularly and naturally as if he were in his usual health. Miss R—— remained
by his couch until some of the regular nurses came into the
ward, and at once informed them of Ashton's condition
and stated that he must not be disturbed under any circumstances, but should be allowed to sleep on until he awoke of
his own accord. She then left the hospital and repaired to
her boarding-house for the purpose of obtaining the rest
and sleep which she so much needed in consequence of her
long and anxious vigil. About noon she awoke and, after
refreshing herself with a sandwich and a cup of coffee,
immediately returned to the hospital to ascertain the condition of Ashton. She found him still sleeping peacefully,
and decided that she would remain with him until he

awoke. It was not long before she noticed in his appearance signs of returning consciousness, and soon thereafter he opened his eyes and began to look around him.

Seeing Miss R——, he looked at her steadily for a moment and then closed his eyes and pressed his hand to his forehead as if trying to collect his thoughts, or recall something that had escaped his memory. His effort appeared to be fruitless, and again opening his eyes and looking at Miss R—— in a half-dazed manner, he said:

"Where am I? And how came I to be here?"

She replied: "You are in a hospital in Washington City, and were brought here in consequence of having been wounded in battle and captured by Federal soldiers about two weeks ago."

"Two weeks ago!" exclaimed Ashton. "Have I been here that long?"

"Not quite so long as that," said Miss R——, "as you were brought here about three days after you were wounded."

Ashton closed his eyes and appeared to be again striving to recall something to remembrance. In a few moments his face brightened and, opening his eyes, he said:

"Yes, I now remember the circumstances under which I was wounded. I had carried a dispatch from General Longstreet to General Jackson the night before, and on the morning of the second day's fighting in the battle of Manassas, was on my way to rejoin General Stuart near Sudley Church. As I was in the rear of General Jackson's line of battle, I had no thought of encountering any Federal soldiers and was carelessly riding along, unconscious of danger, when a small party of Federals suddenly appeared in front of me and began to fire at me. I think I fired twice at them, and was then shot in the breast and fell from my horse. The fall rendered me unconscious for a short time, and when I regained my consciousness I found that I was a prisoner. My wound was dressed and, immediately afterward, I was carried to Centreville, and on the following day brought to this place. I have but an indistinct recollection of my first day's stay here and remember nothing occurring after that time. I am sure that

4

I did **not** see you before I became unconscious, and yet your face seems strangely familiar to me."

"You are correct in your statement that you did not see me before you became unconscious," said Miss R——, "for I was in another ward at that time and did not learn of your case until the next day. I suppose that **the reason why** my face seems familiar to you is because I have frequently been about your bedside since you became delirious and, **although your** brain remained disordered, you were **perhaps at times conscious of my** presence, and my features were then impressed on your mind and, being now recalled, seem familiar to you."

"That is doubtless the correct explanation of the matter," said Ashton, "and what **you** have said enables me, without further information, to understand that you have carefully and assiduously watched **over** me and ministered to my wants during my delirium; **for I** have a recollection that some person, of whose face your own is the counterpart, seemed to exert a strong influence over me and by a simple touch of her hand often soothed and calmed my **troubled** mind. In view of the lengthy period of **my delirium,** I realize the great danger through which **I have** passed and am overwhelmed with a sense of the **debt of** gratitude I owe you for your attention and kindness, **which** I am sure have saved my **life. I cannot find words** to tell you how deeply grateful I am **for what** you have done for me. My gratitude is all the warmer and deeper in view of the fact that I am to you an entire stranger, and also belong to an army that is engaged in war with the section in which you live."

"Do not trouble yourself farther to express your gratitude for what I have done," she replied, "for the pleasure which I feel in having aided in your recovery is ample reward for my exertions. The fact **that you are a Southern soldier, and** which, as it seems, renders **you** all the more grateful **for** what I have done, is really the **reason why I** have had an opportunity for assisting you; for otherwise, you would not have been brought to this hospital, which **is** used only for sick and wounded Confederate prisoners, and I am here solely because **such is its use. Can you** keep a secret? I believe that you can, and will therefore tell you one. Although my home is at New Castle, Delaware, and I am a native of that State, I sympathize with the Southern people in their struggle against the United States, and came here for the express purpose of aiding, as far as possible, sick and wounded Confederate soldiers, knowing that they would need more careful attention than they were likely to receive from mere hired nurses who felt no interest in them and doubtless were inimical to the South. But we will not farther discuss this matter at present, as you are quite feeble and both your mind and body require rest and quiet in order for you to regain your strength. Moreover, I see the surgeon approaching, and, although he is a kind-hearted man and by no means bitter in his feelings toward the South, he must not know that I am a Southern sympathizer."

Immediately after Miss R—— had ceased speaking, the surgeon arrived and, after giving Miss R—— and Ashton a pleasant greeting, said to the latter: "I was truly glad, on making my rounds this morning, to find that your fever had abated and that you were out of danger. As you were quietly sleeping at the time, I gave orders that you should not be disturbed, and should be allowed to sleep on until you awoke of your own accord. I found that in this matter I had been preceded by Miss R——, who had already given similar instructions in regard to you. By the way, I may safely say that to her you are doubtless indebted for your recovery, for in all probability nothing short of the constant and skilful attention which she gave you, would have enabled your system to withstand the continuous and protracted strain to which it was subjected. I thank her for what she has accomplished, and congratulate you on the result of her efforts and your good fortune in having such an efficient nurse."

"Yes, sir," said Ashton, "I am sure that to Miss R—— and yourself I owe my life. I have already endeavored to give her some idea of my gratitude for what she has done for me, and now ask you to accept my earnest and grateful thanks for the efficient service which you have rendered me."

"I will not," said the surgeon, "be guilty of mock modesty and underestimate the service which my professional knowledge and skill have enabled me to render you; but, as I have already intimated, this service would doubtless have proven fruitless without the careful and unremitting attention given you by Miss R——, and I repeat that to her you owe your recovery. However, we will not longer dwell on the means of your recovery. The more important matter is the fact that your recovery is now assured, and I hope that in a short time you will regain your usual health and strength. Now that the fever has been allayed, your body will soon resume its normal condition, and then your wound will rapidly heal. What you now most need are rest and sleep, and in order that you may at once begin to obtain their beneficial effects, Miss R——, and I will leave you to their enjoyment."

The surgeon and Miss R—— then left Ashton and proceeded to visit the other inmates of the ward.

Instead of trying to sleep, Ashton was soon deeply absorbed in reflection on his recent experience and present surroundings. His first thoughts were of Ruth Middleton and his great love for her. He felt that he had but inadequately expressed his love in the letter declaring it, wished that he could have told her of it in person, wondered how she had received his declaration of love, and longed to know whether his love was reciprocated and what had been her reply to his letter. This longing for a knowledge of Ruth's feelings toward him naturally reminded him of the probable cause of his failure to obtain it, viz.: his wound and subsequent captivity; and his thoughts were thereby turned to his experience as a prisoner, and his present surroundings. He thought long and tenderly of the interest that Miss R—— had manifested in him and the unremitting efforts made by her to secure his recovery, and his heart was filled with affectionate gratitude to her for the service she had rendered him. This gratitude was so intense that it had engendered the warmest friendly affection for her, and he felt that if his heart were not already irretrievably given to another, he could and would love her devotedly for the kindness which she had shown him; and yet there was not in this feeling the slightest element of disloyalty to Ruth, for in harboring it he did not really contemplate ever loving Miss R——, or wish that he were free to love her. Thinking of her kindness and attention to him reminded him of the circumstances which called them forth, and he began to wonder what experience awaited him as a prisoner of war. He was satisfied that, as soon as he regained his strength, he would be taken to some one of the Northern prisons to be kept there until regularly exchanged, and the thought of an indefinite and probably a lengthy imprisonment was horrible to him   He determined that he would not wait to be exchanged, but would make an effort to escape if he should have the slightest opportunity for so doing, and thought it possible that Miss R—— might offer some suggestions that would aid him in his purpose. While thinking about this matter, he fell asleep, and did not wake until the next morning.

CHAPTER V.

When Miss R—— arrived at the hospital that morning, she found Ashton greatly refreshed and looking much better as the result of his long sleep. She expressed great gratification at his improved condition, took a seat near his couch, and they were soon conversing with each other as freely as if they had been old acquaintances. In the course of their conversation she told him that during his delirium he had talked in a random manner about various experiences of his which had awakened both her interest and sympathy, and she asked him to tell her as much as he felt inclined to relate of his past life. This he proceeded to do, and the marked attention which she gave the recital showed that she was deeply interested in the story of his life. Similarly friendly and confidential conversations occurred between them every day, and finally their intimacy had become such that Ashton felt authorized to broach the subject of his intended effort to escape when removed from the hospital, and asked Miss R—— if she could offer any suggestion that might aid him in the accomplishment of his purpose.

"Yes," she replied, "and I had already thought of making such a suggestion to you. As I have before stated, my home is in New Castle, Delaware, and if you could succeed in reaching that place it is probable that some means might be provided by which you could get back to the Confederate army. My father is fully in sympathy with the Southern States in the struggle which has resulted from the steps taken by them in the exercise of their constitutional rights and for the preservation of the same, and he would gladly render you any assistance within his power, especially if he were informed of my wishes in the matter. I have already written him about your case, the part I took in the means used for your recovery, and my friendly interest in you, and all that would be necessary to secure his aid would be your identification as the wounded Confederate soldier concerning whom I have written him. This can easily be accomplished, but it must be done in such a man-

ner that there will be no chance to discover your purpose in
seeking my father, or my connection with it; and hence it
would be out of the question for me to give you a **written**
communication to be delivered to him. The plan **of which**
I have been thinking is this: I have a peculiarly **marked**
ring that is an heirloom and has **been in our family more**
than a hundred years, and **when you are ready to leave**
here I will give you an exact drawing **of the ring to be**
delivered to my father, with the request from **me** that he
will render you such assistance as he **may be able** to give
you."

"I am exceedingly **grateful**," said Ashton," for your prof-
fered assistance; but **fear** that its **acceptance** might involve your father and endanger his life or liberty."

She replied: "Of course he will incur some risk in trying
to aid you; but you must not on that account hesitate to
seek his assistance, for if the matter is properly managed
the risk will be slight and he will gladly take it."

"I will gladly accept the drawing," **said Ashton,** "but
cannot positively promise to use it in the manner **suggested,**
for the reason already given. **In any event it will prove a**
precious *souvenir* of the generous purpose that prompted
its execution, and a sweet reminder of the kind-hearted
friend who executed it."

As the days passed by Ashton **rapidly** regained his
strength, and toward the last of September his convales-
cence was such **as** to admit of his removal from the hospital. This removal was perhaps hastened a few days **in**
consequence of the fact that the hospital was somewhat
crowded by an accession of Confederate soldiers who had
been wounded and captured in the battle of Sharpsburg on
the 17th of September. On the day before his removal
Ashton ascertained that it would occur the next morning
and informed Miss R—— of the fact, and told her that he
inferred from what he had heard that he would be confined
for at least two or three weeks in the Old Capitol prison in
the city.

She at once gave him the drawing **which she** had made
of her ring, and again insisted that he must use it in the
event of his succeeding in reaching her father. It had been

made on a small piece of paper, and he easily concealed it under the lining of his coat. During the conversation that ensued, Miss R—— told Ashton that, without any definite reason therefor, she was impressed with the idea that he would succeed in escaping from prison and that her father would in some way aid him in the matter, and gave him full directions for finding her father's residence without the necessity of further inquiry on the subject. At the close of their conversation, Ashton again spoke of his deep and lasting gratitude to Miss R—— for her great kindness to him, and then bade her good-bye with the expressed hope that they would meet again.

On the following morning he was carried to the Old Capitol prison, and placed on the second floor in one of the front rooms overlooking the street between that building and the capitol. He found that there was a small yard in the rear of the building where the prisoners were permitted at stated hours to walk for exercise; and during his stay he made full use of the opportunities thus offered for bodily exercise, as he knew that he would need all of his strength in order to succeed in making his escape should an occasion for so doing arise. He remained in the old capitol building about five weeks, and during that period saw Miss R—— several times from his prison window, as she passed by the building as often as she could safely do so without attracting the attention of the sentinels on the sidewalk in front of the prison. Ashton always greeted her with a friendly bow and a pleasant smile, and she returned his salutations with an answering smile. She feared to give any further evidence of recognition, and gave this with the utmost caution, as the Federal authorities did not permit any exchange of salutations between the Confederate prisoners in the old capitol building and the citizens of Washington, and punished such citizens as were detected in the same.

Although there was no one in the city who more thoroughly sympathized with these prisoners than did Miss R——, yet there were some who were more daring than she was in the manifestation of their sympathy, and it was no unusual sight for the Confederate soldiers, as they looked out through their prison bars, to see some beautiful woman openly salute them with a pleasant bow and smile and an expressive wave of her handkerchief. Such salutations were answered by the raising of battered and weather-stained hats and caps and by other silent tokens of respect and admiration, and would have received a more demonstrative response in the clarion tones of "the rebel yell," but for the fact that this would have attracted the attention of the sentinels below to the conduct of these noble and kind-hearted ladies, and thereby caused their arrest.

About the middle of October Ashton was taken to Fort Delaware, where a prison for Confederate soldiers had been established. Fort Delaware is situated on an island in the Delaware River, opposite Delaware City and about seven miles below New Castle. A considerable part of the island might be said to be artificial, as it is below the level of high tide and is protected from overflow by a broad and high levee that encompasses the island.

On arriving at Fort Delaware, Ashton was greatly pleased that he had been brought to that place as it was so near to New Castle, where Mr. R—— resided; and this close proximity of one whom he believed would befriend him, if called upon for assistance, strengthened his determination to lose no time in arranging some plan by which he would endeavor to escape. Hence, he immediately began to study the topography of the place for the purpose of ascertaining as far as possible what difficulties and dangers he would encounter in attempting to leave the island. He found that the prison for private soldiers and non-commissioned officers consisted of a number of wooden barracks that had been erected just below the fort. The outer row of barracks, together with the long dining-room, formed three sides of a parallelogram, the other side being formed by a high partition separating this inclosure from the prison for commissioned officers, and as this outer row of barracks had no doors or other outlets to the rear, the prison grounds within were thereby completely protected by the same. At the northeast corner of the inclosure there was an opening through which the prisoners had free access at all times to a small space between that point and the levee on the eastern side of the island. This space was inclosed by a high stockade extending almost to the water's edge, and taking in part of the levee. Near the southeast corner of this stockade there was a small gate through which the prisoners passed out to the water when they were occasionally allowed to bathe in the river. As a sentinel was always on guard at a point about twenty paces from this gate, no extraordinary precautions had been taken to prevent its being opened, and it was fastened by means of a common stock-lock.

Ashton decided that when he got ready for his attempt to escape it should be made by way of this gate. The most serious objection to leaving the prison at this place was, that it was the farthest point of the island from the Delaware shore, where he wished to land, and hence he would have to swim nearly half way around the island before he could strike across the river to his proposed landing-place. However, he was satisfied that it was the only place that offered any reasonable chance for him to reach the water without being seen by the sentinels, and for that reason he preferred leaving the prison at this point, notwithstanding the fact that his so doing would necessitate an extra amount of swimming in order for him to land on the Delaware shore. As he believed it would be impossible for him to procure a key that would fit the lock, he was satisfied that he would have to "pick it," and proceeded to construct an instrument by means of which he hoped to do this. Procuring a piece of wire he bent it at a right angle about half an inch from one end, and inserted the other end in a piece of wood to be used as a handle in turning his thus improvised skeleton-key. It was a simple and rude instrument, but he felt confident that it would answer his purpose unless the lock was so constructed as to prevent the point of the wire from coming in contact with the bolt. His next step was to secure some canteens to be used as floats to support him in swimming across the river. As he thought that four canteens would be necessary for his purpose, and the possession of that many by any one person would excite suspicion, he took into his confidence three of his fellow-prisoners whom he could trust, and obtained from them promises that they would let him have their canteens when the time arrived for his attempted escape.

By the first of November Ashton's wound had entirely healed and he had regained his usual strength, and **only** awaited a favorable opportunity for attempting his escape. He knew that the attempt must be made on a very dark night in order to insure its success. On the night of November 9th, the anxiously awaited opportunity arrived. The day had been damp and cloudy, and shortly after sunset the wind commenced blowing strongly from the southeast and by 10 o'clock it had greatly increased in strength and a heavy rain was falling. The darkness was intense, and Ashton decided that he would wait no longer, and proceeded to arrange for his departure. Taking from its place of concealment under his coat-lining, the paper which Miss R—— had given him, he put it in a water-proof match box to protect it while he should be swimming across the river. He had that night obtained the three canteens which had been promised him as before mentioned, and taking off his coat, he strapped them and his own canteen **around** his body so that they rested on his back, just below his shoulder-blades. He then put on his coat, thereby hiding the canteens from view, and quietly left the barracks. At the place where the sentinel near the small gate was posted, there was a lamp that was kept burning all night, and Ashton feared that the light from this lamp might cause his detection. When he had arrived within thirty-five or forty yards of this sentinel's post and at a point where he could have seen the lamp if it had been burning, he was rejoiced to find that it was not lighted. Owing to its exposed position it had shortly before been extinguished by the gale that was blowing, and as the sentinel could not leave his post at this time to procure means for relighting the lamp, he was awaiting the arrival of the relief-guard for the accomplishment of this purpose.

Ashton cautiously advanced toward the gate and succeeded in reaching it without attracting the attention of the sentinel. The latter could not have seen him on account of the intense darkness even if he had been looking directly at the gate, but he was looking in a different direction, for

the gate being somewhat south of his post and the furious
southeast wind having caused him to turn his back to it,
his face was toward the northwest. By passing his fingers
over the face of the lock, Ashton soon found the keyhole
and proceeded to insert into it the instrument that he had
constructed for the purpose of picking the lock. He found
that he had made a correct guess as to the length of the
key, and also that there was nothing to prevent the point
of his instrument from reaching the bolt of the lock, and on
reaching it the instrument caught firmly in the slot of the
bolt. Giving the instrument a strong and steady twist he
was gratified to find that the bolt responded to the force
thus exerted on it and gradually returned to its socket, and
in a moment the gate was unlocked. Withdrawing his
instrument from the lock, he opened the gate, passed
through and closed it, and then inserting the instrument
into the keyhole from the outside succeeded in relocking
the gate. This, as the reader will readily understand, was
done for the purpose of preventing an early discovery of the
fact that a prisoner had escaped. Having thus secured
the gate, Ashton crept down to the water's edge and was
about to enter the river, when the thought occurred to him
that perhaps the exceedingly inclement weather had caused
the sentinels along the levee to be called in nearer to the
barracks and, if so, that he could make the half circuit of
the island on land instead of in the water as he had at first
contemplated doing. Acting on this idea, he cautiously proceeded down the river along the levee, and on reaching a
point where a sentinel was usually posted, discovered that
none was there. He made a similar discovery on arriving
at the next point where a sentinel was accustomed to be
on guard, for his supposition was correct and all of the
sentinels had been called in from that part of the levee and
were on guard nearer the barracks. Hence he proceeded
rapidly along the levee until he had passed around the lower
end of the island and then entered the water and struck out
boldly for the Delaware shore. He was an expert swimmer
and, being buoyed up by his canteens and greatly aided by
the wind and waves coming from the southeast, succeeded
in reaching the Delaware shore in a comparatively short

time. He landed a short distance above Delaware City, having taken a northwest course in order to get the full benefit of the wind and waves that bore him in that direction.

On reaching the shore he unstrapped the canteens from his body, filled them with water and threw them into the river. He then started off in a brisk walk, bearing up the river in the direction of New Castle, as he had decided to comply with Miss R——'s wish and call on her father for assistance. Being unacquainted with the country, he could not advance with any degree of certainty as to whether he was going in the right direction, and only hoped to proceed in a general northerly course. After walking about a mile he entered a road that appeared to lead in the direction that he wished to go, and he decided to keep in it as long as its course remained the same.

He had followed this road for two miles, passing a number of houses in which there was no sign of a light, when he came to a house near the roadside in which there was a bright light burning. As it was now after 12 o'clock, he was surprised to see this light and, on approaching the house, naturally looked in through a window from which the curtains were drawn. The sight which he beheld at once arrested his attention and aroused his sympathy. Near the center of the room was a cradle, and lying in it was a little child that appeared to be very sick and was breathing with great difficulty. By the side of the cradle knelt a well-dressed young woman whose face was intensely sad, and indicated that she was in the deepest distress and perplexity. Standing by her and gazing down upon the face of the child was a young man, whose face was also exceedingly sad and bore a distressed and helpless look, as if he were painfully conscious of his inability to relieve the child, and that his grief had thereby been greatly intensified. So deeply absorbed was Ashton in contemplating the scene before him, and so thoroughly was his sympathy aroused by its sight, that he entirely forgot for the moment his own condition and danger, and thought only of the suffering child and its distressed parents, and felt irresistibly impelled to offer his sympathy to the latter and endeavor to relieve the sufferings of the former. Acting on this impulse, Ashton knocked at the door and, upon its being opened, walked into the room, explained the cause of his apparent intrusion, and asked if he could render any assistance in an effort to relieve the child.

The parents thanked him for the kindly interest he had manifested in the child's condition, and said that there was nothing he could do to aid them in relieving its sufferings. Noticing the wet condition of Ashton's clothes, the man told him he was incurring great danger in wearing them, and suggested that they be immediately exchanged for dry garments.

Ashton gratefully accepted his kind offer, and was at once conducted to an adjoining room where his wet garments were soon exchanged for a plain suit of citizen's clothes. Returning to the room where the mother was still anxiously bending over her sick child, Ashton made such suggestions for its comfort as occurred to him, and although they did not materially help the child, they indicated his anxious concern for its condition and also his great sympathy for its distressed parents.

In the course of an hour the child appeared to be considerably relieved from its suffering and shortly thereafter went to sleep. Its mother then arose and told her husband that she would go into another room to take a short nap, and asked him to awaken her in about an hour, or sooner if the child should awake before the expiration of that time.

Immediately after she retired, Ashton asked her husband if he would permit him to bring his clothes into the room for the purpose of drying them before the fire, so that they would be in a condition to be worn when he got ready to leave.

"Do not concern yourself about drying your clothes," said the gentleman, "as you will have no further use for them."

"You are mistaken," replied Ashton. "I will have a very important use for them as I will have to wear them, for I really have no other clothes."

"I know." said the gentleman, "that you had no other clothes when you came here; but now you have a full suit which, although plain, is comparatively new and much better adapted to your use under existing circumstances than would be the clothes which you have taken off."

The gentleman's use of the expression, "under existing circumstances," in connection with what he said about the two suits of clothes, caused Ashton to start, and look at him with a quick, scrutinizing glance to see if his face gave any additional emphasis to this suggestive expression. Seeing that it did not, Ashton replied:

"I do not at all understand your remark, for the clothes which I have on do not belong to me, and will be returned to you before I leave here, and I cannot see how they should be better adapted to my use than my own clothes, if the latter were only dry."

"If you really do not understand my remark," said the gentleman, "I suppose I will have to explain it, and also make known the purpose I have formed concerning you, although I would have greatly preferred not doing so, as the danger I am incurring would thereby have been lessened. Immediately after you entered the room I noticed that your clothes were of military style, and as they were not blue I knew that you could not be a Federal soldier. As there is a prison for Confederate soldiers at Fort Delaware, which is only a few miles from here, and as you appeared to be too thoroughly drenched from head to foot to have been put in that plight by the rain that has fallen to-night, I at once concluded that you were a Confederate prisoner who had escaped from that prison by swimming the river. The great concern which you manifested in the condition of my child, and your warm sympathy for my wife and myself in our deep distress, touched my heart and awakened in me the liveliest interest in your case, and I determined to aid you in your further efforts to escape, but thought that it would be best, at least for myself, to keep you in ignorance of my purpose. Knowing that your clothes would attract attention, as they were of a military cut and not those of a Federal soldier, I decided to let them remain in their wet condition, and then, when you were ready to leave, I would have an excuse for insisting on

your further use of the clothes I had loaned you, simply suggesting that you could return them when you reached your
destination. Hence it was that I was seemingly lacking in
consideration and courtesy as your host, both in not
promptly having your clothes dried without being asked
and also in offering an excuse for not doing so after your
request in regard to the matter had been made. In addition
to the reasons already given, there is also another why
I was willing to aid you in your effort to escape, and that
is the fact that I do not at all approve of the war of
coercion which is being waged against the Southern Sates,
and they have my sympathy in the struggle. That fact, I
will add, accounts for my presence here at this time; for if
I had believed that the United States were right in attempting, by force of arms, to coerce the seceding States back into
the Union, I would now be at the front as a soldier in the
Federal army."

Ashton had listened with mingled emotions of surprise,
admiration, and gratitude to this explanation, and at its
close, said:

"I cannot hope to repay the kindness you have already
shown me and the still greater kindness which you purpose
concerning me; but I can and will ever cherish the deepest
gratitude for the services you have rendered me, and remember with emotions of highest admiration and warmest
regard the true, noble, and kind-hearted man you have proven
yourself to be. While I would gladly tell you everything
about my recent experience and future plans, I am satisfied,
from what you have said, that it is best that I should tell
you nothing—not even my name—so that if you should be
interrogated concerning me, and it becomes necessary for
you to answer such interrogation, you can truthfully state
that all you know about me is the fact that I sought and
obtained shelter here during the night, and left the next
morning without having given either my name or my destination."

"You have anticipated my wishes," replied the gentleman,
"and expressed my own views in regard to the matter. And
now that you may obtain some sleep and rest before morning, I will conduct you to your bed."

He then conducted Ashton to a bedroom on the opposite side of the house, and, after bidding him goodnight, there left him.

Ashton immediately retired and soon fell asleep. He was awakened by his host about dawn, and ere the sun had risen, had heartily partaken of a substantial breakfast and was ready to resume his journey. He had inquired as to the condition of the sick child, and was rejoiced to learn that it had greatly improved, and that the child was apparently out of danger. Just before Ashton got ready to leave, his host offered to loan him money to defray his traveling expenses, supposing that he probably had only Confederate money, which was entirely worthless in that section.

Ashton thanked him for his kind offer, but declined to accept it, stating that he had sufficient money to meet his immediate wants. This was true, as Ashton, like many other Confederate cavalrymen who were frequently in that part of Virginia which was alternately occupied by each of the contending armies, sometimes had occasion to use United States currency in dealing with the citizens, and hence had accumulated a supply of "greenbacks" for that purpose. Having obtained directions as to the route to New Castle, Ashton again thanked his host for his kindness, bade him and his wife good-bye and left them. As he was leaving, his host laughingly and with a knowing wink, said:

"If you should not find a favorable opportunity for returning the clothes, do not worry yourself about the matter, as they are of no great value."

5

CHAPTER VI.

As the distance to New Castle was short and Ashton was a fast walker, he arrived at that place early in the morning.

Wishing to see Mr. R—— as soon as possible and alone, he immediately proceeded to his house, the location of which he had learned from Miss R——, as before stated. He found that Mr. R—— had not yet gone to his place of business, and shortly after he was ushered into the house, that gentleman made his appearance. He was apparently about fifty years of age, had a ruddy complexion, rather light hair, bright blue eyes and a frank and genial countenance. When he entered the room, Ashton arose and said:

"My name is John Ashton, and I presume that I have the pleasure of addressing Mr. R——."

"Yes sir," said the latter, extending his hand, "that is my name. Please be seated, Mr. Ashton. And now, how can I serve you?"

Resuming his seat, Ashton said:

"You have doubtless been surprised by this informal call on the part of a stranger, especially as I come to your house instead of your place of business. My explanation and excuse for my conduct is the fact that I desired to see you alone and as soon as possible after reaching this place, and hence, on arriving here this morning, I immediately came to your house. As your time is valuable and my business is urgent, I will at once make known the object of my visit. I am a Confederate soldier, was wounded and captured during the battle of Manassas last August, and afterward carried to a hospital in Washington City, and there your kind-hearted and noble daughter, Miss Annie R——, carefully nursed me during a period of dangerous illness and delirium, and ministered to my necessities in such manner as to save my life. After my return to consciousness and during the remainder of my stay in the hospital, she continued to manifest an interest in my welfare, and showed me much kindness. She explained why she had come to the hospital as a nurse, telling me of your sympathy for the South in the war that is now in progress, and of her own feelings in regard to the matter. Just before I left the hospital she stated that, if I could escape from captivity and succeed in reaching this place, you might be able to assist me in returning to the Confederate army, telling me that she had written you concerning me, and the part that she had taken in securing my recovery from sickness. She said that in order to obtain your assistance it would be necessary only to enable you to identify me as the person about whom she had written you, and provided for this identification by giving me a drawing of a peculiarly marked ring belonging to her, and told me to present it to you with the request from her that you would aid me in my effort to get back into the Confederate lines. I stated that I could not positively promise to call on you for assistance as I feared that by giving it you might endanger your life or liberty. She said that if the matter were properly managed the risk would be slight and you would gladly take it. I was taken from Washington City to Fort Delaware about three weeks ago, and last night succeeded in escaping from the latter place by swimming the river, and as I was so near your place of residence I decided that I would come here, have an interview with you and ascertain whether you could render me any assistance without danger to yourself. And now I will deliver the drawing of which I spoke, with the request that if you cannot assist me without danger to yourself, you will not undertake to do so."

Ashton then handed the drawing to Mr. R—— and, after glancing at it, the latter said:

"Your own statement, Mr. Ashton, taken in connection with what my daughter has written me, would have been sufficient to satisfy me as to your identity, and this drawing furnishes perfect proof of the same; for I recognize in it an accurate representation of my daughter's ring. You have acted wisely in coming to me in your present condition; for without the aid of some friend it would be impossible for you to effect your return to the Confederate army, on account of the extensive and thorough system of both military and civil surveillance which has been established by the Federal Government. I cannot deny that I will incur danger in trying to assist you, but this fact will not deter me from the effort, for my daughter correctly stated what would be my course in the matter in saying that I would gladly take the risk in order to aid you. I have no definite plan in view at present, but hope that during the morning I may mature one by means of which I can assist you without any great danger to myself. As it is now near the time at which I should go to my place of business, I must arrange for your concealment here during my absence. Did anyone see you enter my house, or did you make any inquiry as to my place of residence?"

"No one except the servant who ushered me in saw me enter the house," said Ashton, "and I made no inquiry as to your place of residence, your daughter having given me the number and location of the house; and hence I found my way here without having to ask directions in regard to the same."

"That is fortunate," said Mr. R——, "for it is best that your visit to me should not be known and that your presence in the town should, as far as possible, be concealed during your stay. In order that these desirable objects may be accomplished, I will now conduct you to my study, where you will be entirely free from intrusion, as no one enters it except by my direction, or at my call when I am there."

Mr. R—— then conducted Ashton to a room on the second floor of the house, at the rear of the building and overlooking the garden. It contained a large bookcase filled with volumes of the choicest literature, a centre-table on which there were several new magazines and daily papers, a writing-desk, several easy chairs, a luxurious rocker and an inviting lounge; and the contents of the room, together with a bright fire that was burning in the grate, gave it an air of cosy comfortableness that was exceedingly pleasing. Going to his writing-desk, Mr. R—— took from one of the drawers a map and, handing it to Ashton, said:

"This is the latest and most accurate war map of Northern Virginia and, while awaiting my return, it would be well for you to study the same and thoroughly familiarize yourself with the topography of the section through which you will have to pass in your effort to reach the Confederate army. As you doubtless know, General McClellan was removed from the command of the Federal army in Northern Virginia on the 7th day of this month, and General Burnside has been placed in command of the same. Before his removal General McClellan had concentrated the **army** around Warrenton and along the north bank of the Rappahannock river, and it is still there. But in studying the map with a view to your contemplated movements, **you** must do so upon the idea that the Federal army will shortly be at Fredericksburg, for General **Burnside is reported as** favoring its removal to that point. You may expect me back at noon, and I hope that by that time I will have formed some plan by means of which you can succeed in **passing** through the Federal lines."

Mr. R—— then left Ashton, and the latter immediately began a study of the map which had been furnished him. **Being** satisfied that the plan which Mr R—— would suggest for his movements would necessitate his passage through Washington City, he had been gratified to learn that the Federal army would soon be removed **to Fred**ericksburg, as this would leave Fauquier county **(where** that army then was) comparatively free from the presence of Federal soldiers, and thus increase his facilities for reaching the Confederate army by crossing the upper Rappahannock at one of the numerous fords above its junction with the Rapidan. Hence, on examining the map and becoming satisfied that General Burnside's base of supplies would be Acquia Creek, on the Potomac, when his army reached Fred**ericksburg,** Ashton decided that when he should leave Wash**ington City** he would go on the Orange and Alexandria **railroad as** far as he could safely travel toward Rappahannock Station, and then leaving the railroad endeavor to **elude the** Federal pickets along the Rappahannock and cross the river into Culpeper county.

About noon **Mr. R——** returned, and at once made known to Ashton the plan which he had devised for his escape, which we will give in his own words.

"It will be necessary," he said, "for you to go to Washington City and perhaps remain there several days, and in order that you may do this without exciting suspicion, you must **have some ostensible** business calling you there. Hence

I have prepared some orders for merchandise to be presented by you to two wholesale merchants in Washington with whom I occasionally have dealings, and who, like myself, sympathize with the South in the present struggle. I have also written these gentlemen letters introducing you to them as Mr. James Gray, who has recently been employed by me, and in the letters have commended you to their favor. One of these gentlemen, Mr. B——, is so thoroughly in sympathy with the South that you would run no risk in revealing to him your real name and character, and if, as I fear, it should become necessary for you to have a passport in order to leave Washington for the seat of war, you may safely ask his assistance in procuring one. Here is a ticket to Washington which I have purchased for you, and also two hundred dollars to be used as the exigencies of your condition may require. As it is nearly time for the arrival of the train for Wilmington, you had best start to the station, and hence I will not longer detain you."

Ashton was deeply affected by the kindness and generosity of Mr. R——, and gave expression to his grateful appreciation of the same in heartfelt thanks, and assured the latter that the ticket and money given him were accepted as a loan, to be repaid as soon as possible. Mr. R—— then conducted him to the front door and, after they had bidden each other good-bye, Ashton left the house without being seen by any of the family. He immediately repaired to the railroad station and in a few minutes had boarded the train and was on his way to Wilmington. At that place he made close connection with the train for Baltimore and Washington and reached the latter city that night. Getting into a cab he was driven to one of the principal hotels and there registered as "James Gray, Baltimore." Shortly after his arrival he retired to the room which had been assigned him and was soon enjoying a refreshing sleep. The next day he called on the merchants to whom he had letters of introduction, was pleasantly received by them and, after leaving with them the orders sent by Mr. R—— for merchandise, concluded that he would take a stroll over a part of the city.

He had gone down Pennsylvania Avenue from the Capitol, passed the President's house, the State, Navy, and War Departments, and was walking out toward the statue of Washington, when a lady turned into the avenue from Eighteenth Street, and came toward him. On meeting her he was delighted to find that she was Miss R——. She at once recognized him and gave him a cordial greeting. Fearing that he might attract attention by being seen with her on the street, he obtained her address and told her that he would visit her that evening, and then resumed his stroll. At the appointed hour he called on Miss R—— and found her impatiently awaiting his arival, as she was anxious to **ascertain** how he had effected his escape from prison, and **also** wished to see and converse with him as soon as possible. He at once proceeded to give her a full account of the manner in which he escaped from Fort Delaware and his subsequent experience that night, and then told her of the generous and efficient part which her father had taken in aiding him to reach Washington in safety.

"I knew that he would do all in **his** power to aid you," she said, "and I am so glad that you gave him an opportunity for assisting **you**. We must now devise some means by which you can safely **leave** Washington and return to the Confederate army. I learned from the surgeon at the hospital that Captain Neill, of General Burnside's staff was here yesterday with dispatches from General Burnside to General Halleck, and it is reported that the Federal army is about to march down the Rappahannock to Fredericksburg. This **indicates** that an important movement is on hand, and **consequently** the newspapers will send correspondents to the front **in** order to keep fully posted in regard to transpiring events. It has therefore occurred to me that if you could obtain a passport as 'a war correspondent,' an excellent opportunity would thereby be afforded you for reaching a point from which you could easily pass through the Federal lines."

"Your suggestion is an excellent one," said Ashton, "and **if** possible, I will carry it out. By it I am reminded of the **fact** that your father informed me that I might safely reveal myself to Mr. B——, to whom he gave me a letter of introduction, and that he could perhaps obtain a passport for me."

"Yes," said Miss R——, "I think that you might safely reveal yourself to him, but this need not be done by you in person; and, in order to avoid the risk which both you and he might incur by personal interviews, I think it best that the matter should be arranged by a third person. As I am on very friendly terms with him, I will undertake the arrangement of the matter for you."

"There is no limit to your kindness," said Ashton, "and I am overwhelmed by a sense of the obligation under which it has placed me. Your generous desire to befriend me has seemingly rendered you oblivious of the danger which you will incur in the matter, and I must not be so selfish as to let you take this risk."

"You are mistaken," replied Miss R——, "in supposing that I will incur any danger; for if Mr. B—— should excite any suspicion in his effort to secure the passport, this suspicion will rest only on him, as I shall so arrange matters that I will not be known in the undertaking. Hence, you must let me carry out my plan, and while the effort is being made to obtain the passport, you had best leave the hotel where you are now staying and secure lodging in some secluded part of the city."

"I perceive," said Ashton, "that I cannot maintain the position taken by me in the matter, and must submit to your wishes concerning it. As I have assumed the name of James Gray and registered as from Baltimore, I suppose that it will be best to obtain the passport for me under that name and as the representative of a Baltimore paper."

"Yes," said Miss R——, "and another reason for such an arrangement is the fact that, as you are a Southerner and show it in your appearance and speech, you would more readily pass for a Baltimorean than for a Philadelphian, Bostonian, or New Yorker, and it would naturally be supposed that you reside in the place where the paper represented by you is published."

After conversing awhile longer with Miss R——, Ashton left her with the understanding that he should call three days thereafter to ascertain the result of her efforts to obtain the passport.

In accordance with Miss R——'s suggestion, he obtained lodging at a private boarding-house in a retired part of the city, and remained there during the greater part of the next three days. He would have gladly visited Miss R—— several times during this period, as he was anxious to be with her as much as possible, but, at her suggestion, refrained from so doing as she feared that his visits might attract attention to him and perhaps excite suspicion as to the cause of his presence in the city, it being well known by the government officials that she was a volunteer nurse in the hospital for sick and wounded Confederate soldiers.

When he called on Miss R—— at the appointed time, he was rejoiced to learn that she had been successful in her undertaking.

"The passport," said she, "was obtained more easily than I anticipated when I undertook to secure it. The day after you were here I called on Mr. B—— at his residence and gave him a history of your case, told him that I was greatly concerned about securing your return to the Confederate army, and asked him if it were possible for him to obtain for you a passport that would enable you to go safely to the seat of war, and suggested the plan which you and I had discussed as to your going in the character of a newspaper correspondent. He stated that he thought he could obtain the passport for you, and also approved the plan suggested. He farther said that Major W——, the provost-marshal of the city, and he were old friends, and he believed that the major would provide the passport without making any close investigation of the case. I was requested to call again the following day to ascertain the result of his efforts. I did so, and was at once informed by him that he had secured a genuine regulation passport, duly issued for James Gray, correspondent for *The Baltimore Gazette,* and entitling him to uninterrupted passage from Washington City to all points in Virginia within the Federal lines. It is all right and will be respected by the most exacting officials. I now deliver to you this precious docu-

ment with the heartfelt hope that it may enable you to
safely reach your command."

Ashto received the paper from Miss R——, and, grasping
her hand, said in a voice tremulous with emotion: "Words
cannot express my gratitude for your unfailing kindness.
I am already indebted to you for my life, and you now make
me your debtor for the means of its farther enjoyment in
freedom. My unceasing and grateful remembrance of your
kindness, and my abiding friendship for you, will prove how
deeply I feel and appreciate the interest you have manifested in my welfare and the services you have rendered me."

"It has given me the greatest pleasure to aid you," said
she, "and the satisfaction of having been able to assist you
is in itself ample reward for all that I have done. Moreover, has it not given me that rare and priceless treasure, a
true friend? Yes, and although the events of the future
may be such that we will never meet again, it will ever be
to me a source of purest pleasure to believe that your friendship for me is unchanged and that your kindliest wishes
follow me through life."

"Yes, my dear friend," said Ashton, "my best wishes will
ever follow you, and if they could control your fate, your
entire life would be filled with richest blessings. Such I
hope and believe will be the case; for I know that your
noble and generous nature will constantly lead you to perform acts of kindness, and the satisfaction which you will
feel in thus helping others will insure your happiness, as it is
indeed 'more blessed to give than to receive.' I have already
told you of my gratitude for the inestimable benefits which
I have personally received from you, and now, in behalf of
my beloved Southland, where at present your good deeds
are unknown, I thank you with all my heart for your noble
devotion to its cause and your generous kindness and assistance to its sick and wounded soldiers. I must now leave
you and, as I shall start on my journey to-morrow, and
hence will not be able to see you again before my departure,
I will bid you good-bye."

Giving Ashton a cordial grasp of her hand, Miss R——
said: "Good-bye. I shall never forget you. May God
bless and protect you."

And thus these friends, whom the chances of war had so strangely brought together, parted to meet no more until—— but we must not anticipate coming events, as the reader's interest in our story might thereby be lessened.

CHAPTER VII.

The next morning Ashton purchased a suitable outfit for a newspaper correspondent who intended going to the front, a pair of saddle-bags, an overcoat and a pair of blankets.

Immediately after reaching Washington he had returned by express the clothes which he borrowed on the night of his escape from Fort Delaware, and now wore a neat business suit of brown cassimere.

Returning to his boarding-house, he packed his saddle-bags, paid his bill, hired a cab to take him to the station and, after his passport had been duly inspected by the provost-guard, was soon on his way to Alexandria. From this place he was rapidly borne toward Rappahannock Station on the Orange and Alexandria railroad, and on arriving at Manassas was vividly reminded of his having been wounded and captured near that place, and of the varied experiences which had come to him in consequence of that misfortune.

At Catlett's Station several Federal soldiers came into the car where Ashton was, and were soon talking about the movements of the army. He learned from their conversation that it was being rapidly moved toward Fredericksburg, that the greater part of the infantry had left Fauquier county and the remainder would leave early in the morning of the next day, and that only a portion of the cavalry would remain for the purpose of temporarily guarding the fords along the Rappahannock. He had at first thought of going to within a few miles of Rappahannock Station before leaving the railroad, but in view of what he had just heard, decided to leave it at Warrenton Junction, and therefore left the train when it reached that place. His reason for this was, that if he went much farther toward the Rappahannock by rail he would, on leaving the cars, probably encounter some of the Federal cavalry who, upon seeing his passport and thus learning his ostensible business and destination, would cause him to turn back and go down the river in the direction taken by the Federal army; whereas, by stopping at Warrenton Junction he would have an opportunity to go across the country above Rappahannock Station and perhaps entirely flank the Federal pickets at Fox's, Lawson's, Freeman's and other fords up the river.

He spent the night at Warrenton Junction, where he found a small part of General Sickles' division, and learned that one corps of the army was encamped near the place and another corps at Bealeton. These two corps started very early the next morning toward Fredericksburg. About two hours thereafter, Ashton succeeded in purchasing a horse, and rode off as if he were going to Fredericksburg by way of Morrisville. He did not go far in that direction before he turned back, left the road and proceeded in a northwesterly course toward Sulphur Spring. Having some knowledge of the country, and being aided by the examination which he had made of Mr. R——'s map, he made good progress, although he avoided the open roads as much as possible. He soon crossed the Orange and Alexandria railroad a mile or two below Warrenton Junction, and, passing above Fayetteville, crossed the road leading from that place to Warrenton. Thinking that there might still be some Federal troops at Warrenton, and therefore fearing to go any nearer to that place, he changed his course so as to bear down toward the Rappahannock river, and about noon was near the intersection of the roads from Sulphur Spring, Jeffersonton and Fayetteville at Fox's Ford. Finding that he had gone near the river, and that too at a place where there was probably a Federal picket, he turned a little to the right for the purpose of passing above this place, but had not proceeded far before he came in sight of a bivouac of cavalry. Discovering that they were Federal troops he would have turned back, but, being satisfied that they had seen him, feared that by so doing he would excite their suspicion, and hence he boldly rode forward into their midst. He found that he had come upon a small picket force that was guarding Fox's Ford, and had selected the point where he discovered them as picket headquarters, in order that they might the better watch the roads above and below them. The troops were a part of the —— New York cavalry which had been sent out from Bealeton by

General Bayard **to picket Beverly's,** Fox's, Lawson's and Freeman's Fords.

The squad consisted of about twenty men under the command of Lieutenant C——, and when Ashton reached them he was halted and at once carried before that officer. Upon being questioned by the officer as to his name and occupation, Ashton told him that his name was James Gray and that **he** was a correspondent for *The Baltimore Gazette.* **The** officer laughingly informed him that he would not be **likely** to obtain any war news in that quarter, as he was on **the outpost of the** Federal army, which was then moving toward Fredericksburg, and that if he wished to be of any service to his paper as a war correspondent, he would have to turn back and ride down the river to that place. Having inspected his passport and found that it was all right, the officer was about to dismiss Ashton, **when** one of the troopers who had been closely scrutinizing his face, said:

"Heigh-ho! Is that you, Ashton? **I did not** expect to see you here, and especially in citizen's clothes, as I heard that you had joined the Confederate **army."**

Ashton turned toward the speaker, and his heart gave a great throb and began to beat rapidly as he recognized in the Federal trooper, Henry Kuhn, a former acquaintance whom he had met at the University of Virginia, **and who then lived in New York.** Knowing that it would **be impossible for him to overcome the testimony** which Kuhn would give as to his identity, and being conscious of having already manifested such emotion as, if noticed, would prove suspicious, Ashton promptly decided that he would attempt no further deception, but fully explain why he was there in citizen's dress, and conceal only such matters as might implicate others. Replying to Kuhn, he said:

"Yes, Kuhn, this is John Ashton, and you were correctly informed as to my having joined the Confederate army. Although we **were on** friendly terms at the university, I am forced to the impoliteness of saying that I am not at all glad to see you."

Kuhn laughed and said: "Well, I do not blame you for **your aversion to seeing** me under existing circumstances, **nor for the frankness with which you** have expressed it.

Frankness was always one of your leading characteristics, and I cannot reconcile that fact with your present assumed name and occupation. I hope, however, that you can satisfactorily explain your presence here, and my knowledge of your former character may assist you in the matter. If so, I will gladly aid you."

"I thank you for your kind offer," said Ashton, "and with the testimony which you can furnish as to my former character I will be able to give a satisfactory explanation of my presence inside the Federal lines, and show that I am not here voluntarily, or for any improper purpose. And now, lieutenant, if you are willing to hear me, I am ready to give an account of myself."

"Yes," said the officer, "although I have no authority to finally pass on your case, I will listen to what you have to say."

Ashton then proceeded to give a full and truthful account of his movements after he was wounded and captured, telling of his sickness in the hospital at Washington, his temporary stay at the Old Capitol prison, his transfer to Fort Delaware and subsequent escape therefrom, and his immediate return to Washington.

"In this escape," he said, "I was unaided, and none of the officers of your government are in any manner to blame for the same. Of course, I had assistance in obtaining my passport, but the rack could not make me reveal who rendered it. I assumed a fictitious name and character for the sole purpose of trying to escape from captivity, have made no effort to obtain any information for my government, and the party who rendered me assistance knew the circumstances of my case and merely wished to aid me in avoiding a recapture in my effort to return to the Confederate army."

"I am satisfied, lieutenant," said Kuhn, "that Ashton has told the truth, for my knowledge of his exemplary character and high sense of honor when at college, convinces me beyond doubt that he would not, under any circumstances, stoop to the position of a spy."

"I, too," said Lieutenant C——, "am convinced as to the truthfulness of his story, and trust that he may be able likewise to convince those who will have to deal with his case. But under the circumstances, I can do nothing more than send him to General Bayard at Bealeton, and report the facts attending his capture. Tell a corporal to detail two men, including yourself, and report here at once for the purpose of conveying the prisoner to General Bayard."

In a few moments a corporal, accompanied by Kuhn and another trooper, appeared on horseback ready to do the lieutenant's bidding. Lieutenant C—— had written a short note in regard to Ashton's capture, and, handing it and the passport to the corporal, directed him to conduct Ashton to General Bayard and deliver the papers with the statement that Private Kuhn would give him the details of the case.

Ashton was then directed to mount his horse and was in the act of doing so, when the clatter of horses' feet was heard on the road from Sulphur Spring, and in a few moments a column of Confederate cavalry came dashing toward the encampment at full speed. The Federal troopers rushed for their horses, but before they could get in the saddle the Confederates were in their midst, and seeing that resistance would be useless, they surrendered without firing a shot.

The corporal, having been charged with the delivery of an important paper to General Bayard, felt bound to make a desperate effort to escape for this purpose, and at once dashed off on the road leading to Fayetteville. His movements were immediately discovered by the Confederates, and instantly from the head of their column there darted out, as if propelled by a catapult, a fleet gray mare bearing the slender, wiry form of a man of medium height whose body seemed instinct with life and energy, and whose seat in the saddle proclaimed the practiced rider. Dashing across to the Fayetteville road he was soon in hot pursuit of the fleeing corporal. The latter had about fifty yards the start of him, and, being excellently mounted, thought he could distance the Confederate in the race and make his escape. But he was not aware of the difficulties with which he would have to contend, for he did not know of the phenomenal speed of his pursuer's horse, nor the fiery zeal, tireless energy, and daring courage of her rider. **Both** horses soon reached their full speed, and the corporal, on glancing back, saw that his pursuer was rapidly gaining on him. Seeing that his pursuer was alone, he determined that he would not surrender without **first attempting** to kill the Confederate. When the latter was within fifteen or twenty paces of the corporal he called to him to halt and surrender. Instead of doing so the corporal turned in his saddle and quickly fired at his pursuer, but his aim had been faulty in consequence of the movement of his body in turning to fire, and the ball passed more than a foot to the left of his enemy. The next **moment he saw** the flash **of his** pursuer's pistol, and instantly **felt a sharp pain** in **his** right arm, which dropped powerless to his side, and his pistol fell from his hand, the Confederate having shot through the muscle of his arm just above the elbow. Being now defenseless, the corporal checked his horse and surrendered to the Confederate, and the two rode back to the Federal picket-post. On their arrival there one of the Confederates, addressing the corporal's captor, said:

"Well, captain, I see that you caught him. **We were confident** that you **would** do so and knew that you would not need any assistance in the matter, and hence none of us followed you, especially as we saw plenty of other game to be bagged out here."

The person addressed, **replied:**

"**You** did exactly right, Randolph, as it was not necessary **that more** than one of us should follow a single **man. According to** strict military rules it was improper that I **should have** left the command to follow **a** single fugitive, **and I would** have directed some one else to do this, but for **the fact that I saw** at a glance that he was riding a fleet horse, and feared to risk in his pursuit any horse less fleet than my own. Moreover, I suspected that there might be some special reason, other than the mere fear of captivity, why he was making such a desperate effort to escape, and I was therefore all **the more anxious to** make certain his capture."

Ashton had been listening to this conversation, and now **stepped** forward and said:

"Your suspicion was well-founded, Captain Mosby, for the fugitive was the bearer of a note from the Federal lieutenant here to General Bayard, telling of my capture at this place about an hour ago, and inclosing a passport that had been issued for me in a fictitious name."

Captain Mosby (for the person addressed by Ashton was that famous partisan officer), scrutinizing Ashton's face, said: "Well, this is marvelous! You here, John Ashton? How can that be when you were killed near Manassas last August? There must be some mistake, and I guess that it was in the report that you were killed; for I cannot be mistaken in that face."

"Yes, Captain, the mistake was made in reporting me as being killed at that time, if such report has been made. I was painfully wounded and captured, and have but recently made my escape from imprisonment at Fort Delaware, and was endeavoring to get back into our lines, when my identity was discovered here to-day by an old college-mate who is a member of this Federal troop, and I was about to be carried to General Bayard's headquarters at Bealeton when you and your command so opportunely arrived and disarranged the plans of my captors. You have thereby placed me under everlasting obligation to you, especially as you saved my passport from falling into the hands of those who would have made such investigation concerning it as might have endangered the life or liberty of the person who secured it for me. I will thank you to have the passport at once taken from the man whom you captured and return it to me."

Captain Mosby had one of his men to obtain the passport and, after having glanced at it, returned it to Ashton and said:

"I am truly glad to see you again, and congratulate you on both your escape from prison and the recovery of your passport. While you will no longer need the passport, I appreciate the danger which it might have brought to others if it had not been recovered, and hence its recovery has been exceedingly fortunate. I have been so much interested in your case that I have entirely neglected to look after our prisoners, and this I will now do."

Captain Mosby then directed that the prisoners should be collected at a spot near by, and that preparations be made to march in a few minutes. Turning to the Federal lieutenant, he said:

"Lieutenant, I occasionally parole prisoners captured by me; but there are reasons why I will have to detain you and your men until you are regularly exchanged. This I regret, but it cannot be avoided. I had hoped to capture your post without bloodshed, and am sorry that I was compelled to shoot your corporal. I avoided doing so as long as possible, and did not fire at him until after he had answered my demand for his surrender with a pistol shot. I then fired at his right arm for the purpose of so disabling it that I might capture him without further danger to myself, or the necessity of killing him. The ball passed through his arm without breaking any bones and the wound is not a dangerous one."

Lieutenant C—— replied: "I thank you, captain, for the consideration manifested by you for the life of my corporal, and also for your courteous conduct toward myself. I am glad to know that the reports in circulation at the North concerning your character are false, and that instead of being a cruel and remorseless guerilla, delighting in scenes of slaughter, you are an affable and gentlemanly officer engaged in legitimate partisan warfare and averse to the shedding of blood."

After thanking the lieutenant for his manifestation of fairness and justice in thus readily discrediting the false reports that had been circulated concerning him, Mosby ordered his men to mount and proceeded to cross the river.

The Federal vedette who was on guard at the ford when the other troopers were captured, was also captured immediately thereafter, and the way was thus opened for Mosby's passage across the river without his movements being detected.

The reader will perhaps wish to know how Mosby happened to be in that section at the time, and succeeded in so easily surprising and capturing the Federal pickets, and we will therefore explain the matter.

Some time before this occurrence, Mosby had been detailed by General Stuart **as a scout or** partisan whose duty it was to penetrate the **Federal** lines, obtain information as to the **location,** numbers and movements of the enemy, and, when occasion was offered for so doing, to capture wagon trains, pickets and detached parties of Federal troops; **and for** the accomplishment of these objects he was authorized **to take** with him small detachments of enlistd cavalry **and such volunteer troopers as he could obtain.** He had no commission **from the Confederate Government at** this time, **but was** *de facto* "Captain of Partisan Rangers" and this title **was** uniformly applied to him. Having learned that the Federal army was evacuating Fauquier county and moving down to Fredericksburg, and knowing **that the** fords along the Rappahannock above Rappahannock Station would still be guarded for a day or two by the **Federal cavalry,** Mosby determined to make an **incursion into** Fauquier county for the purpose of **trying to capture some of their** pickets. Hence, he had gathered together **about thirty men, and a** few hours before the occurrence we have related, crossed the river between Fox's Ford and Sulphur Spring **at a place** where it was unguarded, as it was not supposed **to be ford-**able at that point. Being thoroughly acquainted with every by-road and bridle-path in that section of the country, he easily and secretly made his way down the **river** toward Fox's **Ford, at** which place he knew **there was a** Federal picket-post. When within a short distance of **the** ford he entered **the road** leading to it **from Sulphur** Spring, rode rapidly forward and charged the picket-post with the results already narrated.

After crossing the river, Mosby halted his men and calling Ashton to him, said:

"**I suppose that you** will wish to join your regiment as soon as possible, and hence we will have to separate here as **my route lies up** the river, and your regiment **is** now near **Fredericksburg.** By the way, **your** regiment has a new commander in the person of Colonel R. L. T. Beale. Colonel W. H. F. Lee was recently made a brigadier-general and on the **10th of this month assigned to the command of** a brigade **to which your regiment has been transferred** from General

Fitzhugh Lee's brigade. I will have some of my men detailed to take these prisoners to Culpeper to be forwarded to Richmond, and you had best go with them that **far on your** journey. **As I see that you** are riding an **inferior horse,** I will allow you to exchange him for the **Federal** corporal's horse captured by me, which is quite fleet and appears to be an excellent animal, and moreover, will serve to remind you of your happy extrication from a distressing and dangerous predicament."

"I thank **you** very warmly, Captain," said Ashton, "for your kind and generous offer, and accept it with the greatest pleasure. Your valuable souvenir will serve to remind me not only of my deliverance from danger, but also of the **brave and daring** officer to whose extraordinary skill, pluck **and** enterprise as a partisan commander, I am indebted for **my** deliverance. As soon as possible I shall give General Stuart a full account of your exploit in order that **he may** know that of which he is already satisfied, viz.; that you are actively engaged in the work to which he has assigned you, and successfully executing the commission intrusted to you."

Mosby then had eight men detailed **with instructions to** conduct the prisoners to Culpeper for transportation to Richmond and then to join him near Woodville the next day, from which point he contemplated starting on another expedition into the enemy's country. He then bade Ashton good-bye and started up the river with the remainder of his command.

Ashton and the detail in charge of the prisoners took the **road to** Culpeper by way of Brandy Station, and reached their destination that evening. There the prisoners were **turned over** to the proper authorities for transportation to Richmond, and after bidding his companions good-bye, Ashton sought and obtained accommodations for himself and his horse for the night. Early the next morning he started for Fredericksburg and reached that place about night. He learned that his regiment was six miles below the town, near Hamilton's crossing, and on the following morning he found it, rode into camp and reported for duty.

Great was the astonishment and gratification of the members of his company when he made his appearance, for,

as before stated, they fully believed that he was dead. They
gathered around him by the score, eager to learn his experience since they had last seen him, and he gave them a full
account of his adventures.

Having made inquiry as to whether any letters had come
for him during his absence, he was informed that one arrived just after the battle of Manassas and, as he was supposed to have been killed, was forwarded to the Dead
Letter Office at Richmond to be returned to its writer. His
informant stated that the postmark on the letter was that
of some town in Georgia, the name of which he had forgotten. As Ashton's only correspondent in Georgia had been
Ruth Middleton, he was satisfied that the letter had come
from her and was an answer to the one in which he had told
her of his love. During his varied experiences and the
strange and trying scenes through which he had passed
since writing that letter, he had almost constantly thought
of Ruth and intensely longed to know what her answer
would be, and the anxiety for this knowledge and the hope
of obtaining it as soon as he reached his regiment had
served to buoy him up in the midst of the depressing surroundings of his captivity, and also to encourage him in his
efforts to escape; and now, when he learned that the letter
from which he expected to obtain this knowledge had been
returned to its writer, and reflected that it might be weeks,
or perhaps months, before he would know his fate, his heart
was chilled by the disappointment which he had experienced, and for the moment his spirit was almost crushed
beneath the weight of despondency that was resting upon
it. His despondency continued for hours, and so absorbingly did he brood over his disappointment and distress in
not having received an answer to his letter, that he felt that
he was grieving over an unfavorable answer to the same,
forgetting that this answer had merely failed to reach him,
and might have been as favorable as he could have desired.
At last awaking to a sense of this fact, he realized the use-
lessness and folly of longer grieving over the mere failure
to obtain the knowledge that he wished, at a particular
time, and felt that the proper and sensible thing to do would
be to immediately write again to Ruth and thus shorten the

period of **his** uncertainty as **to her** feelings toward him.
Acting **on** this idea, he wrote her a long letter in which he
again told her of his deep and absorbing love for her, **ex-**
plained why he had not received her answer to his last letter, gave her an account of his captivity and subsequent
escape therefrom, and urged her to write at once and relieve
him from the harrowing effect produced on his mind by the
uncertainty as to her feelings toward him and his intense
longing to hear from her. The writing of the letter was **a**
great relief to him, and when it was finished he felt as if **a**
weight had been lifted from his heart; and with this revul-
sion of feeling there came what was almost a spirit of joyousness born of the thought that he would soon hear from
Ruth, and the hope that her message would be one of **love,**
that would bring peace and gladness to his soul.

When he handed his letter to the regimental mail-carrier to
be posted, he breathed a fervent prayer that it might **be**
swiftly and safely borne to its destination. Had his prayer
been answered, he would have been spared much disappointment and pain, and perhaps some of the incidents hereinafter related would never have occurred. **But, alas, for the
peace and** happiness of two loving hearts, the message of
tenderness and devotion from one which would have blessed
and brightened the other was sent in vain. In order that
the reader may understand why this was so, it will be neces-
sary to return to Ruth Middleton and give an account of
her experience after receiving the crushing news of Ashton's
death.

CHAPTER **VIII**.

We left Ruth clasped in the loving embrace of her cousin, who, by this tender manifestation of sympathy, was seeking to lighten the weight of woe that was crushing her heart. But there are sorrows that human sympathy cannot relieve, and wounds which only the hand of time can heal; and such was the sorrow that Ruth had experienced and the wound which she had received from the reported death of her lover. She had never loved before and, constituted as she was, would never love again; for with her love was not an ephemeral state of emotion resulting from extraneous influences and dependent on their continuance for its existence, but was a permanent growth of feeling springing up within her heart in response to the wants of her nature, and it had taken such complete possession of her soul as to become a part of her being and as lasting as life itself. Her love for Ashton being thus a part of herself, her entire nature felt the shock of the blow inflicted by the news of his death, and both mind and body were seriously affected by the same. Hence, although she gave no expression to her grief, her usual buoyancy of spirits was gone, and a permanent feeling of sadness took possession of her mind and heart, and manifested itself in her appearance and actions. Owing to the influence which the mind at times exerts upon the body, her physical constitution was affected and her health impaired by her mental suffering and the all-absorbing grief that had taken possession of her. Hence, in the course of a few weeks, she appeared to be gradually wasting away, and her physician recommended a change of climate as the most promising remedy for her condition.

It was now the first of November and, as winter was near at hand, the physician decided that she had best go to Florida, whose mild and comparatively uniform climate and salubrious sea breezes it was thought would greatly aid in restoring her health. Therefore, about the middle of the month and just before Ashton's return to his regiment, she and Bertha Gray left B—— with the intention of going to Jacksonville, but, while on their journey, they learned that

the place was garrisoned by Federal troops, and, therefore,
changed their course and proceeded to Ocala in Central
Florida. Ruth had instructed the postmaster at B—— to
forward her mail to Jacksonville, and hence, when Ashton's
letter arrived at B——, it was forwarded in accordance with
this instruction. Owing to the occupation of Jacksonville
by the Federals, the letter was not carried to that place
but was brought back and eventually reached the Dead
Letter Office at Richmond, from which place it was finally
returned to Ashton about two months after it was written.
As he saw that it had been forwarded from B—— to Jacksonville and then sent to the Dead Letter Office, he was satisfied that Ruth was at neither of those places, and having no
idea as to where she was, he deemed it unnecessary to make
another effort at that time to communicate with her.

After her arrival at Ocala, Ruth wrote to the postmaster
at B——, changing the instruction she had given in regard to
her mail, and requested that it be forwarded to Ocala.
Unfortunately he did not receive this request until after he
had forwarded Ashton's letter to Jacksonville, n l therefore it did not reach her, for the reason already given.

On their arrival in Ocala, Ruth and Bertha stopped at a
hotel, but in a day or two secured board with Mrs. Mary
Austin, whose husband, Captain Wil iam Austin, was in the
Confederate army. Mrs. Austin was a refined and cultured
woman, unassuming in her manners, and exceedingly kind-
hearted and sympathetic. The sad expression on Ruth's face
at once attracted her attention and deeply touched her
heart. Being satisfied that Ruth had experienced some great
grief which had imbued her life with sorrow, she determined to do all in her power to arouse her from the state of
melancholy into which she appeared to have lapsed, and endeavor to restore her to a condition of cheerfulness. Believing that she could best accomplish her object by seemingly
ignoring Ruth's sadness, she never alluded to it, and was
constantly arranging plans for her enjoyment of such quiet
recreations as would please and amuse her without jarring
her melancholy feelings. In conversing with Ruth, she
talked of such things as were calculated to interest her, excite her mind to action and draw her thoughts away from

herself. Taking her cue from Mrs. Austin's conduct, Bertha also endeavored to prevent her **cousin from** dwelling on **the** past, by keeping her mind directed into pleasing channels of thought, and inducing her as often as **possible** to participate in the quiet pleasures which their surroundings afforded. The scenery of the surrounding country **was both novel and** attractive, and Bertha quite often induced **Ruth to join** her in its enjoyment through the medium of a walk or **drive in the midst of its beauties.**

It was not very long before Ruth's surroundings **began to** produce a salutary effect upon her, and the delightful and salubrious climate, beautiful scenery and pleasant companionship which she enjoyed, rapidly improved her health and **tended to** dissipate her melancholy feelings. By the end of winter her health was restored, and she had, in a measure, **recovered her wonted cheerfulness, but** her face still wore **a sad expression and at times she experienced fits of melancholy.**

At the opening of spring she and Bertha returned to their **home,** and naturally this return to the scenes where she had **first met Ashton, and amidst which their mutual love had sprung into existence, revived the sad memories of the past, and opened afresh the wound in her heart. At first she made no effort to put away the sad thoughts that filled her mind, but took a melancholy pleasure in dwelling on the past and living over in imagination the hours spent with Ashton, and which had led to her brief enjoyment of perfect** happiness in the reception of his love and the gift of **her** own, and that other hour in which her happiness had been blasted and her heart broken by the news of his death. **But** she soon realized, from the injurious consequences of **these** melancholy moods, that she would wrong herself **and unnecessarily distress others by longer indulging in them, and** therefore determined to find some means for so employing her time and engaging her mind as to divert her thoughts from herself and also enable her **to be of service to** others.

Being thoroughly imbued with a spirit of patriotism, and fully alive to a sense of the sufferings of those who had left their homes in defense of the South, she naturally thought **that some means for aiding them would be** the most appropriate and serviceable plan that she could adopt. After mature deliberation, she decided on the adoption of a plan for the accomplishment of this purpose, and **soon thereaf-**ter revealed it to her cousin in the following conversation:

"Bertha," said she, "I have something to tell you which I know will make you sad, and is also painfully distressing to me. I find that I will soon have to leave you for **an in-**definite length **of time.**"

"Leave me!" exclaimed Bertha. "What do you mean? Surely **you** cannot be in earnest, and moreover, I will not **let you leave me.**"

"**Yes," said Ruth, "I am certainly in** earnest, and you **must not try** to dissuade **me from** the purpose which I have **formed, for it is necessary that** I should go away, and I will now **give you** the reasons for this necessity. Of course you have noticed that since returning home I have lapsed into my former state of melancholy and dejection, and you doubtless understand that this was caused by the fact that my surroundings here have awakened and serve to keep alive the memory of that which produced **my sadness, and will** naturally tend to perpetuate it. I **have decided that for my** own sake I **must** do something to **divert my** thoughts from myself; and, as I desire to be of some service to others, I can think of no better **plan** for the accomplishment of these objects than that of rendering assistance to our soldiers. Hence I have determined to follow the noble example furnished by Florence Nightingale during the Crimean War, **and shall** devote my services to the sick and wounded Con-**federate** soldiers in the hospitals **at** Richmond."

"Oh, **Ruth,** you could not endure such service," said Bertha, "**and** must not think of the undertaking. You know that **you** are not as strong as you once were, and the tax on your physical powers would soon exhaust them."

"You forget," replied Ruth, "that my loss of strength was to a great extent caused by my constant contemplation of my condition and a persistent brooding **over** my sorrow, and the plan that I **have formed** will enable me to avoid a repetition of such conduct, and to that extent tend to pre-**serve** my strength. Besides, I am influenced in the matter by a sense of duty and my devotion to the holy cause for which our armies are contending, and the more I think of it the more like an inspiration it seems that I have been led to form this plan for the relief of our suffering soldiers."

"I find as usual," said Bertha, "that I cannot meet your arguments. I wonder if this is because you are so much wiser than I, or is it because I always act from impulse, while you act from reason and duty? Well, if **you** will go, I shall go **with** you."

"No," said Ruth, "that would not do; for you **could not,** with your lively and restless disposition, long endure the **con-**finement and tedium incident to the occupation of even a *volunteer* nurse in a hospital, and you would soon become dissatisfied with your work and it would become correspondingly inefficient."

"**I suppose,**" said Bertha, "that I must yield to your judgment in the matter; but it will almost break my heart **to** be separated from you, especially as we have been constant companions for so many years. **Of course, you** will not object to my visiting you occasionally?"

"Oh no," said Ruth, "and I was just about to suggest **that plan** as a means of mitigating the sadness of our separation. It will not only be a source of comfort and pleasure **for** us to thus occasionally be together, but you will have opportunities for seeing the attractions of the Confederate Capital, and these will interest and amuse you."

Having thus decided on her future course of conduct, Ruth made all necessary arrangements for carrying it out, and by the first of April she had gone to Richmond, offered her services as a volunteer nurse, and had been assigned to duty at one of the hospitals in the city.

Leaving her to learn, **and familiarize** herself with the duties incident to the occupation in which she had engaged, we will return to Ashton whom we left in camp below Fredericksburg just after he had, with a fervent prayer for its speedy delivery, handed to the regimental mail-carrier his second love-letter to Ruth and which, as we have incidentally explained, failed to reach its destination and several months afterward was returned to him.

Ashton learned that his regiment had reached its present camp only the day before, all of General W. H. F. Lee's

brigade, except the Thirteenth Virginia Cavalry, having
been ordered to the vicinity of Fredericksburg on that day
to co-operate with the troops already there in resisting **any**
effort that might be made by the Federals to cross the Rappahannock at that place. General R E. Lee rapidly concentrated his army at Fredericksburg to meet the threatened attack at that point, and in a few days General W. H. F. Lee's
brigade was sent farther down the river to guard and **operate** along the Lower Rappahannock. Both the Federal
and Confederate commanders were busily engaged in making preparations for a battle which, in some respects, proved
to be one of the most notable of the Civil War. As before
stated, General Burnside had been massing his army in the
vicinity of Fredericksburg and it now occupied the lofty
range of hills, known as Stafford Heights, overlooking the
Rappahannock river at their base and the town of Fredericksburg on the south side of that stream. He had hoped
to conceal his movements sufficiently long to effect a passage of the river at this point, before General **Lee could con-**
centrate an adequate force to check his progress; but **the**
ever-watchful and sagacious commander of the Confeder-
ate army had discovered his design, and now confronted
him with the greater part of the army on the opposite side
of the river. The two armies retained their respective positions for about two weeks before the battle to which we
have referred began. As this battle was a notable one, **we
trust** that a description of it will **not prove** uninteresting
to the reader.

In order to give an intelligible account of the engagement,
some description of the topography of the battle-ground
and its surroundings will be necessary. As before indicated,
the Rappahannock river at this point flows along the base
of a range of highlands on its northern bank, known as
Stafford Heights. The town of Fredericksburg, situated
on the south side of the river, extended about a mile and a
quarter along the bank of the stream and about a half mile
backward from the same. From a point on the river above
the town another range of highlands, known as Spottsyl-
vania Heights, extends in a southeasterly direction for
several miles, and then changing its course and gradually

diminishing in height, again approaches the river below the town until it terminates at the valley of Massaponax Creek, about four miles from Fredericksburg. Hence it will be seen that the town was situated in a basin or valley, and this valley was an open plain varying in width from one to two or three miles. Near the middle of this plain was a road, known as the River Road, extending down the river at a distance of about a mile and a half from the Spottsylvania Heights, and at the time of the engagement there were on each side of it earthen embankments and hedgerows of cedars and other trees which afforded the Federals the advantage of a double line of intrenchments. Opposite the point where the Telegraph Road, leading southward, issues from the town is a lofty eminence known as Marye's Hill, and at its base this road turns abruptly eastward and runs parallel with the south side of the town for several hundred yards. The side of this road next to the town was protected by a massive stone fence, and between it and the town was a narrow, open and level field. The Richmond, Fredericksburg and Potomac railroad, issuing from the eastern end of the town, passed through the plain below, parallel with the road already described, and out into the interior at a way-station called Hamilton's Crossing.

Having endeavored to give the reader an idea of what was to be the battle-ground of the opposing armies, we will try to describe the locations of their respective forces. On the 11th and 12th of December, General Burnside succeeded in placing most of his army on the south side of the river by means of pontoon bridges, and under cover of a heavy fog that prevailed during the 12th, a large part of his troops, consisting of General Franklin's grand division and one of General Hooker's corps, had taken position along the River Road below the town. During this day, General Sumner's grand division also crossed the river, while the remainder of General Hooker's grand division was held in readiness to cross, at a moment's notice, to the support of Sumner on the right or Franklin on the left. According to General Burnside's report, the line that had been established was as follows:

"The second corps held the center and right of the town; the ninth corps was on the left of the second corps, and connected with General Franklin's right at Deep Run, the whole of this force being nearly parallel to the river; the sixth corps was formed on the left of the ninth corps, nearly parallel with the old Richmond road, and the first corps on the left of the sixth, nearly at right angles with it, its left resting on the river."

On the morning of December 13th, the Federal army, with the exception of General Hooker's reserves, was formed in lines of battle along the River Road below the town, and within the streets of the same. Stafford Heights for miles were crowned with numerous batteries that commanded the plain below, and the heights on its southern side. Along the latter heights the Confederate army was posted, and, according to General Lee's report, from which we quote, the respective positions of its several divisions were as follows:

"Longstreet's corps constituted the left, with Anderson's division resting upon the river, and those of McLaws, Pickett, and Hood extending to the right in the order named. Ransom's division supported the batteries on Marye's and Willis' hills, at the foot of which Cobb's brigade, of McLaws' division, and the 24th North Carolina, of Ransom's division, were stationed, protected by a stone wall. The immediate care of this point was committed to General Ransom. The Washington Artillery occupied the redoubts on the crest of Marye's Hill, and those on the heights to the right and left were held by a part of the reserved artillery, Col. E. P. Alexander's battalion, and the division batteries of Anderson, Ransom, and McLaws. A. P. Hill, of Jackson's corps, was posted between Hood's right and Hamilton's Crossing, on the railroad. His front line, consisting of the brigades of Pender, Lane, and Archer, occupied the edge of a wood. Lieutenant-colonel Walker, with fourteen pieces of artillery, was posted near the right, supported by the 40th and 35th Virginia regiments, of Field's brigade, commanded by Colonel Brockenborough. Lane's brigade, thrown forward in advance of the general line, held the woods, which here project into the open ground. Thomas' brigade was stationed behind the interval between Lane and Pender, and Gregg's in rear of that, between Lane and Archer. These two brigades, with the 47th Virginia regiment, and 22d Virginia battalion of Field's brigade, constituted General Hill's reserve. Early's and Taliaferro's divisions composed Jackson's second line— D. **H.** Hill's division **his reserve.** His artillery was distributed along his line in **the most** eligible position so **as to** command the open **ground in** front. General Stuart, with two brigades of cavalry, **and** his horse artillery, occupied the plain on Jackson's right, extending to Massaponax Creek."

On the morning of December 13th, **a** dense fog enveloped the plain on which the Federal army lay, and it was impossible for the Confederate army to discern its operations for several hours. At an early hour the opening guns of the battle were fired, **when the Federal batteries on** Stafford Heights began to play on Longstreet's position, and under cover of this fire the Federal army was formed for attack, Franklin's grand division occupying the left and Sumner's the right of their line of battle. Shortly after 9 o'clock **the** rising of the fog disclosed to the view of the Confederate army a spectacle such as they had never before seen, and one which brought vividly before their eyes the imposing pomp and awful grandeur of war, for, looking down from their elevated position on Spottsylvania Heights, **they saw** marshaled on the plain beneath more than one hundred thousand foemen with glistening muskets and numerous batteries of field guns, awaiting but the order to advance, and apparently capable of overwhelming them by sheer force of numbers. This myriad host did not long await the order of attack; and soon Franklin began his advance toward Hamilton's Crossing against Jackson, and **dense** masses of Federal soldiers moved out in front of A. P. Hill, extending far up the river toward Fredericksburg. The Federal batteries on Stafford Heights, numbering one hundred **and fifty guns,** and those with Franklin on the plain below, numbering one hundred and sixteen guns began to belch forth their deadly shot and shell, and were answered by the Confederate batteries on Spottsylvania Heights, and **amidst their** mimic thunders and the noise of bursting shells, the Federal troops pressed forward to the attack. The attack was made by General Reynolds' corps, being led by General Meade's division, composed entirely of Pennsylvania troops, which was supported on the right by General Gibbon's division and on the left by General Doubleday's division. The Federals moved forward in gallant style, but when they crossed the River Road the dauntless boy-hero, John Pelham, of Stuart's Horse Artillery, dashed out into the open plain between them and Massaponax Creek with two of his guns, and began a destructive enfilading fire on their left flank which, for awhile, stopped their advance. Four of General Reynolds' batteries and some of the heavy guns on Stafford Heights were at once turned upon him; but notwithstanding this terrific fire, the peerless Pelham **held** his ground for at least an hour, fighting his guns with that marvelous coolness, gallantry and skill for which he was noted, and did not retire from his perilous position until recalled by positive orders from General Stuart. When Pelham was withdrawn, General Franklin's left was extended down the River Road and his numerous batteries began a rapid and furious fire upon General Jackson's line, shelling for about a half hour the wood in which Lane's brigade was posted, and on the right of which Lieutenant-colonel Lindsay Walker's artillery was located.

As there was no response from the Confederate artillery, the Federal infantry moved forward to seize the position held by Lieutenant-colonel Walker. He reserved his fire **until** they were within less than eight hundred yards of his **position,** and then shelled them with such destructive **effect that** they were checked in their advance, began to waver and soon retreated in confusion. About 1 o'clock P. M., Franklin's main attack was made on General Lee's right and, under cover of a heavy cannonade, **three com-** pact lines of battle were advanced against Hill's front. As before, the Federals were received by a furious fire from the Confederate batteries and momentarily checked, but they soon pressed forward with gallantry and determination, and **when** they came within range of the Confederate infantry, the battle became fierce and bloody. Generals Lane and Archer repulsed the Federal lines immediately in front of

them, but unfortunately there was an interval between
their brigades, and, before it could be closed, the Federals
pressed through it in overwhelming numbers and turned
Lane's right and Archer's left. Being attacked in front and
flank, two of Archer's regiments and Lane's **brigade gave**
way after having made a gallant and determined resist-
ance to the superior force opposing them. Archer, **however,**
with the remainder of his brigade, stubbornly and gallantly
held his line until the arrival of reinforcements. **General**
E. L. Thomas with his valiant Georgia brigade quickly **and**
gallantly came to the relief of Lane, and being joined by
the 7th and 18th North Carolina regiments, of Lane's brigade, repulsed the column that had broken Lane's line and
drove it back to the railroad. In the meantime, a large
force of Federals had advanced into the wood as far as
Hill's reserve and attacked Gregg's brigade. So sudden and
unexpected was this attack that **a** part of Gregg's brigade
was thrown into confusion, they having mistaken the Federals for Confederates whom they supposed were retiring.
Their gallant general was mortally wounded while in the
act of rallying them, but Colonel D. H. Hamilton, of the 1st
South Carolina regiment, at once took command of the
brigade and checked the further progress of the Federals.
At this time General Jackson brought up his second line,
consisting of the divisions of Early and Taliaferro, and the
Federals were quickly routed, driven out of the wood with
heavy loss and, although largely reinforced, were forced
back and pursued to the railroad embankment where they
took shelter. From this position they were gallantly dislodged by Lawton's and Trimble's brigades under Colonels
E. N. Atkinson and E. F. Hoke, and driven across the plain
to the protection of their batteries. Colonel Atkinson pursued the Federals too far into the plain, and his flank became exposed to an enfilading fire, while at the same time
his front was subjected to a heavy fire of musketry and
artillery. Colonel Atkinson being severely wounded, Captain E. P. Lawton, assistant adjutant-general, being mortally wounded, and the ammunition of the brigade having
been exhausted, the brigade was compelled to fall back to
the main body, which at this time occupied the original line

of battle. The attack that had been made on Hill's left was successfully repulsed by Walker's artillery, notwithstanding the fact that it was constantly under a furious fire from twenty-four guns. One brigade of Federals advanced some distance up the channel of Deep Run, being protected by its high banks from the Confederate artillery, but they were gallantly charged and routed by the 16th North Carolina regiment of Pender's brigade and the 54th and 57th North Carolina regiments of Law's brigade, Hood's division. The two last mentioned regiments had never before been under fire, but their bravery was marvelous, and they greatly distinguished themselves by the impetuosity **and** **routing the** Federals, they pursued them across the railroad and far out into the plain, although their ranks were being raked by a heavy flank fire from the channel of Deep Run, and did not return until frequent messages recalling them had been sent by Hood. It is said that as they returned, some of them were seen weeping with vexation because they had been, as it were, dragged back from their pursuit of the enemy and, in speaking of General Hood's conduct in recalling them, they exclaimed: "It is because he has not confidence in Carolinians. If we had been some of his Texans, he would have let us go on."

The repulse of the Federals on the Confederate right had been complete and decisive, and **the attack** was not renewed, but their batteries kept up an active fire at intervals during the remainder of the afternoon.

While the events just narrated were occurring on the Confederate right, desperate and repeated assaults were made by the Federals in great force on the left of the Confederate line. About 11 o'clock A. M., General Sumner massed his troops under cover of the houses of Fredericksburg, and soon moved out in strong columns toward the Plank and Telegraph roads for the purpose of seizing Marye's and Willis' Hills, at the foot of which those roads come nearly together a short distance from the town. General Ransom, who, as before stated, had the immediate care of this point, at once advanced Cooke's brigade to the top of the hill, and placed his own, with the exception of the

24th North Carolina, **a short distance in** the rear, this North Carolina regiment being with Cobb's brigade of Georgians in the Telegraph road at the foot of Marye's Hill. The numerous batteries on Stafford Heights concentrated their fire on the Confederate artillery for the purpose of trying to silence it and cover the advance of the Federal infantry. The Confederate batteries, however, disregarded this furious cannonade, and poured a rapid and destructive fire into the dense lines of Federal infantry as they advanced to the attack from the outskirts of the town, frequently breaking their ranks and driving them back to the shelter of the houses. Notwithstanding the extensive and terrible slaughter effected by the Confederate artillery, the Federals pressed forward six times with great gallantry to within one hundred yards of the foot of the hill, but here they received the well-directed and destructive fire of the Confederate infantry, by which their columns were shattered, and the survivors fled in confusion to the town. The havoc made in their ranks was horrible, and immediately in front of the position held by Cobb's brigade the ground was literally covered with dead and wounded men. The brave and noble commander of this brigade, General Thomas R. R. Cobb, fell during the third assault of the Federals. He was distinguished as an orator and a statesman as well as a soldier, and his untimely death was deeply lamented by every Southerner who had heard of his Christian virtues, civil renown and military fame. The fighting at this point continued until nightfall and every attack of the Federals was successfully repulsed. During the day General Sumner used the entire force of the Right Grand Division in his efforts to take Marye's and Willis' Hills, and the order of his several assaults was as follows:

Toward noon the division of Hancock, composed of Caldwell's brigade, Meagher's (Irish) brigade, and Zook's brigade, and the division of French, composed of Kimball's, Palmer's and Andrews' brigades, pressed forward from the town toward Marye's and Willis' Hills. They advanced with great gallantry and determination across the open ground, but were met with such a destructive fire of artillery and musketry that their ranks were quickly shattered, their progress was checked, **and** finally they fled in confusion to the town. The casualties in the three first mentioned brigades were exceedingly great, as they lost in killed, wounded **and** captured nearly half of the troops engaged. They fought bravely and well, but no troops could have withstood the rapid and deadly fire to which **they** were subjected. Howard's division, composed of Sully's, Owens' and Hall's brigades, Sturgis' division, composed of Nagle's and Ferrero's brigades, and Getty's division, composed of Hawkins' and Harland's brigades, were next advanced by Sumner **to renew** the attack. This they did **with** great spirit and **gallantry, but,** like the troops who had preceded them, **they were repulsed** with fearful **slaughter** and driven back by the destructive fire **of** the **Confederates. It** was now about 2 o'clock P. M., and the **repeated** and ineffectual efforts which had been made to take the Confederate works should have convinced General Burnside that it was impossible for him to take them; but he appeared not to realize the fact and, although he **had** that **morning learned from a Confederate** prisoner **that** Longstreet's position was impregnable and that **the** Confederates desired an attack at that point, he determined to make another **effort to carry** Marye's and Willis' Hills, and ordered General **Hooker to make the attack** with Butterfield's corps. Griffin's **division of this corps had been sent to** support General **Sturgis, and the remaining** divisions of Humphreys and Sykes **constituted the force** with which **Hooker** was expected **to** do that **which Couch's** entire **corps and** two divisions of Willcox's corps had failed to **accomplish** by repeated efforts during the greater part of **the day.** Being fully convinced that it would be a useless **waste** of life **to** make the attack with the force at his command, General Hooker dispatched an aide to General Burnside advising **him not** to attack. Burnside replied that the attack must be **made.** Hooker **then in** person gave Burnside a more **thorough** explanation of the difficulties that would render **the** attack fruitless, and endeavored to dissuade him from making it, but Burnside insisted upon its being made. Hooker then brought up every available battery **at his** disposal, posting one of them (Hazzard's, of the

1st Rhode Island Artillery) within about five hundred yards of the Confederate line, and a furious cannonade was begun upon the Confederate position. This artillery fire was continued with great vigor until near sunset, and then the direct attack with bayonet was made by Humphrey's division, Sykes' division advancing on its right to assault *en echelon* and support.

Notwithstanding the desperate character of their undertaking and the bloody repulses of those who had preceded them, the troops moved bravely forward and the attack was made with great gallantry and determination, but, like all of the attacks that preceded it and at about the same place on the plain, it was quickly checked by the fatal fire of the Confederates, and the attacking columns were driven back with heavy loss.

This was the last attack made on the Confederate left, and marked the close of a hard-fought battle, in which the Confederates had achieved a signal victory over nearly five times their numbers; for, while the greater part of General Burnside's army of one hundred and twenty-two thousand was engaged in the battle, the whole number of General Lee's troops actually engaged did not exceed twenty-five thousand. The Confederate loss in killed, wounded and captured was four thousand two hundred and one, and that of the Federals was twelve thousand six hundred and fifty-three.

Ashton did not take part in the general engagement at Fredericksburg and, during most of the time occupied by it, was only a spectator, as General Stuart's cavalry was guarding the right wing of Lee's army, and only occasionally attacking the Federal left when a favorable opportunity for so doing occurred. The respective positions of the two armies and the nature of the ground were such as to prevent a more extensive operation of Stuart's command.

We should have mentioned, however, that about ten days before the battle, Ashton was one of a party of dismounted men who went on an expedition into Westmoreland county and captured the Federal pickets at Leedstown. The party consisted of a detachment of sixty men

from the **9th** Virginia cavalry, under **the** command of
Major **T.** Waller. They left their horses on the south side
of the Rappahannock, and crossed the river in skiffs a short
distance above Leedstown on the night of December 1st,
and after making a detour of several miles, approached **the**
town from the **rear or north side** of the same. **They**
waited in concealment until just before the setting of the
moon between 2 and 3 o'clock A. M., and then cautiously
but quickly proceeded to accomplish the object of the expedition. **A short distance** above the town they surprised and
captured a sentinel posted on the Port Conway road, in
the **town** they captured eight men, and just below **the**
town, within a short distance of the river, they captured
two more sentinels and the entire picket force, with the ex-
ception of one man who escaped in the darkness. The
whole number captured was forty-nine, including the officer
in command, Captain Wilson of the 8th Pennsylvania cavalry. They also captured fifty horses, and recaptured two
Confederates who had previously fallen into the hands of
the Federals. The party recrossed the river in safety that
morning without having suffered any casualty during the
expedition, except the accidental wounding of one man by
one of his comrades.

CHAPTER IX.

About ten days after the battle of **Fredericksburg**, General Stuart planned a raid on Dumfries and **other points near** the Potomac. The force organized **for this expedition consisted** of detachments from the brigades **of Generals Hampton, Fitzhugh Lee** and W. H. F. Lee, aggregating **in all one thousand eight hundred** men, and four pieces **of the Stuart Horse Artillery.** These detachments were under the immediate command of their respective brigade commanders and, **having crossed the** Rappahannock at Kelly's Ford, bivouacked near Morrisville on the night of December 26th, 1862. In accordance with the plan marked out by General Stuart, General Hampton was to move around to the left toward Occoquan, General Fitzhugh Lee was to strike the Telegraph road between Dumfries and Acquia Creek, and General W. H. F. Lee was to march between the two directly upon Dumfries. Ashton was, of course, with the detachment of his new brigade commander, General W. H. F. Lee, and it proceeded on its march without meeting any Federals until it reached Wheat's Mill on the Quantico Creek. Here they found an infantry picket consisting of twelve men, which was charged and captured by one squadron of Ashton's regiment under Captain S. Bolling. This squadron at once crossed the Quantico Creek supported by two other squadrons, but on arriving at the suburbs of Dumfries it was driven back by two regiments of infantry. A squadron of Federal cavalry then advanced, but was quickly repulsed and hastily retreated. About this time General Stuart arrived and ordered up Henry's battery of horse artillery, which opened on the Federals and soon drove them from their position. The Federals promptly brought forward their artillery and an engagement ensued between it and the Confederate battery. The Federals soon evacuated the town and took position in a pine thicket on a high ridge overlooking the town, their force consisting of a brigade of infantry and a battery of artillery. In the meantime, General Fitzhugh Lee's command had struck the Telegraph road about two miles below Dumfries, captured twenty-four men, and nine wagons laden with sutler's stores, and now arrived at Dumfries. General Stuart then arranged to assault the Federals and capture the town; but, upon reflection, abandoned the undertaking, as the capture of the place was of no especial importance and would not have compensated for the loss of life that would have resulted from the movement, and General Fitzhugh Lee was ordered to engage the Federals with dismounted skirmishes and artillery, while the remainder of the command moved around on the Brentsville road. These dismounted men and two guns of Breathed's battery kept up the engagement until dark. In this engagement, while gallantly leading the sharpshooters, Captain J. W. Bullock, of the 5th Virginia cavalry was mortally wounded. General Hampton in the meantime had moved in the direction of Occoquan, captured a picket at Cole's store, and a part of his command dashed into Occoquan, dispersing several hundred Federal cavalry, and capturing nineteen prisoners and eight wagons, with the loss of only one man wounded. That night Stuart's entire command bivouacked near Cole's store and the next morning (December 28th) moved forward toward the Occoquan River. On reaching Greenwood Church, Colonel M. C. Butler, of the 2nd South Carolina, was detached and ordered to take his command to Bacon Race Church for the purpose of cutting off a detachment of Federals reported to be in front of the advancing column.

Soon after leaving Greenwood Church, Stuart's command came in sight of two regiments of Federal cavalry drawn up in line of battle near a dense piece of woods. The intervening ground was open and favorable for a cavalry charge, and General Stuart at once ordered Fitzhugh Lee's brigade (which happened to be in front) to make the charge. The order was promptly obeyed and at the sound of the bugle, the brigade, led by the 1st Virginia cavalry, under Colonel James H. Drake, bore down upon the Federal cavalry at full speed in the face of heavy volleys from the enemy's carbines. The sight of the charging columns, with glittering sabres flashing in the sunlight, the sound of the horses' clattering feet upon the road and, high above the clang of

sabres, the din of horses' feet and the crack of carbines, the
"wild Confederate yell," all conspired to make the occasion
thrilling and grand beyond description.

So stirring was the sight that General **Hampton, ever**
ready for the fray, dashed forward with drawn sabre and
joined the Virginians in their gallant charge, and so rapidly
did he ride that he succeeded in unhorsing some of the
enemy with his own hand. The Federals, terrified by the
avalanche of steel that was being hurled against them, did
not await its descent upon their ranks, but turned and fled
in confusion before its rapid approach. Then began a rapid
pursuit by the Confederates, which continued for five or
six miles and resulted in the killing of eight or ten, and the
capture of more than one hundred Federals.

The Federals fled across the Occoquan at Selectman's
Ford, and on arriving there General Fitzhugh Lee found
that the northern bank of the stream was occupied by a
considerable force of dismounted sharpshooters. Without
waiting to exchange shots with them, the brigade, led by
the 5th Virginia cavalry under Colonel T. L. Rosser,
charged gallantly across the narrow and rocky ford in single
file in the face of heavy volleys from the Federal sharpshooters, and soon captured or dispersed the entire party.
Pushing rapidly forward, Lee found and destroyed a large
camp, captured a number of horses, mules, wagons, blankets
and stores of various kinds, and burned the tents and everything else that could not be carried away.

Colonel Butler rejoined the command at Selectman's
Ford, having encountered a division of Federal infantry
that was moving from Fairfax to the support of the
troops at Dumfries, and extricated his command from a
critical situation by his coolness and presence of mind.
Just after Colonel Butler rejoined the command, General
Hampton went with a part of his brigade down toward
Accotink, while the main body moved across toward Burke's
Station. Hampton encountered a small party of Federals
and at once put them to flight, but owing to the darkness
did not follow them far and soon returned to the main
command. The head of the column reached Burke's Station on the Orange and Alexandria railroad some time af-

ter dark. The telegraph operator was captured before he could give the alarm, and as General Stuart had an operator with him he was enabled to ascertain what preparations had been made to receive him, the news of his raid having already reached Washington and dispatches being at that time sent over the wire between General S. P. Heintzelman at Washington and the commanding officer at Fairfax Station.

General Stuart, who was fond of and ever ready for a joke, having obtained all the information that he desired as to the wide-spread alarm and extensive defensive preparations which his raid had occasioned, facetiously sent some messages to General M. C. Meigs, quartermaster-general of the United States army, at Washington, in which he complained of the inferior quality of the mules recently furnished, as their condition seriously interfered with the moving of the wagons that he had captured.

After sending a small detachment under General Fitzhugh Lee to burn the bridge across the Accotink (which was promptly done), General Stuart left Burke's Station and proceeded to the Little River turnpike, and there halting the rest of the command, he advanced toward Fairfax Court-house with Fitzhugh Lee's brigade for the purpose of surprising and capturing the town if practicable. The place, however, was well-garrisoned and Stuart was saluted with a heavy volley from the Federal infantry who were guarding it, and, after keeping up the appearance of an attack for a short time, he moved off by way of Vienna toward Frying Pan, near which the command was halted, and the horses fed about dawn, the whole division having been in the saddle and constantly marching or fighting all of the preceding night and day.

After resting at Frying Pan for an hour or two, General Stuart proceeded to Middleburg, and from that place Colonel Rosser, with fifteen men, went by way of Snicker's Gap into the Valley, and, having captured the Federal picket near Leetown, penetrated the enemy's lines, ascertained the strength and position of the forces in that section and returned by way of Ashby's Gap without the loss of a single man. From Middleburg, General Stuart's com-

mand returned by easy marches to Culpeper Court-house,
reaching that place on December 31st, and from there the
three brigades repaired to their respective camps, having
been on the march or engaged in fighting for seven days
and several nights, and during that time the saddles were
not taken from their horses except on the night of December 26th. General Stuart's loss during the expedition was
exceedingly small, being one officer (Captain J. W. Bullock)
killed, Lieutenant-colonel Watts and twelve men wounded,
and one non-commissioned officer and twelve privates captured. He captured over two hundred prisoners, a large
number of horses, mules, wagons, saddles, bridles, pistols
and sabres, and destroyed the telegraph line between
Chopawamsie and the Occoquan, the tents and other property of the 2nd Pennsylvania cavalry, fired the bridge over
the Accotink and destroyed a portion of the Orange and
Alexandria railroad, and, moreover, obtained valuable information as to the forces of the Federals at Winchester,
Martinsburg and other points in the Valley. The expedition
was a brilliant and successful one, and "the gay cavaliers"
who engaged in it returned to camp in jubilant spirits,
and many a time for months afterward, around their blazing camp-fires did they revive, by interchange of reminis-
cences, the memories of those stirring scenes and thrilling
incidents that marked the manner in which they spent the
Christmas holidays of 1862 at Dumfries, Cole's store,
Greenwood Church, Fairfax Court-house and on the
Occoquan.

Whenever an occasion for so doing was afforded him,
Ashton had displayed his usual gallantry throughout the
raid, and thereby maintained the high esteem in which he
was held by both officers and men for his soldierly qualities. Although of a quiet disposition and at times somewhat reserved in his manner, he was quite popular with the
members of his company; for he never held himself aloof
from the humblest one of them, and was ever ready to render an act of kindness for his comrades when any opportunity for so doing presented itself. After remaining a
month or two longer on the Lower Rappahannock, the
brigade to which his regiment belonged moved up to the

vicinity of Culpeper Court-house, and began to picket the line of the Upper Rappahannock and the Hazel River. At some points, little more space than the width of the rivers separated the Confederate and Federal pickets, and they were thus in full view and easy range of each other; but there was a tacit understanding between them that there should be no firing by either side, and hence for Ashton and his comrades, who from time to time were sent on picket, the first weeks of the opening spring passed quietly by, without any incident worthy of notice.

However, about the middle of April, 1863, their routine experience of picket duty and camp life was suddenly interrupted, and the services of the brigade were called into requisition to check a threatened advance of the Federals. On the 13th of that month, a heavy force of Federals, consisting of cavalry and artillery moved up the Rappahannock from Fredericksburg to Kelly's Ford, and General W. H. F. Lee promptly sent a part of Ashton's regiment to meet them. About dawn the next morning the Federal cavalry, supported by a regiment of dismounted sharpshooters, made a dash for the ford, but were quickly repulsed by the sharpshooters of Ashton's regiment and hastily retired in disorder. During that morning they forced a passage of the river a short distance above, at Rappahannock Station, but were again driven back. The Confederate Horse Artillery then engaged the Federal batteries and firing was kept up between the artillery and sharpshooters on both sides during the remainder of the day.

The next day the Federal cavalry forced a passage of the river at Welford's Ford, driving in the Confederate pickets, and also attacked a force of Confederates at Beverly's Ford. General Lee at once advanced rapidly to Beverly's Ford with a part of his brigade, and soon Ashton and his comrades were in the midst of the fray. The Federals could not withstand the rapid and vigorous onslaught of the Confederate troopers, and were soon routed and driven back across the river. Some of them, however, were not so fortunate as to get across, for their rear guard, consisting of two squadrons, was driven into the river in a confused mass, where a number of them were drowned and fourteen prisoners and sixteen horses were captured. Although Ashton had become so much accustomed to scenes of death caused by sabre blade, bullet and cannon ball that he could bear them with some degree of composure, yet the sight of these drowning men was shocking to his feelings and greatly enlisted his sympathy in their behalf and he would have gladly saved them if it had been possible to do so. Indeed he did succeed in saving one poor fellow who, in his struggles, had managed to reach the south side of the stream, but owing to the steepness of the bank at that point could not extricate himself from the water. Seeing his helpless and critical condition, Ashton leaped from his horse and, at great peril to himself from the firing of the enemy on the other side of the river, ran to the assistance of the floundering Federal and succeeded in drawing him out of the water. General Lee had completely repulsed the Federals at all points, and they did not again attempt to cross the river. His force, as compared with that of the enemy, was exceedingly small, and his own gallantry and that of his officers and men were highly commended by General Stuart in forwarding a report of the two days fighting to General R. E. Lee.

Ashton and his comrades enjoyed but a short respite from the duties and dangers of war, for about two weeks after the occurrences just related, they were again called on to meet an advance of the enemy, and this time the force to which they were opposed was far more formidable than that which they had before successfully checked and routed. On the 29th of April the Federal army began to concentrate at and near Chancellorsville and a large force also crossed the Rappahannock at Kelly's Ford on that day. On the same day General George Stoneman crossed the river at that place with about five thousand cavalry for the purpose of starting on his (afterward) celebrated raid, the object of which was "the cutting of General Lee's communication with Richmond by the Fredericksburg route," and "the checking" of what General Hooker (who had succeeded General Burnside in the command of the Federal army, thought would be "his retreat" over that route when he attacked him at Chancellorsville.

Owing to the fact that Hampton's brigade had gone into the interior to recruit their horses, and Fitzhugh Lee's brigade had been taken by General Stuart to Chancellorsville, and only two regiments, the 9th and 13th Virginia cavalry, of his brigade had been left with General W. H. F. Lee at Culpeper Court-house, he had merely these two regiments with which to meet the advancing Federals. With this small force of cavalry and one piece of artillery, he marched from Culpeper to Rapidan Station on April 30th. On May 1st his little band was engaged all day with one or two brigades of Federal cavalry, stubbornly contesting the ground over which they passed in their forward movement, and that night he withdrew to Gordonsville. On May 2d he was informed that the Federals were at Trevilian's Station, and sent the 9th Virginia cavalry in that direction. The regiment met and gallantly charged the Federals, drove them back three miles and captured thirty-two of their number. On the following day General Lee learned that the Federals were moving from Louisa Court-house toward Columbia, and, believing that their object was to destroy the James River and Kanawha canal, he at once started in pursuit of them. He arrived at Columbia that night but the Federals had heard of his approach and precipitately fled without having destroyed the canal, and on learning this, General Lee continued his pursuit of them during the entire night. At daybreak he had ridden about sixty miles and halted for a short time to rest his horses. Having given the horses a short rest, General Lee moved forward and soon came upon the Federals drawn up in column at Flemming's Crossroads.

The squadron to which Ashton belonged was a few hundred yards ahead of General Lee's main force and at once charged the Federal cavalry. The Federals charged at the same time, and in a few moments the two opposing forces were engaged in a hand-to-hand fight. The engagement lasted only about five minutes, when the Federals were completely routed and driven back with the loss of six men killed, a number of others wounded and thirty-three captured, among whom were Captain Wesley Owens and Lieutenant Temple Buford of the 5th United States cavalry. Although short, the fight was a fierce and vigorous one and sabres were freely used, especially by the Confederate squadron. Ashton was in the front rank of fours and hence got into the thickest of the fray. He became engaged in a hand-to-hand encounter with a Federal trooper who had previously fired at him twice without effect and hence drew his sabre to defend himself from Ashton's fierce attack upon him with his own sabre. The Federal was successful only to the extent of weakening Ashton's blows and preventing them from being fatal, for he carried off in his subsequent flight no less than seven sabre cuts as evidence of the rapidity and skill with which Ashton had used his weapon. So vigorous had been the charge, accompanied, of course, with "the wild Confederate yell," and so fierce had been the attack upon the Federal column, that Captain James E. Harrison, commanding the Federal cavalry, appears to have greatly exaggerated the numbers of the attacking squadron, as he says in his official report of the fight: "I found that I had become engaged with at least one thousand men. The shock of the charge was so great that my foremost horses were completely knocked over."

They were "knocked over," not by the supposed large number of the attacking force that charged his column, but by the impetuosity and vigor with which the charge was made by that gallant little squadron (two companies) of Confederate cavalry.

General Lee's entire force numbered only about eight hundred men, and but one squadron took part in the charge. After their rout the Federals retreated to Yanceyville and subsequently, by forced marches day and night, succeeded in recrossing the Rappahannock at Kelly's Ford. General Lee was informed by one of the captured officers that General Buford was only three miles distant, but owing to the smallness of his force and the jaded condition of his horses, he decided not to pursue him and returned to Gordonsville.

Having learned on May 6th that a force of Federals was recrossing the Central railroad below Gordonsville, General

Lee started in pursuit of them and came up with the rear guard of their column at the North Anna river, where he captured seventeen prisoners. They had crossed the river and destroyed the bridge, and as the stream was swollen and not fordable he could not farther pursue them. Learning that another column of Federals was moving farther down the river, he went in pursuit of them, but found that they, too, had crossed the river and destroyed the bridges behind them. On the following day he moved toward Orange Court-house, and learned from his scouts that the Federals had crossed the Rapidan and were beyond his reach.

This terminated the part taken by the brigade to which Ashton belonged in the efforts that were made to check Stoneman's raid, and in view of the smallness of the Confederate force (two regiments), their work was bravely and efficiently done.

In the meantime, the main body of General R. E. Lee's army had fought and won the battles of Chancellorsville and Salem Church, and driven General Hooker's army back across the Rappahannock with a loss of more than seventeen thousand men, about twenty thousand muskets, thirteen pieces of artillery, seventeen colors and an immense quantity of ammunition, the Confederate loss being about eleven thousand.

These victories were achieved by the Confederates over greatly superior numbers and in the face of apparently insurmountable obstacles; for, while General Lee's force was greatly reduced by the absence of General Longstreet, with Hood's, Pickett's and Ransom's divisions in southeastern Virginia, and consisted only of Jackson's corps, Anderson's and McLaws' divisions of Longstreet's corps and one brigade of cavalry and aggregated something over forty thousand men, that of General Hooker consisted of his entire army of seven corps and part of the cavalry corps, numbering over one hundred and ten thousand, and, at Chancellorsville, was intrenched in the heart of a tangled wilderness behind strong earthworks, the approaches to which were protected by abattis and barricades of heavy timber.

8

The victory of the Confederates at Chancellorsville was mainly due to the rapid and successful flank movement of General "Stonewall" Jackson, by means of which he turned General Hooker's right flank, attacked him unexpectedly in the rear, in the afternoon of May 2d, and in about two hours drove the right wing of his army pell-mell more than three miles over a succession of outer works, and into his strongly intrenched central position at Chancellorsville. In this movement, General Jackson had only D. H. Hill's division, commanded by Brigadier-general R. E. Rodes, Isaac R. Trimble's division, commanded by Brigadier-general R. E. Colston, and A. P. Hill's division, and the first-mentioned division, under the superb leadership of the gallant Rodes, completely routed and put to ignominious flight the 11th corps, commanded by General O. O. Howard, which sustained a loss of one thousand, four hundred and twenty-eight killed and wounded, and nine hundred and seventy-four captured; and, moreover, in their headlong flight disarranged, demoralized and swept back another corps that had come to their assistance. This victorious movement was checked about 8 o'clock P. M., when in the darkness the Confederates became entangled in a heavy abattis in front of the intrenchments between them and Chancellorsville, and their first and second lines were thereby mingled in great confusion. General Jackson promptly reformed his line, with A. P. Hill's division in front, and soon thereafter rode forward a short distance to reconnoitre, intending to renew the attack that night, and giving orders to his men not to fire unless cavalry should approach from the direction of the Federals. He had gone about one hundred yards when he discovered that no pickets had been placed in front of his line and, having finished his inspection, sent an order to General A. P. Hill to advance, and started to return to his troops. He failed to notify them of his approach and, while riding back, he and his escort were fired upon by some of his own men, who supposed them to be Federal cavalry. From this fire General Jackson received several wounds that completely disabled him, and from the effects of which he died on May 10th.

But for this occurrence, General Hooker's army would have been annihilated or captured, for it was General Jackson's purpose to move his troops still farther to the left, get completely in General Hooker's rear, occupy the roads leading to Ely's Ford on the Rapidan and the United States Ford on the Rappahannock, thus cutting off his line of retreat, and, on the following day, after remaining on the defensive for a few hours and repulsing the efforts that General Hooker would have naturally made to open his line of retreat, he intended to attack the Federal commander from the rear with his whole force, while General Lee pressed him in front, and in this way the Federal army would have been crushed between the two Confederate forces thus closing in upon it. General J. E. B. Stuart, who was unexpectedly called to the command of the troops that night on account of the fact that General A. P. Hill had been wounded, being unfamiliar with the ground and uninformed as to General Jackson's plans, pursued a different policy and, on renewing the battle the next morning, moved his troops to the right until he had formed a junction with General Lee. The united forces of the two then stormed and captured the Federal stronghold at Chancellorsville, but Hooker's line of retreat toward the Rappahannock being open, he succeeded in escaping in that direction, and took refuge in a strong line of intrenchments covering the United States Ford.

General Lee made preparations to renew his attack on General Hooker and drive him across the Rappahannock, but was deterred from so doing by the receipt of information that General Sedgwick, with a large force, was marching against him from the direction of Fredericksburg, with only General C. M. Wilcox's brigade to impede his progress. General Lee at once ordered General McLaws, with Kershaw's, Wofford's, Semmes' and Mahone's brigades, to the assistance of General Wilcox. When these reinforcements reached him, General Wilcox, with only about two thousand men, was gallantly holding in check General Sedgwick's force of about twenty thousand at Salem Church, and had formed his brigade in line of battle across the plank-road to receive an attack that was about to be made by the advancing Federals. General McLaws quickly lengthened his line of battle by placing Kershaw's and Wofford's brigades on the right and Semmes' and Mahone's brigades on the left of Wilcox's brigade; but before his troops were fully in position the Federals had pressed forward in heavy force and attacked the brigades of Wilcox, Semmes and Mahone, the 50th and 53rd Georgia regiments of Semmes' brigade having to take position under a storm of bullets.

The attack of the Federals was gallantly made, but it was still more gallantly and successfully repulsed by the Confederates, the brigades of Wilcox and Semmes bearing the brunt of the battle; and after a fierce and desperate conflict, the Federals were routed and driven back in great confusion. Wilcox's brigade and the 10th and 51st Georgia regiments, of Semmes' brigade, pursued the fleeing Federals, and another line coming up the plank-road to the support of their retreating comrades was quickly broken by the Confederates and driven back in a perfect rout upon the Federal reserves. It was now dark, and the conflict ceased for the night.

During the next day General Lee came in person with the remainder of General R. H. Anderson's division (Perry's, Posey's and Wright's brigades) to reinforce General Mc-Laws, and about 6 P.M. renewed the attack on General Sedgwick, who was rapidly driven back toward the Rappahannock until darkness prevented farther pursuit, and he made his escape that night by crossing the river at Banks' Ford.

On the following day, General Lee returned to Chancellorsville for the purpose of attacking General Hooker, but was prevented from so doing by the retreat of the latter that night across the Rappahannock at the United States Ford.

Thus ended General Hooker's brief, bloody and unsuccessful Chancellorsville campaign, and his complete and disastrous defeat, culminating in the strange spectacle of an immense army fleeing before a force about one-third as large as its own, presented a picture in strikingly ridiculous contrast to the imaginary one drawn by him on April 30, when, after he had crossed the Rappahannock with but little opposition and massed his troops around Chancellorsville, he issued "General Orders, No. 47," and therein said:

"It is with heartfelt satisfaction the commanding general announces to the army that the operations of the last three days have determined that our enemy must either ingloriously fly, or come out from behind his defenses and give us battle on our own ground, where certain destruction awaits him."

The "enemy" did not "ingloriously fly," but had "come out from behind his defenses" and given the Federals "battle on their own ground," and instead of meeting with "certain destruction," had achieved a marked and brilliant victory over vastly superior numbers, thereby demonstrating the superior prowess of the Confederate troops, and also administering a severe and wholesome rebuke to the premature boastfulness of the over-confident Federal commander.

General Hooker's effort to conceal the disastrous failure of his inglorious campaign, as shown by "General Orders, No. 49," issued May 6, 1863, was supremely absurd and ridiculous; for in that paper he says:

"The major-general commanding tenders to this army his congratulations on its achievements of the last seven days. If it has not accomplished all that was expected, the reasons are well known to the army. It is sufficient to say they were of a character not to be foreseen or prevented by human sagacity or resource.

"In withdrawing from the south bank of the Rappahannock before delivering a general battle to our adversaries, the army has given renewed evidence of its confidence in itself and its fidelity to the principles it represents. In fighting at a disadvantage, we would have been recreant to our trust, to ourselves, our cause, and our country.

"Profoundly loyal, and conscious of its strength, the army of the Potomac will give or decline battle whenever its interest or honor may demand. It will also be the guardian of its own history and its own fame.

"By our celerity and secrecy of movement, our advance and passage of the rivers were undisputed, and on our withdrawal not a rebel ventured to follow.

"The events of the last week may swell with pride the heart of every officer and soldier of this army. We have added new luster to its former renown. We have made long marches, crossed rivers, surprised the enemy in his intrenchments, and whenever we have fought, have inflicted heavier blows than we have received."

Comment on this remarkable rodomontade would be superfluous, as its ludicrous fancifulness will be perfectly apparent to the reader in view of the facts previously narrated in regard to the results of the Chancellorsville campaign.

Although that campaign had resulted in a marked and brilliant victory for the Confederates, their success had been dearly purchased; for they had lost many brave private soldiers and some of their most gallant and efficient officers. Among the latter, as already mentioned, was that military prodigy, General T. J. Jackson, whose phenomenal achievements had made him the idol of his friends and a terror to his foes, and not only stamped him as the best corps commander of any age, but also indicated that if he had been at the head of an army he would have taken rank with the greatest generals that ever lived.

After the close of the Chancellorsville campaign, the remainder of the month of May became a period of comparative rest to all branches of the army of Northern Virginia, and this rest was especially acceptable to Ashton and his comrades, in view of the arduous service which they had rendered during Stoneman's raid. At its close they went into camp in Orange county, where there was an abundance of clover on which to graze their horses.

Although we have seemingly forgotten our heroine, the reader must not suppose that Ashton had forgotten her amid the varied and exciting scenes through which he had passed during the preceding five months. Such was not the case, for he had been constantly thinking of her, and was greatly troubled in consequence of the fact that he had failed to hear from her, his last letter, as before stated, having been returned to him. And now, while enjoying temporary rest from the labors and dangers of active service during the bright and beautiful days of May, and lolling in the genial sunshine, amid the blooming clover fields of Orange county, watching his faithful horse as he contentedly grazed upon the rich herbage rising knee-high around him, Ashton thought more constantly **than ever before of Ruth** Middleton and his ardent love for her. As he reflected **on** the depth and tenderness of his love for **her, he realized how** completely that love had possessed his heart, and how thoroughly it would dominate his after life. Although his failure to hear from Ruth in answer to his declaration of love, and the uncertainty as to how that declaration had been received, greatly troubled him, he was not altogether unhappy and found much pleasure in thinking of her and, with the utmost *abandon*, giving full sway to his affection for her. While it was true that he had idealized her and felt that he was unworthy of her love, yet, seeming contradiction, **he** was somehow confident that he would eventually **become** the object and possessor of that love. Leaving him to indulge in his tender and loving musings of Ruth, we will return to her and give some account of the manner in which her life had been spent in Richmond.

CHAPTER X.

Shortly after Ruth's arrival in Richmond, she secured a
pleasant boarding-place with a family on Franklin street,
near the Capitol. The family consisted of Mrs. Julia
Slaughter, whose husband, Colonel Percy Slaughter, had
been killed at the second battle of Manassas, her daughter
Kate, about eighteen years of age, and her son Randolph,
about thirteen years of age. Mrs. Slaughter was well
educated, refined in her manners and exceedingly kind-
hearted, and her conduct was marked by that gentle, ever-
watchful and yet unobtrusive solicitude for the comfort
and pleasure of others which would have caused one to
speak of her as "a motherly woman." Kate was a high-
spirited, bright and lively creature, thoroughly independent
in her thoughts and actions, slightly headstrong and
inclined to have her own way, but withal utterly incapable
of doing a small or selfish thing, and as warm-hearted and
affectionate as any child. Randolph's disposition was the
counterpart of his sister's except in this, that it was more
equable and tractable than hers and invariably caused him
to show deference to the opinions and wishes of his
superiors. Ruth was charmed with the family among
whom her lot had been cast, and in a very short time all of
its members had become quite fond of her. By the kindly
interest which she manifested in Randolph she at once won
his heart, and soon this manly, warm-hearted boy was as
loyal to the lovely lady who had come among them as ever
knight of old was to the fair maiden in whose honor he
engaged in the peaceful joust of the tourney lists, or rode
in martial mood to the battle-field. Surrounded by such
kind-hearted and considerate friends, Ruth passed most
pleasantly the time spent in their company, and the affectionate interest which they manifested in her welfare tended
greatly to soothe her sorrowing heart and restore her
former peace of mind. During the day the greater part of
her time was spent at the hospital where her services as a
volunteer nurse had been accepted, as before stated; and
she had become deeply interested in the work in which she

was engaged, and also in the patients who had come under her care. She possessed all the qualifications necessary to make a good nurse and this fact, together with the deep interest felt by her in those to whose wants she was ministering, rendered her not only eminently successful in her new vocation but also exceedingly popular with her patients.

In making her rounds each day, she always had a pleasant greeting, a kindly smile and a cheering word for every one of her patients, and at her approach the faces of even the most despondent would be brightened by the pleasant emotions which her presence invariably inspired. Nearly all of the inmates of the ward to which her duties called her were soldiers who had been wounded in battle, and this fact kept her constantly reminded of Ashton, and at first tended greatly to depress her feelings and partially unfit her for the discharge of her duties in that cheerful manner in which she knew that they should be discharged in order to render them the most efficacious. In a short time, however, she succeeded in overcoming this depressing influence, and that which at first had caused it now helped to better fit her for her work; for, thinking of Ashton and, in imagination, picturing to herself the ghastly wound by which she supposed he had met his death, made her more solicitous for the recovery of those who, like him, had been wounded in defense of their country, and caused her to do all in her power to alleviate their sufferings and hasten their recovery.

Toward the latter part of April Ruth received a very affectionate but doleful letter from Bertha, in which the latter told her of how greatly she missed her and how sad and lonely her life had been since she left, and closed with the statement that she could not longer endure their separation and would be in Richmond on the 25th of that month. At the time mentioned, Bertha arrived in the city, and the meeting between her and Ruth was so affectionate and joyous that any one witnessing it would have been impressed with the idea that they had been separated for at least a year. As Bertha possessed the happy faculty of adapting herself to her surroundings, she would soon have been at ease in any household, and in consequence of the genial dispositions and affable manners of the Slaughters, she at once felt at home among them, and was soon on very friendly terms with the entire family. She found Kate especially congenial and, although the latter's nature was the stronger of the two, they possessed sufficient similarity of tastes and feelings to quickly engender a warm mutual attachment that brought about a loyal and delightful comradeship between them. As a natural result of this, they were almost constantly together and to some extent Kate's associates also became Bertha's. Kate's frank, bright and high-spirited nature and cordial manners had rendered her quite popular with the gentlemen of her acquaintance as was manifested by the number of her visitors. The *personnel* of her visitors was constantly changing, as nearly all of them were soldiers in active service and only temporarily in the city on short furloughs, or called there by business connected with the army; for so thoroughly did Kate believe that every young man who was able to shoulder a musket or wield a sabre should be at the front, that she would have scorned the attentions of any such who refrained from offering their services to the Confederate Government.

When, through the medium of Kate's existing acquaintances, it became known that the attractions of Mrs. Slaughter's house had been enhanced by the presence of two charming girls from Georgia, the number of visitors proportionately increased and scarcely an evening passed without the presence there of several young soldiers. And such is human nature and the buoyancy of youth, that these young men who, in many instances, were fresh from scenes of carnage and suffering and would soon return to similar scenes, were as gay and light-hearted as schoolboys and passed the time in lively chat and merry jest, seemingly oblivious of the fact that a gigantic and destructive war was in progress with all of its attendant incidents of suffering and death.

Amid these gay parties that nightly filled Mrs. Slaughter's parlors, there was one who was not in harmony with her surroundings and did not participate in the lively badinage that was freely indulged in by the others, for Ruth Middleton's heart was too full of grief for her lost lover, and solicitude for the wounded soldiers to whom she daily ministered, to have any room therein for merriment. Occasionally, however, there were those among these visitors who were inclined to serious discourse, and Ruth found pleasure in conversing with them.

Shortly after Bertha's arrival she had accompanied Ruth on one of her visits to the hospital, and although at first so much affected by the distressing scenes around her that she felt inclined to hasten away from them, after awhile her sympathy was so thoroughly aroused in behalf of the suffering soldiers that she either forgot or overcame the disagreeable feelings which she had previously experienced at sight of their condition, and was suddenly inspired with an earnest desire to do what she could to relieve them. Hence, on leaving the hospital she proposed to assist Ruth in her work. Ruth was naturally surprised by this proposition, but told her that if the hospital authorities would consent to the arrangement she would gladly accept her assistance. On the following day Ruth submitted the matter to the surgeon in charge of the hospital. Having ascertained the relation which Bertha sustained to Ruth, he promptly consented to the proposed arrangement and after that Bertha went to the hospital at least once each day to assist Ruth in her duties. She soon became deeply interested in her work, and correspondingly efficient in its performance. Bertha had been assisting Ruth for about a week when a number of soldiers who had been wounded during the battle of Chancellorsville were brought to the hospital. Among them was Captain Philip Carrington, of the 4th Georgia regiment of infantry, who had been wounded while gallantly leading his company in a charge on May 2d. He was shot through the right arm and as the bone was broken it was at first thought that amputation would be necessary; but on close examination the regimental surgeon decided that the wounded arm could be saved by proper attention. The wound was promptly dressed; all particles of bone were extracted, and Carrington was carried to Richmond where he could receive better treatment than in the field hospital. As he has thus suddenly come into our story and will figure

in its future development, the reader will doubtless wish
to know something about him. **He** was about twenty-five
years of age, of medium stature, well-proportioned, and
had a strikingly handsome and attractive **face and an easy**
and graceful carriage. His complexion was dark, his hair and
mustache were almost black, and his eyes dark **brown. He
was quite intellectual,** highly educated, and a man **of exalted**
moral character. His disposition was genial and **lively, and**
he readily made friends of all who came in contact with **him,
and that too, without** the slightest effort to **win their**
favor. **He was a physician and** had left a lucrative practice at the outbreak of the war in order to devote himself
to the service of the South. Such was Phil Carrington, as
his friends familiarly called him; and he at once attracted
the attention of Ruth and Bertha and aroused their warmest
**sympathy in his behalf. Although they were accustomed
to minister alike and impartially to the wants of all of the
soldiers in their ward, there was something in the appear-**
ance and manner of this handsome young officer that irresistibly **called forth more than ordinary care and attention**
on their part. He was deeply touched by the **solicitude**
which they manifested in his case, and plainly **showed by**
his manner that he was truly grateful for **the same.
Even under ordinary circumstances, the gentle and** kindly
ministrations of two lovely girls would have greatly interested and gratified him, and when he ascertained that Ruth
and Bertha were natives and residents of his own State,
who had left the comforts and pleasures of home and
come to Virginia to try to alleviate the sufferings of
unknown soldiers, Carrington became all the more interested in them, and his heart was filled with pride and
gratitude at the thought of their patriotic and self-
sacrificing devotion to the cause of the Confederacy. As he
became better acquainted with them, his respect and admiration for them rapidly increased, and soon he was on
quite friendly terms with them. **In a short time, he had so**
far recovered from the debilitating effects of his wound
that he was able to take a little exercise each day, and
after that he rapidly regained his strength and
health. As soon as the surgeon pronounced him out of

danger and consented that he might be discharged from the hospital, he secured a boarding-place in the city and became a frequent visitor at Mrs. Slaughter's residence. Although he greatly admired both Ruth and Bertha, he had been especially attracted to the latter, and it soon became evident to those who saw them together that Carrington was in a fair way of becoming the willing captive of this bright and charming Georgia girl. It was also evident that she was deeply interested in him and preferred his society to that of any of the numerous visitors who, from time to time, called at Mrs. Slaughter's. As Carrington's interest in and regard for Bertha increased, he naturally became anxious to enjoy more of her society than he had opportunities for enjoying in Mrs. Slaughter's parlors while other visitors were present, and hence he began to take her out driving to various points of interest in and around the city. He made full use of the opportunities thus afforded for manifesting his increasing interest in and warm regard for Bertha and, erelong, noticed with joyous emotions evidences of the fact that his lover-like attentions were acceptable to her and that her interest in him was daily increasing. Shortly after Carrington left the hospital and began his visits to the young ladies at Mrs. Slaughter's, one of Kate Slaughter's acquaintances, Lieutenant Henry Harris of the——artillery, called at Mrs. Slaughter's one evening and brought with him a young man whom he introduced as Sergeant Paul, of Mosby's cavalry. Harris had met Paul a few days before in the reading-room of the Exchange Hotel, when a lengthy conversation ensued between them. The intelligent and ready manner in which Paul discussed the various topics that formed the subjects of their conversation, and his easy and affable manners made quite a favorable impression on Harris, and on meeting Paul again the next day, he gave him a very cordial greeting. The latter not only heartily responded to the cordial greeting of Harris, but so demeaned himself in their subsequent conversation as to impress Harris with the idea that he desired to cultivate his acquaintance. Harris, being of a social disposition and finding Paul's conversation entertaining, readily acquiesced in this desire, and they were soon on friendly terms. As a result of the acquaintance thus begun, Harris had invited Paul to join him in a visit to the young ladies at Mrs. Slaughter's; and hence his appearance there at the time before mentioned. Carrington was present on the occasion and, although Paul was a man of fine personal appearance, easy bearing, affable manners, and apparently frank disposition, he was somewhat unfavorably impressed by him and could not avoid wondering whether his supposed frankness was real or assumed. If he had been called on to give a reason for this unfavorable impression, he could not, perhaps, have given one that would have been satisfactory to any one else, nor could he, in reflecting on the matter afterward, attribute it to any cause that was entirely clear or satisfactory to himself. However, the impression had been made and continued to exist without any tangible cause. It was one of those sudden, instinctive, and inexplicable feelings of distrust and antipathy which are engendered by what may be termed the exhalations from an evil or hypocritical nature, independent of overt act or outward appearance, just as one's sense of smell is offended by the noxious odors of a poisonous flower, although in appearance it may be the perfection of beauty. Notwithstanding the fact that Sergeant Paul ignored (if he were aware of its existence) the unfavorable impression which he had made on Carrington, and was perfectly easy and affable in his conduct toward him, doing and saying nothing that was apparently insincere or offensive, Carrington could not get rid of the sense of distrust that he experienced in regard to him. Having formed the acquaintance of the young ladies at Mrs. Slaughter's, and being apparently well pleased with their society, Paul continued to visit them, and by his bright and sprightly conversations and pertinent and intelligent observations on the conduct and progress of the war, invariably succeeded in interesting and entertaining his listeners. Moreover, he occasionally presented to their view certain phases of the war, with which not even the most experienced soldiers present were familiar, by giving them graphic pictures of Mosby and his little band of partisan rangers when engaged in their irregular but efficient system of border warfare, telling, with the spirit and perspicuity of an eye-witness and participant, of their silent, midnight marches through the darksome woods in their frequent incursions **into** the enemy's lines, their unexpected and vigorous assault upon and capture of some outlying Federal picket-post, and their rapid return into the Confederate lines and sudden dispersion to their secret haunts in Fauquier and Rappahannock counties and amid the mountain fastnesses of the Blue Ridge. Such incidents were not only interesting, but also novel to Paul's listeners, for, as Mosby was not with the regular army and was operating outside of the Confederate lines, even the soldiers present had no means of acquiring full information in regard to his movements. Hence, those to whom Paul related Mosby's gallant and successful achievements, were naturally deeply interested in their narration and consequently pleased with the narrator. **He** had seemingly incidentally explained his presence **in** Richmond at this time by stating that he had been sent there with dispatches for the War Department and had leave of absence from his command for two **or three** weeks. This explanation of his presence in the city was a plausible one and entirely satisfactory to those who had heard it.

It was now the first of June and about two weeks after Paul began his visits at Mrs. Slaughter's, when, during one of his visits, he announced that he expected to return to his command in a day or two. The next afternoon Carrington and Bertha took a long drive which **was** the occasion of certain developments that were of sufficient interest to **entitle** them to a place in our story. Leaving Franklin **street near** the southwest corner of Capitol Square, they **drove** up Ninth street into Broad, and out East Broad beyond Shockoe Creek to Seventeenth street, and up that street to where it is called Valley street, and out Valley street for about a mile and a half along the Central rail-road. Recrossing the railroad, they drove around **by** Shockoe Hill Cemetery into Second street, and down Second street to Marshal, and out West Marshal to Henry street, and passing down Henry street, they drove by the public square and along what is now Belvidere street to Albemarle street and out Albemarle to Hollywood cemetery. Here they alighted from their buggy, entered the cemetery, and began to stroll amid its beautiful shrubbery and handsome monuments. Although they were seemingly engaged in looking at the many attractions of nature and of art that abounded in this beautiful city of the dead, their surroundings had but a small place in their thoughts, **and** the fact that they were in the presence of the **emblems of** decay and death only served to awe them into comparative silence and temporarily check what would otherwise **have** been an exuberant flow of joyous feeling; for they **were** quietly and yet supremely happy. From what has previously been said in regard to their increasing interest in each other, the reader can readily guess the secret of their happiness, and we will simply state that, as Carrington's wound had about healed and he expected to return to his regiment in a few days, he had seized the opportunity afforded him by their lengthy drive to tell Bertha of his love, and received the happy assurance that her heart **was** all his own. No wonder, therefore, that they were supremely happy **and,** in a measure, oblivious of their surroundings. Continuing their walk, unconscious of the distance that they had strolled, they at last reached a point not far from **where** the James River and Kanawha Canal passes by the southern extremity of the cemetery, and here they found a **rustic** seat in the recess of a beautiful bower of overarching vines and shrubbery. The sight of the seat reminded Bertha of the fact that she was somewhat fatigued by the long walk she had taken, and she readily adopted Carrington's suggestion that they should rest awhile in this inviting retreat. On entering it they were effectually screened from view from all directions except that immediately in front of its opening, and as the shrubbery and bushes in the rear of the bower and toward the canal were quite dense, it would have been almost impossible for anyone to have discovered their presence except by approaching the bower directly in front. They had been seated only a few moments when they heard the sound of voices in rear of the bower and discovered that the persons talking were approaching them from the direction of the canal. When these persons had approached within eight or ten paces of

Carrington and Bertha, they stopped, and although the latter could neither see nor be seen by them, they could hear what they were saying. Greatly to the surprise of the lovers, they immediately recognized one of the voices as that of Sergeant Paul, and the first remark made by him **not** only fixed their attention but also caused them to listen with intense interest to the conversation thus begun, which was as follows:

"Well, Fox, I have played my cards successfully, and the game is won. The 'Mosby's man' dodge has worked like a charm, as it has increased my opportunities for observation and decreased the dangers of detection; for it is known that **many of** Mosby's men are not regularly enlisted in the Rebel army and hence they have greater freedom of action **in** Richmond than regular soldiers, and do not have to give such a strict account of themselves as the latter. I have made several friends among the Rebel officers, and used them efficiently in obtaining the information for which I came. I have learned that Lee is concentrating his army in Orange and Culpeper counties with a view to an important movement. I am preparing in cipher information as to the details of this movement and will have it ready for you to-morrow night. It is best that you should at once take this to General Hooker at Falmouth. I will remain here a few days longer and then leave for the Rebel army, where I hope to acquire some additional information in regard to **Lee's** plans before returning into our lines."

The person addressed as Fox replied:

"**You** have certainly played your cards well, Mr. Craft, **and I** congratulate you on the success of your game. I doubt whether there is another one of our emissaries who would have done half so well. I hope that your reward will be proportionate to the service rendered, and in view of the dangers incident to such service, your compensation should be very great."

"No doubt," said Paul, "I will be handsomely rewarded for the information furnished, **as** its value to the Federal commander will be incalculable. Among all of the Rebels **whom** I have met, a certain Captain Carrington is the only one who appears to have distrusted me, and he has been so

9

much engaged in his courtship of a Rebel girl, who is on a visit here from the South, that he has made no effort to have me shadowed, or, so far as I am informed, attempted to ascertain anything in regard to me. I am sure he has not even suspected my real character, or the object of my presence in the Rebel Capital."

"You have been quite fortunate," said Fox, "in having escaped suspicion as to the object of your presence here, and I hope that you may be equally as fortunate during the remainder of your stay. Now let us have an understanding as to when and where I am to meet you to-morrow night for the purpose of receiving your cipher dispatches and any further instructions you may wish to give me."

"I have been thinking about that matter," replied Paul, "and have concluded that it would be rather risky for us to meet at our former rendezvous in the city, as that quarter is now under complete surveillance by the police. It will be best for us to have our interview at some point in or near the public square, and I will meet you there to-morrow evening about dusk. I will be near the southeast entrance of the square at that time, and if I do not immediately find an opportunity for delivering the papers we can stroll out toward the Richmond, Fredericksburg, and Potomac railroad, and I can deliver them during our walk. As there is nothing further to be said or done at present, we will now separate."

The speakers then retired in the direction from which they had come, and Carrington and Bertha at once returned to their buggy and drove back to Mrs. Slaughter's. They were profoundly interested in what they had heard, and Carrington told Bertha that he would take immediate action to arrange for the arrest of the two spies, and thereby prevent Paul's dispatches from being forwarded to the Federal commander. He suggested to Bertha that she had best spend the next day away from her boarding-house, so that, in the event that Paul should call there, she would not have to meet him; as he knew that it would be very disagreeable to her to meet him after what she had heard, and also feared that her manner toward him might be such as to awaken his suspicions. Bertha readily promised that she would adopt his suggestion and thanked him for making it, stating that the thought of again meeting Paul was extremely repugnant to her. After leaving Bertha, Carrington immediately sought an interview with the provost-marshal of the city and related to him all that he had heard of the conversation between the two spies. The provost-marshal assured him that prompt and effectual measures would be adopted for the apprehension of the spies and on the following morning he made arrangements for the accomplishment of this object. Knowing that the presence of policemen at or near the public square at the time appointed for the meeting of the spies would excite less suspicion than that of soldiers, the provost-marshal, after consulting with the chief of police, had ten policemen detailed for the work in hand and gave them full instructions as to the steps to be taken in making the contemplated arrests. It was arranged that the policemen should be stationed as follows: Four near the southeast corner of the public square, four at the junction of Henry and West Franklin streets, and the two others at the corner of Smith and West Grace streets, as this disposition of the men would enable them to watch the movements of the spies in the event that they should not hold their interview at or near the southeast entrance to the square as contemplated by them, but should go out toward the Richmond, Fredericksburg, and Potomac railroad to give Paul an opportunity for delivering his dispatches to Fox. A little before dusk that evening, all of the policemen had reached the positions to which they had been respectively assigned. A few minutes afterward, Sergeant Paul sauntered into the square from Henry street, and after strolling around for a short time, returned to the southeast entrance. A moment afterward, a man in citizen's dress approached the entrance from Main street and walked in. On seeing Paul, he walked briskly toward him and when he had reached him extended his hand and said:

"Why, how are you, sergeant? I am glad to see you. When did you reach the city?"

"Good evening, Mr. Phillips," said Paul. "This is an unexpected pleasure, for I had supposed that you were out of the city, as I have been here for several weeks without meeting you. I am really glad to see you again and regret that we did not meet before now, especially as I will leave for the army in a few days. Let us take a stroll, as I would like to have a chat with you and hear about Mrs. Phillips and your daughters."

"Very well," replied Paul's companion, "nothing **would** please me better."

Paul and his companion then turned around and **began to** walk off toward the north entrance of the square, **and** immediately the four policemen who were near them, **but** concealed by some shrubbery, made their appearance and started toward them. The man called Phillips caught sight of them and at once darted off through the square toward **the northwest corner of it.** Two of the policemen pursued him, firing several shots as they ran. He ran with great speed and soon so far distanced his pursuers as to get out of their sight **in** the gathering gloom and thus make his escape. In the meantime, the other two policemen had seized Paul, and one of them said:

"Edward Craft, alias Sergeant Paul, by authority of the provost-marshal of Richmond and in the name of the Con- **federate** Government, I arrest you as a Federal spy."

"**Arrest** me as a Federal spy?" replied Paul. "Ha! ha! **What a blunder!** That is certainly a capital joke. Now if I had been arrested as a Confederate spy, there might have been some foundation for the act, for the Major (that's Mosby) frequently sends me into the Yankee lines under such circumstances and on such missions that, if I were caught, appearances would be so greatly against me I would doubtless be treated as a spy. But the idea of my being a Federal spy is so preposterous that it is really **amusing.** Why, my friend, I am one of Mosby's men, and have been connected with his command for more than six months."

The policeman replied: "Your arrest may appear amusing **to you, but** I think you will soon find that it is a very **serious matter.** However, it is not my business to discuss the affair with you, but simply to obey orders and conduct you to the provost-marshal to be disposed of by him. And **as we have some distance to** walk, we will start at once."

Having relieved him of his pistol, and the other policemen having returned from their fruitless chase after Fox, **the party** started off with Paul, making him walk between two of their number. On reaching Franklin street a messenger was sent for the policemen at the junction of Smith and West Grace streets, and when they arrived the entire party returned into the city and conducted their prisoner to the provost-marshal, who was at his office awaiting their arrival. Paul was at once informed that he had been arrested on the charge of being a Federal spy and that he would have to submit to being searched. **At** this statement he turned slightly pale and appeared to be somewhat excited; but recovering his composure in a moment, he protested against the indignity of such a proceeding and **demanded** to know upon whose accusation he had been arrested. At that moment Captain Carrington entered the office and said:

"You were arrested upon my accusation, and I am prepared to establish its truthfulness. If the persons who arrested you did their duty, and prevented you from delivering to your confederate a certain document which was to have been delivered to him this evening at or near the public square, there will be found on your person cipher dispatches to the Federal commander at Falmouth giving what you claim to be definite information as to the contemplated movements of General Lee's army."

While Carrington was speaking, Paul turned deathly pale, **and** gave unmistakable signs of great nervousness and embarrassment. His confusion was such that he did not attempt any reply to Carrington's statement; and he was **at once** subjected to a thorough search. Just as had been **expected, a** lengthy document in cipher was found on his person. It was in a sealed envelope without direction, was not addressed to any one, and was simply signed, "C."

As this paper was the only suspicious article found on his person, and the provost-marshal appeared unable to read **it,** Paul experienced momentary relief from the feeling of despair that had seized him when it was discovered. This relief, however, was only momentary, for the provost-marshal handed the writing to his clerk and said:

"Mr. Sharp, examine this document and see if you can read it?"

After examining the document for a moment the clerk said: "Yes, sir; although it is written in a peculiar cipher, I can readily read it."

He then proceeded to read the contents of the paper, which embodied a detailed statement of the recent increase of General Lee's army, the aggregate force under his command, his contemplated invasion of Pennsylvania, the route by which he expected to march, and the means to be used in concealing his movements and ultimate destination from General Hooker, and also other information that would have been of incalculable value to the latter at that particular time. When the clerk had finished reading the paper the provost-marshal turned to Paul and said:

"What have you now to say in answer to the accusation against you?"

"Nothing," replied Paul with an air of seeming indifference.

The provost-marshal then stated that the case would be investigated by a court-martial the next day, and ordered that Paul be conducted to prison to await his trial. This was immediately done, and soon Paul was safely lodged in a prison cell.

Shortly after he was placed in prison, he requested the guard to furnish him some paper and a pencil for the purpose of writing a note to one of his friends in the city to procure counsel for him in his approaching trial. The guard complied with his request, and he at once began to write. When he had finished writing he told the guard that he would wait until morning to send the note, blew out the light in his cell and went to bed.

When the jailer went to the door of Paul's cell the next morning for the purpose of giving him his breakfast, he discovered that Paul had not arisen from his bunk. Having called him two or three times without receiving an answer, the jailer asked the guard to watch the door while he was in the cell and immediately entered it.

Upon reaching the bunk on which Paul was lying, he was startled and horrified to find that he was dead. He reported the fact to the sentinel at the door, and upon an examination of the body, they discovered that it was cold and stiff, thereby indicating that life had been extinct for six or eight hours. Lying on the floor beside the bunk they found a folded paper, and on examining it at once ascertained the cause and manner of Paul's death. So intent were they on immediately learning the contents of the paper, they did not go to the light to read it, but there, in the semi-darkness of the prison cell and within touch of the dead hand that had written it, they read with absorbing interest the following statement:

"Knowing that there is ample evidence to convict me, and abhorring beyond expression the ignominious death of a spy, I have deliberately arranged to take my own life by means of a poisonous drug which was long ago provided for just such a contingency as the present. I earnestly request that as little publicity as possible be given to my case in order that no suspicion as to my identity may be excited in the minds of my family, which is a highly respectable one, and no member of it has the remotest idea as to where or what I am. Not one of those whom I have been serving suspects my real name, and inside the Federal lines I am known only by the name which will be hereunto signed. While the name of Paul, by which I am here known, is an assumed one, my claim to membership in Mosby's command is not without foundation; for nominally I belong to the command, and have frequently aided in its operations. I joined and have operated with the command in order to acquire freedom of action and ample opportunities for plying my trade, and also to lessen the chances of my detection and arrest.

"As to the motive that prompted me in becoming a Federal spy, I suppose that my case is peculiar; for it was neither love for the Union, hatred of the South, nor a desire for gain that caused me to enter upon the work in which I have been engaged. I began it purely in a spirit of adventure and soon became so much interested in and infatuated with the work that, in my thoughts, I idealized it and thereby was rendered oblivious to its ignominious character. Its dangers but enhanced its attractions, and so

fascinating did it become **that I was never for a moment**
inclined to relinquish it, although I **realized** that it would
probably lead to my death.

"I do not fear death in any ordinary **form, as the act**
which I am about to perform will prove. **But it is with**
sickening dread and horror that I contemplate the ignominy
of being hung as a spy, and in order to escape that infamous
fate, I now, with a species of gladness, take the **poisonous
drug which** is to launch into eternity the spirit of

"EDWARD CRAFT."

When the jailer and sentinel had finished reading this
singular communication, they expressed great surprise at
its contents and agreed in thinking that the writer was not
altogether as **bad** as they had supposed him to be when he
was brought to the prison as a spy. Moreover, they could
not avoid feeling a species of admiration for the man's
courage and the measure which he adopted to prevent his
public and ignominious execution and save his family from
the pain and humiliation which they would have experienced in consequence of a knowledge of his fate.

The provost-marshal was at once informed of Paul's
suicide and, after reading the communication which the lat-
ter had left, decided that he would endeavor to induce the
**War Department to comply with Paul's request that no
unnecessary publicity be given as** to the circumstances of
his death.

In **this he** was successful, and, the matter having been
kept out of the papers, comparatively few persons in the
city knew that a Federal spy had been captured in their
midst and had committed suicide in order to escape the dis-
graceful penalty of his infamous crime.

The military operations which occurred shortly there-
after plainly indicated that General Hooker was ignorant
of General Lee's movements and the ultimate object of the
same; and hence, the interception of Paul's cipher dispatches to the Federal commander naturally leads one to
speculate as to whether those operations would have
occurred, or different movements been inaugurated, if General Hooker had received the information which these dis-
patches contained. If Hooker had known of the steps that

were being taken for the concentration of the Confederate army at Culpeper Court-house and General Lee's contemplated invasion of Pennsylvania, and that only A. P. Hill's corps confronted him at Fredericksburg, it is probable that instead of throwing Sedgwick's corps across the Rappahannock at Deep Run on the 6th of June for purposes of observation, the Federal commander would have waited until General Ewell's corps left Culpeper Court-house on June 10th and was well on its march to the Valley, and then he could have crossed the Rappahannock with the bulk of his army, crushed A. P. Hill's corps, and either pressed forward toward Richmond, or marched against Longstreet's corps at Culpeper Court-house with decided chances in favor of his defeating General Lee before Ewell could return to Lee's assistance. If he had received the aforesaid information, General Hooker would not have found it necessary to have sent General Pleasanton with two divisions of cavalry and two brigades of infantry across the Rappahannock at Kelly's and Beverly's Fords on the 9th of June on a reconnoissance that resulted in the desperate and protracted cavalry fight that day at Fleetwood Heights and Brandy Station.

Ashton having taken an active part in that engagement, we are reminded to return to him and give some account of his experience and the movements of his regiment after we left him basking in the sunshine amid the clover fields of Orange county and thinking tenderly of Ruth Middleton. For a week or two, he had ample time and opportunities for frequent musings in regard to his relation to Ruth; for, with the exception of an occasional skirmish drill, or a day on picket, there was but little to interrupt him in his daily occupation of taking his horse out to graze for hours at a time in the clover fields near which his regiment was encamped. Lying at full length amid the blooming clover and listening to the humming of the bees around him and the more distant music of numerous birds that were pouring out in sweetest strains the flood-tide of joy which filled their hearts to overflowing at the gladsome advent of spring, Ashton was thoroughly imbued with the spirit of joyousness that pervaded his surroundings, and thereby rendered more cheerful than he had been for several months.

About a month after his letter to Ruth **was returned to** him from the Dead Letter Office, he wrote to **her again, but** received no answer to his letter, and in consequence thereof became exceedingly despondent; but in the happy state of mind which he now enjoyed, it was easy for him to imagine and accept as satisfactory, various reasons why he had not heard from her. Hence, to a great extent, he dispelled his despondency, gave full sway to his absorbing love for Ruth, and dreamed of the time when **her silence would be explained,** and he should learn that she loved him. The tender love and happy hopefulness which he was thus cherishing, **not only** engendered in his heart a feeling of contentment, **but also had a reflex action on his outer life, and,** although he was uniformly affable in his manner, his comrades found him livelier and more genial than usual, and noticed with pleasure his increased cheerfulness and sociability.

Those halcyon days were of short duration and constituted merely an interlude in Ashton's soldier life—a calm before the impending storm—for, as before mentioned, a great military movement was imminent, and soon Stuart's entire division of cavalry was concentrated in Culpeper county, where the bulk of General Lee's army was assembling preparatory to the invasion of Pennsylvania.

CHAPTER XI.

On Sunday, June 7th, 1863, there was a grand review of the cavalry by General Lee, and as they passed in martial array before the noble commander-in-chief, the sight thereby presented was extremely imposing. The review of each regiment closed with a charge, at full speed, against imaginary foes, and this mimic warfare with its accompaniments of clattering hoof-strokes, flaunting banners, flashing sabres, and the inevitable "Rebel yell," gave the beholder some idea of what could be accomplished by those gallant troopers when engaged in real battle. They did not, at the time, suspect that in less than forty-eight hours they would thus be riding against real foes amidst the din and dangers of actual conflict, and returned to camp that evening in merry mood, thinking only of the gala day which had just closed.

The several brigades of General Stuart's division spent the following day in their respective encampments in a quiet and uneventful manner. But about 5 o'clock on the morning of June 9th, a large Federal force, under General Buford, drove in the pickets of General W. E. Jones' brigade at Beverly's Ford and crossed the Rappahannock at that point, and shortly thereafter the remainder of General Pleasanton's command, under General Gregg, began to cross the river at Kelly's Ford. General Jones promptly went with his brigade to the support of his pickets, and at the same time General W. H. F. Lee moved his brigade toward Beverly's Ford. General Fitzhugh Lee's brigade moved in the same direction. General Hampton's brigade moved forward toward a central position between the roads leading to Beverly's and Kelly's Fords, and General Robertson's brigade advanced on General Hampton's right toward Kelly's Ford. Jones' brigade soon became hotly engaged with the Federal cavalry and infantry that was advancing through the woods along the Beverly's Ford road, and being assisted by W. H. F. Lee's brigade on the left and sharpshooters from Hampton's brigade on the right, the Confederates succeeded in temporarily checking the advance of the Federals at this point.

In a short time the entire Federal **force had** crossed the river, and General Gregg's division of cavalry, with several batteries of artillery and three regiments of infantry, advanced from Kelly's Ford toward Fleetwood Heights. General Stuart, with a view to making a stand on these heights, moved forward to occupy them. Two regiments of Jones' brigade led the advance and reached the **heights** about fifty yards ahead of the Federals, and then ensued a long and hot contest for the possession of the heights. The foremost Federal force was driven back by the 12th Virginia cavalry under Colonel A. W Harman, but this regiment was in turn driven back by the Federal reserves, and in retiring deranged the ranks of White's battalion, which was advancing to charge. However, the charge was made by Colonel E. V. White in a **gallant** and vigorous manner, and his battalion broke the advance of the Federals and reached their artillery, but they greatly outnumbered his small force, and the 6th Virginia **cavalry, under** Major C. E. Flournoy, was sent to his assistance. This regiment also reached the Federal battery but was unable to hold it.

At this critical period in the engagement, **the gallant** Cobb's Legion under Colonel P. M. B. Young, being directed by General Hampton to charge, came up the steep hill at full speed in **obedience to** the ringing bugle-notes that had sounded the charge, brandishing their gleaming sabres and shouting the **wild** Confederate yell. Rapidly nearing their foes, they soon struck the flank of the Federals with the force of a catapult and **swept** them entirely from the hill in a perfect rout. At the **same** time, the 1st North Carolina cavalry, under Colonel L. S. Baker, supported by the Jeff Davis Legion, under Lieutenant-colonel J. F. Waring, swept around Colonel Young's left and made several dashing **and** successful charges, driving the Federals back each time. Colonel L. L. Lomax with the 11th Virginia cavalry charged directly **over the crest of** the hill, captured three pieces of artillery with their cannoneers, pushed **forward to** Brandy Station,

routed the Federals there and drove them back toward Kelly's Ford.

The charge made by Colonel Young with Cobb's Legion turned the scale of battle in favor of the Confederates, as by means of it the Federals were routed and driven from Fleetwood Hill; the Federal artillery subsequently captured **by** Colonel Lomax, **was** prevented from reaching the top of the hill, and the Federal forces were so disordered as to render the work of routing them much easier to the other regiments that subsequently attacked them.

Just after the Federals had been driven back toward Kelly's Ford, **a large** force of Federal cavalry with infantry and artillery rapidly advanced from the direction of St. James church on the Beverly's Ford road and threatened an im-**mediate** attack on Fleetwood Hill. Jones' brigade was posted behind Fleetwood with artillery on the heights, and his sharpshooters were engaged with the Federal infantry on his left.

Hampton's brigade was in position on Jones' right, and W. H. F. Lee's brigade was on Jones' left and confronted by Buford's division which, as before stated, had crossed the river at Beverly's Ford and had been temporarily checked early in the engagement by the brigades of Jones and W. H. F. Lee and Hampton's sharpshooters. General W. H. F. Lee attacked the Federals in a series of gallant and vigorous charges with his respective regiments, rout-**ing** them each time, but, on account of their superior num-**bers**, had to fall back to re-form his ranks. In one of these **charges, he** received a severe wound in the leg which unfitted him for duty for some time.

At this point, the 9th Virginia cavalry made several dash-**ing charges,** driving the Federals back to the cover of the woods behind them, where they were protected by their infantry supports.

Ashton was in each of these charges and, as usual, used his sabre well. While engaged in a hand-to-hand fight with **two** Federal troopers, he was **slightly** wounded by a sabre-stroke from one of them and his position became decidedly critical. Just at this moment, one of his comrades came to his assistance and shot one of his antagonists. Being thus placed on an equal footing with the other, Ashton soon unhorsed him by a vigorous and well-directed stroke of his sabre, and was thus extricated from his perilous position. At this time, Fitzhugh Lee's brigade, under Colonel Thomas T. Munford, came up and attacked the Federals in the flank. They at once began to retreat and were soon driven across the river at Beverly's Ford.

Thus closed the most extensive and hotly contested cavalry fight of the war, and the brilliancy of the victory won by the Confederates was enhanced by reason of the superior numbers of the Federal cavalry and their large infantry supports. The Confederate forces consisted of four brigades of cavalry, composed of twenty-one regiments and five batteries of artillery—Robertson's brigade of cavalry (two regiments) not being engaged in the fight. According to the report of General A. Pleasanton, who commanded the expedition, the Federal forces consisted of seven brigades of cavalry, composed of twenty-four regiments and Orton's company of the District of Columbia, two brigades of infantry, composed of eight regiments, and six batteries of artillery.

His report shows that his total effective force of cavalry and infantry was ten thousand nine hundred and eighty-one, consisting of seven thousand nine hundred and eighty-one cavalry and three thousand infantry. No report having been given by General Stuart as to the strength of his division, we are unable to state the number of the Confederate forces engaged in the battle, but it was several thousand less than that of the Federals. The official reports of the casualties on both sides show that the Confederate loss, in killed, wounded, and missing, was four hundred and eighty-five and that of the Federals was nine hundred and thirty-six. It would seem, however, from a report made by General Pleasanton as to the strength of his forces just two days afterward, that the Federal loss was even greater than reported. The following is an extract from the report:

"Cavalry and artillery present on review, Warrenton Junction, June 11th, four thousand nine hundred and seventy-three; absent on scout and picket, one thousand six hundred and eighty; total effective strength of cavalry, June 11th, six thousand six hundred and fifty-three."

This shows that the total effective strength of the Federal cavalry was one thousand three hundred and twenty-eight less on June 11th than when it entered the fight two days before. In the engagement the Confederates, in addition to taking several hundred prisoners, captured a number of horses, three pieces of artillery, four hundred and twenty-one carbines, rifles and pistols, one hundred and fifty-five sabres, and six battle-flags.

The Federals obtained no definite information in regard to General Lee's movements, and hence their reconnoissance was not only practically useless but caused them to be severely punished for their temerity in making it. However, it revealed to General Hooker the presence, in Culpeper county, of a larger force than he had supposed was there, and hence, on June 11th, he moved the 3d corps of his army to Rappahannock Station and Beverly's Ford, and posted his cavalry along the upper waters of the Rappahannock river. He was still ignorant as to General Lee's object, and supposed that his movements were being directed against his communications with Washington. Having completely puzzled Hooker as to his object, General Lee put his army in motion for Pennsylvania, General Ewell taking the advance with his corps and leaving Culpeper Court-house on June 10th. By June 14th, General Ewell had captured Berryville, Winchester, and Martinsburg, with several thousand prisoners. General Hooker, having received news of General Ewell's movements in the Valley, became satisfied that he had been deceived by General Lee, and on the night of June 13th had Sedgwick's corps to recross the Rappahannock from its position below Fredericksburg, and the next day his entire army was withdrawn from the line of that river and marched toward Manassas.

General Lee at once ordered A. P. Hill's corps from Fredericksburg to the Valley, and in order to conceal its march and draw General Hooker still farther away from Washington, Longstreet's corps left Culpeper Court-house on June 15th, passing along the east side of the Blue Ridge, and occupied Ashby's and Snicker's Gaps, thus cutting off

Hooker's means of communication with that part of the Valley over which A. P. Hill was to march. In this way General Hooker was drawn away from Washington toward the mountains, and A. P. Hill soon crossed the Blue Ridge and took position at Winchester. By means of these strategic movements, General Lee had, in a masterly manner and in a few days, drawn General Hooker away from the Rappahannock to the Upper Potomac and placed **the three** corps of his army in strong positions within supporting distance of each other, and from which they could begin **their** march into Pennsylvania without the risk of interference **or** attack by General Hooker. As General Lee had succeeded **in** placing his army in position for its advance into Pennsylvania, it was now necessary to conceal and protect the forward movement as long as possible; and hence he directed General Stuart to leave a sufficient force on the Rappahannock to watch General Hooker and move the main body of his cavalry parallel to the Blue Ridge and on Longstreet's right flank, who was to move near the base of the mountains through Fauquier and Loudoun counties. As soon as the Federal army should enter Maryland, General Stuart was to cross the Potomac, moving either east or west of the Blue Ridge as he thought best, and take his position on the right of the Confederate army in its forward movement. In consequence of these directions, General Steuart placed Hampton's and Jones' brigades in observation along the Rappahannock and Hazel rivers, with instructions for them to follow the main body of his command as soon as Hill's corps had passed that point, and on June 15th he directed Fitzhugh Lee's brigade to cross the Rappahannock at Rockford and take the advance of Longstreet's corps by way of Barbeer's Crossroads, and started W. H. F. Lee's and Robertson's brigades to cross lower down the river at Hinson's Mills. The movement thus begun resulted in a series of hotly contested engagements between the Confederate and Federal cavalry in which our hero took an active part; and hence, its progress may prove of interest to the **reader.**

Ashton's wound being a slight one, he was ready for duty in a day two after he received it, and marched with his

regiment when it left camp on June 15th. As the Federals had retired to Centerville, General **Stuart** proceeded without interruption to within a few miles of Salem, and there bivouacked for the night. **On June 17th, Fitzhugh Lee's brigade** moved toward Aldie for the purpose of holding the gap in Bull Run Mountain in order to conceal Longstreet's movements. W. H. F. Lee's brigade was kept near **the** plains to reconnoitre Thoroughfare Gap, and Robertson's brigade was halted near Rectortown, within supporting distance of the other two brigades. When Fitzhugh Lee's brigade arrived within a short distance of Dover, it was halted and pickets **were** sent forward **to the Aldie** Gap. **These** pickets were soon attacked by Federal cavalry advancing from **the direction of Fairfax, and driven back on** the brigade, which took position west of Aldie. At the same time **that** this attack was made, General Stuart, who was at Middleburg, received information that the Federals were advancing on Middleburg from the direction of Hopewell. He had only his staff and a few pickets with him, and **retired toward Rector's Crossroads, sending orders to Colonel** Thomas T. Munford, commanding Fitzhugh Lee's brigade, to watch the road to Middleburg, and also sent orders for General Robertson to march at once for Middleburg, and Colonel John **R. Chambliss, commanding W.** H. F. Lee's brigade, **to take the Salem road to the same place.** The **attack that was made** on Fitzhugh **Lee's** brigade near Aldie resulted in a desperate and bloody engagement in **which** the Federals were repulsed with loss, the Confederates holding their position until General Stuart's dispatch to Colonel Munford rendered it necessary for him to retire on account **of** the threatened attack from the Federal force at Middleburg. The Federals had been so thoroughly punished that they did not attempt to follow Munford. General Robertson arrived at Middleburg about dark and was at once ordered **to** attack the Federals. This he did, and with his two regiments drove them out of the place and pursued them for several miles **on** the Hopewell road. Colonel Chambliss, approaching Middleburg from that direction with W. H. F. Lee's brigade, intercepted the fleeing Federals and captured the greater part of one regiment.

10

General Stuart occupied Middleburg that night, and on June 18th took position around the place with W. H. F. Lee's and Robertson's brigades, while Fitzhugh Lee's brigade took position at Union, on General Stewart's left. The Federals soon made such advances on General Stewart's left that he thought it necessary to leave Middleburg, and did so, keeping out pickets near to the enemy. As Hampton's and Jones' brigades had not yet arrived, Stuart did not wish a general engagement, and devoted his attention to procuring information of the movements of the Federals through scouts and reconnoitering parties. In one of these expeditions, our old friend Mosby, whose gallant achievements had won for him the rank of major about three months before, with his accustomed daring, penetrated the Federal lines and captured Major Stirling, of General Hooker's staff, bearing dispatches from the latter to General Pleasanton at Aldie. The dispatches disclosed the fact that Hooker was greatly concerned about Aldie; that Pleasanton occupied the place with both cavalry and infantry, and that a reconnoissance in considerable force was contemplated in the direction of Warrenton and Culpeper Court-house. General Stuart at once dispatched this information to General Hampton, who was coming by way of Warrenton from the direction of Beverly's Ford, and directed him to meet this advance at Warrenton. General Hampton did this and easily drove back the Federals, but was prevented from pursuing them in consequence of the approach of night and a heavy storm, under cover of which they retreated. On the morning of June 19th the Confederate pickets beyond Middleburg were driven in on Robertson's and W. H. F. Lee's brigades, which were posted to the west of the town, and the Federals advanced with a large force of cavalry and dismounted men deployed as infantry. The force consisted of three brigades, composed of twelve regiments, under General D. McM Gregg, and greatly outnumbered the two Confederate brigades, which contained only six regiments. The Federal attack was met in a spirited and determined manner, but they finally obtained possession of a piece of woods in front of the Confederate line, and although the Confederates met and repelled every effort of the enemy to advance from this position, yet whenever they charged the Federals, they were subjected to a heavy carbine fire from these woods, and also a furious fire from the Federal artillery beyond. General Stuart, therefore, withdrew his command to a more advantageous position about a half mile farther back and waited a renewal of the attack, but the Federals did not again attack him that day.

On the evening of that day Jones' brigade arrived and was posted near Union, Fitzhugh Lee's brigade being still farther to the left, watching Snicker's Gap and the Snickersville pike. General Hampton's brigade arrived on June 20th, but too late for General Stuart to attack the Federals that day. There was continuous skirmishing on the left beyond Goose Creek, and the 5th Virginia cavalry, under Colonel Rosser, drove the Federals across the stream in a brilliant manner. Having been reinforced by Jones' and Hampton's brigades, General Stuart was anxious to attack the Federals as soon as possible, but the next day (June 21st) being Sunday, he decided to suspend hostilities and devote the day to rest. The Federals, however, showed no regard for its sanctity, and about 8 o'clock that morning they renewed the attack.

General Pleasanton had, the day before, learned from a captured infantryman of Longstreet's corps that Longstreet had passed through Ashby's Gap into the Shenandoah Valley on June 19th, and that only Stuart's division of cavalry was east of the Blue Ridge. In consequence of this information, he sent a dispatch to General Hooker requesting permission to take his entire corps and attack Stuart the next morning (June 21st), and also asked for a division of infantry to aid him in the movement. Both requests were granted, and General James Barnes' division, consisting of three brigades of infantry with one battery, reinforced General Pleasanton's corps at 3 o'clock on the morning of June 21st. General Pleasanton advanced with his entire corps and one brigade of infantry, the latter being on the left of Gregg's column of cavalry, on the Ashby Gap road.

General Stuart sent forward the brigades of Hampton and Robertson, and they occupied a strong position which they could easily have held against a force of equal size with their own, or against cavalry alone; but although they repulsed the attack of the Federals and gallantly maintained their position for a long time, the Federal cavalry greatly outnumbering them and being aided in the attack by a brigade of infantry which moved around on their right flank, it became necessary for them to retire from that position. Hence, General Stuart directed General Hampton to withdraw to the next height in rear of him as soon as his position should be hard pressed, and ordered Colonel Chambliss and General Jones to resist the Federals as far as possible and for the latter to connect with Hampton's left and, retiring with the main body, effect a junction with it at Upperville, where Stuart contemplated a more determined stand than could be made with his forces separated as they then were, the several brigades of his division being from four to six miles apart.

While retiring from the first position before Middleburg, one of the pieces of Captain J. F. Hart's battery of horse-artillery had the axle broken by a shot from a Federal gun and had to be abandoned, and in referring to the matter in his official report, General Stuart said: "It is the first piece of my horse-artillery that has ever fallen into the enemy's hands. Its full value was paid in the slaughter it made in the enemy's ranks, and it was well sold."

The next stand made by General Stuart was on the west bank of Goose Creek, and although his two brigades were again attacked by a superior force of Federal cavalry and the brigade of infantry, he repulsed the attack with considerable slaughter, checked them for awhile and then withdrew his command in plain view of them and under the fire of their guns. In the meantime, the brigades of Jones and W. H. F. Lee had become hotly engaged with another heavy column of Federals, and were gradually retiring toward Upperville, and before they reached that place, the enemy had passed up so close as to render it hazardous for these brigades to attempt a junction there, and also made it necessary for Hampton's and Robertson's

brigades to move out immediately to the west of Upperville
to avoid being flanked by the Federals through the medium
of the various roads converging at that place. On
account of the women and children in the place, the Confederates were anxious to avoid a conflict in the village,
but the Federals, reckless of the injury that might be done
to these helpless persons, and seemingly taking advantage
of this disinclination of the Confederates to fight there, made
a furious attack on the rear guard. In an instant a part
of General Hampton's brigade, led by its peerless commander, wheeled about and charged the Federals with their
accustomed dash and bravery, and drove them back in the
greatest confusion, killing, wounding, and capturing a
great many of their number. After this repulse, General
Stuart leisurely retired to the mountain gap west of
Upperville and took position to dispute any further
advance of the Federals. They made no attack, and went
into camp at Upperville that night. The next morning
they retired and were pursued to within a short distance of
Aldie, a number of them being captured. General Stuart
resumed his position at Rector's Crossroads and remained
there until June 24th. In his official reports of the several
engagements at Aldie, Middleburg, and Upperville, from
June 17th to June 22d, General Pleasanton was quite
boastful as to the achievements of the Federals, claiming
in substance, that they had defeated the Confederates in
every engagement with heavy loss to the latter, as compared with that of his own troops. This claim was made
during the excitement incident to his surroundings and
before he had obtained full and reliable information as to
the casualties among his own and the Confederate troops;
for the official tabulated returns of these losses show that
in those engagements, the Federal loss was eighty-three
killed, three hundred and twenty-eight wounded and four
hundred and sixty-seven captured or missing, and the Confederate loss was fifty-six killed, two hundred and seventy-
nine wounded, and one hundred and sixty-six captured or
missing. Moreover, the Confederates were not "defeated"
at all in the proper sense of that word, for while it became
necessary for General Stuart to retire three or four miles

in order to get together his widely separated brigades, this was done in good order in the face of largely superior forces, and when he had thus concentrated his forces, the Federals failed to attack him and retreated, leaving him master of the situation, as he was still in possession of the mountain gaps and the section of country which he had been protecting in order to screen Longstreet's movements. On the night of June 24th, General Stuart left Robertson's and Jones' brigades to watch the Federals, and with the brigades of Hampton, Fitzhugh Lee and W. H. F. Lee, moved out from near Salem Depot on his march to the Potomac. His first objective point on the route was Dranesville, and in order to reach that place it was necessary for him to pass through Bull Run Mountains. Learning that General Hancock's corps occupied Thoroughfare Gap, General Stuart moved with his command to the right of that point and succeeded in passing through Glasscock's Gap and marched toward Haymarket. As they neared that place they found that Hancock's corps was passing through there toward Gum Spring, and General Stuart opened on his moving column with artillery, doing considerable damage to his train and disabling one of his caissons, which was abandoned. Sending a dispatch to General Lee informing him of General Hancock's movements, General Stuart retired to Buckland in order to deceive the Federals as to his own movements. He had at first contemplated passing west of Centerville, but the presence of the Federals in that quarter caused him to decide to cross the Bull Run lower down and march through Fairfax for the Potomac. On the next day he marched through Brentsville to the vicinity of Wolf Run Shoals on the Occoquan, where he halted for the purpose of grazing his horses. On the following day (June 27th), he marched for Fairfax Station, sending General Fitzhugh Lee with his brigade by Burke's Station with instructions to rejoin the main command at Fairfax Court-house, or farther on if circumstances should so require.

Near Fairfax Station, General Hampton's front regiment, the 1st North Carolina, charged a detachment of Federal cavalry called "Scott's Nine Hundred," and killed, wounded, and captured the greater part of them. On reaching Fairfax Court-house and receiving a communication from General Fitzhugh Lee, General Stuart became satisfied that the main body of the Federal army had moved toward Leesburg, and that the remainder had retired to the fortifications of Washington, and hence that the chances were favorable for his march to the Potomac between the rear of the Federal army and Washington. Reaching Dranesville late that afternoon, General Stuart ordered Hampton's brigade to march at once to Rowser's Ford on the Potomac, W. H. F. Lee's brigade remaining at Dranesville to await the arrival of Fitzhugh Lee's brigade. Hampton's brigade crossed the Potomac early that night, but reported to General Stuart that it would be impossible for his artillery to cross at that ford, and this opinion was also expressed by several citizens of the vicinity. However General Stuart, with his accustomed sanguine disregard for opposing difficulties and dangers, decided to make an effort to cross his artillery at that point, and before 12 o'clock that night, by indomitable energy and perseverance, in the face of seemingly insurmountable obstacles, every gun was carried safely over the river and the entire command, bivouacked on the Maryland side of the stream.

A lock-gate in the Chesapeake and Ohio Canal was soon broken, and steps were taken to intercept boats. About a dozen were intercepted, and the following morning several boats loaded with negro troops and army stores were captured by the rear guard of Stuart's command. Realizing the importance of joining the Confederate army in Pennsylvania as soon as possible, General Stuart resumed his march northward early on the morning of June 28th, sending Hampton's brigade by way of Dranestown to Rockville, while he, with the two other brigades, took the direct route to the same place. General Hampton reached Rockville in advance of the main body, having captured several small parties of Federals and a number of wagons and teams on the route. While the main body of the command was on the way to Rockville, the advance guard of W. H. F Lee's brigade, in which Ashton happened to be at the time, had a running fight with the ——New York cavalry, whose picket, as the reader will remember, captured Ashton near Fox's Ford on the Rappahannock the preceding November and was in turn captured by Mosby. The horses of the Confederates were in bad condition and greatly jaded, while those of the Federals were fresh and in good condition, and hence the latter soon distanced the former and bore their riders beyond the reach of their pursuers. Ashton was still riding the corporal's horse which Mosby had given him, and the result of the chase brought vividly before his mind the unfavorable contrast between his horse's condition and speed then, and what they were when its former owner was captured by Mosby.

There was a Federal force at Rockville, but they retreated on the approach of the Confederates, and General Stuart immediately took possession of the town. Soon after he had occupied the place, a long train of wagons approached from the direction of Washington, and, although those in charge of them made a desperate effort to escape with the wagons, every one of them was captured. There were more than one hundred and twenty-five wagons and teams and the hindmost wagon was within four miles of Washington, the train being eight miles long. Under some circumstances this capture would have been not only valuable but also a fortunate one, but the time and labor subsequently devoted to the safe conduct of the train, as well as its presence with his command, retarded General Stuart's movements and rendered his operations less successful than they would otherwise have been. Having paroled about four hundred prisoners at Brookville, General Stuart pushed forward that night to the Baltimore and Ohio railroad, and Fitzhugh Lee's brigade reached the railroad about daylight the next morning. The bridge at Sikesville was burned, and the track torn up at Hood's Mills. That afternoon the head of the column reached Westminster and had a skirmish with a squadron of the 1st Delaware cavalry, in which Lieutenants Pierce Gibson and John W. Murray, of the 4th Virginia cavalry, were killed. Although they had fallen in a strange land, it was evident that their deaths had occurred in the midst of those who sympathized with the cause in defense of which they had given up their lives;

for some of the ladies of the place requested that they might have the privilege of superintending the burial of these gallant young soldiers. Their request was granted, and these noble women enjoyed the melancholy pleasure of paying a loving tribute to the South, and honoring her dead, by superintending the burial rites of two of her fallen heroes.

On the following morning (June 30th), General **Stuart** marched directly toward Hanover, W. H. F. Lee's brigade being in advance, Hampton's brigade in the rear of the wagon train, and Fitzhugh Lee's brigade on the left flank. About 10 o'clock A. M., the head of the column reached Hanover, Pennsylvania, and was attacked by a large force of Federal cavalry. The 9th Virginia cavalry **was in** advance and met this attack by a gallant and vigorous charge, and not only repulsed the Federals, but drove them **in** confusion through the town and captured many prisoners. Ashton was among the foremost in the charge, had several close encounters with Federal troopers and unhorsed more than one of his antagonists. Moreover, he **rendered** his captain a timely service **which, doubtless, saved his** life; for while the latter **was hotly engaged in a saber** contest with one **of the Federal troopers, another Federal** came to his comrade's **assistance** and **was in the act of** dealing Captain B—— a blow with his saber, **when** Ashton caught the descending saber on his own, parried **a** fierce and vigorous thrust made with it at himself, and with **a rapid** and well-directed right cut cleft the Federal's right jaw in twain and instantly unhorsed him. Ashton's conduct throughout the fight was marked by the greatest gallantry, and evoked unstinted praise from the officers and men of his company. The Federals rallied their forces and, as only a portion of Stuart's command had arrived, succeeded in regaining the town; **but** when General Hampton's brigade arrived, they were again attacked and driven from the place. The Federals did not retreat, but moved **around** to the left of Stuart's command and continued to press **the** left flank **with** dismounted sharpshooters. The immense wagon train captured by the Confederates, **and** about four hundred prisoners who had been captured since

those were paroled at Brookville, now became the source
of great embarrassment to General Stuart; but having
reasons to believe that the Confederate army was near the
Susquehanna river, he thought that he could save the train
by making a detour to the right by Jefferson, and hence
put Fitzhugh Lee's brigade at the head of the column with
instructions to push on with the wagon train through
Jefferson to York, and communicate as soon as possible with General Lee's army, and directed Hampton's
brigade to bring up the rear of the column. In this order
the command continued the march throughout the entire
night, and it was exceedingly trying to both men and
horses on account of the many hardships experienced during
the past fifteen days of constant service. Entire regiments
slept in their saddles, and in some instances the men fell
from their horses, being completely overcome by fatigue
and sleepiness. General Stuart reached Dover, Pa., on the
morning of July 1st, but could obtain no definite information as to the location of the Confederate army. In the
afternoon he arrived at Carlisle, and found that it was
occupied by a considerable force of Federal militia concealed in the houses with a view to entrapping the Confederates upon their entrance into the place. General Stuart
did not wish to subject the town to the injurious consequences of an attack, but as his men were entirely out of
rations it was necessary that they should obtain a supply
of food, and hence he sent in, under a flag of truce, a demand for the unconditional surrender of the place with the
alternative of a bombardment if his demand should be
refused. The demand was refused, and after placing his
artillery in position he repeated the demand. It was again
refused and he was forced to shell the town, but none of
the buildings except the United States cavalry barracks
were burned.

General Stuart was still uninformed as to the where-
abouts of General Lee's army, but during the night received
a dispatch from him stating that the army was at Gettysburg and had been engaged that day with the advance of
the Federal army. He at once sent an order to General
Hampton to march ten miles that night toward Gettysburg

and, arranging for the other brigades to reach there early the next morning, he started in person for the place that night.

General Hampton arrived at Gettysburg July 2d, just in time to meet and check a movement of the Federal cavalry upon the rear of the Confederates, by way of Hunterstown; and his brigade, by a series of gallant charges, routed the Federals and defeated their purpose. General Stuart took position that day on the York and Heidlersburg road on the left wing of the Confederate army.

On the morning of July 3d, in pursuance of instructions from General Lee, he moved forward to a position to the left of, and in advance of General Ewell's left, where an elevated ridge commanded a wide plain of cultivated fields between that point and the base of the mountain spurs, where the Federals were posted. His command had been increased by the addition of General Jenkins' brigade, and he moved this and General W. H. F. Lee's brigade secretly through the woods with a view to an attack on the rear of the Federals; but Hampton's and Fitzhugh Lee's brigades, which had been ordered to follow Stuart, unfortunately marched out into the open ground and thereby disclosed the movement and caused a counter-movement of the Federals to meet it. Before General Hampton reached General Stuart, the Federals deployed a heavy line of sharpshooters and advanced toward Stuart's position. In the meantime, Hampton's and Fitzhugh Lee's brigades had become hotly engaged as dismounted skirmishers. The Federals sent forward a small force of cavalry and were about to cut off a part of the Confederate sharpshooters, and General Stuart ordered the 9th Virginia cavalry to quickly charge this cavalry force. The regiment promptly responded to the order and made a gallant and irresistible charge. At the same time the 1st Virginia cavalry made a similar charge on the left; but having gone too far, their jaded horses failed under the prolonged strain upon them, and the Federals, perceiving this, turned upon them with fresh horses. The 1st North Carolina and Jeff Davis Legion were sent to their support, and this hand-to-hand fighting gradually involved the greater portion of Stuart's com-

mand and continued until the Federals were driven from
the field with heavy loss, including many prisoners. General Hampton, ever foremost in the fray, was twice
wounded in this engagement and in consequence thereof
had to leave the field. During that night General Lee withdrew the main body of his army to the ridges west of Gettysburg and on the next night began his march back to the
Potomac.

General Stuart having received from General Lee instructions as to the order of march, disposed of the cavalry in
such manner as to cover and protect the flanks of the retiring army. The brigades of Jenkins and W. H. F. Lee
under the immediate command of General Stuart, proceeded by way of Emmitsburg and Cavetown toward Ha-
gerstown and, after one or two skirmishes on the route,
reached the latter place on July 6th. General Stuart found
a large force of Federal cavalry in possession of the town
and at once attacked them. At this time the Confederate
wagon trains were at Williamsport, six miles from Hagers-
town, and were unable to cross the Potomac on account of
the swollen condition of the river. Being satisfied that the
Federals contemplated an attack on Williamsport for the
purpose of capturing these trains, General Stuart determined to defeat their purpose, if possible, by a vigorous
attack on them. They were finally driven out of Hagers-
town and at first took the road to Sharpsburg, but afterward turned into the one leading to Williamsport. W.
H. F. Lee's brigade was pushed down the Williamsport
road after the Federals, and Robertson's and Jenkins' brigades, taking the left of the road, moved parallel with
Lee's brigade. The 9th Virginia cavalry was in advance
and, when the order was given to charge, it dashed forward along the pike at full speed and soon struck the Federal column with irresistible force, driving it back in great
confusion.

The charge was a brilliant one, and the fighting, though
brief, was furious and sanguinary, and Ashton engaged in
the same with even more than his usual zeal, energy, and
gallantry. His usually calm and quiet countenance was
aglow with excitement and enthusiasm, his whole body

was instinct with animation, his soul seemed to be imbued
with the spirit of battle, and he rushed into the thickest of
the fight with headlong impetuosity, apparently unconscious of danger and bent solely on the destruction of his
foes. Riding at the head of the column, he was one of the
first to reach the Federal troopers and at once began to use
his saber with telling effect, cutting right and left with
lightning-like rapidity; and almost every stroke of his
flashing blade disabled the unfortunate foeman on whom
it fell. His comrades had long known and marked his skill
and gallantry in battle, but they had never before seen him
display such impetuosity and seemingly reckless bravery as
characterized his conduct on this occasion. The Federals
did not long withstand the vigorous onslaught of the Confederates and soon began to retreat. At this time Jenkins'
brigade, which, as before stated, was moving parallel with
W. H. F. Lee's brigade on the left of the road, was hurried
up to attack the Federals in the flank, but several fences
obstructed their march and delayed their movements to
such an extent that the Federals had time to rally their
forces and obtain a sheltered position behind a crest of
rocks. Jenkins' brigade was then dismounted and at once
advanced on the Federals and soon drove them out of the
position which they had taken. As soon as they were dislodged by the dismounted men, the mounted men renewed
the attack upon them and drove them back. The Federals
made one effort at a countercharge, which was bravely met
and completely repulsed by a fragment of the 5th North
Carolina cavalry under its gallant commander, Colonel
James B. Gordon. Immediately after this, Colonel L. L.
Lomax arrived with the 11th Virginia cavalry, of Jones'
brigade, from the direction of Cavetown. Moving his regiment parallel with the pike until within about five hundred yards of the Federals, he turned into the pike under a
heavy fire from the Federal batteries, advanced rapidly
toward the Federals, and when within two hundred yards
of them, his regiment began a charge that was a gallant
and effective one, resulting in the complete rout of the Federals and the capture of a number of prisoners. By this
vigorous and persistent attack, General Stuart not only

inflicted a severe blow on the Federals, but also, as he had expected, caused them to raise their siege of Williamsport, and thereby saved the army trains congregated at that place; for they hastily left that night by the Downsville road.

On the next day (July 7th), General Stuart proceeded to Downsville, and on the following day advanced toward Boonsborough. At Beaver Creek Bridge, the Federals were first encountered on the Boonsborough road by Jones' brigade, and from that point to Boonsborough, the fighting was continuous, Hampton's, Fitzhugh Lee's, and W. H. F. Lee's brigades participating in the same. Owing to the fact that the ground was very soft from the effects of recent heavy rains, cavalry operations were impracticable, and most of the fighting was done on foot. It was done in a gallant and spirited manner by the Confederates, and they steadily drove back the Federals before them.

The 9th Virginia cavalry furnished its quota of dismounted men to act as sharpshooters in driving back the Federals, and Ashton was among the first to dismount and press forward to the attack. He was an excellent shot and did good service with his carbine during this forward movement. Just as the Federals reached the outskirts of Boonsborough in their retreat, and while Ashton was in the act of firing, he was wounded by a shot from a carbine. The ball entered his left shoulder just below the collar-bone and passed out at the point of the shoulder-blade, inflicting a painful and dangerous wound. He was at once taken to the rear and carried with other wounded Confederates to Williamsport. There his wound was examined and dressed and his condition rendered as comfortable as possible.

Owing to the swollen condition of the Potomac, General Lee had not yet begun to move his army across the stream, which was too deep to be forded, and his pontoon bridges had not been laid. However, the wounded were being carried over in ferry-boats, and on the following day Ashton was taken across in that manner. On the night of the 13th and the morning of the 14th of July, the entire army crossed the river and after several skirmishes, principally by the cavalry, resumed its former line along the Rappa-

hannock on July 25th, but ultimately occupied the line of
the Rapidan about August 4th.

In the meantime, Ashton had been subjected to a trying
and painful experience. After he was carried across the
Potomac on July 9th, he remained near that point until
the army crossed the river. On July 15th he was carried
to Bunker Hill, about twelve miles north of Winchester,
where the army encamped until July 21st, and during that
time arrangements were made for the removal to Staunton
of all of the sick and wounded soldiers who could bear transportation. Although Ashton's wound was exceedingly painful and caused him intense suffering, he insisted on being taken
to Staunton, as he had a horror of again falling into the
hands of the enemy. His request was granted, and in company with other wounded soldiers, he was transported up
the Valley turnpike to Staunton. At Mount Jackson and
Harrisonburg wayside hospitals had been established, and
at each of these places Ashton remained for a day or two,
and his wound was redressed, and he was refreshed with
food and much-needed rest.

The ladies at these places were exceedingly kind to the
sick and wounded Confederate soldiers, bringing them
food and drink suitable for their condition and doing all in
their power to alleviate their sufferings. Indeed, such had
been the conduct of the noble and patriotic citizens all
along the route from Winchester whenever they had opportunities for ministering to the sick and wounded of the
retiring army. This was the second time they had manifested their kindness and liberality in contributing to the
necessities of the sick and wounded of the Confederate
army; for in the preceding September, after the battle of
Sharpsburg and General Lee's return from Maryland, the
sick and wounded of his army were transported from
Winchester by way of the Valley turnpike. Nobly and
generously did the people along the route respond to the
calls that were thereby made upon their kindness and liberality; and many a war-worn, battle-scarred Confederate
veteran to-day holds in highest honor and in his heart
blesses the patriotic, generous, self-sacrificing and kind-
hearted citizens of the Shenandoah Valley. We might add,
in passing, that in contrast with this feeling of honor and

gratitude for the kindness and generosity of these noble citizens, there is also in the hearts and minds of those Confederate veterans an ineradicable **feeling of** utter condemnation and abhorrence of the barbarous, brutal and cruel conduct of General Sheridan in his treatment **of those citizens** and the wholesale destruction of their property during the fall **of** 1864, whereby that once beautiful and pro-**ductive** valley was almost made a desert.

In order that the reader may see that this comment on **Sheridan's** conduct is just, and that the effect of **his barbarous deeds** has not been exaggerated, we will let **him** speak for himself by quoting from the dispatch sent **by** him just after he had driven General Early back to Staunton in September, 1864, and withdrawn his own army behind **Cedar Creek.** In that dispatch, he says:

"**In moving back to this point, the whole country, from the Blue Ridge to the North Mountains, has been made en-**entirely **untenable for a rebel army.** I have destroyed over two **thousand** barns filled with wheat and hay and farming implements, over seventy mills filled with flour and wheat; have driven in front of the army over four thousand head of stock; and have killed and issued to the troops **not** less than three thousand sheep. This destruction embraces the **Luray Valley and the Little** Fork Valley, as well as the main valley."

Asking the reader to excuse this digression **we will** return **to** Ashton. After arriving at **Staunton, he was** allowed to remain there for a few days and was then transferred over the Virginia Central railroad to Gordonsville, reaching that place on August 1st. Gordonsville, at this time, **was** a distributing point for the sick **and** wounded soldiers, **and** from there they were sent to the various general hospitals. **On the day** after his arrival at Gordonsville, Ashton was **sent, in** company with a number of other wounded soldiers, to Richmond, and arrived there in the evening of that day. **He** was assigned to the hospital **at** which Ruth Middleton **and Bertha** Gray were doing duty as volunteer nurses two months before, but they were not there at this time. In order that the reader may understand the cause of their absence, it will be necessary to relate something of their experience since they last appeared in our story.

CHAPTER XII.

A few days after the suicide of Sergeant Paul, alias Edward Craft, Captain Carrington returned to his command, which was then near Culpeper Court-house and about to start on the march to Pennsylvania. These few days had been rife with happiness to him and Bertha, and their parting was exceedingly sad to both, as they felt that it might be a final one. For several days after Carrington's departure, Bertha was very sad and dejected, but on June 11th her feelings were greatly revived by the receipt of a letter from him, written the night before he left Culpeper Court-house with Ewell's corps on its march to the Valley. The letter was characterized by a spirit of tenderest devotion that was very sweet and comforting to her heart, and written in such a joyous and hopeful strain that it partially banished her sadness and tended to restore her cheerfulness. Carrington promised to write as often as he had opportunities for so doing, but told her that these opportunities would necessarily be quite few, as the army was about to invade the enemy's country and it might be weeks before he could send a letter back into the Confederacy, and hence that she must not be uneasy should she fail to hear from him for some time after he had crossed the border.

It had now been nearly two months since Bertha arrived in Richmond, and she decided to terminate her visit and return to B——. Hence, a few days thereafter, she bade Ruth good-bye and returned to her Southern home. Ruth's interest in her work at the hospital was unabated, but she now had comparatively little to do, as most of the wounded soldiers who were brought to the hospital just after the battle of Chancellorsville, had recovered from the effects of their wounds and been discharged. This gave her a great deal of leisure time, and much of it was spent in walking about the city in company with her devoted little friend, Randolph Slaughter, who took the greatest delight in acting as her escort and showing her various places of interest in the Confederate Capital.

About the middle of July, they were one day walking in
Capitol Square and, while approaching Clay Monument,
suddenly came face to face with a lady and gentleman
walking toward them. The lady at once rushed forward,
exclaiming:

"Why, how do you do, Ruth! You dear old girl. I am so
glad to see you!"

Ruth instantly recognized the lady as Belle Preston, who
had been one of her classmates when she attended Augusta
Female Seminary, at Staunton, several years before, and,
springing forward to meet her, the girls were soon em-
bracing each other in a very affectionate manner. After
this affectionate greeting was over, Belle introduced the
gentleman as her brother, Lieutenant Frank Preston of the
—— artillery, which was then stationed near the city and
constituted part of the defensive force of the Confederate
Capital. Ruth, in turn, introduced Randolph Slaughter to
Belle and Lieutenant Preston and opened the conversation
by saying:

"I am delighted to see you, Belle, and have several times
thought of writing you to let you know that I was
here, so that you might make me a visit."

"You don't mean to say," said Belle, "that you have been
in Richmond for any length of time? What in the world
have you been doing? And why did you not come to see
me?"

"Yes," replied Ruth, "I have been here for several months,
and my time has been occupied in attending on the
wounded soldiers at one of the hospitals, where I am a
volunteer nurse. I have really had no opportunity for visiting you and, moreover, did not know whether or not you
were at home."

"Yes," said Belle, "I have been at home all the year, and
am so sorry that I did not know that you were here; for if
I had, I would certainly have come to see you immediately.
I was greatly surprised to find you here, but am not now
surprised to learn what you are doing; for, in view of my
knowledge of your character, it seems perfectly natural to
find you acting the part of a Florence Nightingale. Now
that I have found you, I am bent on seeing something of

you and intend to take you home with me. You need not offer any excuses, for I will not accept them, and you must get ready to go home with us. Isn't that so, Frank?"

Lieutenant Preston replied: "Of course, Belle, we must not try to influence Miss Middleton to act contrary to her sense of duty as to the claims of her patients at the hospital, but, if she can consistently leave them for two or three weeks, I agree with you in thinking that she ought to make you a visit. And I hope, Miss Middleton, that their condition is such that you can safely and consistently with your sense of duty leave them for that length of time; for our family will be delighted to have you with them and, moreover, the salubrious climate of Lexington and the bracing breezes from the Blue Ridge mountains will be a pleasant and salutary change from the atmosphere of this crowded city and the confinement of hospital duties."

"I thank both of you," said Ruth, "for your kind invitation for me to visit your home, and am glad that I can at this time consistently accept it. Nearly all of the wounded soldiers have been discharged from the hospital where I am performing the duties of a nurse, and hence my services can very well be spared at present. I will, therefore, be delighted to make Belle a short visit."

"I am so glad," said Belle, "and you must get ready at once, for we expect to leave for home to-morrow. Frank has obtained a short leave of absence from his company, as there is at this time no force threatening Richmond, and his services are not especially needed here."

Ruth promised to make arrangements to accompany Belle and her brother home the next day, and the parties separated. She at once communicated with the hospital authorities in regard to her contemplated visit, obtained their consent to the same, and made all necessary preparations for her departure.

The next morning Frank Preston and his sister called for Ruth in a cab, and the three were at once driven to the railway station and were soon on their way to Lexington. Ruth received a hearty welcome from Mr. and Mrs. Preston and at once felt at home in the household. She found that Frank Preston had by no means exaggerated the cli-

matic advantages of Lexington as contrasted with her surroundings in Richmond, and soon **felt** the beneficial effects
of her change of locality in an increase of strength, **vital-
ity,** and buoyancy of spirits. Indeed, **not** only **was the**
climate all that could be desired in point **of salubrity, but
Rockbridge county, in which** Lexington is **situated, proved
exceedingly attractive to her,** being one of the **most beautiful and** picturesque portions **of** the great **Valley of Vir-**
ginia. Lying between the Blue Ridge on the east **and Alle-**
ghany Mountains on the west, and near the **foot of the**
former, the county is quite fertile, its climate is exceedingly
healthful, and the country surrounding it is peculiarly beautiful and attractive.

During Ruth's visit, Frank Preston constantly exerted
himself to contribute to her pleasure, and before its close he
had given her **the full benefit of the mountain breezes** and
beautiful scenery, and taken her and Belle to various points
of interest in the county. **Among** these was the Natural
Bridge, whose single arch of solid rock spans a yawning
chasm and forms an adamantine causeway across its dizzy
depths. Here the party spent several hours in **viewing this**
curious freak of **nature,** and the attractions of the deep
chasm which it spans, whose rocky and perpendicular sides
and rugged surroundings present a sight of nature in one
of her most weird and **picturesque forms.** The time
allowed for Ruth's stay with her friends passed pleasantly
and swiftly by, and at its close she was loth to leave
them, and would have prolonged her visit but for the fact
that she was informed that her services were needed in
Richmond in consequence of the arrival there of many of
the soldiers who had been wounded during the Gettysburg campaign. Hence, on August 3d, she left for Richmond,
accompanied by Lieutenant Preston, and arrived there that
evening. On **the** following morning she repaired to the
hospital, reported for duty, and immediately resumed her
work. On entering the ward into which her duties called
her, she was shocked to see that every bunk was occupied,
and her heart was greatly pained by the sound of an occasional groan from some poor fellow who was still suffering from the effects of his wound.

Ruth had thought that her familiarity with distressing scenes incident to her service at the hospital was such that she would never be unnerved by them, but on this occasion she was so affected by the sights and sounds around her that it was several moments before she felt equal to the discharge of her duties. Having finally regained her composure, she began her work at the entrance to the ward and moved on down the row of bunks on that side of the room, rendering to each of their respective occupants such service as his case required. She had assisted in dressing several ghastly wounds and looked with pain upon the pinched and haggard faces of a number of soldiers who had been almost reduced to skeletons by loss of blood and intense suffering, and when she arrived near the lower end of the row of bunks, her feelings had become so affected that she was completely unnerved.

At that moment she approachd the bunk on which Ashton was lying. His face was partially turned from her, and he was dozing at the time. As she caught sight of his face, something familiar in its appearance arrested her attention and caused her to stop. In a moment, she quickly and nervously advanced to obtain a better view of his features, and, as she did so, the sound of her footsteps awakened him. Opening his eyes, he turned his face and looked at her in a startled manner. Starting back in affright, she exclaimed:

"Great heavens! Is that an illusion? Or has the grave given up its dead?"

At the sound of Ruth's voice, Ashton's face was illumined by an expression of happiness, and quickly rising to a sitting posture, he joyously said:

"Neither, Ruth, my darling; for 'tis I, John Ashton, in the flesh."

With a cry of intense gladness, Ruth sprang forward and fell on Ashton's breast, exclaiming:

"Thank God, my darling is alive," and fainted from excess of joy.

Ashton called to one of the attendants in the ward and at once had the surgeon and a female nurse summoned to Ruth's assistance. They bore her to the matron's apart-

ment, and, by the use of proper remedies, she was soon
restored to consciousness. About an hour afterward she
returned to Ashton's bedside. Although their surroundings
prevented a full and free expression of the joyous feelings
that filled their hearts, each read in the other's face the
sweet story of perfect love and supreme happiness.

Mutual explanations were given, and, although from
what had occurred, Ashton could easily have guessed the
contents of Ruth's lost letter, he learned from her for the
first time the story it told of her reciprocal love, and Ruth
became aware of the fact that it had never reached its destination. He also learned why the letter he wrote Ruth
just after his return from captivity failed to reach her and
was returned to him, that his last letter was never
received, and that, in consequence of his reported death and
her failure to hear from him, Ruth had mourned for him as
dead for nearly a year. This led her to explain her presence
at the hospital and the circumstances which had brought
about their fortunate meeting. Ashton then explained how
he came to be reported among those who were killed at the
second battle of Manassas, and gave Ruth a full account
of his capture on that occasion, his experience in the
hospital at Washington, the services of Miss R —— in rescuing him, as he believed, from imminent death, his removal
to Fort Delaware and subsequent escape therefrom and
ultimate return to his command. In the hearts of some
women Ashton's grateful and glowing account of Miss
R——'s untiring attention to him during his dangerous illness, and her subsequent services in securing the means for
his safe return to the Confederacy, and his warm tribute to
her worth would have awakened feelings of jealousy; but
no such effect was thereby produced in Ruth's heart, in
which there dwelt that "perfect love that casteth out fear,"
and she experienced only emotions of highest admiration
for, and deepest gratitude to, this noble and self-sacrificing
girl for what she had done, and longed to see and thank her
for having saved the life of her lover.

Ashton naturally told Ruth of his sickening disappointment in failing to receive her letter in answer to the one in
which he declared his love for her, the harrowing uncer-

tainty thereby occasioned as to whether his love was returned, and the almost constant anxiety and despondency that he subsequently experienced in consequence of his continued failure to hear from her. Ruth was deeply affected by the knowledge of all that he had suffered in consequence of his failure to receive her letter, and told him how keenly she regretted the unfortunate occurrence. After giving her an account of his service in the army subsequent to his escape from captivity, and the circumstances under which he received the wound that caused him to be brought to the hospital, Ashton told Ruth that, notwithstanding the intense suffering which he had experienced from his **wound, he** did not regret having received it, as it had been the means of revealing her love for him and relieving her from the sorrow occasioned by his supposed death. She was deeply touched by this manifestation of his exalted appreciation of her love, and his absorbing love for her and great solicitude for her happiness, and shed tears of gratitude and joy at the thought that she was the honored object of such perfect devotion. She expressed the tenderest sympathy **for him in his wounded condition and told** him how glad she was that her hospital experience had prepared her to render him efficient service in alleviating his suffering and restoring his lost strength.

Their conversation was greatly prolonged, and when Ruth finally left him, it was done reluctantly and with the assurance that she would return as early as possible **the** next morning. The reader can readily imagine what cheerful feelings filled the mind and heart of Ashton in consequence **of the** incidents of that day; and such is the effect of cheerfulness and happiness on the physical nature that there was a marked improvement in his condition when Ruth arrived at his bedside the following morning. She instantly noticed his improved appearance and joyously said:

"I am glad to see that you are looking so much better. Some fairy must have given you a draught of the elixir **of** life during the night."

"No," said Ashton, "but an angel gave me a sip of the

elixir of love on yesterday, and its vivifying effects have been magical."

Blushing at this compliment, Ruth replied: "I saw at a glance that you were looking better, and now I know you are *feeling* better than when I left you; for persons don't flatter when they are feeling badly. Rejecting as fanciful your idea of the giver, and accepting as a fact the alleged effect of the gift, I, as your *nurse*, promise you such an abundant supply of the elixir of which you speak as will secure your speedy recovery."

"A thousand thanks, my darling, for that assurance," said Ashton. "While I did not need it to satisfy me of your continued love, it is very sweet and comforting to me, and, in all seriousness, I assure you that the knowledge of your priceless love and the perfect peace and happiness which your presence gives me will greatly hasten my recovery. It is true that my wound is still troublesome and will require some time in which to heal; but the sweet contentment that I experience in your companionship and love will wonderfully assist both nature and science in the work of healing."

"It makes me inexpressibly happy," said Ruth, "to know that I can be instrumental in contributing to your happiness and aiding in your recovery. And you must now let me begin one branch of this labor of love by dressing your wound."

Ruth then performed this operation in a very gentle and careful manner, and with that ease and deftness which frequent practice in similar work had given her. When she had finished, and Ashton, by both words and looks, had expressed his grateful thanks for her service, Ruth said:

"I have been so absorbed in my thoughts of you and the happiness I experience in the fact that you were not killed, as I had long believed, that I have entirely forgotten to tell you anything about my cousin, Bertha Gray. Of course, you remember her and would doubtless like to hear about her."

"Yes," said Ashton, "I remember her with great pleasure, and think of her as one of my best and most highly prized friends. Moreover, if I had not admired and liked her for her intrinsic worth, her perfect devotion to you would have attached me to her; for, you know, 'a fellow feeling makes us wondrous kind.' Please tell me all about her, as I shall be interested in everything concerning her."

"Well," said Ruth, "I will begin by stating that she has 'met her fate' and is deeply in love. The fortunate possessor of her heart is a handsome, talented, and gallant officer of the 4th Georgia infantry, and I believe that he fully appreciates her love and is in all respects worthy of it. The gentleman alluded to is Captain Philip Carrington and strange to say, she met him in this very ward and under circumstances similar to those which reunited us; for, like yourself, he was brought here in a wounded condition, and Bertha met him while assisting me in my hospital duties. And now I will tell you all about the affair."

Ruth then proceeded to give Ashton an account of Bertha's visit to Richmond, her meeting with Carrington, and her subsequent experience in the Confederate Capital.

Leaving her thus engaged, we will give the reader some account of Carrington's experience and the movements of his command after he left Bertha the preceding month. He reached Culpeper Court-house June 7th in time to rejoin his regiment on its arrival there that day, and resumed the command of his company the next morning. He was exceedingly popular, both with his company and the entire regiment, and when it became known that he had returned to camp, scores of persons from all parts of the regiment came to his tent to congratulate him on his recovery from the effects of his wound, and heartily welcomed him back to the army. The 4th Georgia regiment, to which he belonged, was in General George Doles' brigade of General Robert E. Rodes' division, and on June 9th the division was moved out toward Brandy Station to support the Confederate cavalry in the engagement which we have described in a former part of our story, but did not take part in the fight, as the Federals had been repulsed and driven back by General Stuart.

On the next day, the division began its march to the Shenandoah Valley, crossed the Blue Ridge on June 12th, and moved toward Berryville on June 13th for the purpose of capturing the Federal garrison at that place. The Federals discovered the movement and escaped by retreating that night. Ascertaining this fact the next day, General Rodes pressed forward to Martinsburg and reached that place late in the afternoon. At this time the cavalry brigade of General Jenkins was skirmishing with the Federals, and General Rodes at once attacked the latter and quickly routed them, capturing five pieces of artillery and a number of horses, and also some commissary stores, artillery ammunition and small arms which were stored in the town. The division marched to Williamsport the next day, and the brigades of Doles, Iverson, and Ramseur were at once sent across the Potomac. The division reached Greencastle, Pennsylvania, June 22d and from that place it marched through Chambersburg to Carlisle, arriving there June 27th. Receiving orders on June 30th to rejoin the main body of the army, General Rodes marched to Heidlersburg, and on July 1st proceeded to Middletown, where he learned that A. P. Hill's corps was advancing on Gettysburg and, by order of General Ewell, the division was moved toward that place. Before reaching the town, the Federals were encountered in large force, and Rodes' entire division was soon engaged in a hot and sanguinary contest with him. Iverson's brigade was in advance on the right center, supported on the right by Daniel's brigade and on the left by Rodes' brigade, under Colonel Edward A. O'Neal. In advancing, Iverson's brigade changed its direction to the left and soon encountered a heavy force of Federals strongly posted in the woods and behind a concealed stone wall and became engaged in a desperate and unequal conflict with them. Discovering General Iverson's change of direction, General Daniel moved his brigade by the left flank to support Iverson's right, and soon encountered a large force of Federals whose line of battle was almost at right angles with Iverson's line, and in a few moments the Federals were pouring a destructive fire of artillery and musketry into his own left and Iverson's right flank About this time Rodes' brigade advanced on Iverson's left and was almost instantly driven back, and the Federals in overwhelming numbers charged Iverson's brigade and captured nearly all of three of his regiments that had not already been shot down. These brave North Carolinians had made a gallant fight and about five hundred of **them** were lying dead **and** wounded in line of battle as straight as **was** ever formed on dress parade. Doles' brigade was on the extreme left of the line of battle and maintained a fierce contest with a much larger force **of** Federals until relieved by the **arrival** of General Early's division on its left. Notwithstanding the fact that General Doles was greatly outnumbered, he at once, and without awaiting orders, attacked the dense masses of Federals in his front and the brigade pressed forward **with** its wonted spirit and gallantry. The 4th Georgia regiment maintained its well-earned reputation for **intrepid** dash and daring, and Captain Carrington led his company with unsurpassed gallantry in the fierce and vigorous charge that was made on the Federal lines. Waving his sword aloft with flashing eye and glowing countenance, Carrington pressed forward in the charge, seemingly unconscious of danger and unmindful of the countless bullets that were whizzing around and above him, and the hurtling shot and shell that were being **hurled at the** advancing lines by the **Federal batteries.** The **contest** was hot and desperate, but of short duration, and Doles' brigade rapidly drove the enemy back before them, and in line with the other brigades of Rodes' division, followed the Federals into and through Gettysburg, Doles' brigade being the first **to** reach the center of the town, and there had two vigorous and successful conflicts in the streets with the **retreating** forces of the enemy. In this engagement the division captured two thousand and five hundred prisoners.

General Rodes having been informed by General Ewell that General Lee did not wish to bring on at that time a general engagement, as Longstreet's corps had not arrived, and the Federals having occupied a strong position on the heights back of Gettysburg, halted his division on the outskirts of the town and there awaited orders. This position was held by the division until the next afternoon, when about dark an attack was begun but not carried out on account of the fact that there was not full concert of action between this division and the one immediately on its right,

the latter having attacked and then fallen back by the time
the former had driven in the Federal skirmishers. However, General Rodes did not fall back, but established his
front line in the plain to the right of Gettysburg and held
this position during the remainder of the battle. In the
meantime a vigorous attack had been made by other portions of the Confederate army on the right and in front of
the Federal position on Cemetery Hill. The Federals
occupied an exceedingly strong position, with their right
resting upon two commanding elevations near each other,
south and southeast of Gettysburg, the former being
known as Cemetery Hill. Their line extended from these
two hills along a steep and elevated ridge, parallel with the
Emmitsburg pike, for about a mile to another high hill
known as Round Top. This ridge and the hills above mentioned were difficult of ascent, and along the slope there
were numerous rail and stone fences which afforded protection to the Federals, who were posted in strong force
behind them and also upon the crest of the ridge, which was
lined with artillery. The ground in front of the Federals,
and over which the Confederates had to pass in making the
attack, was mostly open for about three-quarters of a mile,
and hence the assault was made under very disadvantageous and trying circumstances.

The attack was begun against the Federal left by Hood's
division of Longstreet's corps, on the extreme right of the
Confederate line and followed up by McLaws' division of
the same corps, supported on his left by Wilcox's, Wright's,
Perry's, and Posey's brigades, of Anderson's division of
Hill's corps. The Confederates pressed gallantly forward
across the open ground under a heavy and destructive fire
of artillery and musketry, quickly drove the Federals from
their advance position on the Emmitsburg pike to the cover
of a ravine and a line of stone fences at the foot of the
ridge, and after a severe struggle, dislodged them from this
position and drove them to the crest of the ridge, capturing
several of their batteries. General C. M. Wilcox's brigade
reached the foot of the ridge, having broken two lines of
infantry and captured six pieces of artillery on the way,
and there had a severe struggle with the Federals for

about half an hour, and would have carried the heights if there had been a supporting line at hand, but for lack of support was compelled to withdraw. General A. R. Wright's brigade, composed of the 3d, 22d, and 48th Georgia regiments and the 2d Georgia battalion, not only gained the crest of the ridge but drove the Federals into a rocky gorge on the eastern side of the same and captured about twenty pieces of artillery; but as there was no protecting force on the left and a brigade on the right having been driven back, Wright's brigade was forced to retire and had to abandon the captured artillery, especially as the Federals had advanced on both flanks of the brigade and were about to surround it. In the meantime, General Edward Johnson with Jones', Nicholls', and Stuart's brigades, of his division, assaulted the Federal position on the steep and rugged hill next to Cemetery Hill, and under a heavy fire drove the Federals into their intrenchments, a part of which was taken by Stuart's brigade.

Soon after General Johnson's division became engaged, General Early ordered Hays' Louisiana brigade and Hoke's North Carolina brigade, commanded by Colonel I. E. Avery, to advance and carry the Federal works on Cemetery Hill. These two brigades advanced in gallant style across the open ground over which they had to pass under a heavy fire of artillery, attacked and drove back a large force of infantry at the foot of Cemetery Hill, pressed forward up the hill, and soon broke and drove back a second line of Federals posted behind a stone wall. Again advancing, they reached the third line of Federals posted in rifle-pits behind a strong abattis of heavy timber and having broken this line they quickly gained the summit of the hill and by a rapid charge drove back the Federals on its crest and captured several pieces of artillery, four stand of colors, and a number of prisoners. These brave Louisianians and North Carolinians had fully and gallantly executed General Early's orders and were now in possession of the Federal stronghold on Cemetery Hill; but as they were entirely without support (that which was expected having failed to arrive), and the routed Federals having been heavily reinforced, they were soon compelled to retire before overwhelming numbers. This was done in a deliberate and orderly manner and with but little loss.

Thus for lack of sufficient support, the Confederates had been unable to hold much of the ground which they had taken from a superior force occupying exceedingly strong and advantageous positions. However, some ground had been gained on the right by General Longstreet, and his troops were so disposed that night as to hold it. The result of that day's operations induced General Lee to believe that, with proper concert of action and with the increased support which the positions gained on the right would enable the artillery to render the assaulting columns, he would ultimately succeed in defeating the Federals; and hence, he determined to renew the attack, the general plan of the same remaining unchanged. General Longstreet, reinforced by the arrival of Pickett's division, was ordered to attack the next morning, and General Ewell was directed to assail the enemy's right at the same time. On the following morning General Longstreet, instead of attacking the Federals in front as was contemplated in General Lee's plan of attack, arranged for renewing the attack by his right, "with a view," as he says in his report, "to pass around the hill occupied by the enemy on his left, and to gain it by flank and reverse attack," and had given orders for the execution of this plan, when General Lee reached him and ordered that the assault be made against the main position of the Federals on Cemetery Hill. Before General Ewell could be notified of the delay in General Longstreet's dispositions for attacking the Federals, General Edward Johnson had become engaged, and it was too late to recall him. He drove the Federals out of part of their intrenchments but failed to carry their stronghold. The contemplated attack on their left not having been made, the Federals were enabled to hold their right with a force much larger than that of General Johnson, and finally to so threaten his flank and rear as to render it necessary for him to retire to his original position As there was a force on the extreme left of the Federals which could attack General Longstreet's troops in reverse as they advanced, he thought it necessary to protect his flank and rear with Hood's and

McLaws' divisions, and hence he was reinforced by **Heth's** division and two brigades of **Pender's division**, of A. P. Hill's corps. General Hill was directed to hold his line with the remainder of his corps, "afford General Longstreet **further** assistance, **if** required, and avail himself of any success that might be gained."

About 1 p. m., the Confederate artillery opened fire along the entire line, and the Federal artillery promptly replied.

For two hours an incessant and unprecedentedly terrific artillery contest was waged between the opposing armies, and before its close, some of the Federal batteries on the left had been silenced and a number of **those at and near** Cemetery Hill were disabled or driven off and had **to be** **replaced by** fresh ones. **At the close of the cannonade, General Longstreet ordered** forward the column of attack, consisting of Pickett's division with Wilcox's brigade in rear of its right flank to guard the same, and Heth's division, under General James J. Pettigrew, supported by Lane's and Scales' brigades of Pender's division, commanded by General Isaac R. Trimble. The position which they were to attack was the Federal stronghold and was occupied by the **1st and 2d corps and part of the 3d corps, with other** troops in supporting distance. The Federals not only occupied a **naturally** strong position, but **were posted** behind barricades erected the preceding night, and **rail and** stone fences; and hence, as the Confederates had to pass **over** open ground **in** making their attack, the dangerous and desperate character of the undertaking **in which this** assaulting column of about twelve thousand men was to **engage, is** fully apparent.

At the word of command, the troops promptly began to advance and moved steadily forward to within seven hundred yards of Cemetery Hill, when the Federal artillery along the ridge and on Round Top opened upon them a heavy fire of grape, canister, and shell, which rapidly thinned **their** ranks. Undaunted by this, the troops quickly closed up the gaps in their **ranks and** continued to press gallantly forward in almost **perfect order, although** they had to **climb** several high fences in their route, and soon met the **advance** line of the Federals **about one** hundred yards in

front of the second line, which was posted behind the rail
and stone fences and barricades to which reference has been
made. The front line of the Federals was quickly routed
and driven back in confusion on the second line. The Confederates continued to press gallantly and steadily forward
under a destructive fire of both artillery and musketry,
reached the strongly intrenched position of the Federals on
Cemetery Ridge, engaged them in a hand-to-hand conflict,
broke their line at a point where the left of Pickett's division and Archer's brigade, of Heth's division, charged in concert and planted the Confederate flag inside their works,
where General L. A. Armistead was killed at the head of
his brigade, General R..B. Garnett having been shot from
his horse just outside the works. The success of the
Confederates was but momentary, for the Federals rapidly
reinforced their broken line by concentrating at that point
troops from both sides of the breach, and, by a front and
flank attack on those who had reached the works, soon
overpowered and captured the greater part of them, as they
were compelled to surrender for lack of a supporting force.
That force would have been at hand if General Lee's directions had been fully carried out, and it appears that one
who has assumed to criticise that matchless military leader
for ordering the assault was to blame for the absence of
such supporting force, and the consequently disastrous
result of the assault; for General Longstreet not only
failed to call for support from General Hill, who had been
directed to "afford him further assistance, if required," but
also checked a movement which was about to be made by
General R. H. Anderson, of Hill's corps, for the purpose of
rendering such assistance, as is shown by his report of the
engagement, in which he says: "Wilcox's and Perry's
brigades had been moved forward, so as to be in position
to render assistance or take advantage of any success gained
by the assaulting column, and at what I supposed to be the
proper time, I was about to move forward Wright's and
Posey's brigades, when Lieutenant-general Longstreet
directed me to stop the movement, adding that it was useless,
and would only involve unnecessary loss, the assault having failed."

If the assaulting column had received from Hill's corps the assistance for which General Lee's instructions provided, and General Longstreet had at the same time moved forward the divisions of Hood and McLaws against the Federal left and thereby prevented the movement of troops from that point to aid in meeting the assault upon Cemetery Ridge, instead of holding those divisions in reserve "to defend his flank and rear," the position gained by the assaulting column would have been held, and the battle of Gettysburg, instead of resulting in a repulse of the Confederates, would have been a complete victory for them; for Cemetery Ridge was the key to the entire Federal line, and its possession would have enabled General Lee to rout General Meade's army.

The brief outline which we have given of the gallant but fruitless assault of the Confederates on the Federal stronghold conveys but an imperfect idea of the matchless heroism displayed by that comparatively small assaulting column in thus storming an almost impregnable position, held by a greatly superior force, and literally lined with artillery which was constantly pouring a heavy fire of shot, shell, and canister into the advancing lines, and mowing wide swaths in their rapidly decreasing ranks. Even their enemies were moved to admiration by their chivalrous daring, and in reporting the engagement, paid tributes of praise to their valor and heroism.

General W. S. Hancock wrote: "I have never seen a more formidable attack."

General John Gibbon wrote: "The line moved steadily to the front in a way to excite the admiration of every one."

Colonel Norman J. Hall wrote: "The perfect order and steady but rapid advance of the enemy called forth praise from our troops, but gave their line an appearance of being fearfully irresistible."

General A. S. Webb wrote: "Their march was as steady as if impelled by machinery, unbroken by our artillery, which played upon them a storm of missiles."

General Henry J. Hunt, chief of artillery, wrote: "The enemy advanced magnificently, unshaken by the shot and

12

shell which tore through his ranks from his front and from our left."

During the three days' fighting, the losses were heavy on both sides, those of the Confederates being two thousand five hundred and ninety-two killed, twelve thousand seven hundred and nine wounded, and five thousand one hundred and fifty captured or missing; and those of the Federals being three thousand one hundred and fifty-five killed, fourteen thousand four hundred and twenty-nine wounded, and five thousand two hundred and sixty-five captured or missing. The Federal force greatly outnumbered that of the Confederates, being one hundred and four thousand strong; while the strength of the latter was about sixty-eight thousand.

Owing to the great strength of the Federal position and **the scarcity of** ammunition, General Lee would not risk another attack, and as it was exceedingly difficult to procure supplies, it was impossible for the army to continue longer where it was. Hence, after remaining at Gettysburg during July 4th, the Confederate army began to retire toward the Potomac that night. On reaching the Potomac, General Lee found that it was greatly swollen and unfordable in consequence of recent rains, and that a pontoon bridge which he had left at Falling Waters had been partially destroyed by the Federals. Hence, his army had to await the subsiding of the waters, and the construction of a new pontoon bridge before a passage of the river could be effected. They were thus detained for four or five days, having occasional skirmishes with the advance troops of the Federals, and on July 12th the main body of General Meade's army arrived. The Confederate army at once took a position, previously selected by General Lee, covering the Potomac from Williamsport to Falling Waters, and there remained for two days awaiting an attack from the Federals; but the latter, instead of attacking, prepared for an expected attack from the former by throwing up intrenchments along their entire line. By July 13th the river at Williamsport, although still deep, had become fordable, and the bridge at Falling Waters had been completed; and as further delay would have enabled the Federals to obtain reinforcements, General Lee decided to await an attack no longer, and gave orders for the passage of the Potomac that night. During that night and the following day, the Confederate army safely crossed the river, Ewell's corps fording it at Williamsport and Hill's and Longstreet's corps crossing on the pontoon bridge at Falling Waters. After resting several days near Bunker Hill and Darkesville, the army retired up the Shenandoah Valley, crossed the Blue Ridge, and on August 4th took position along the Rapidan.

During this retrograde movement, the division to which Carrington belonged was ordered to Manassas Gap to relieve Wright's brigade, which was holding the gap against a large attacking force supported by two corps of the Federal army. General Rodes' sharpshooters (about two hundred and fifty men) were promptly sent to strengthen General Wright's line, and O'Neal's brigade was deployed behind Wright's brigade about three hundred yards in his rear. The Federals in large force attacked and slowly drove back the front line of skirmishers for a short distance; but were soon checked by the stubborn fighting and fatal fire of this handful of gallant men, who frequently broke the solid lines of the enemy, and finally a few shots from the artillery completely stopped their advance and ended the engagement. During that night, Rodes' division fell back and bivouacked near Front Royal. From this point it resumed the backward march, crossed the Blue Ridge at Thornton's Gap, and reached Madison Court-house on July 29th, and thus ended the part taken by this division in the Gettysburg campaign. While all of the troops who engaged in this celebrated and exceptionally trying campaign under the leadership of the matchless Lee won great renown, none are deserving of more honor and praise than the brave and gallant Georgians, Alabamians, and North Carolinians, who constituted Rodes' division. They were almost constantly on the march, or engaged in fighting, for six consecutive weeks, and even when they crossed the Blue Ridge at Chester's Gap on June 12th in the forward movement many of the men were barefooted, and long before they recrossed it at Thornton's Gap nearly half of the men and many of the officers were in like condition. Notwithstanding this and the fact that they had to travel over rough and rocky roads during the hottest days of summer, these shoeless heroes, with bruised and bleeding feet, kept up with the moving column, and in ranks, during its rapid march, and, when they had opportunity for so doing, fought with dauntless courage and unabated zeal and enthusiasm.

The names and fame of Pickett's and Heth's divisions and Lane's and Scales' brigades of Pender's division are inseparably connected with the battle of Gettysburg, and their intrepid charge against the Federal stronghold on Cemetery Hill, on July 3d, has justly immortalized them; and alongside of their heroic deeds should be recorded in the annals of war the impetuous charges and determined assaults made by Rodes' division, under a heavy fire of artillery, on the dense masses of infantry pressing it in front and flank on July 1st, and by means of which a force greatly outnumbering this division was completely repulsed, and, by the aid of the brigades of the gallant John B. Gordon and Harry T. Hays and Hoke's brigade led by the brave and lamented Colonel Isaac E. Avery, was routed and driven back through Gettysburg and compelled to take shelter behind their intrenchments on Cemetery Hill.

General Lee witnessed the attack made by Rodes' division on that occasion, and afterward said to its brave commander, "I am proud of your division." Such praise from the lips of that peerless chieftain was proof of the dauntless courage and hardy heroism of those on whom it was bestowed. These were the true and valiant soldiers whom Captain Carrington helped to command, and the examples of fortitude, bravery, and patriotic devotion set by officers like himself greatly aided in making these soldiers what they were.

Carrington had written Bertha several letters after leaving Culpeper Court-house on June 10th, and she had answered them, but none of her letters had yet reached him, as many letters for the Confederate soldiers were not forwarded while the army was in Maryland and Pennsylvania, and these happened to be among the number. However, in a day or two after Carrington reached Madison Court-house, he received the letters and immediately devoured their contents with an avidity and a delight known only to the impassioned and heart-hungry lover. Yielding to the promptings of her **impulsive and** affectionate nature, Bertha had written with perfect *abandon* and put her whole heart in her letters, and hence they gave full expression to her ardent and absorbing love for him to whom they were addressed, and manifested the deepest and tenderest solicitude for the safety and happiness of her lover. Carrington was deeply touched by this manifestation of Bertha's love and devotion and, realizing more fully than ever before the rich blessing that he had received in the gift **of that pure** and unselfish love, his heart was filled with happiness. He at once wrote Bertha a **long** and loving letter in which he endeavored to give her some idea of how completely his love for her had taken possession of his nature and become a part of his being, and told of the sweet contentment and perfect happiness that had come into his life through the medium of her love, and of his ever-present and yearning desire to make her supremely happy. **In clos**ing his letter, he urged her to visit her cousin in Richmond, as soon as possible, stating that if she should do so he would obtain **a short** leave of absence from his command and visit her while she was there. On receipt of this letter, Bertha wrote Carrington that she would visit Ruth the last of August or the first of September.

We will now return to Ashton, whom we left listening to **Ruth's** account of Bertha's love affair and subsequent experience in Richmond. He was greatly interested in all that she **told** him about her cousin and Captain Carrington, and especially so in regard to the experience which they had at Hollywood Cemetery that led to the detection and capture of **the** Federal spy, Sergeant Paul, alias Edward Craft. Although Ashton abhorred the occupation of a spy and utterly despised those who engaged in it, yet, after hearing of Craft's confession, the reasons given by him for having engaged in that calling, and the steps which he took **to** prevent his family from learning of his conduct and **fate, he** could not avoid feeling a species of admiration for him, and expressed the opinion that he did not think that

Craft was an utterly depraved man, as he appeared to
have been actuated by no sinister or sordid motive in
what he had done. Ruth agreed with him in this opinion,
spoke of Craft's attractive social qualities, and stated that
she had really regretted his death.

Ashton's wound did not heal very rapidly and was occasionally somewhat troublesome; but he did not become
disheartened or worry himself about his condition, for,
being cheered and made happy by the daily companionship
of Ruth, he was content to patiently await the results of
the combined agencies of science and nature in their cura-
tive processes. It was about the first of September and
nearly two months after he was wounded before he had
sufficiently recovered from the effects of his wound to
authorize his discharge from the hospital. He was still
unfit for active service, and, having obtained from the surgeon a certificate to that effect and a recommendation for a
thirty days' furlough, he sent the same to the captain of
his company, and shortly thereafter received the furlough
thus recommended. After leaving the hospital, he secured
a pleasant boarding-place in the city and, of course, became
a constant visitor at Mrs. Slaughter's residence, where
Ruth was still boarding.

About this time Bertha arrived on her contemplated visit,
and a few days thereafter Carrington came to the city in
accordance with his previously expressed purpose of visiting her. The avidity and constancy with which they
mutually monopolized each other's society at once indicated
that they intended to fully utilize in heart-communion the
short leave of absence which Carrington had obtained. The
meeting of two such men as Ashton and Carrington would
have naturally been cordial under ordinary circumstances,
and it was especially so in view of the relations which they
respectively sustained to Ruth and Bertha, and the fact
that they had thereby been brought into close companionship from widely different branches of the army. They at
once became good friends, and when opportunity offered,
found great pleasure in exchanging recitals of their respective experiences in the Pennsylvania campaign. In this
way they learned that they had fought in close proximity

to each other during the battle of Gettysburg when Stuart's
cavalry was immediately on the left of Ewell's corps and
protected it from the attempted flank **movement of the**
Federals.

Ruth and Bertha were greatly interested in these conversations between their lovers, and their hearts throbbed
with enthusiasm **and** their minds were filled with admiration when they heard of the gallant and impetuous attacks
made by the Confederates upon the Federals, and which fell
short of final success because of inadequate supporting
force resulting from a failure to fully execute General Lee's
orders.

The days passed swiftly by, and all too soon for the hap-
piness of Bertha and Carrington the latter's leave of
absence expired, and the time for his departure arrived.
With the assurance that she should hear from him frequently,
and the promise that he would visit her as soon as possible,
he returned to his regiment about the middle of September.
Although Bertha was naturally saddened and depressed by
his departure, she bore it better than she had borne their
former separation, as there was not **at** this time any indi-
cation of an impending battle, and hence she did not think
of Carrington as exposed **to** immediate danger, as when he
started on the Pennsylvania campaign three months before.
She had resumed the work of assisting Ruth at the hospital, and now devoted herself assiduously to the discharge
of the duties incident to the same. Indeed, **she insisted on**
doing the greater part of Ruth's work, and thereby gave
the latter more opportunities than she would have otherwise had for being with Ashton, and, moreover, kept her
own time **and** attention so constantly occupied in ministering to her patients, that she was prevented from morbidly
dwelling on **the** sadness caused by the departure **of her**
lover. Both Ashton and Ruth fully appreciated this generous thoughtfulness **and solicitude** for their happiness and
were deeply grateful to Bertha **for the same.** In consequence of Ruth's partial relief from her hospital duties, she
and Ashton were enabled to spend a considerable portion of
each day in private conversations that were in all respects
real heart-and-soul communions, which not only intensified

and strengthened their love, but also revealed to each a thorough knowledge of the other's character. Ashton had thought that he already understood Ruth's character, but during these happy days when, in consequence of her warm and trustful love, her inmost soul was revealed to him, he felt that he had but caught a glimpse of the beauty and worth of her moral nature, wherein breadth and depth of thought, refinement and tenderness of feeling, and warmth and unselfishness of affection combined to make the perfect woman. In her he found his heart's high ideal fully realized; her companionship and love entirely satisfied the wants and longings of his nature and he was perfectly happy. She was also supremely happy, for, in his noble character, embodying loftiness of purpose, strength, depth and tenderness of feeling and ardency of affection, she had found her ideal of true manhood and her soul was satisfied. Being thus happy in each other's companionship and love, Ashton and Ruth were almost oblivious of the flight of time, and about the first of October they experienced a painful shock on realizing that his furlough would expire in a few days. His wound had healed, but occasionally he felt some unpleasantness from its effects and was not fully fitted for active service. However, he was unwilling to ask for an extension of his furlough and determined that at its expiration he would promptly return to his regiment. His furlough extended to October 6th, and on October 5th he left Richmond to rejoin his regiment. The parting between him and Ruth was exceedingly painful, but as duty called him to the front, they bore it uncomplainingly, and neither would have had it delayed at the expense of loyalty to the cause in which he was engaged.

CHAPTER XIII.

Ashton reached his regiment the day after he left Richmond and found it encamped on the right of General Lee's
army near the **Rapidan river.** After exchanging cordial
greetings with the members of his company and receiving
their hearty congratulations on his recovering from the
effects of his wound, he at once made inquiry about his
horse, and was delighted to learn that the animal was
brought safely to camp on the return of the army from
Maryland, had since been well cared for by one of Ashton's comrades and was now in excellent condition.

The true cavalryman is always attached to his horse, and
Ashton was especially fond of his, both on account of the
faithful service which it had rendered him and the peculiar
circumstances under which it had come into his possession;
for it was none other than Mosby's parting gift to him just
after his rescue from the Federal picket near Fox's Ford.

At this time the Confederate army occupied a position
along the south side of the Rapidan **river, and the Federal**
army, under General Meade, was lying around Culpeper
Court-house and extended to the north side of the Rapidan.
There was nothing to indicate that a general movement
of either army was imminent, and Ashton looked forward
to no other occurrences than those incident to the usual
routine of camp life and picket duty. However,
"Marse Robert," as his soldiers affectionately called General
Lee, was maturing a plan which would soon put the entire
army in motion. That plan was to bring on a general
engagement with Meade, and in order to increase the
chances of success, General Lee determined to turn Meade's
right flank and strike him in the rear. Hence, in pursuance
of this plan, the infantry and artillery of the army marched
toward Madison Court-house on October 9th, and on the
following day proceeded by a circuitous route in the direction of Culpeper Court-house, which was reached on October 11th, when it was discovered that the Federal army had
retreated toward Washington along the line of the Orange
and Alexandria railroad. General Lee made another effort

to engage General Meade by crossing the Rappahannock and pressing forward through Warrenton, but the latter continued his retreat to Centreville, and there intrenched his army. In the meantime the Confederate cavalry had not experienced the same difficulty as the main body of the army in meeting the Federals, and had **had** a series of engagements with them.

As Ashton took part in several of these, we will give some **account of the operations of the** cavalry in this **forward movement.** On October 10th, Buford's division **of cavalry** crossed the Rapidan at Germanna Ford and, after capturing a portion of a company of the 1st Maryland cavalry **of** Lomax's brigade, moved up the river toward Morton's Ford. General Fitzhugh Lee (who had recently been made a major-general), with his division, consisting of Lomax's brigade, W. H. F. Lee's brigade, commanded by Colonel John R. Chambliss, and Wickham's brigade, commanded by Colonel T. H. Owen and also with Johnson's brigade of infantry, attacked the Federals early on the morning of October 11th. Lee's and Lomax's brigades moved directly against them, and General Fitzhugh Lee, with Wickham's and the infantry brigade crossed the river at Raccoon Ford **and moved down upon** their flank and rear. Lomax and Chambliss drove the Federals across the river at Morton's Ford, and pressed them closely in their rapid retreat toward Stevensburg. At this place they attempted to make a stand, but were promptly dislodged from their position and driven back to Brandy Station. On reaching Brandy Station, General Fitzhugh Lee found a portion of Hampton's division, under command of General Stuart, engaged with General Kilpatrick's division and a part of General Gregg's division, and at once joined in the engagement. Colonel Chambliss ordered Major Waller, commanding the 9th Virginia cavalry, to charge **the** Federals, and it was gallantly and vigorously done. Thus, before Ashton had fully recovered from the effects of his wound, he was again actively engaged in battle, and participated in this charge with his wonted spirit and gallantry. This charge was followed by another by the 13th Virginia cavalry, and the Federals were driven back with loss. General Stuart and

General Fitzhugh Lee, having united their forces, advanced on the Federals at Fleetwood Heights, where the forces of Buford and Kilpatrick had also been united, and a fierce and obstinate engagement there ensued. The fighting became general and there were a series of charges and counter-charges made in rapid succession, the regiments of Lomax's brigade making no less than five in one part of the field, while the Confederate sharpshooters were constantly engaged with the enemy on foot. At times these sharpshooters were entirely surrounded by the Federal cavalry but would not surrender and, bravely defending themselves, were each time rescued by the well-directed charges of the Confederate cavalry.

The Federals were finally routed and driven back toward the Rappahannock, which they crossed that night. The day had been won by the Confederates by fierce, persistent, and skillful fighting, in which the 9th Virginia cavalry fully bore its part, and Ashton, both in the saddle and on foot, rendered gallant and efficient service. On the following morning General Stuart left the 5th Virginia cavalry, under Colonel T. L. Rosser, and one piece of artillery below Fleetwood for the purpose of meeting any advance that might be made by the Federals toward Culpeper Court-house, and proceeded with Fitzhugh Lee's division and Funsten's and Gordon's brigades toward Warrenton. After a brief but hot engagement at Jeffersonton between the 7th and 12th Virginia cavalry and a regiment of Federal cavalry, in which the latter was completely routed, General Stuart pushed forward to the Rappahannock river and forced a passage of the stream at Warrenton Springs, the 12th Virginia cavalry charging across the river in a gallant manner in the face of a heavy fire from the Federals on the opposite side. This charge was especially creditable to those who participated in the same, as it was made under peculiarly trying circumstances. The regiment expected to cross the river on the bridge at this point, but on charging up to it, discovered that the flooring had been taken up and that the bridge was impassable. Although the troops were exposed to a heavy fire from the Federals across the river, they did not become confused or waver in their purpose, but turned to the right, dashed down the road to the ford below, plunged into the stream, and pushed rapidly across under a heavy fire from the Federal sharpshooters, a number of whom were captured before they could make their escape. General Stuart soon had the bridge repaired for the passage of the infantry, and sent Funsten's and Gordon's brigades to Warrenton, where they bivouacked that night.

During that day Colonel P. M. B. Young, of Cobb's Legion, commanding Hampton's old brigade, was the hero of an engagement which occurred near Brandy Station, and in view of the boldness and success of Colonel Young's conduct and the important results thereby accomplished, we trust that the reader will indulge us in an account of the same. On October 10th, General Stuart engaged the Federals nearly all day near James City with Gordon's and Young's brigades, and ascertaining the next morning that they had retreated, he marched toward Culpeper Courthouse with Gordon's brigade, leaving Colonel Young to hold his position at James City until further orders. Colonel Young remained there until the morning of October 12th, and then in obedience to orders received from General Stuart, proceeded to Culpeper Court-house. He arrived there about 3 P. M., and just after the head of his column entered the town firing was heard in the direction of Brandy Station, and a courier from Colonel T. L. Rosser, of the 5th Virginia cavalry, reported that the Federals were advancing in heavy force from Brandy Station, having driven Colonel Rosser back from below Fleetwood, where, as the reader will remember, General Stuart had left him with his regiment and one piece of artillery the day before.

A few moments before the firing was heard, the column had halted, many of the troopers had dismounted and details were being made to be sent out after provisions for the men, who were really suffering from hunger, as no rations had been issued to them that day. At the sound of the firing, the troopers hastily remounted their horses, the column was instantly put in motion and galloped rapidly through Culpeper and on toward Brandy Station. As it passed at rapid speed and with clattering noise over the rocky streets of Culpeper, the horsemen were greeted all along the way by

the sight of lovely and loyal ladies at almost every door-
way enthusiastically waving their handkerchiefs, clapping
their hands, and smiling approval on the men in gray.
Dashing out of the town, with no slackening of their speed,
the Confederate cavalry rode rapidly on in the direction of the
firing, which was each moment becoming heavier and approaching nearer to Culpeper. Riding at this rapid pace
for about two miles, the Confederates reached a wooded
ridge called Slaughter's Hill and Colonel Young quickly
deployed his brigade along the ridge, his right resting on
the Orange and Alexandria railroad, dismounted about
three-fourths of the command as sharpshooters, and had
five pieces of artillery placed at intervals along the ridge so
as to sweep the road to Brandy Station and both flanks of
the Federals, who were seen advancing from the direction
of Brandy Station in heavy force. They had driven
Colonel Rosser back some distance and were closely pressing him when Colonel Young arrived, and just as the latter
got his brigade in position, Colonel Rosser's regiment fell
back on Cobb's Legion and formed in the rear of the latter
regiment, which was on the extreme right of Young's line,
and supporting a battery stationed in the Brandy Station
road near the edge of a heavy body of woods. At this time
Colonel Young, who had just galloped down his line from
the left, halted in front of Cobb's Legion, made a short and
stirring speech to the men, which set them to cheering in a
loud and enthusiastic manner, and then galloped back to
the left of the line, which was about a mile in length. The
cheering begun by Cobb's Legion was taken up and continued by the whole brigade as Colonel Young rode along
the line, and its heartiness and volume were calculated to
impress the Federals with the idea that at least an army
corps confronted them, whereas the brigade numbered only
about twelve hundred men. The Federal force, as was afterward ascertained, consisted of Buford's division of
cavalry, several pieces of artillery, and the 5th and 6th
corps of infantry, under General Sedgwick, numbering
twenty-five thousand men; and hence the reader will understand that Colonel Young was playing a bluff game in
presenting such a bold front to this overwhelming force.

Just after Colonel Rosser's regiment was driven back on Young's line, the Federals advanced in large force, their front consisting of a heavy line of infantry skirmishers and their center and flanks supported by heavy columns of cavalry. They were met and temporarily checked by a volley from the dismounted sharpshooters and a well-directed fire of the Confederate artillery. The skirmishing then became general along the line, and in accordance with instructions from Colonel Young, a constant fire was kept up by the artillery.

In a few minutes, a heavy force of Federals charged on foot through the woods on the right, and came within a short distance of the edge of the timber, the noise of their many feet upon the leaves with which the ground was thickly covered resembling the sound of a tempest sweeping through a forest in Autumn. On they came, shouting their "hip, hip, hurrahs" in varied tones of unequal volume, but the gallant sharphooters of Cobb's Legion were calmly awaiting them, and when the Federals arrived within short range of this little band of sharpshooters, the latter raised the wild Confederate yell and poured a volley into their ranks which effectually checked their farther advance. They had come so close to the battery which Cobb's Legion was supporting that the officer in charge of the gun, fearing that it would be captured, ordered it limbered up and started to move it. At this moment Colonel Young came galloping down the line at full speed and, when in about forty yards of the retiring gun, called to the officer in charge of the same, saying: "Where are you going with that gun? Bring it back at once." When Colonel Young reached him, the officer explained his conduct by telling of the close proximity of the enemy and the consequent danger of the capture of the gun. Colonel Young instantly replied, "Unlimber that gun and put it in position," and when this was done, he said: "Now fire that gun, and keep firing it. It don't make a bit of difference whether or not you *see* anything. I want a noise kept up here."

His command was literally and faithfully obeyed, and never was a gun better served or more rapidly fired than that one from then until dark, and although the gunners were often without a visible target, the gun was incessantly fired and a continuous noise kept up at that point. The artillery fire and sharpshooting continued until night, and, immediately after dark, in obedience to orders from Colonel Young, the troops built hundreds of fires all along the line of battle and kept them burning through the night. The Federals retreated during the night, the infantry crossing the Rappahannock at 12 o'clock and the cavalry about daylight. The object of this movement on the part of the Federals and the force engaged in the same, will be seen from the following copy of an order received that day by General Buford:

"(Orders.) HEADQUARTERS ARMY OF THE POTOMAC,
October 12, 1863, 10:30 A. M.

"Major-general Sedgwick will, in addition to his own corps, take command of the 5th corps and Buford's division of cavalry and advance immediately to Brandy Station and take position at the heights there, driving the enemy and holding the position. He will report his progress to the commanding general, and also the force, position and movements of the enemy.

"By command of Major-general Meade.

S. WILLIAMS,
Assistant Adjutant-general.

"Official copy furnished for General Buford's information.

"By command of Major-general Pleasanton.

"C. C. SUYDAM,
"Assistant Adjutant-general."

In his official report of the movement, General Buford says:

"At 12 M., the division was across the river again and in motion. After advancing about two miles, the enemy's pickets were driven in, and the advance command skirmishing with the enemy. Finding his force insignificant, a general advance was ordered, and he was driven to one and one-half miles of Culpeper. The object of the expedition being accomplished, the division returned and bivouacked on the left of the infantry near Brandy.

"At 12 that night the infantry withdrew beyond the Rappahannock, my division bringing up the rear, and recrossed by daylight on the 13th."

As compared with the Federal force, that of the Confederates *was* "insignificant," but the only force that "was driven to one and one-half miles of Culpeper" by the Federals was the one regiment of Colonel Rosser, and when they struck Young's brigade the driving ceased, and their forward movement was completely checked. Notwithstanding General Buford's statement to the contrary, "the object of the expedition" was not "accomplished;" for General Sedgwick failed in "driving the enemy" as directed and also failed to advance sufficiently far to enable him to correctly "report the force, position, and movements of the enemy" to General Meade. Hence "the expedition" was a failure, and the cause of its failure is found in the fact that the Federals did not, as they could easily have done with their overwhelming force, drive Young from his position and thereby ascertain the exceedingly small force that confronted them. If they had displayed one-half the gallantry in attacking the Confederates that the latter manifested in meeting and checking their movement, they could have easily driven Young back by advancing two hundred yards through the woods on the right of his line and about a quarter of a mile across the open ground on the left of the same, and on reaching his position would have instantly discovered what a mere handful of men were opposing them, as the country was entirely open from that point to Culpeper, and Young's whole command could have been captured or annihilated unless it had sought safety in flight, as there was no supporting force within ten miles of it. If the Federals had thus advanced and then moved forward to Culpeper, "the expedition" would indeed have been a success and yielded fruits of which General Meade did not dream when he ordered it; for at that very time the commissary and quartermaster's trains of General Lee's army were loading with supplies at the depot in Culpeper, and these, of course, would have fallen into the hands of the Federals, thereby entailing an almost inestimable loss upon the Confederate army. The Federals were doubtless deterred from attacking more vigorously than they did and also from making any farther forward movement, by the marvelous amount of "noise" that Young's command had "kept up," and the impression thereby made that a large force confronted them. Young's bluff game had proven a perfect success, and for months afterward it was a matter of merriment among his men that they had so completely bluffed the Yankees at Brandy Station.

We will now return to that part of General Stuart's corps with which Ashton was connected, viz.: Fitzhugh Lee's division. After the Federals were driven across the Rappahannock on October 11th, as heretofore mentioned, General Fitzhugh Lee, with W. H. F. Lee's and Wickham's brigades, camped near Welford's Ford on the Hazel river that night, and on the following day moved to Fox's Mill on the Rappahannock, where he encamped for the night. On October 13th he moved by way of Warrenton to Auburn, where he had a slight engagement with a force of Federal infantry which was marching by that place. On October 14th the division marched by way of New Baltimore and Gainesville to Bristow Station, and there encamped that night. The next day it moved to Manassas, where the Federals were found deployed on the plains. Colonel Chambliss, commanding W. H. F. Lee's brigade, was ordered to advance and take possession of Mitchell's Ford on Bull Run, and this was quickly done by his dismounted sharpshooters in an impetuous charge down to the river under the immediate command of Captain Haynes, of the 9th Virginia cavalry, who was seriously wounded in the charge. On the following day Lee's brigade moved to the rear of Manassas, and about sunset it was met by a superior force of Federals.

The 9th Virginia cavalry made a gallant charge on them, in which Ashton participated, but the regiment being greatly outnumbered, was repulsed. The brigade then retired to Bristow Station, where it remained until the morning of October 17th, and then moved to Catlett's Station. On October 19th the division marched to Buckland, and arrived there in time to participate in the engagement at that place in which General Kilpatrick was so completely routed and came near losing his entire command by means of a trap which had been laid for him by Generals Fitzhugh

Lee and Stuart. Two days before, General Stuart had
marched with Hampton's division to the vicinity of Chan-
tilly, on the right flank and partly in the rear of the Federal
army, and had a skirmish with a portion of General Sedgwick's corps at Frying Pan Church. On October 18th he
retired to Gainesville and toward night moved with the
division above Haymarket for the purpose of obtaining
forage and supplies, and encamped along the roadside.
During the night he learned from his scouts that General
Kilpatrick's division of cavalry, with six pieces of artillery,
and a column of infantry in the rear, had left Fairfax
Court-House the day before and were advancing on him. On
the morning of October 19th General Stuart passed through
Gainesville and moved back toward Buckland, being closely
followed by Kilpatrick whose advance troops were engaged with one regiment of Young's brigade until the latter
reached Buckland about 10 A. M. General Stuart having
crossed Broad Run, placed his artillery and sharpshooters
in advantageous positions along that stream and awaited
the advance of General Kilpatrick, having determined to
hold him in check at that point until General Fitzhugh Lee
could come to his support, in accordance with a notification
previously given. The Federals made several desperate
efforts to force a passage across the stream, but were each
time repulsed by the Confederates. After a while they ceased
their efforts to cross the stream in General Stuart's front
and sent out forces on his flanks. About this time General
Stuart received a dispatch from General Fitzhugh Lee, who
was advancing from Auburn, stating that he was coming
to General Stuart's support and suggesting that the latter
should retire with Hampton's division toward Warrenton,
drawing the Federals after him, and that he would come in
from the direction of Auburn and attack them in the flank
and rear. General Stuart at once adopted the suggestion
and, sending word to General Lee that he would be ready
to turn upon the Federals as soon as he heard Lee's signal
guns, he retired slowly with Hampton's division until he
reached Chestnut Hill, about two miles and a half from
Warrenton. General Kilpatrick, confidently believing that
he was really driving the Confederates, walked right into

the trap thus laid for him and followed General Stuart until the latter had reached Chestnut Hill, when the sound of artillery near Buckland indicating that General Lee had arrived and begun the attack, General Stuart, turning back, pressed the Federals suddenly and vigorously in front with Gordon's brigade and on the flanks with Young's and Rosser's brigades.

This attack was at first firmly resisted by the Federals, but they were so gallantly and impetuously charged by Gordon's brigade (the 1st North Carolina cavalry leading the charge) that they soon gave way and were completely routed. General Fitzhugh Lee had come in on the Auburn pike and struck the Federals on their right flank ; Young was moving with his brigade around on their left flank to get in their rear at or near Buckland ; and Gordon, advancing on the Warrenton pike, attacked them in front, as before stated, striking the head of their column near New Baltimore. At this place General Kilpatrick narrowly escaped being captured by a member of the 1st North Carolina cavalry. Confidently believing, as before stated, that he was really driving General Stuart back with perfect ease, and apparently intrusting the further management of the movement to his subordinates, he stopped at a house in New Baltimore and ordered dinner. Before he had time to partake of the meal that was being prepared for him, his troops had been routed by General Stuart and came dashing down the Warrenton pike and on through New Baltimore as fast as their horses could carry them. Hastily leaving the house where he had hoped to enjoy an excellent dinner, General Kilpatrick mounted his horse and started for the pike to join his fleeing troopers in their pell-mell flight. The aforesaid North Carolinian happened to espy him, and at once dashed out of the pike to intercept him. This movement caused General Kilpatrick to change his course, and wheeling his horse, he galloped off in another direction rapidly followed by the North Carolinian. Being closely pressed by the latter, General Kilpatrick dashed into a garden and rode rapidly across it, his pursuer being only a short distance behind him. Indeed he was so close to the fugitive that he could easily have shot and killed him, but, knowing his rank, he had set his heart on capturing the general—therefore refrained from shooting. Just as General Kilpatrick reached the farther side of the garden, and when the North Carolinian was within a few paces of him, the horse of the latter stumbled and fell, thereby enabling the fugitive to escape.

When the Federals were attacked in front and flank, as before mentioned, they turned and fled in the utmost confusion; and then began a rapid and exciting chase such as had not before been seen during the Civil War. The routed and demoralized Federals were pursued by the Confederates at full speed through Buckland, and for miles beyond, one column fleeing toward Haymarket and the other toward Gainesville, until both had been driven behind their infantry supports, a number of the latter being killed and captured. About four hundred prisoners were captured by the Confederates, and dead and wounded Federals were scattered all along the road for miles. If General Fitzhugh Lee's attack had been delayed for a half hour, and thus given Young time to get in the rear of the Federals, General Kilpatrick's entire division would have been killed or captured. As it was, the route was complete, and the pell-mell flight of the division was afterward described by a Federal writer as presenting "the deplorable spectacle of seven thousand cavalry dashing riderless, hatless, and panic-stricken through the ranks of their infantry."

The 9th Virginia cavalry participated in the flank attack that was made by Fitzhugh Lee's division, and Ashton was among the sharpshooters who gallantly pressed the Federals on foot near New Baltimore until their ranks were completely broken, and then remounting their horses engaged in chasing the demoralized fugitives in their rapid and disorderly flight through and beyond Buckland. In this, as in previous engagements, he maintained his reputation for dash and gallantry and won the renewed admiration of his comrades and commanding officers.

This engagement, which the Confederates facetiously called "the Buckland races," terminated the brief, but brilliant campaign of Stuart's cavalry in October 1863, during which they captured between one thousand and five hundred and two thousand prisoners, and killed and wounded a great many of the Federals. On the following day the Confederate cavalry recrossed the Rappahannock and repaired to their respective camps.

Shortly thereafter the brigade to which Ashton belonged went into camp in Madison county and there remained until the latter part of November, when it and the other brigades of Lee's division moved to the vicinity of Morton's and Raccoon Fords on the Rapidan and relieved General Ewell's corps of infantry during General Meade's movement across the river lower down, which resulted in his disastrous repulse at Locust Grove and Mine Run. During Meade's movement against Lee's army, Kilpatrick's division of cavalry crossed the Rapidan two or three times at Morton's and Raccoon Fords, but was repulsed and driven back each time by Fitzhugh Lee's division. On December 2d, the division was relieved by the return of Ewell's corps, and moved back to Madison county. From there a part of the division, including the regiment to which Ashton belonged, moved to the vicinity of Charlottesville, on December 12th, for the purpose of going into winter quarters, but left there December 14th to aid in checking the raid of General Averell on the Virginia and Tennessee railroad. Owing to incorrect information given him as to Averell's movements, General Fitzhugh Lee failed to intercept or overtake him, and the command returned to camp after a week's hard riding, having marched about three hundred miles in pursuit of the enemy.

CHAPTER XIV.

Just after Ashton's regiment returned to Madison county,
he received a letter from Ruth in which she informed him
that her cousin, Bertha Gray, and Captain Carrington were
to be married on Christmas eve, and urged him to obtain
leave of absence from his command in order that he might
be present on the occasion, and also spend the following
week in Richmond. Ashton immediately made application
for leave of absence during Christmas week, and in due time
the same was granted.

This information in regard to the approaching marriage
of Carrington and Bertha naturally aroused in Ashton's
heart an intense longing for the speedy consummation of his
his own engagement with Ruth Middleton, and he was
prompted to write the latter urging that there might be a
double wedding on the occasion, in which she and he would
take prominent parts. On reflection, he decided that such a
request would be supremely selfish, and at once discarded
the thought of asking Ruth to link her fate with his, under
existing circumstances. While he knew that Bertha would
make a great sacrifice in marrying a soldier in active service,
he also knew that this sacrifice would not be so great as
that which Ruth would have to make if she should marry
him; for he was but a private soldier in the cavalry, which
was usually on the outposts of the army and liable to be
moved from place to place at any time, while Captain Carrington was an infantry officer, with more privileges and
much better pay than he enjoyed, and, moreover, would be
in a position to have his wife with him during a considerable part of the time, especially in the winter months.
Having thus in a measure stifled his longing for a speedy
marriage with Ruth, and summarily curbed his inclination
to request the same, Ashton consoled himself for his disappointment in the matter by thinking of the inestimable blessing which he enjoyed in the possession of Ruth's
love, although the time of their marriage was indefinite,
and, philosopher-like, resumed the discharge of his daily
duties with his wonted alacrity and cheerfulness, looking

forward with gladsome anticipation to his enjoyment of Ruth's companionship on the occasion of Bertha's marriage to Captain Carrington.

As Carrington has found a permanent place in our story, and we have really come to like the brave, bright, and genial fellow, and hope that the reader has done likewise, it is natural and, we trust, pardonable, that some account should be given of his movements since his return to the army at the expiration of his visit to Bertha in September.

From that time till October 9th, his regiment remained quietly in camp near the Rapidan, and he had no experiences worthy of notice. On that day, as the reader will remember, the infantry and artillery of the Confederate army marched toward Madison Court-House, and the brigade (Doles') to which Carrington belonged participated in the flank movement thus begun, but had no serious fighting to do, as General Lee failed to secure a general engagement with the Federal army. After the Confederate army returned from this movement, Doles' brigade was stationed near Kelly's Ford on the Rappahannock, and participated in the engagement at that point on November 7th, which preceded the unfortunate capture of a part of Hays' and Hoke's brigades on the north side of the river above the ford. On November 27th the brigade was actively engaged in conjunction with General Edward Johnson's division in the fight at Payne's farm near Locust Grove, where the Federals under General French were repulsed with considerable loss. The next day the brigade rejoined Rodes' division on Mine Run, and after the Federals had been repulsed all along the line and begun their retreat on December 2d, Carrington's regiment took an active part in following them up in their retreat, and nineteen of the sharpshooters of the regiment charged about three hundred Federals posted behind an embankment on the plank-road, and captured one hundred and thirty-seven of them. On November 27th in the fight at Payne's farm, this regiment, in conjunction with the 12th Georgia, rendered timely and efficient service to General G. H. Stuart's brigade. It was nearly dark, General Stuart's brigade had been engaged for some time, was hard pressed, and its extreme left about to be overpowered by superior numbers, having exhausted its ammunition, when the 4th and 12th Georgia regiments were ordered to its support. Moving forward at a double quick, they charged the Federals, drove them back and re-established the Confederate line, relieving the left of Stuart's brigade from the heavy pressure that was upon it. After this Carrington and the other members of his regiment had no heavy fighting during General Meade's farther demonstrations along Mine Run, and the Federals having crossed the Rapidan and made good their retreat, the regiment, together with the remainder of the brigade, returned to Morton's Ford and resumed the position which it had occupied when relieved a few days before by a part of General Fitzhugh Lee's division. Ashton and Carrington had thus twice been in close proximity to each other within less than a week; but, as they were not aware of the fact, they did not meet or have any communication with one another.

At this time Bertha Gray was at home, where she had gone a few days before to make preparations for her approaching marriage. She had remained in Richmond assisting Ruth in her hospital duties until the last of November, and then returned home for the purpose just mentioned. Ruth had been constantly engaged at the hospital ever since Ashton's departure to rejoin his regiment, but her duties at this time were not so taxing as when he left, as many of the soldiers who were wounded in the Gettysburg campaign had been discharged from the hospital, and, consequently, she had some leisure time every day. During the preceding month, Belle Preston spent a week with her, and both girls derived much pleasure from the visit. Belle was at once impressed by the fact that Ruth was much brighter and happier than when the latter visited her the preceding summer, and having expressed her gratification at this change, Ruth was led to explain its cause. As the girls had been intimate friends at school and there formed an enduring attachment for each other, the utmost confidence now existed between them, and hence Ruth did not hesitate to relate the sad experience which she had before meeting Belle in the summer, and the subsequent events that had wrought such a complete change in her appearance and feelings. She told Belle of her love for Ashton, her long settled opinion that he was dead, the singular **manner** in which she had discovered her mistake as to his supposed death, their subsequent engagement, and the great happiness that she experienced in loving and being loved by him. On being asked by Belle at what time she expected to marry him, Ruth stated that she did not expect to marry him until the close of the war, as, from her knowledge of his character, she was satisfied that he would consider it selfish for him to request an earlier consummation of their engagement, and hence would not do **so**. Having thus alluded to Ashton's character, **Ruth was** thereby led to give a description of the same, and as the description was based on a thorough knowledge of her subject and somewhat influenced by her love, **it** impressed **Belle** with the idea that Ruth's lover was a remarkable and exceptional man, and caused her to express an earnest desire to meet and know him. Ruth informed her that she would soon have an opportunity for gratifying this desire, stating that Bertha wished her to attend her marriage and that Ashton would be present on the occasion.

It had been arranged that the marriage should occur in Richmond, and Mrs. Slaughter's family were looking forward with pleasurable anticipations to the coming event, and making suitable preparations for the same. While Ruth rejoiced with Bertha in the happiness which she had found in Carrington's love, she was at times saddened by the thought that her cousin's approaching marriage would terminate their almost lifelong companionship and thereby make her own life for awhile a comparatively lonely one. Hence **she** looked forward to that event with mingled emotions of pleasure and pain. The intervening time between the close **of** Belle Preston's visit and Bertha's return to Richmond was spent by Ruth in the customary discharge of her hospital duties and in aiding the Slaughters in the preparations that were being made for Bertha's marriage. As before stated, the marriage was to occur on Christmas eve, and Bertha arrived in Richmond a few days before that time. Carrington, Ashton and Belle, and Lieutenant Preston reached the city on December 23d, and, in accordance with an arrangement previously made, all of them repaired to Mrs. Slaughter's residence that evening. Lieutenant Harris of the——artillery, who, as the reader will remember, introduced Sergeant Paul to the ladies at Mrs. Slaughter's, was also present. When it was discovered that Sergeant Paul was an impostor and spy, Kate Slaughter, in her impulsive way, became very indignant and was greatly displeased with Lieutenant Harris for having brought Paul to the house, and scolded him for what she termed his lack of prudence in the matter; but on reflection she recognized how naturally the mistake had been made by Harris and promptly apologized for her hasty condemnation of his conduct, and they were now good friends.

In view of the occasion that had called them together and the pleasant relations which existed between them, it is doubtful as to whether a happier party could have been found within the bounds of the Southern Confederacy than was assembled that evening at Mrs. Slaughter's residence. Their surroundings, too, were such as to inspire cheerfulness and gayety; for the house was brilliantly lighted, blazing fires were burning in the grates, and the rooms were tastefully decorated with branches of holly and sprigs of mistletoe, whose fresh green leaves, together with numerous vases of beautiful flowers in various parts of the house, presented a gladsome picture, suggestive of sweet springtime, and in delightful contrast with the snow-clad world without, where the wintry winds were shrilly whistling through the shivering branches of the leafless trees. This joyous picture had its counterpart in the breasts of those who were delightedly feasting their eyes upon its animating beauties, for in the midst of cold and dreary winter the coming Christmas-tide and the occasion which called them together, had brought warm and gladsome springtime to their hearts. Forgetting for the time the scenes of strife and bloodshed on the battle-fields, and the privations and hardships of camp life which some of them had but recently left, and with which all were more or less familiar, they gave themselves entirely up to the enjoyment of the occasion.

For a time the conversation was general and the members of the party remained together engaged in lively chat and merry jest; but after awhile the law of affinity began its operation, and soon they were sitting apart or promenading in pairs, as follows: Ashton with Ruth, Carrington with Bertha, Lieutenant Preston with Kate Slaughter, and Lieutenant Harris with Belle Preston.

Although Lieutenant Harris had known Belle only a short time, having formed her acquaintance during her visit to Ruth the preceding month, he was charmed with her girlish impulsiveness and unaffected warm-heartedness, frank and sunny disposition, and bright and sprightly intellect, and had become deeply interested in her. Indeed it was apparent to those who witnessed the devoted air which marked his conduct toward her, and the absorbing interest with which he talked to her, that if he had not already succumbed to the power of the divine passion, he was in a fair way of yielding to its sway. The same was also true as to the effect that had been produced on Lieutenant Preston by the many virtues of high-spirited, headstrong, and yet charming Kate Slaughter, whose acquaintance he had assiduously cultivated since meeting her the preceding summer. As the conversations of the several couples, though deeply interesting to the parties therein, would not, perhaps, entertain the reader, we refrain from repeating them.

After partaking of a delicious supper and spending an hour or two in general conversation, interspersed with some of Ruth's soul-enchanting songs, the party dispersed for the night, looking forward with delightful anticipations to their reunion at the wedding on the following evening. The next morning dawned clear and bright, and Bertha, accepting this as a favorable omen, felt that no expectant bride could ask for a more auspicious wedding-day than that which had been vouchsafed to her.

The marriage was to occur at 8 o'clock P. M., at Mrs. Slaughter's residence, and only those who were gathered there the preceding evening and the officiating clergyman were to be present. Shortly before that time the entire wedding party had assembled, and at the appointed hour Carrington and Bertha were duly united in the holy bonds of matrimony. After the congratulations and good wishes of the assembled guests had been extended to the happy pair, the party repaired to the dining-room and partook of a sumptuous repast, the savory substantials and delicious delicacies of which would have satisfied the most exacting taste of a confirmed epicure. It is needless to say that they did full justice to the wedding supper, and at its close were in that proverbially happy frame of mind which a delicious feast **invariably produces. The** evening passed pleasantly and **swiftly by, and at its** close it was agreed that the party should go sleigh-riding on the morrow. Hence, shortly after breakfast, the next morning, the entire wedding **party** were swiftly gliding over the snow-clad streets of the city **on** their way to the country. They drove out toward Meadow Bridge on the Chickahominy river, passing by and examining the fortifications north of the city and catching a glimpse of the —— artillery, **with** which Lieutenant Preston was connected. Some of the company, recognizing Preston, waved their caps and in hearty tones wished **the party a merry** Christmas. They were certainly **having a** merry Christmas, and the sweet-toned sleigh-bells making glad music on the clear, crisp air, found an echo, as it were, in the still sweeter joy-bells that were softly ringing in their happy hearts. After crossing the Chickahominy at **Meadow** Bridge, the party drove out beyond Mechanicsville, **and** after passing over a part of the ground where the fierce and bloody battle of June 26, 1862, was fought, returned to Richmond by the Mechanicsville turnpike. During the remainder of the Christmas holidays the members of the wedding party were together every day, and the time was **passed in a round of** gayeties that rendered it one of the **happiest weeks** of their lives. With its close the parting **hour** drew nigh, and their hearts were saddened at thought **of the separation that** must ensue with the coming **of the New Year.**

New Year's day dawned fair and bright, and shortly after breakfast all of the party were assembled at Mrs. Slaughter's residence for the purpose of bidding each other good-bye. The beauty and brightness of the day and the feeling of joyousness which the New Year invariably inspires, tended to counteract the natural depression which they felt in view of their approaching separation, and they managed to keep up a show of cheerfulness to the last. As Carrington's regiment was in winter quarters, and not expected to move until the opening of the spring campaign, it was arranged that his **wife should** return with **him,** and he had secured a pleasant boarding-house for her **near** the encampment of the regiment. At last the parting hour arrived and the parties separated after bidding each other an affectionate good-bye.

Belle Preston went to her home in Lexington, and Lieutenants Preston and Harris returned to their respective commands. Carrington and Bertha traveled by rail to Rapidan Station, and from that point by a hired conveyance to their temporary home near Morton's Ford.

Ashton had accompanied them as far as Gordonsville and, **having** there bidden them good-bye, proceeded **to** Charlottesville. **On reaching** Charlottesville he found **his horse** awaiting him, in accordance with instructions previously given in regard to the matter, and from there he rode out to the encampment of his regiment. As he rode along **he** lived over in imagination the happy hours **recently spent** with Ruth, and intensely longed for **the time when he could** claim her **as his wife. As he was still fixed** in his purpose **not to request the appointment of this time until** the close of the war, he had no hope of its speedy arrival, for the fall of Vicksburg and other reverses **to the** Confederate army in the Southwest during the preceding summer and fall, and **the** unsuccessful issue of the Gettysburg campaign so greatly encouraged the North in the prosecution of the war that an indefinite continuation of hostilities was probable. **In view of** this fact, and **the** poorly clad and half-starved condition **of** General Lee's army, Ashton regarded **the** outlook as exceedingly gloomy, and for the moment was greatly depressed. However, he soon shook off this feeling of despondency and rode into camp that evening in a comparatively cheerful frame of mind, ready for the prompt and faithful discharge of any duty that might be **as**signed him.

When Ashton left Richmond, Ruth keenly felt the pangs of their separation and was naturally heavy-hearted for several days after his departure. But she did not let this feeling of depression deter her from, or unfit her for her work, and resumed her labors at the hospital with unabated interest and efficiency.

We have alluded to the condition of the Confederate army in Virginia, and will farther state that at this time it was deplorable, as the soldiers were daily experiencing the greatest hardships and suffering. They did not have sufficient clothing to protect them against the cold and inclement weather, and, the meager supply of food received by them being entirely inadequate to meet the demands of nature, many of them were half-starved. The horses in both the cavalry and artillery also suffered greatly for lack of food, and many of them were entirely unfit for service.

Some time before this Victor Hugo's masterpiece in literature, "*Les Miserables*," had found its way into the army and was extensively read by the soldiers. An Anglicized pronunciation of the title so forcibly suggested and aptly described the wretched condition of the troops, that they promptly and pertinently dubbed themselves "Lee's Miserables," and both the name and the wretchedness which it implied clung to them during the remainder of the war.

The deplorable state of affairs to which we have referred, naturally caused a number of desertions from the army, but, to the honor of that peerless army be it said, nearly all of the troops bore their hardships and sufferings with uncomplaining fortitude and displayed a degree of patriotic devotion and exalted heroism that has never been equaled in the annals of war. The winter passed by without any general or important engagement between the two armies; but the Federals made two efforts to capture Richmond by means of raiding parties. The first effort was made under the direction of General B. F. Butler, who was in command of the Federal forces on the Peninsula. His plan was to send a raiding party of cavalry up the Peninsula to surprise Richmond, which he believed was practically defenseless; and in order to cover this movement and thereby increase the chances of its success, the Federal army on the Rapidan was to make a demonstration against General Lee's army lying south of that stream. The Federal raiding party, under General Wistar, marched up the Peninsula and reached Bot-

tom's bridge on the Chickahominy on February 6th, 1864,
but, **finding** that the road to Richmond was strongly
guarded, advanced no farther, and returned from the expedition without having accomplished anything by the movement. In pursuance of the plan before mentioned, **the**
Federal army on February 7th made a demonstration against
General Lee's army along the lower **fords** of the Rapidan,
failed to accomplish anything by the movement, **and lost**
several hundred men.

A second and more serious attempt to capture **the** Confederate Capital was made about three weeks after the first
had failed. **At** that time an expedition consisting of four
thousand cavalry was organized and equipped with great
care for the purpose of **capturing the** city and releasing
the Federal prisoners who were confined there. General Kil-
patrick had command of the expedition, and an important
part in the same was assigned to Colonel Ulric Dahlgren, a
young officer who had previously won distinction by his
skill and daring. The plan marked out for the movement
was as follows:

A column under **General Custer was to advance on Char-**
lottesville for the purpose of **drawing attention from the**
main body, which was to march to Beaver Dam Station on
the Virginia Central **railroad. On arriving at Beaver Dam**
Station, the main column **was to be divided, a part of the**
troops, under **General Kilpatrick, moving on Richmond**
along the north bank of the James river, and **the remain-**
der, under Colonel Dahlgren, crossing to the **south side of**
the stream, were to march down the right bank of **the same,**
release the prisoners at Belle Isle, **recross the river, burn**
the bridges, and rejoin Kilpatrick in the city, destroy the
city and **kill** President Davis **and his cabinet.** The movement was **begun** on February 28th, and General Custer
attempted to carry out the part assigned to him by marching toward Charlottesville, but on arriving in the vicinity
of the place, he **was** repulsed **and driven back by** Stuart's
Horse artillery and at once retreated to **Madison** Court-
house. On reaching Beaver Dam Station, the main column
of the Federals divided, and Kilpatrick, with the greater
part of the same, marched toward Richmond, while Dahlgren

with five hundred picked men, moved toward the James river. Kilpatrick approached Richmond by the Brook turnpike, but seemingly made no real effort to capture the city, and without much show of fighting, changed his course and marched down the Peninsula. Dahlgren reached the James river, but found that it could not be forded, and moved toward Richmond on the Westham plank-road, moving parallel with that stream, expecting to join Kilpatrick near the city. He arrived within four miles of Richmond on the night of March 1st, only a short time after Kilpatrick's retreat, and was met by a small force of department clerks and laborers in the government workshops that had been hastily collected and armed to aid in defending the city. Colonel Dahlgren, with his five hundred picked horsemen, was perfectly confident that he could easily disperse the small force opposing him and ordered his men to charge "the militia." The charge was made, but the result was very disappointing to the over-confident officer who ordered it, for "the militia" boldly stood their ground and received **the charge** with a well-directed fire which emptied about a dozen saddles, repulsed the raiders and scattered them in confusion. Discomfited by this bold and vigorous reception, Dahlgren did not renew his attack on the Confederates, but moved off around the city for the purpose of reaching the road leading down the Peninsula in order that he might escape by that route, as he now realized that the expedition had failed, and that he was in imminent danger of capture. A part of his command succeeded in making their escape by that route, but during his retreat Dahlgren and about one hundred of his men became separated from the rest of the command, and on the night of March 3d rode up to the camp of a detachment of **the** 24th Virginia cavalry and some horse-guards and militia who were on the watch for them. As soon as Dahlgren saw the Confederates he ordered them **to** surrender, but instead of doing this they poured a volley into his ranks, killing him instantly, and routing his command, which fled in confusion, leaving their dead com**mander** behind them. These fugitives were captured the next day, and thus terminated a well-planned but poorly executed raid which threatened the capture and destruction of

Richmond. If the Federals had reached Richmond on the morning of March 1st, it would have been captured and destroyed, as there was then no sufficient force at hand to prevent their entrance into the city.

On Colonel Dahlgren's person were found an address to his command, some special orders, and his private note-book, from the contents of which it clearly appeared that the murderous and incendiary design of killing President Davis and his cabinet and burning the Confederate Capital had been deliberately planned, and that ample preparations for its execution had been made before the raid began.

Copies of these documents were published in the Richmond newspapers and their authenticity was subsequently denied by Colonel Dahlgren's father and others; but the denial was not sustained by proof, and the genuineness of the papers was fully established by a report from General Fitzhugh Lee, who personally delivered them to the War Department, and also by a lengthy statement of Edward W. Halback, a school-teacher, giving a full account of the circumstances under which Colonel Dahlgren was killed, and how, immediately after his death, the papers were taken from his person by William Littlepage, one of Mr. Halback's pupils, about thirteen years of age. Moreover, circumstantial evidence of Colonel Dahlgren's incendiary design is furnished by a communication of his addressed to Major-general Hooker, May 23d, 1863, in which he asks permission to prepare and attempt a cavalry expedition similar to the one we have described, and says: "The object of the expedition would be to destroy everything along the route, and especially on the south side of the James river, and attempt to enter Richmond and Petersburg. If the general proposition should meet with your approval, I will submit more minute details."

14

CHAPTER XV.

On May 4th, 1864, General U. S. Grant crossed the Rapidan with the Federal army and began a movement that resulted in a series of the severest and bloodiest battles of the war. Having already devoted so much space to descriptions of the various operations of the commands to which Ashton and Carrington respectively belonged, we will refrain from giving a detailed account of the series of engagements in which they participated during General Grant's movement from the Rapidan to the James, in which, with an army of one hundred and forty-eight thousand men that was constantly being recruited and reinforced, he was repeatedly repulsed by General Lee with an army of originally about sixty thousand men which was gradually being decreased, and received but few recruits or reinforcements. In this movement General Grant lost in killed, wounded, and captured fifty-four thousand nine hundred and twenty-six men without accomplishing his purpose of getting between General Lee's army and Richmond, and was finally forced to transfer his army to the south side of the James and take a position which he could have occupied with scarcely the firing of a gun; and by November 1st, 1864, when he suspended for a time active operations in front of Richmond and Petersburg, his loss had reached the enormous aggregate of eighty-eight thousand three hundred and eighty-seven men. While General Grant, during this movement, was constantly endeavoring to flank General Lee and get between him and Richmond, it is true that this was not his sole or ultimate object; for his purpose, as he has expressed it, was not only "to beat Lee's army, if possible, north of Richmond, then, after destroying his communication north of the James, to transfer the army to the south side and besiege Lee in Richmond, or follow him south if he should retreat," but also "to hammer continuously against the armed forces of the enemy and his resources, until, by mere attrition, if in no other way, there should be nothing left to him but submission." Although General Grant did not succeed in his first object of "beating **Lee north of** Richmond," being constantly repulsed in every engagement from the Rapidan to the James, and sacrificed more than a third of the army with which he started, in transferring it to the **south** side of the James and placing it in a position to "besiege Lee in Richmond," yet the hammering process which he had inaugurated resulted in incalculable **and** irreparable injury to the Confederate cause; for much valuable property and army stores were destroyed, and the places of the Confederate soldiers who were killed, wounded and captured by the Federals could not be filled. Indeed, it was by means of this hammering process and as the result **of "mere** attrition" that the hitherto invincible army of Northern Virginia was ultimately vanquished, and it required **the** constant efforts of **almost four times** its numbers for nearly twelve months to accomplish this result.

Many gallant men and officers of General Lee's army lost their lives during the campaign from the Rapidan to **the** James, and among the latter was General J. E. B. Stuart, the prince of cavaliers, **who was mortally wounded on** May 11th, 1864, at Yellow Tavern while engaged in checking General P. H. Sheridan's raid on the Virginia Central railroad and the Richmond, Fredericksburg, and Potomac railroad. It is supposed that he was shot by John A. Huff, of Company E, 5th Michigan cavalry and formerly of Berdan's sharpshooters, who was himself mortally wounded shortly afterward at Haw's Shop. This regiment and others of Custer's brigade were severely punished by General Hampton at Haw's Shop, May 28th, and also defeated by Hampton at Trevilian Station, June 11th; but the destruction of Custer's entire brigade would by no **means have** compensated the Confederacy for the loss of its great cavalry commander. **It is** true that there **was** a worthy successor to the illustrious and lamented Stuart, and the command **of** the cavalry corps **was** soon given to General Wade Hamp**ton,** who was, in all that constitutes the ideal soldier and commander, the peer of his predecessor, but the Confederacy had urgent need for the services of both of these matchless **men,** and the **loss of** General Stuart was irreparable.

After General Grant's army had **reached** the James **river** and commenced crossing it at Wilcox's Landing on **June** 14th, he at once proceeded to Bermuda Hundred and gave General B. F. Butler orders for the immediate capture **of** Petersburg, knowing that the possession of this place by his army would force General Lee to abandon Richmond. In **accordance with the instructions** given by General Grant, General W. F. Smith, commanding the 18th army **corps, a** division of negro troops under General Hinks and a **division** of cavalry under General Kautz, was ordered to march **that** night to Petersburg and capture the city. General **Smith** began his march as directed, and arrived in front of **the Confederate pickets near Petersburg before** daylight the next morning, but made no assault on the main lines until late in the afternoon. The city was practically defenseless **against the force that then assailed it, the Confederate** force consisting of only a part of General Wise's brigade, the militia of Petersburg and four batteries of artillery; but the gallant defense made by **this little band** doubtless caused General Smith to suppose that the garrison was a large one. The Federals made three assaults which **were** repulsed, but the fourth assault was successful and by **dark the entire line of outer works for a distance of more than two miles had** been captured. General Hancock's corps arrived just after dark and, although he outranked General Smith, he waived this fact and offered the services of his troops to the latter, believing that General Smith best understood the situation of affairs and what disposition should be made of the troops under the circumstances. If General Smith had now seized the opportunity offered for so doing, he could easily have entered the city and taken possession of it. But he failed to do this, merely used the fresh troops of General Hancock to relieve a part of his **own** in the captured works and awaited the arrival of General Grant, who was marching on Petersburg with the rest of his army. General Grant arrived the next morning, and by his orders an attack was made at 6 o'clock that afternoon by three corps of his army, and the fighting continued all **night**, resulting in the capture of one line **of** works; but **General Lee had, in the meantime, succeeded** in reinforcing

the troops who were defending the city, and the further
advance of the Federals was completely checked. He arrived there that night with the greater part of his army
and soon recaptured the line of works that had been taken,
and drove the Federals back to their original line. They renewed the attack on June 17th, and the entire day was spent
in heavy fighting, the Confederates constantly repulsing the
repeated assaults that were made on their works. General
Grant's entire army having arrived, he ordered a general
attack on the morning of June 18th; but his opportunity
for a successful assault had passed, for General Lee had
constructed a strong interior line of works immediately
around the city, and on the next morning withdrew from
his former line to this one, which proved to be impregnable.
Having ascertained that the works which he expected to
assail were abandoned, General Grant ordered an assault
upon General Lee's new line, and the attack was made
about noon by a part of the 2d corps and promptly repulsed. After that attacks were successively made by the
2d, 5th, and 9th corps of Grant's army, and each attack
was repulsed with heavy loss to the Federals. General
Grant now realized that it would be impossible for him to
capture Petersburg by a direct assault, and hence he
determined to besiege the city, and his army proceeded to
envelop it toward the South Side railroad as far as possible without attacking the Confederate fortifications. This
knowledge had been obtained by General Grant at immense
cost, for in the several assaults made on the Confederate
fortifications he had lost nine thousand six hundred and
sixty-five men, as shown by the Federal official reports.

We refrain from a description of the memorable siege
which was thus begun and continued from June 18th, 1864,
to April 2d, 1865, during which period General Lee with a
poorly clad, half-starved, and defectively armed force of
less than forty thousand troops successfully held a line forty
miles in length against a well clothed, well fed, and perfectly armed force of more than three times their numbers.
The marvelously successful resistance made by this band of
heroes to the constantly recurring assaults of the myriad
hosts assailing them, and their daily deeds of valor have

never been equaled in the history of the world. Even to the last General Grant's powerful army failed to carry the Confederate works by assault and General Lee finally abandoned them on the night of April 2d, 1865, only because of the fact that General Grant had moved his army to a point from which he could flank the Confederate army on its right and reach its rear, unless General Lee retreated from Petersburg and Richmond.

We will now return to Carrington and Ashton and give some account of the movements, during the siege of Richmond and Petersburg, of the commands to which they respectively belonged. Carrington's regiment had distinguished itself in the several battles in the Wilderness and at Spottsylvania Court-house, and also in the other engagements occurring during General Grant's movement from the Rapidan to the James. It was by a sharpshooter of this regiment that General Grant's best corps commander, General John Sedgwick, was killed on May 9th, 1864, near Spottsylvania Court-house.

Immediately after General Grant reached the James a large Federal force under General David Hunter began a movement on Lynchburg, and in order to meet this movement it became necessary for General Lee to detach a part of his army. Ewell's corps, to which Carrington's regiment belonged, was detached for this purpose, and General Jubal A. Early was placed in command of the same, as General R. S. Ewell was at the time unfitted for active service in consequence of wounds which he had previously received.

General Early reached Lynchburg June 17th and the next day met and repulsed an attack made by General Hunter on the Confederate works around the place. Hunter retreated the following day and was so closely pressed by Early that he did not return by way of the Valley but took a more circuitous route through Western Virginia. This left the Valley of Virginia comparatively clear of Federal troops and enabled General Early to carry out instructions previously received from General Lee to cross the Potomac and threaten Washington. Hunter retreated toward Lewisburg, and Early followed and harassed the fleeing Federals until they had passed through Botetourt county, some of the

Confederate cavalry pursuing them as far as Newcastle. Early then moved to the vicinity of Staunton and on June 28th started down the Valley on his contemplated expedition **across** the border.

Thus Carrington was again to pass over much of the ground that he had traveled about a year before on the march to Pennsylvania, and he naturally thought of the hardships and dangers to which he and his fellow-soldiers had been exposed during that disastrous campaign. The thought of these, however, did not lessen his interest in or dampen his ardor for the cause which he had espoused, and although he felt that the expedition on which General Early had started would not, on account of his small force, accomplish any great results in the enemy's country and might terminate in disaster, yet he knew that an invasion **of** Maryland would cause the detachment of troops from General Grant's army to meet it, and thus materially aid and greatly relieve the beleaguered Confederate army at Richmond and Petersburg, and in order to accomplish this desirable result he was willing to endure any hardship and encounter any danger. General Early marched rapidly down the Valley and by July 3d had captured Martinsburg, a large quantity of army stores, and a number of prisoners and on the next day captured Bolivar Heights, and that night the Federals evacuated Harper's Ferry. On the following day General Early crossed the Potomac into Maryland and on July 8th began his movement on Washington. On the **next** day, after driving the enemy's pickets through Frederick City toward Monocacy Junction, General Early attacked and completely routed the Federals on the Monocacy river, where they occupied two block-houses and a strong line of earthworks. On July 10th the Federals retreated toward Baltimore, and the Confederates, after destroying the iron bridge across the Monocacy and the block-houses at Monocacy Junction, continued their march toward Washington. On July 11th the division to which Carrington belonged (Rodes') advanced to the border of the District of Columbia, engaged the Federal skirmishers and drove them into the fortifications of Washington. General Early found the Federal fortifications exceedingly strong and too fully manned to justify an assault upon them with his small force, and hence refrained from making such an assault and encamped that day in the vicinity of Silver Spring.

McCausland's brigade of cavalry advanced into the **Dis**trict of Columbia by the Georgetown road and engaged the Federals near Tennallytown, about three miles from Washington, and at the same time Colonel Mosby with his **command made** a demonstration at Chain Bridge on the Virginia side of the Potomac. General Early spent July 12th in front of Washington, and during that day **Carring**ton's regiment took part in a heavy skirmish with the enemy on the Seventh street turnpike. That night General Early began to retire from before Washington, continued his backward movement the next day, recrossed the Potomac on July 14th, and slowly retired up the Valley toward Strasburg, reaching that place July 22d, after having had several skirmishes with the Federals who had cautiously followed his retiring army. The movement on Washington caused great excitement in the North; and it was generally believed that Early would capture the city. This he would doubtless have done if the troops defending Washington had not been promptly and heavily reinforced by General **Grant, who sent to** their relief the 6th corps from the armies besieging Richmond and Petersburg, and the 19th corps which had just arrived in Hampton Roads from the Gulf Department. On July 24th General Early began another movement toward the border, and by the 29th had driven the Federal forces in the Shenandoah Valley across the Potomac, and on the following day McCausland's brigade of cavalry made a raid into Pennsylvania and burned the town of Chambersburg in retaliation for the repeated outrages of the Federal troops in Virginia. In consequence of this movement, General Grant greatly increased the forces against which General Early had been operating, by adding to them the 6th and 19th corps and Torbert's and Wilson's divisons of cavalry which were detached from the army of the Potomac, and on August 7th General P. H. Sheridan was placed in command of the army thus constituted, and consisting of at least forty thousand men. To oppose this

large army General Early had only about eight thousand
and five hundred infantry, less than three thousand cavalry,
and thirty-six pieces of artillery, and hence about the middle of August he was forced to retreat up the Valley to
Fisher's Hill. General Anderson, with Kershaw's division
of infantry and Fitzhugh Lee's division of cavalry, coming
to the assistance of General Early, August 17th, the two
Confederate columns advanced on the Federals, drove them
back through Winchester and, pursuing them the following
day, forced them to withdraw to Harper's Ferry and Maryland Heights.

On September 15th General Anderson started to Culpeper
Court-house with Kershaw's division, leaving General Early
near Winchester with his original small force to oppose
General Sheridan's large army, which at the time was
between Charlestown and Berryville and occupied a favora-
ble position for a successful attack on the Confederate
forces in the event that General Early should make any disposition of his troops that would invite an attack. This
he did by committing the blunder of posting Ramseur's
division of infantry and Wickham's division **of cavalry at**
Winchester, Breckinridge's division of infantry, and Lomax's
division of cavalry at Stephenson's Depot, about five miles
from Winchester, and marching with Rodes' and Gordon's
divisions to Martinsburg for the purpose of destroying the
Baltimore and Ohio railroad, thus scattering his forces over
twenty miles of territory and greatly hazarding their
destruction in detail if attacked by the largely superior
forces of his enemy. About this time General Grant came
from City Point to Charlestown to confer with General
Sheridan as to whether an attack should be made on General Early's forces, and after ascertaining their widely
scattered condition he at once ordered the attack. It was
made at daylight on September 19th, and at that time
General Early was returning from his expedition to Martinsburg, but had not reached Winchester, Gordon's division
being twelve miles away at Bunker Hill, and Rodes' division being at Stephenson's Depot, where it had arrived the
night before on its way back from Martinsburg. The
attack was made by the 6th corps and Wilson's division of

cavalry and was met by Ramseur's division consisting of
about fifteen hundred men, and Wickham's division of
cavalry consisting of about the same number of men; and
this little band of heroes bravely held their ground against
sixteen thousand infantry and twenty-four pieces of artillery
and three thousand cavalry, successfully resisting for
hours the repeated attacks of the Federals, and holding the
latter in check until the arrival of General Early with
Rodes' division. Immediately thereafter Gordon's division
arrived, and at this time the Federals had massed a heavy
force on Ramseur's left and were pressing forward for the
purpose of overwhelming him. General Early at once
attacked the advancing columns with Rodes' and Gordon's
division and rapidly drove them back with great slaughter.

The charge made by Rodes' division was led by General Rodes in person, and as Carrington advanced with
his company to the attack of the Federals, he marked with
pride and enthusiasm the fervid zeal and reckless daring of
his brave commander, gallantly leading his troops against
at least three times their number. While thus leading them
he was killed, and his loss was deeply mourned, not only by
his own division, but also by the entire army. The Federals
in front of General Early made no further attack for some
time, but in the afternoon a heavy force of cavalry
advanced on his left flank from the direction of Charlestown by way of Brucetown and Stephenson's Depot, and
although this force was checked by General Breckinridge's
division, yet as soon as the firing was heard from this
direction, which was in rear of Early's left flank, the infantry all along the line began to fall back and the Federal
infantry again renewed their attack. This was repulsed by
General Early and he could still have remained master of
the field if he had only had sufficient cavalry to check the
progress of the overwhelming force of Federal cavalry
that was pressing toward his rear; but as he lacked this
force the Federal cavalry turned his left flank and his men
again began to give way and he was forced to retire
through Winchester. He promptly formed line of battle
near the town, reorganized his army and deliberately re-

tired to Newtown, and on the following day fell back to Fisher's Hill.

The Federals claimed that in the battle of Winchester they won a great victory, but if the comparative losses of the two armies be made a test of the truthfulness of this claim it will be found groundless; for the official reports of the casualties on both sides show that the Federal loss in killed and wounded was four thousand six hundred and eighty, and that of the Confederates was one thousand seven hundred and seven. On September 22d General Early was flanked in his position at Fisher's Hill and compelled to retreat up the Valley with the loss of twenty-four killed, one hundred and ninety-four wounded, and several hundred prisoners, and twelve pieces of artillery. He had no further engagements of importance with the Federals until the morning of October 19th, when, after a long and arduous flank movement during the preceding night by Gordon's, Ramseur's (formerly Rodes'), and Pegram's divisions, under the immediate command of General Gordon, the rear of the Federal army on Cedar Creek was reached, and, by a simultaneous attack by Gordon's forces in the rear and Kershaw's division in front, the 8th and 19th corps of Sheridan's army were completely routed and one thousand and three hundred prisoners and eighteen pieces of artillery captured. The 6th corps was shortly afterward attacked and, after making some resistance, fell back beyond Middletown. The successful movement thus begun would soon have terminated in a glorious victory but for the inexcusable and insubordinate conduct of many of the Confederates, who abandoned the pursuit of the routed Federals and stopped to plunder their captured camp. General H. G. Wright was in command of the Federals, on account of the temporary absence of General Sheridan, and after retreating a short distance beyond Middletown he rallied his men, re-formed his line, and awaited the expected advance of General Early. The advance was not made, as General Early's ranks had been so depleted by the absence of the camp plunderers that his force at the front was insufficient to authorize an attack. About this time General Sheridan arrived on the field and, after waiting some time

for General Early to attack him and finding that he did not
advance, put his army in motion to attack the Confederates
and regain his captured camp.

The attack was at first gallantly met and the force in
front of the division to which Carrington belonged (now
Ramseur's) was driven back, but subsequently Gordon's
division, on the left, gave way and then Kershaw's and
Ramseur's divisions also gave way through fear of being
flanked when they perceived Gordon's line falling back.
Carrington, in common with other officers who had kept
their wits about them, endeavored to check their retreating
troops and some of them were rallied and made another
stand against the Federals. However, it was only temporary, for soon the left again gave way, the brave and gallant Ramseur was shot down while courageously commanding his division, and the entire command became
demoralized and precipitately retreated in a disorderly and
panic-stricken manner, heedless of threats and deaf to
entreaties that were earnestly made by their officers. Although Sheridan did not follow with his infantry, and the
organized efforts of five hundred men would have saved
the captured artillery, wagons, and ambulances of the Federals and Early's own guns, which had all been carried
across Cedar Creek, yet the Confederate troops were so
completely demoralized and panic-stricken that a small
force of Federal cavalry crossed the creek without opposition, and was allowed to pass through the Confederate
troops and the retiring train upon the pike, tear up a bridge
in front of the latter and thus capture the greater part of
the artillery and a number of ordnance and medical wagons and ambulances. The glorious victory of the morning
had been converted into an inglorious disaster in the after
noon by the lack of discipline and the cupidity of the Confederates, which caused them to abandon the results of
their signal success at the outset, and their subsequent
strange and causeless panic when the Federals returned to
attack them. That this panic was causeless is shown by
the fact that when it began the Confederate loss in killed,
wounded and prisoners had been exceedingly small, and at
the close of the engagement amounted to only about two

thousand men, while that of the Federals was five thousand six hundred and sixty-five men.

This battle practically terminated **Early's operations in** the Valley, which Sheridan's barbarities, as we have before stated, had rendered desolate, and about two months afterward the remnants of Ewell's old corps, under General Gordon, returned to the army of Northern Virginia and rejoined their former comrades-in-arms in the trenches around Petersburg. There Carrington did his full duty during the protracted siege, gallantly led his company in Gordon's brilliant assault upon and capture of Fort Steadman **on March** 5th, 1865, where his new brigade commander, General Philip Cook, was wounded, cheerfully and heroically shared with his men the hardships and dangers of General Lee's subsequent retreat, and bravely led the few survivors of his company in Gordon's final charge upon the Federal lines, just before General Lee's surrender, in which the last piece of artillery taken by the army of Northern Virginia was captured by Cook's brigade, and it was the battle-scarred flag of the regiment to which Carrington belonged that was planted upon the captured gun.

Immediately after General Lee's **surrender,** Carrington hastened to Richmond to rejoin his wife, who had been staying with Ruth Middleton during the siege. The latter had remained at her post in the discharge of her hospital duties ever since the bridal party left her on January 1st, 1864, **and** many Confederate soldiers who were wounded in the trenches in front of Richmond and Petersburg remembered long afterward with warmest gratitude the cheering smile and kindly attention of the pure and noble Georgia girl who, like an angel of mercy, hovered around their bedsides, ministered to their necessities, and did all within her power to restore them **to** health and strength. She did not leave her post when the city was evacuated and, while thousands of terror-stricken citizens were hastily fleeing from the abandoned capital, which was partly in flames, and the streets were thronged with Federal soldiers, and drunken and dangerous mobs, wild with want and bent on plunder, she remained behind to minister to the sick and wounded Confederates in the hospital where she had begun her noble and patriotic work.

CHAPTER XVI.

Some time after the last mentioned **operations of the**
brigade to which Ashton belonged, its former commander,
General W. H. F. Lee, was made a major-general and **com-**
manded a division of cavalry when the campaign opened in
May 1864, and General John R. Chambliss, Jr., was in command of the brigade. This brigade participated in the fight
at Todd's Tavern, May 7th, the engagement at Spottsylvania, May 12th, and in other engagements during General
Grant's movement from the Rapidan to the James, **and**
hence Ashton was frequently subjected to the hardships
and peril of that exceptionally severe campaign.

On June 17th General R. E. Lee ordered the brigade to
operate with General Wade Hampton who had just de-
feated an aggressive movement of General P. H. Sheridan's
cavalry on Gordonsville and Charlottesville, General Sheridan's object having been to destroy **the Virginia railroad**
from Trevilian Station to Louisa Court-house **and from**
Cobham Station to Charlottesville, unite with General Hunter in his attack on Lynchburg (the successful repulse of
which by General Early has been previously mentioned) and
then aid Hunter in reaching General Grant's army. At the
time the brigade reached General **Hampton, General Sheri-**
dan had retreated to the White House and started with his
command and a large **wagon train to cross the** James and
join General Grant's army. **Chambliss' brigade** had a skirmish with a portion of Sheridan's command at the Forge
Bridges on the Chickahominy June 23d, and on the following day that brigade and the brigade of General Martin **W.**
Gary displayed great gallantry in an engagement which
General Hampton had with Gregg's division at Saint
Mary's Church, and materially aided in securing a complete
victory for the Confederates. **The** Federals were intrenched in a strong position, but **by** a vigorous assault on
their flank by Chambliss' and Gary's brigades and a similar
attack in front by the other troops under the immediate
command of General Fitzhugh Lee, they were soon driven
from their works in confusion, leaving their dead and

wounded on the field. As they retreated, the Phillips and Jeff Davis legions, of Young's brigades, raising "the Rebel yell," bore down upon them with gleaming sabres in one of those resistless charges for which these regiments were noted, and drove them for three miles in a perfect rout. The 12th Virginia and the 42d Virginia battalion participated in a part of this charge, and the Federals were ultimately driven within two and a half miles of Charles City Court-house, a distance of six miles, being pursued until nearly 10 o'clock that night. The attack by Chambliss' and Gary's brigades was made on foot, and Ashton was among the dismounted troopers who engaged in the same. For a short time he and his comrades were subjected to a furious fire of artillery and small arms, as the Federals made a stubborn resistance at first; but, undaunted by this, the Confederates pressed gallantly forward, loudly cheering as they charged, and soon drove the Federals from their works, as already mentioned.

Ashton's conduct throughout the engagement was in keeping with his previous acts of bravery, and he and his comrades had become so accustomed to fighting on foot that their gallant achievements in this engagement would have reflected honor on a brigade of veteran infantry.

The Federal loss in killed, wounded, and captured was three hundred and fifty-seven, about two hundred of these being killed and wounded, and the entire loss of the Confederates was about one hundred. The Federals retreated to Douthat's Landing the next day, and on June 27th crossed the James river. Before the crossing was completed, General Sheridan was ordered to march rapidly to the support of General James H. Wilson, who was then returning from a raid, the object of which had been the destruction of parts of the South Side and Richmond and Danville railroads for the purpose of breaking General Lee's connections south of Petersburg.

General Hampton being notified of this raid, also crossed the James and moved rapidly to Stony Creek Depot on June 28th, to intercept General Wilson. Having ascertained the route of the Federals, General Hampton marched toward Sappony Church, and soon after crossing Sappony

Creek the head of the Federal column was charged by Ashton's regiment (the 9th Virginia) and driven back behind the church, where the charge was checked by a considerable force of dismounted men posted in a strong position. General Chambliss immediately dismounted his men, formed a line near the church and was soon attacked by the Federals. He bravely held his ground and, being reinforced by the 7th Virginia cavalry and about two hundred infantry of Holcomb's Legion, repulsed the attack all along the line. Young's brigade, under Colonel G. J. Wright, of Cobb's Legion, was dismounted and put in position, and the line thus formed remained unbroken during the night, although the Federals used their artillery freely and made frequent attacks on the Confederates. The Federals had two lines of breastworks and their position was too strong for a front attack, and hence at daylight General Hampton threw portions of Young's and Rosser's brigades upon their left flank, and at the same time General Chambliss attacked with the front line, and in a few moments the Federals were driven out of their works and retreated in confusion, leaving their dead and wounded behind them. They were closely pursued for several miles when, finding that they had taken the road to Reams Station, General Hampton moved by Stony Creek Depot to the Halifax road to intercept them. Soon after crossing Rowanty Creek, he met an advance of Federals who had crossed the Halifax road, and at once charged and routed them with a portion of Chambliss' brigade. Immediately afterward another party of Federals who were crossing the Halifax road were charged by General Hampton with a portion of the 13th Virginia of Chambliss' brigade, and driven back, and Lieutenant-colonel Phillips, of that regiment, was sent forward to get possession of the bridge over Rowanty Creek. Finding that a portion of the Federals had crossed the creek and taken a road leading east, Colonel R. L. T. Beale was sent with two or three squadrons of the 9th Virginia in pursuit of them, Ashton being with the detachment. The Federals were so completely demoralized that Ashton and his comrades had but little fighting to do, but had some very hard riding in their pursuit of the fugitives, which continued for four miles and

resulted in the capture of a large number of the Federals
and the dispersion of the rest.

General Hampton had been successful at all points; the
Federal force was completely broken and the fragments
were seeking safety in flight in various directions when
darkness terminated their pursuit. They continued their
flight during the night, and, although vigorously pursued
the next day, succeeded in rejoining the Federal army.

In the fight at Sappony Church and during the next day
the Federals lost heavily in killed and wounded, and the
Confederates captured eight hundred and six prisoners and
also one hundred and twenty-seven negroes whom the Federals were endeavoring to carry into their lines. The loss
in Hampton's division was two killed, eighteen wounded,
and two missing.

The pursuit of the Federals which terminated near Pe-
ters' bridge on the Nottaway, closed the active operations
of General Hampton's command beginning on June 8th.
During that time the command had no rest, was scantily
supplied with rations and forage, marched more than four
hundred miles, fought the greater part of six days and one
night, killed and wounded many Federals, captured over
two thousand prisoners, many guns, small arms, horses,
wagons and other material of war, and succeeded in defeating two formidable and well-organized expeditions of the
Federals. In the accomplishment of this, General Hampton's loss was seven hundred and nineteen killed, wounded,
and missing.

In the operation against General Wilson, Ashton's regiment had captured three Federal flags, and Colonel Beale
presented them to General Hampton, but, owing to the
army regulations, the latter could not retain them, and it
was a source of regret to him that he had to part with
these tokens of the admiration entertained for him by the
commanding officer of the gallant Virginians who had so
recently begun to operate with his command.

During the month of July the cavalry on the right of
General Lee's army were comparatively inactive, and hence
Ashton and his comrades had but little service to perform,
except that of picket duty. The infantry of the army was

15

not so fortunate, for, on the night of July 26th, General Grant sent the 2d corps, under General W. S. Hancock, and three divisions of cavalry, under General P. H. Sheridan, to the north side of the James for the purpose of surprising the troops on General Lee's left, breaking through his lines at that point, and destroying the railroads from near Richmond out to the South Anna. The Federals were repulsed by a portion of General Longstreet's corps, and the expedition proved a complete failure.

This demonstration having caused General Lee **to** send from Petersburg all of his troops except three divisions, General Grant decided to assault the works in front of that place, hoping that he could carry them and capture the city, especially **as** "Burnside's mine," which extended under a part of the works in front of Cemetery Hill, was ready for explosion. Hence, about 5 o'clock A. M. on July 30th, the mine, containing eight thousand pounds of powder, was exploded and **blew up a part of the Confederate** works, known as Pegram's salient, and occupied by a part of Pegram's artillery and the **18th and** 22d South Carolina regiments. The explosion formed a crater one hundred and thirty-five feet long, ninety-seven feet wide, and thirty feet deep, made a considerable breach in the lines, and killed and wounded two hundred and seventy-eight men. The assault **was** then made by the 9th corps, fifteen thousand two hundred and seventy-two strong, under General A. E. Burnside, supported by the 18th corps, fifteen thousand nine hundred and thirty-four strong, under General E. O. C. Ord and the 5th corps, eleven thousand nine hundred and twenty-seven strong, under General G. K. Warren—the entire force aggregating forty-three thousand one hundred and twenty-three **men.** To meet this attack the Confederates had only the divisions of Generals Bushrod R. Johnson, E. F. Hoke, and William Mahone, and they were extended along the works a considerable distance on each side of the breach that had been made by the explosion, General S. Elliott's brigade, of Johnson's division, occupying the salient, and the remainder of the division the line adjacent thereto, Mahone's division being on the right and Hoke's division on the left of Johnson's division.

When the dense smoke and dust caused by the explosion had cleared away, the Confederates discovered that the advance forces of the Federals had occupied the breach, and thousands of othe troops were pressing forward to their support. Two hundred and fifty-six men of the 18th and 22d South Carolina regiments of Elliott's brigade had been killed and wounded by the explosion, and General Johnson promptly concentrated the remainder of the brigade at and near the breach and sent to Generals Hoke and Mahone for reinforcements. The former could not at first furnish any troops on account of the weakness of his line, but after awhile sent the 61st North Carolina regiment, and about the same time General Mahone arrived with Wright's and Sanders' brigades. In the meantime a furious conflict had been waged in front of and on both sides of the breach in the Confederate line, General Johnson having repulsed and held in check for hours an overwhelming force of Federals with a little more than three regiments of Elliott's brigade, two regiments of Ransom's brigade and two regiments of Wise's brigade, and a part of the artillery. After the arrival of General Mahone two charges were made by the Confederates and the Federals were partially dislodged from their position by 12 o'clock; and at 2 o'clock P. M. by a third charge they were routed and driven back and the Confederates obtained possession of the crater and the adjacent works, thereby completely re-establishing their lines. Before this last charge was made the crater had become densely crowded with Federal soldiers who had there sought safety from the fatal fire of the Confederates and failed to find it, for the latter pressed forward to the edge of the crater and by a rapid and destructive fire made of that place of refuge a veritable slaughter-pen. Hence, when the Confederates entered it in their final charge they found its bottom and sides literally covered with dead and wounded Federals. Their surviving comrades were soon captured, and greatly increased the large number of prisoners already taken.

Considering the great disparity in numbers on the side of the Confederates, and the signal success achieved by them, this was one of the most notable victories of the Civil War,

and the brave and successful defense of the breach in their
lines by General Johnson and his gallant little band against
the assaults of the 9th corps should take rank in military
annals with the courageous conduct of "Leonidas and his
brave three hundred at the pass of Thermopylæ."

The loss of the Federals, as reported by General Meade,
was four thousand four hundred killed, wounded, and missing; and the Confederate loss was about one third as
great.

In a communication to General Meade, August 1st, 1864,
General Grant referred to this movement of the Federal
army · as a "miserable failure," and said: "So fair an opportunity will probably never occur again for carrying
fortifications. Preparations were good, orders ample, and
everything, so far as I could see, subsequent to the explosion of the mine, shows that almost without loss, the crest
beyond the mine could have been carried."

This inference of General Grant's might have been correct
if "the crest beyond the mine" had been defended by hireling
soldiers, but was entirely groundless in view of the fact
that it was defended by patriots, whose courage was
phenomenal and who were fighting a cause dearer to them
than life.

In August Chambliss' brigade was moved north of the
James to the left flank of General Lee's army. As it passed
through Richmond on the route, Ashton secured an hour's
leave of absence from his regiment for the purpose of visiting Ruth Middleton. She was still boarding at Mrs.
Slaughter's, and had been constantly engaged in the performance of her hospital duties since Ashton left her nearly
eight months before Bertha had been with her ever since
the opening of the Spottsylvania campaign in May and was
now, as formerly, assisting her at the hospital. Ashton's
unexpected visit was naturally a source of great delight to
Ruth and Bertha and the former was deeply comforted by
it, as she had been earnestly longing to see him. He
received a warm welcome from Mrs. Slaughter and Kate,
with whom he was quite a favorite. Randolph Slaughter
was not at home, for, although but a lad of fifteen, he had
joined the Confederate troops in the Department of Rich-

mond, and was serving in the trenches as a member of the
2d battalion Virginia Reserves, in General George W. C.
Lee's brigade.

Although there had been great changes **for the** worse in
the affairs of the Confederacy since Ashton last saw these
ladies, and they, in the meantime, had experienced many
trials and discomforts, he saw no sign of gloom in their
faces and found them exceedingly cheerful and hopeful, for
they still had an abiding faith in the ultimate success of the
Confederate arms, confidently believing that, in accordance
with the fitness of things and the operation of the principles
of justice, right would finally triumph over might. This spirit
of hopefulness and the confidence shown by his lady friends
in **the** final success of the **sacred cause** for which he was
fighting, fired Ashton**'s soul** with renewed **zeal and** enthusi-
asm, and, although he was just from the field of battle
where the unequal contest was being almost daily waged
beween the friends and the foes of that cause, with stupendous odds in favor of the latter, he received fresh inspiration and encouragement to aid in prosecuting **the contest**
with even greater energy and persistency than **ever before.**
Hence, when his brief visit had ended and he galloped away
to overtake his **comrades, his heart was not** only throbbing
with delight in **consequence of the joy** which he had experienced in being with **the object** of his love, but it was also
filled with increased hopefulness, ardor, and enthusiasm in
regard to the heroic contest which the South was waging
in defense of her constitutional rights.

By **rapid** riding Ashton overtook his regiment in a short
time, **and** was back in ranks long before it reached its place
of encampment that evening. He and his comrades learned
the next **day that** the brigade had been transferred to the
north side **of the** James to aid in checking a movement
which was about to be made by a large part of General
Grant's army against the Confederate line between the
Darbytown and Charles City **roads.** A part of the brigade
was posted at Deep Creek on **the** latter road, and it was
suddenly attacked on August 16th by **General** D. McM.
Gregg's division of cavalry and General Nelson A. Miles'
brigade of infantry. General Chambliss made a gallant

defense with his small force, but was driven back toward
White's Tavern by overwhelming numbers, and while
bravely commanding his men and stubbornly resisting the
advance of the Federals, was killed by some member of
Miles' brigade. In a few moments after he fell several of
his barbarous foes rushed forward, and in a spirit of vandalism cut some of the buttons and ornaments off his uniform.
Shortly after this the Confederates were reinforced, and
turning upon the Federals they attacked them vigorously
and fiercely and drove them back beyond White Oak
swamp. The blood of Ashton and his comrades had boiled
with fiery indignation when they witnessed the barbarous
treatment to which the body of General Chambliss had
been subjected, and in their subsequent attack on the Federals they strove with unwonted vigor and fury to punish
the perpetrators of the dastardly deed. They were strongly
attached to him and deeply lamented his tragic death.
This sense of loss in the death of their gallant leader was
not confined to his immediate command; for General R. E.
Lee, in writing to General Hampton August 19th, said:
"The loss sustained by the cavalry in the fall of General
Chambliss will be felt throughout the army in which, by his
courage, energy and skill, he had won for himself an honorable name."

The reader will doubtless remember that during the Gettysburg campaign Chambliss, then colonel of the 13th Virginia regiment, was commanding the brigade in consequence
of the fact that General W. H. F. Lee had been wounded at
Brandy Station, and for some time after General Chambliss' death it was known as Chambliss' brigade. As such
we will continue to designate it.

After General Grant's movement north of the James was
repulsed, Chambliss' brigade returned to its former position
on the right of General Lee's army, and on August 25th this
and three other brigades of the cavalry corps, to the command of which General Hampton had been assigned August
11th, had a severe engagement with the Federals in their
intrenchments at Reams' Station, where they were endeavoring to destroy the Petersburg and Weldon railroad.
In this engagement General Hampton was co-operating

with General A. P. Hill, whose force consisted of Cook's and McRae's brigades, under General Henry Heth, Lane's brigade, under General James Conner, and Pegram's artillery, and they were opposed by the 2d corps under General W. S. Hancock and General D. McM. Gregg's division of cavalry. The Federals were driven out of their breastworks and completely defeated with a loss of two thousand seven hundred and forty-two killed, wounded, and captured, twelve stand of colors, nine pieces of artillery, three thousand one hundred stand of small arms, and thirty-two horses. The Confederates lost seven hundred and twenty killed, wounded, and captured. General Hampton's command carried one line of intrenchments with great gallantry and captured seven hundred and eighteen prisoners. Chambliss' brigade was foremost in the fray, and Ashton and his comrades fought with such fury and fierce persistency as indicated that they were again bent on severely punishing their foes for the barbarous indignity to which the dead body of their former commander had recently been subjected, and by a singular coincidence this well-merited punishment was being inflicted upon the proper objects of it, for a part of the Federals whom they were fighting consisted of Miles' brigade and Gregg's division o cavalry, some members of which had been the perpetrators of that barbarous outrage.

In his report of the engagement General Hampton said: "Chambliss' brigade was in advance when we met the enemy, and it was engaged all day, displaying through the whole fight marked gallantry."

To have won such praise from a leader who was the embodiment of valor, and the commander of a corps whose chivalrous achievements have never been surpassed, was proof of the fact that Ashton and his brave comrades had displayed signal courage on this occasion, and they were naturally proud of the commendation received from the bold and gallant leader who had taken the place made vacant by the death of their former corps commander, the daring and chivalrous Stuart.

For nearly three weeks after this engagement Ashton and his comrades were on outpost duty near Reams' Station, the regiment to which he belonged being encamped about five miles west of that place. On September 13th, they were summoned to take part in a novel and daring expedition planned by General Hampton, the object of which was the capture of a large herd of cattle which one of his scouts, Sergeant George D. Shadburne, had reported to be grazing near Coggins' Point, on the James river. On the following morning General Hampton took the division of General W. H. F. Lee, the brigades of Generals Rosser and Dearing and a detachment of one hundred men from the brigades of Generals Young and Dunovant, under the command of Lieutenant-colonel Miller, of the 6th South Carolina cavalry, and marched down the west side of Rowanty Creek to Wilkinson's Bridge and bivouacked there that night.

In order to accomplish the object of the expedition it was necessary to get in the rear of the Federal army, and this could be done only by breaking through their lines at some point. General Hampton selected Sycamore church, in Prince George county, as the point to be attacked, and on the next day marched rapidly to a place on the Blackwater where Cooke's Bridge had formerly stood, but which, as he knew, had been destroyed; and it was for that reason that he had chosen this route, as he thought that in consequence of the destruction of the bridge the Federals would not expect an attack from that direction. A new bridge having been constructed by his men, he crossed the stream, and at 12 o'clock that night the command resumed its march, General Lee going to the left of Sycamore church, General Dearing proceeding to Cooke's mill to the right of the church, and General Hampton, with Rosser's brigade and the detachment under Lieutenant-colonel Miller, moving directly to the church, General Rosser being charged with the duty of driving the Federals from their position at the church and securing the cattle when that was accomplished. The three columns reached the points to which they were ordered, without being discovered, and at 5 o'clock A. M. on the 16th, General Rosser attacked the Federals. They had a strong position and for awhile stubbornly resisted Rosser's attack, but were finally driven back and completely routed, leaving their dead and wounded on the field and their camp in the possession of the Confederates. In the meantime General Lee, on the left, and General Dearing on the right, had successfully attacked and routed the Federals at the points to which they had gone, thereby insuring the easy capture and safe withdrawal of the cattle, which numbered two thousand four hundred and eighty-six.

The object of the expedition having been accomplished, General Hampton retired before 8 o'clock A. M., sent the cattle across the Nottaway at Freeman's Bridge and, after defeating the division of General Henry E. Davies, Jr., in a fight on the Jerusalem plank-road, recrossed Rowanty creek at Wilkinson's Bridge, and on the following day arrived within the Confederate lines. The Confederates brought in, as the fruits of the expedition, two thousand four hundred and sixty-eight of the captured cattle, eleven wagons, some valuable stores, including a large number of blankets, three guidons, and three hundred and four prisoners, two hundred and twelve of whom belonged to the First District of Columbia cavalry, there being among the latter two majors, one captain, and six lieutenants. The capture of the cattle was a windfall for the Confederate troops who were, as usual, on short rations and in a half-starved condition.

Returning to their former camp, Ashton and his comrades enjoyed a short respite from the hardships and dangers of the battle-field; but on September 29th, they were unexpectedly called upon to meet an advance of the Federals near Hatcher's Run, to which point General M. C. Butler's pickets had been driven back that morning. In the fight that ensued the Federals were driven back with the loss of a number of prisoners, and the Confederate picket-line was re-established. On the following morning General Hampton learned that General Dearing's brigade had been driven from their works and that the Federals were then in possession of them. He at once held a consultation with General Heth and they decided to attack the Federals, it being arranged that General Heth should assault them in front and General Hampton should strike them on their left flank. For the purpose of executing this plan, General Hampton moved Chambliss' and Barringer's brigades down the Vaughn road to the left of the Federals and occupied some

works that were found there. In the meantime General
Heth's division of infantry had begun their attack, and as
the Federals moved up to reinforce their front line their
flank was exposed to General Hampton. He at once
ordered General W. H. F. Lee to attack them, and the latter, leading his men in person, made the attack with the 9th
and 10th Virginia regiments, dismounted, who moved
steadily and gallantly forward in line of battle, reserving
their fire until very near the Federals. They then coolly
delivered a well-directed volley, dashed forward in an impetuous charge, completely routed the Federals and captured about nine hundred prisoners and ten standards.
General Heth's troops were also successful in their attack
and the entire Federal force, consisting of the 5th and 9th
corps and Gregg's division of cavalry, was driven back with
a loss of over two thousand and five hundred men killed,
wounded, and captured. In his report of the charge made
by his men, General Hampton said: "The whole affair was
one of the handsomest I have seen, and it reflects the highest
credit on the troops engaged in it." The Federal troops
whom these two cavalry regiments had attacked and
routed were infantry who greatly outnumbered them, and
Ashton and his brave comrades were naturally and justly
proud of their brilliant victory.

Shortly after the termination of this engagement Butler's
brigade was attacked on the Vaughn road, and General
Hampton at once took the 9th and 13th Virginia regiments
and went to the assistance of that brigade. Moving by a
short route across the country, General Hampton reached
the Squirrel Level road, gained the rear of the Federals, and
his two regiments bore down upon them in a rapid and successful charge. This movement relieved General Butler's
troops, and the Federals fell back to a strong position on
the Vaughn road.

In the charge made upon the rear of the Federals, Ashton
narrowly escaped death; for his horse, having been mortally wounded, fell to the ground with him and for a few
moments he was in great danger of being crushed beneath
the hoofs of the numerous horses behind him, as some of
them dashed over him at full speed. Having regained his

feet, Ashton gazed tenderly and sorrowfully at his dying animal and was moved almost to tears as he thought of the numerous hardships and dangers that they had shared together, and realized that the service and companionship of his faithful friend had ended; for the stricken animal was the horse that Mosby gave him and had borne him safely through many conflicts during the past two years.

For a few days after his horse was killed, Ashton thought that he would be forced to join the ranks of the dismounted cavalry, as Confederate cavalrymen had to mount themselves, and at that time horses were exceedingly scarce and difficult to obtain. However, after repeated efforts he succeeded in procuring, at a fabulous price, another horse, and was thus enabled to remain with his regiment and participate in the future operations of the cavalry. Shortly afterward he was again in the saddle, and distinguished himself in an engagement which Generals Hampton and Heth had with the Federals on the Boydton plank-road and at Hatcher's Run on October 27th, in which the latter were defeated and driven back with a loss of one hundred and sixty-six killed, one thousand and twenty-eight wounded, and five hundred and sixty-four captured, the Confederate loss being comparatively small. The Federal force consisted of the 2d, 5th, and 9th corps, under General W. S. Hancock, G. K. Warren, and John G. Parke, respectively, and General D. McM. Gregg's division of cavalry, while the Confederate force consisted of one brigade of Heth's division and three brigades of Mahone's division, under General William Mahone, and five brigades of cavalry, under General Hampton; and in view of the comparatively small force of the Confederates, their victory was all the more brilliant and remarkable.

The movement which the Confederates had checked was intended to be one of great magnitude that should result in signal success to the Federal arms, and General Meade was near at hand to watch and direct its progress, General Grant also being present during a part of the day. The immediate object of the movement, as shown by General Meade's orders issued October 25th, was to attack with the 9th corps, supported by the 5th, the right of the Confederate in-

fantry between Hatcher's Run and their new works, which
were supposed to be incomplete, and by a secret and sudden
assault surprise the Confederates and carry these works,
while the 2d corps, aided by Gregg's division of cavalry,
was, by a concealed march, to move beyond the Confederate right, press on to the South Side railroad and endeavor
to seize a commanding position on that road. If the
movement had been successful, General Lee's right flank
would have been turned, and General Meade would have
been in his rear with fifty-two thousand men to be encountered outside of intrenchments by the comparatively small
force holding the Confederate lines from Hatcher's Run to
Petersburg. The consequences would necessarily have been
disastrous to the Confederates, especially as General Lee could
have sent no reinforcements from the left of his lines, as General B. F. Butler, with the 10th and 18th corps, and a division
of cavalry under Colonel Robert M. West, aggregating twenty-eight thousand men, had made a similar and simultaneous
attack on the Confederate lines north of the James on the
Darbytown and Williamsburg roads for the purpose of
turning the left flank of General Lee's army. General Longstreet repulsed this attack with General C. W. Field's
division and General Martin W. Gary's brigade of cavalry,
and the Federals were defeated with a loss of one thousand
six hundred and three killed, wounded, and captured, and
eleven standards, the Confederate loss being very light,
General Field having lost only sixty-four men, killed,
wounded, and captured.

In view of the fact that both flanks of the Confederate
army were simultaneously attacked by the bulk of General
Grant's army, it is evident that he hoped by this sudden
movement to capture both Richmond and Petersburg, and
this view is strengthened by a statement, in a dispatch sent
that day to Honorable Edwin M. Stanton, virtually
acknowledging the defeat of the movement, where he says:
"This reconnoissance, which I had intended for more, points
out to me what is to be done.'" Hence, the complete defeat
of the movement by Generals Hampton, Heth, and Longstreet not only reflected great credit on them and the gallant men by whom it was effected, but also prevented

incalculable injury to the Confederate cause. General Lee, had, several weeks before, **contemplated** the probability of such a movement, and **naturally** feared its consequences, as **is shown** by a communication **to** Honorable James A. Seddon, Secretary of **War,** October 4th, 1864, asking for reinforcements, in **which he** says: "The enemy's numerical superiority enables him to hold his lines with an adequate **force** and extend **on each** flank with numbers so much greater than **ours** that we can only meet his corps, increased by recent **recruits,** with a division reduced by long and arduous **service.** We cannot fight to advantage with such odds, and **there** is the **greatest** reason to apprehend the result of every encounter."

The Confederate cavalry under General Hampton were **naturally** elated **at the** success which they had achieved over 'Gregg's cavalry and Hancock's and Warren's infantry in **the fight on** and near the Boydton plank-road, but to their **peerless** leader **the** glory of victory was darkened by the gloom of grief; for his brave and noble son, Lieutenant Thomas Preston Hampton, aid-de-camp, while gallantly leading a charge against the Federals, was mortally wounded, and Lieutenant Wade Hampton received a severe wound.

After this **fight General** Hampton's command was not actively engaged **with the Federals for** more than a month, **and** during that **time Ashton** enjoyed a period of comparative rest, occasionally doing picket duty on the Rowanty. But **on December 7th** General Hampton marched with the command **to meet a movement** of General G. K. Warren's on Hicksford with twenty-two thousand infantry, four thousand **cavalry,** and six batteries of artillery, the object of **which was the** destruction of a part of the Weldon railroad. The numbers **of** the Federals were so great that General Hampton **could** not afford to attack the entire force with **his** two divisions of **cavalry,** but he successfully defended Hicksford, **saved** the bridge over the Meherrin, at that place, interrupted their destruction of the railroad, defeated their cavalry in several skirmishes, and harassed them on their retreat, capturing over two hundred and fifty prisoners. On their retreat the Federals were guilty of the vilest vandalism, for, as shown by General Warren's report, "almost every house was set on fire along the route," and these houses were occupied only by helpless women and children.

This movement closed the active operation of General Hampton's command for 1864. In January 1865, he was sent with General M. C. Butler's division to join the Confederate forces in South Carolina and, at the same time, General W. H. F. Lee was placed in command of the remainder of the cavalry corps operating on the right of General Lee's army. During that month the division to which Ashton belonged had no serious engagements, and was moved down to Belfield in order that forage for the horses might be more easily obtained; but on February 5th, it was suddenly recalled to aid in checking an advance of the Federals on the Confederate right. On that day the Federals moved in heavy force to Hatcher's Run, forced a crossing at the Vaughn road, and advanced in the direction of Dinwiddie Court-house. The movement was promptly met by the Confederates, and during that afternoon and the next two days there was severe fighting at Armstrong's and Dabney's Mills and other points, resulting in comparatively heavy losses to the Federals. Their force consisted of the 2d and 5th corps, parts of the 6th and 9th corps and Gregg's division of cavalry, but, although opposed by only Pegram's, Gordon's, and Mahone's divisions, and W. H. F. Lee's division of cavalry, was unable to break through General Lee's main line at any point, merely capturing a part of his rifle-pits on the picket-line, and was finally driven back.

By marching nearly all of the night of February 5th, Lee's division reached the Confederate right in time to meet and drive back Gregg's division on the Boydton plank-road, and Ashton and his comrades thus found themselves again fighting the Federals over ground made memorable by former conflicts.

Although the Federals had accomplished nothing except the extension of their lines a short distance beyond Hatcher's Run, their movement had been the means of subjecting the Confederates to the greatest hardships; for the weather was exceedingly inclement and intensely cold, and in consequence of exposure to it during this movement, in their half-clad and half-starved condition, the Confederate troops experienced indescribable suffering. On February 8th, in a communication to Honorable James A. Seddon, Secretary of War, General Lee wrote in regard to the suffering of the troops, as follows: "Yesterday, the most inclement day of the winter, they had to be kept in line of battle, having been in the same condition the two previous days and nights. I regret to have to state that under these circumstances, heightened by assaults and fire of the enemy, some of the men had been without meat for three days, and all were suffering from reduced rations and scant clothing, exposed to battle, cold, hail, and sleet. I have directed Colonel Cole, chief commissary, who reports that he has not a pound of meat at his disposal, to visit Richmond and see if nothing can be done. If some change is not made and the commissary department reorganized, I apprehend dire results. The physical strength of the men, if their courage survives, must fail under this treatment. Our cavalry has to be dispersed for want of forage. Fitz Lee's and Lomax's divisions are scattered because supplies cannot be transported where their services are required. I had to bring William H. F. Lee's division forty miles Sunday night to get him in position. Taking these facts in connection with the paucity of our numbers, you must not be surprised if calamity befalls us."

This communication was sent to President Davis for perusal, and on it he wrote the following indorsement:

"This is too sad to be patiently considered and cannot have occurred without criminal neglect or gross incapacity Let supplies be had by purchase, or borrowing, or other possible mode."

The foregoing extract from General Lee's communication to the secretary of war will give the reader an idea of the wretched condition of the troops defending Richmond and Petersburg, and the intense suffering that they were daily enduring in behalf of the cause which they had espoused. Instead of improving, the condition of the beleaguered army constantly grew worse, and its numbers were daily decreased by sickness and death resulting from lack of food and clothing, and exposure to the inclement weather, and also by frequent desertions caused by the severe hardships to which the troops were subjected and, in many instances, the knowledge of the fact that their loved ones at home were suffering for lack of the necessaries of life. In the meantime the besieging army had been reinforced by the arrival of General P H. Sheridan, from the Shenandoah Valley, with nine thousand cavalry, and also the addition of large numbers of recruits; and hence, toward the end of March it was evident that General Lee could not hold Richmond and Petersburg much longer, especially if General Grant should move his armies to the left and turn the Confederate right beyond Hatcher's Run. General Grant decided to make such a movement, which was to begin on March 29th, as shown by the following extract from instructions issued to Generals Meade, Ord, and Sheridan, March 25th, to wit: "On the 29th instant the armies operating against Richmond will be moved by our left, for the double purpose of turning the enemy out of his present position around Petersburg and to insure the success of the cavalry under General Sheridan, which will start at the same time in its efforts to reach and destroy the South Side and Danville railroad."

The movement began on the morning of March 29th, and by night General Sheridan's cavalry was at Dinwiddie Court-house and the left of the Federal infantry line extended to the Quaker road near its intersection with the Boydton plank-road.

On the next day General Fitzhugh Lee, by order of General R. E. Lee, marched with his division of cavalry from Sutherland Station toward Dinwiddie Court-house, via Five Forks, to meet this threatened movement of Sheridan's cavalry.

General Sheridan was to be supported in his operations by the 5th and 2d corps, under command of Generals G. K. Warren and A. A. Humphreys, respectively, aggregating thirty-eight thousand two hundred and twenty effective men; and his own force, under the immediate command of General Wesley Merritt, consisted of the 1st, 2d, and 3d divisions of cavalry respectively commanded by Generals Thomas C. Devin, George Crook, and G. A. Custer, and numbered nine thousand effective men.

In the afternoon of March 30th, General Fitzhugh Lee encountered the advance of General Sheridan's cavalry beyond Five Forks and drove them back on the main force at Dinwiddie Court-house. During the evening he was joined by the divisions of General W. H. F. Lee and Thomas L. Rosser, and, by order of General R. E. Lee, took command of the cavalry corps, consisting of his own division, commanded by General Thomas T. Munford and the two other divisions just mentioned. On the following day General George E. Pickett arrived with five small brigades of infantry, to wit: Stewart's, Corse's, and Terry's of his own division and Wallace's and Ransom's of General Bushrod Johnson's division, and General Sheridan's large force of cavalry (which had begun to advance) was attacked by the Confederates beyond Five Forks. A severe engagement ensued in which the Federals were finally driven back with heavy loss to within half a mile of Dinwiddie Court-house. The fighting was fiercest at two crossings on Chamberlain's Creek, where the Confederates effected a passage of the stream in the face of heavy forces strongly posted on the opposite side. When the Confederates had forced a passage of the stream and could fight the Federals on equal ground, the latter were rapidly driven back until darkness closed the conflict. In their reports of the engagement, Generals Sheridan, Merritt, Devin, Cook, and Custer endeavored to excuse their complete and disastrous defeat by claiming that they were "forced to fall back before overwhelming numbers," and General Merritt represented that the Confederate force "consisted of Pickett's and Johnson's divisions of infantry, since ascertained to have been over fourteen thousand strong, and all the enemy's cavalry."

The unreasonableness of this claim and the incorrectness of General Merritt's statement as to the number of the Confederate infantry engaged in the fight are apparent to any one who is at all informed as to the greatly reduced ranks of General Lee's army at that time. More than a month before, to wit: February 28th, 1865, as shown by the monthly returns of the army, the effective force of Pickett's entire division was six thousand one hundred and fifty-seven and that of Johnson's division was six thousand two hundred and seventy-seven, making an aggregate of twelve thousand four hundred and twenty-eight, and in the meantime this number had been greatly reduced by losses in battle, sickness, and death, resulting from lack of food and clothing and constant exposure to the **inclement weather,** and also by numerous and almost daily desertions. Moreover, as already stated, General Pickett had with him only three of his brigades and two of Johnson's, **all** of which were quite small. His entire force was less than four thou**sand** men. The Confederate cavalry consisted **of seven** small brigades containing twenty-six regiments and **num**bered something over three thousand men, and hence **the** entire Confederate force was about seven thousand. General Sheridan's force consisted **of** nine large brigades containing thirty-nine regiments, and according to his official report, was nine thousand strong. Therefore, it will be seen that the Federals were not "forced to fall back before overwhelming **numbers,"** but were fairly whipped in open fight, and driven back by **inferior numbers. This, by the** way, was not an uncommon experience **with them, as** the Confederates had often defeated forces much larger **than** their own. Indeed, the 5th corps had that day had **a similar** experience just before Sheridan was driven back by inferior numbers; for General Bushrod Johnson with Moody's and **Wise's brigades of his own division, Hunton's** brigade of Pickett's division, **and McGowan's** brigade of Wilcox's **division, attacked** and drove back that corps on the White Oak road with a loss of **one thousand** four hundred and seven killed, wounded, **and captured, the** Confederate loss being about eight hundred killed, wounded, and captured

In the fight beyond Five Forks the losses of the Confed**erate** cavalry were comparatively light, the heaviest loss being in the command to which Ashton belonged (W. H. F. Lee's division), **and** having occurred while it was forcing a passage of Chamberlain's Creek. Ashton had frequently been under heavy fire, but at this point for a short time, he felt that he and **his** comrades were being subjected to the heaviest and hottest fire that they had ever been called upon to **face; for the** Federals occupied a strong and advantageous position on the opposite side of the stream and stubbornly defended it until the Confederates dashed forward with the utmost gallantry and dislodged them. This being done, the Federals were steadily driven back toward Dinwiddie Court-House, as already stated.

At daylight the next morning Generals Fitzhugh Lee and Pickett retired to their former position at Five Forks and so disposed their troops as to form connection by a thin line (Robert's brigade of two regiments) on their left with the right of General Lee's army at Burgess' Mill. About 3 o'clock that afternoon General Sheridan, having been reinforced by Mackenzie's cavalry brigade of one thousand effective men and the 5th corps, under General Warren, attacked Generals Pickett and Fitzhugh Lee by a flank movement on their left, drove Roberts' brigade back across Hatcher's Run, turned General Pickett's left flank, and drove him back several miles with heavy loss, separating him from General Fitzhugh Lee. The Confederates made a gallant defense, but it was impossible for their force of seven thousand men to withstand the combined attack of the overwhelming force of infantry and cavalry assailing them, which consisted of more than twenty-six thousand men and, by reason of greatly superior numbers, had been enabled to flank them. General Fitzhugh Lee remained in position near Five Forks that night and was joined by General R. H. Anderson, with Wise's and Gracie's brigades, which had been brought up from Burgess' Mills to reinforce the Confederates at Five Forks, but did not arrive in time to participate in the fight, as they had come by a long and circuitous route.

On April 3d Generals Anderson and Fitzhugh Lee learned that the Confederate army was withdrawing from the vicinity of Richmond and Petersburg, and began to retire toward Amelia Court-house, the cavalry acting as rear guard on the route. General Fitzhugh Lee had several fights with the advance guard of the Federals in his route to Amelia Court house, which was reached on April 5th. Here he found the main body of the army under General R. E. Lee, and from that point to Appomattox Court-house the cavalry under his command protected the rear and marching flanks of the retreating army, fighting every day

with undiminished ardor and gallantry, notwithstanding
the apparent hopelessness of ultimate success in the unequal struggle between the weary, half-starved and half-
armed remnant of the Army of Northern Virginia and the
myriad of vigorous, well fed and excellently equipped troops
that were rapidly enveloping it. These gallant troopers,
whose chivalrous achievements in brighter days, under the
leadership of Stuart and Hampton, had immortalized the
cavalry corps of the Virginia army, now in these dark
days of adversity, under their new and valiant leader, displayed their wonted valor, and successfully defeated the
Federal forces with whom they came in conflict at Paineville,
High Bridge, Farmville, and beyond the latter place on
their route to Appomattox Court-house. In the final conflict at that place on April 9th, assisted by about one thousand six hundred infantry under General John B. Gordon,
they drove back Sheridan's cavalry corps until checked by
the 5th, 24th, and part of the 25th corps of infantry, numbering over twenty thousand, under General E. O. C. Ord,
who had just arrived on the field, and in his report of the
engagement says: "Our cavalry were falling back in confusion," and adds: "We were barely in time."

   In order that the reader may understand the circumstances under which this conflict occurred, we will briefly
narrate the experience of the main body of the Confederate army the preceding week.

CHAPTER XVII.

When General Lee began his retreat on the night of April 2nd, he hoped to effect a junction with General Joseph E. Johnston's army, and might have done so if, as he had directed, supplies for his army had been deposited at Amelia Court-house to await his arrival there. But this was not done; hence, when General Lee arrived at Amelia Court-house on the morning of April 4th, he found nothing there on which to feed his army, which had been without food for nearly two days. It required nearly twenty-four hours in which to procure food for the army, and the time thus lost enabled Generals Sheridan and Ord to get between General Lee and Danville, thereby cutting off that line of retreat, and effectually preventing a junction with General Johnston's army. The only route now open for General Lee's retreat was by way of Farmville, where he ordered supplies from Lynchburg, and he started for that place on the night of April 5th. The scenes and incidents of the next three days presented a pathetic yet thrilling picture of sublime fortitude and heroism that beggars description. Marching by night and fighting by day, pressed from behind by overwhelming numbers of infantry and artillery, and harassed on the flank by the Federal cavalry, the small remnant of the Army of Northern Virginia under its matchless commander passed through an experience of unparalleled hardships, and suffering without murmuring at its fate, or flinching from the full discharge of duty. The men were so completely exhausted by loss of sleep, fatigue, and hunger that they could scarcely stand up in ranks; and yet in this desperate condition the remnant of General Ewell's command, consisting of Kershaw's and G. W. C. Lee's divisions, and Tucker's naval brigade, and aggregating less than four thousand men, on April 6th at Sailor's Creek, met and for a time repulsed more than five times their number, and not until they were hemmed in on all sides and overwhelmed by numbers did they finally surrender. With the remainder of his army, reduced to two corps, under Longstreet and Gordon, General Lee reached Farmville on the morning of April 7th, having marched all of the preceding night. He continued his retreat toward Lynchburg that day, and about five miles from Farmville was attacked by the 2nd corps under General A. A. Humphreys, and quickly repulsed the Federals with considerable loss.

During the night of April 7th and the following day, General Lee continued his retreat, and about dark that evening the head of his army arrived at Appomattox Court-house. There had been no fighting of any consequence that day, and as Lynchburg was only twenty-four miles distant, the Confederate soldiers had some hope of reaching that place in safety. This hope, however, was of short duration, for suddenly they heard heavy firing in front of them and it was soon ascertained that Sheridan's cavalry by rapid riding had got ahead of them and cut off their line of retreat. On the preceding day General Grant, then at Farmville, believing that General Lee could not possibly extricate the remnant of his army from the overwhelming force that was forming a complete cordon around it, wrote the latter as follows:

"April 7th, 1865.

"General R. E. Lee,

"General:—The result of the last week must convince you of the hopelessness of further resistance on the part of the Army of Northern Virginia in this struggle. I feel that it is so, and regard it as my duty to shift from myself the responsibility of any further effusion of blood by asking of you the surrender of that portion of the Confederate States army known as the Army of Northern Virginia.

"U. S. Grant,
Lieutenant-general."

To this General Lee gave the following answer:

"April 7th, 1865.

"Lieutenant-General U. S. Grant,

"General:—I have received your note of this date. Though not entertaining the opinion you express on the hopelessness of further resistance on the part of the Army of Northern Virginia, I reciprocate your desire to avoid useless effusion of blood, and, therefore, before considering your proposition, ask the terms you will offer on condition of its surrender.

> "R. E. LEE,
> General."

General Grant received this note early on the morning of the next day, before **leaving** Farmville, and immediately replied as follows:

> "April 8th, 1865.

"GENERAL R. E. LEE,

"General:—Your note of last evening in reply to mine of same date, asking the conditions on which I will accept the surrender of the Army of Northern Virginia, is just received. In reply I would say that, peace **being my** great **desire,** there is but one condition I would insist upon, namely, **that** the men and officers surrendered shall be disqualified from taking up arms again against the government of the United States until properly exchanged. I will meet you, **or will** designate officers to meet any officers you may name for the same purpose, at any point agreeable to you, for the purpose of arranging definitely the terms upon **which** the surrender of the Army of Northern Virginia will be **received.**

> "U. S. GRANT,
> Lieutenant-general."

In the note to which this **was a** reply, General Lee did not intend to convey the idea that he was ready to immediately surrender his army, and, as before stated, had continued his retreat on April 8th and reached Appomattox Court-house about dark that evening. About midnight General Grant **received** from him the following communication:

> "April 8th, 1865.

"LIEUTENANT-GENERAL U. S. GRANT,

"General:—I received at a late hour your note of to-day. In mine of yesterday I did not intend to propose the surrender of the Army of Northern Virginia, but to ask the terms of your proposition. To be frank, I do not think the emergency has arisen to call for the surrender of this army, but **as the** restoration of peace should be the sole object of all. I desire to know whether your proposals would lead to that end. I cannot, therefore, meet **you with** a view to surrender the Army of Northern Virginia, but as far as your proposal may affect the Confederate **States forces under** my command, and tend to the restoration of peace, I should be pleased to meet you at 10 A. M. to-morrow, **between the** picket-lines of the two armies.

> "R. E. LEE,
> General."

That night Generals **Longstreet,** Gordon, and **Fitzhugh Lee met General R. E. Lee at** his headquarters, and **the lat-**ter explained to them the condition of affairs and **showed** them the correspondence that had passed between himself **and General Grant.** A conference was then held, and it was decided that General Fitzhugh Lee with the Confeder-ate cavalry should at daylight attack the Federal cavalry which was reported as obstructing the line of retreat; Gen-eral Gordon was to support Lee and, if only cavalry should **be discovered,** they were to clear it from the route of the Confederates and open the **way** for the remainder of the army; but in case the Federal cavalry should be supported by a heavy force of infantry, General Lee was to be at once notified of the fact in order that a flag of truce might be sent to arrange for a surrender of the army.

Early the next morning, General Grant wrote General Lee as follows:

> "April 9th, 1865.

"**GENERAL R. E. LEE,**

"General:—Your note of yesterday is received. I have no authority to treat on the subject of peace; the meeting pro-posed **for 10** A. M. **to-day would** lead to no good. I will **state,** however, General, that I am equally anxious for peace with yourself, **and** the whole North entertains the same **feeling.** The **terms** upon which peace can be had are well understood. By the South laying down their arms they **will hasten that most** desirable event, save thousands of human lives, and hundreds of millions of property not yet destroyed. Seriously hoping that all our difficulties may be settled without the loss of **another life,** I subscribe **myself, etc.**

> "U. S. GRANT,
> Lieutenant-general."

In the meantime and at daybreak that morning, General Gordon, with the remnant of his corps, consisting of about one thousand and six hundred men, formed a line of battle on the Lynchburg road about half a mile west of Appomattox Court-house. The cavalry corps, consisting of about two thousand four hundred horsemen under General Fitzhugh Lee, was formed on General Gordon's right in the following order: W. H. F. Lee's division next to the infantry, Rosser's division in the center and Munford's division on the extreme right. At sunrise this comparatively small force moved forward with their accustomed gallantry and vigorously attacked the Federals in front of them, who proved to be a large force of dismounted cavalry. The Federals were quickly driven back in great confusion with the loss of two pieces of artillery and a number of prisoners. At this time General E. O. C. Ord arrived with two corps and part of a third of Federal infantry, numbering over twenty thousand men, who were immediately thrown into the fight, and the Confederates were compelled to retire before this overwhelming force. General Gordon withdrew across the Appomattox river, General W. H. F. Lee retired in the same direction and Generals Rosser and Munford with their divisions moved out toward Lynchburg, having cleared that route of the Federals, and thus escaped capture.

The timely arrival of the army of the James under General Ord, had thus prevented General Lee from opening a line of retreat toward Lynchburg in accordance with the plan that had been adopted the preceding night; and hence as soon as General Gordon was forced to retire before the Federal infantry he notified General Lee of his situation When General Lee received this message he realized that he could not reach Lynchburg, that further resistance would cause a useless sacrifice of life and that the time for the surrender of his army had arrived. He at once dispatched a flag of truce to General Sheridan, requesting a suspension of hostilities with a view to such surrender, and at the same time sent General Grant the following note:

"April 9th, **1865.**

"Lieutenant-General U. S. Grant,

"General:—I received your note of this morning on the picket-line, whither I had come to meet you and ascertain definitely what terms were embraced in your proposal of yesterday with reference to the surrender of this army. I now ask an interview in accordance with the offer contained in **your** letter of yesterday for that purpose.

"R. E. Lee,
General."

The interview between the commanders of the two armies occurred at the house of Mr. Wilmer McLean, in Appomattox Court-house, and there they entered into an agreement, by the terms of which the hitherto invincible Army of Northern Virginia was to take up arms no more against the United States until properly exchanged. When it became known that General Lee had decided to surrender the army, the emotions of the soldiers were indescribable. Their glorious achievements in the past, the constantly recurring victories that had crowned their arms in numerous engagements with greatly superior forces, and their indomitable courage had inspired them during the past week to boldly meet and fearlessly fight the overwhelming numbers that were pressing them on flank and rear, and in the face of apparently certain defeat and destruction they had persistently cherished the hope of ultimately escaping from their enemies; and hence, when apprised of the fact that they could fight no more, and must lay down their arms, they were at first dazed by the startling intelligence and could scarcely realize its full significance, and when they did this, their disappointment and grief were almost heartrending in their effects. While they experienced a feeling of relief in consequence of the termination of the long, harassing, and unequal conflict in which they had been engaged, there was mingled with it an agonizing regret at the failure of the cherished cause for which they had so earnestly and faithfully contended. As General Lee came riding back from his interview with General Grant, his men were completely overcome by the distressing emotions which the occasion had engendered, and hundreds of them, regardless of disciplinary regulations, broke ranks, crowded around him, and with tears and sobs told him of their sympathy and affection for him, and struggled with each other in their efforts to obtain a farewell grasp of his hand. He was deeply affected by this manifestation of their love and sympathy, and with tears streaming down his face, he said:

"I have done what I thought was best for you."

They had not questioned this, nor had they for a single moment lost confidence in their noble commander, and now in this dark hour of disaster and defeat, they loved and honored him even more, if that were possible, than in the bright days of his greatest victories. The next day he bade his troops an affectionate farewell in a noble and touching address, and on April 12th, the Army of Northern Virginia was formally surrendered, stacked their arms and furled forever the stainless flag which they had followed so long and loved so well, realizing that their cause was lost, and yet feeling the truth of the poet's strain:

> "Though right trampled, be counted for wrong,
> And that pass for right which is evil victorious,
> Here, when virtue is feeble and villainy strong,
> 'Tis a cause, not the *fate* of a cause, that is glorious."

Ashton had passed unhurt through the frequent conflicts in which the cavalry had been engaged on its retreat from Hatcher's Run to Appomattox Court-house, and was one of the brave little band of horsemen who boldly rode forth on the morning of April 9th charged with the duty of attacking more than three times their number and opening a line of retreat for the remnant of General Lee's army. This duty was fearlessly and faithfully done, and the Federal cavalry, as before stated, were driven back in confusion before them, until the advance of General Ord's overwhelming force of infantry caused them to retire with the handful of Confederate infantry that had joined in the attack.

Throughout the brief engagement Ashton had fought with unabated ardor and gallantry in the face of stupendous odds, conscious of the fact that he was defending a failing cause; and by his chivalrous conduct added one more leaf to the wreath of laurel which he had won as a true and typical private soldier in the knightliest army the

world has ever seen. At the time Generals Rosser and Munford escaped with their commands by the road to Lynchburg, which had been opened by the Confederate cavalry,
General Fitzhugh Lee also rode out with a portion of General W. H. F. Lee's division, but Ashton remained with his
division commander and was one of the two hundred and
ninety-eight men constituting the remnant of **that** division
which surrendered at Appomattox on April 9th. **The entire**
Confederate force which surrendered at that time, including
officers, was twenty-eight thousand two hundred and **thirty-**
one, consisting of two hundred and eighty-one at general
headquarters, twenty-two thousand three hundred and
forty-nine infantry, one thousand five hundred and fifty-
nine cavalry, two thousand, five hundred and seventy-six
artillery, and fourteen hundred and sixty-six miscellaneous
troops composed of detachments of engineers, invalids, naval
brigade, **provost guards, etc. On the morning** of April 9th,
when Generals Gordon and Fitzhugh Lee, with their little
band of about four **thousand men marched forth to open a**
way for farther retreat, they had with them **more than a**
third of the armed forces of the Army of Northern Virginia,
for, according to the reports of the ordnance officers that
morning, there were only seven thousand eight hundred and
ninety-two organized infantry with arms, and all of the
cavalry participated in the movement. According to the
official returns showing the effective strength of General
Grant's army on April 10th, 1865, it consisted of one hundred and seven thousand four hundred and ninety-six men,
exclusive of General Sheridan's cavalry corps of about nine
thousand men, not included in the **report. It** was under
these circumstances that General Lee was forced to surrender, and the wonder is, not that he surrendered at that time,
but that for six consecutive days, with a half-starved and
defectively armed force of about thirty thousand men, he
repulsed the repeated assaults of the immense army that
was gradually enveloping him, and successfully conducted
the retreat of his army for many miles over difficult roads,
through a country where it was impossible to obtain food
for man or beast.

As we have before stated, General Lee bade farewell to
his troops in a **touching address, and as** it embodies a just

and exalted tribute to the valor and patriotism of those to
whom this work is dedicated, we believe that it will find a
fitting place in these pages, and, therefore, deem it unnecessary to apologize to the **reader for giving a** copy of the
address, which was as follows:

'GENERAL ORDERS, **No. 9.**

"HEADQUARTERS ARMY OF NORTHERN VIRGINIA,
April 10th, 1865.

"After four **years** of arduous service, marked by unsurpassed courage and fortitude, the Army of Northern Virginia
has been compelled to yield to overwhelming numbers and
resources. I need not tell the brave **survivors of so** many
hard-**fought** battles, who **have remained steadfast to** the
last, that I have consented to the result from no distrust of
them. But, feeling that valor and devotion could accomplish nothing that could compensate for the loss that must
have attended the continuance of the contest, I determined
to avoid the useless sacrifice of those whose past services
have endeared them to their countrymen. **By the** terms of
the agreement, officers and men can **return to their homes,**
and remain **until exchanged. You will take with you the**
satisfaction that proceeds from the consciousness **of** duty
faithfully performed. I earnestly **pray** that a merciful God
will extend to you his blessing and protection.

"With an increasing admiration of your constancy and
devotion to your country and a grateful remembrance of
your kind and generous consideration of myself, I bid you
all an affectionate farewell.

"R. E. LEE,
General."

By the terms of the surrender, couriers and mounted men
of the artillery and cavalry, whose horses were owned by
them, were allowed to retain them, and as Ashton's horse
belonged to him, he was permitted to keep the animal, and
shortly after the surrender of the army he rode out to
where the 4th Georgia regiment was encamped, in search of
Carrington, but failed to find him, as he had left for Richmond. Returning to where the small remnant of W. H. F.
Lee's division had bivouacked, Ashton dismounted and
began to make preparations for his departure, and the

reader will readily understand that his place of destination
was to be Richmond, which, now **that** the Confederacy
had practically fallen, contained in the person of Ruth Middleton, all that to him made life worth living. **His first act**
was to seek out **among the** disbanded troops every member
of his company for **the** purpose of personally bidding them
good-bye, and, although there were but few **of** them left,
this **occupied some time, for each** one of them **had some**
special and kindly words of adieu for Ashton, whom they
greatly honored and admired. These leave-takings were intensely sad, and men who had borne the brunt of battle **for
four** years and never quailed under shot and shell or shrunk
from threatened sabre-stroke, were **now** overcome by
emotion, and could not restrain their tears at the thought
of this final parting and the crushing calamity which had
caused it. When Ashton had bidden his comrades good-bye,
he mounted his horse and rode off toward Richmond,
where he arrived in the afternoon of the third day thereafter, and about six hours **after Carrington had reached the**
city. Having **secured a lodging place for himself and**
accommodations for his horse, he at once repaired to **the**
residence of Mrs. Slaughter. There he found **Carrington
and his wife** and Ruth Middleton, and, notwithstanding
their sorrowful surroundings, the meeting was a **happy one.**
The soft love-light which he saw in Ruth's **tender and
trustful eyes, and the glad welcome** which she gave him as
he grasped **her hand, made Ashton** almost forget, for the
moment, **the calamity that had** befallen his country, and he
thought **only of his supreme** happiness in possessing the
perfect **love of the** pure and noble woman before him.

After their greetings **were over, the friends** began to discuss their plans for **the immediate** future, and **it was
promptly decided that** the party should leave for Georgia
as soon as preparations for their departure could be made.

In view of the **fact** that Confederate money had become
worthless, the matter of arranging for the payment of the
traveling expenses of the ladies and providing for their
comfort during the journey home, at once suggested itself
to the minds of **Ashton** and Carrington, but they refrained
from mentioning it in the presence of the former. As soon

as they were alone, Ashton mentioned the matter to Carrington and arranged a settlement of it. He informed the latter that he had not had occasion to spend all of the money which he borrowed from Mr. R——, and still had some of the same; that he intended selling his horse in Richmond, as it would be difficult and perhaps impossible to obtain transportation for the animal, and that he would thus have ample means to defray the traveling expenses of the ladies, and requested that Carrington accept an amount sufficient for that purpose, concealing from the ladies the source from which it had been obtained. Carrington agreed to this, and the matter was thus arranged between them.

Ashton succeeded in selling his horse the next day and it was with regret and sadness that he parted with the animal for, although he had owned him only about six months, he had become greatly attached to the faithful creature, and nothing but necessity would have induced him to sell the horse. He exacted of the purchaser a promise that he would take good care of him, and that if at any time within the next twelve months he should decide to sell the animal, he would write Ashton at B——, giving him the privilege of purchasing him.

By the following morning our friends were ready to leave Richmond. Ruth had made a final visit to the hospital and taken leave of her patients, and the many grateful thanks for her kindness to them, and the fervent wishes for her happiness which were mingled with their parting words, showed how truly and deeply they had become attached to her during the time she had patiently and tenderly ministered to their necessities.

After warmly thanking the Slaughters for their many acts of kindness and bidding them an affectionate good-bye, our friends were driven to the railway station, and were soon on the way to their Southern home. Their journey was comparatively slow in consequence of the damage that had been recently done by military operations against the railroads south of Richmond, but in the course of a week they arrived at B——. A few days thereafter the army of General Joseph E. Johnston, in North Carolina, surrendered to General Sherman, and this event practically terminated the war, as farther resistance to the Federal troops east of the Mississippi was impracticable, and the Confederate force under General Kirby Smith in the Trans-Mississippi department was too small to successfully prolong the struggle.

In the meantime, Ashton had not wasted a single day in fruitless regrets at the fate of the cause for which he had bravely contended for four years, but accepted the result of the struggle as a calamity that must be patiently and courageously endured, and its disastrous consequences overcome by bold and manly effort.

Hence, on the day after his arrival in B——, Ashton began to make arrangements for resuming the practice of his profession. He sought an interview with the gentleman to whom he had sold his law library just before leaving B—— to join the Confederate army, and informed him that he desired to repurchase it, but was unable to do so at that time, and would have to ask indulgence until he could make the money to pay for the books. As the gentleman had perfect confidence in Ashton's integrity, and also in his professional ability, he unhesitatingly sold him the books and granted the requested indulgence. Having thus secured a library, Ashton immediately opened an office, and through the medium of the village paper announced that he had resumed the practice of law.

On arriving in B——, Carrington and his wife had gone home with Ruth, intending to remain there only a few days and then proceed to E——, his former place of residence, where he expected to resume the practice of medicine. But the existence of certain circumstances, that were either unknown or not considered at the time, caused a complete change in their plans. In order that the reason for this change may be fully understood, it will be necessary for us to give the reader some account of the financial affairs of Ruth Middleton and her cousin Bertha, and in so doing, we will have to begin at a period antedating the opening of our story.

CHAPTER XVIII.

James Middleton and Herbert Gray were intimate friends and classmates at the University of Georgia, where they graduated in 1838 After taking a course **of lectures in** Jefferson Medical College, at Philadelphia, and obtaining a diploma from that institution, Middleton began the practice of medicine in B——. Shortly thereafter Gray visited Middleton **and** spent about a month with him. During this time Middleton and Gray formed the acquaintance of Mary and Annie Ansley, daughters and only children of Mr. Robert Ansley, a wealthy planter who resided about three **miles** from B——. They were greatly pleased with **the Misses** Ansley and consequently made frequent visits to "The Oaks," as Mr. Ansley's residence was called on account of the magnificent grove of forest oaks in which his handsome house was situated. As a result of the acquaintance thus begun, the two friends subsequently wooed and won the maidens of their choice, and **the following winter** there was a brilliant and happy double marriage at "The Oaks" in which James Middleton **and Mary Ansley, and** Herbert Gray and Annie Ansley respect**ively,** were the contracting parties.

A few months after this event Mr. Ansley died intestate and, as his wife had previously died, his two daughters became his only heirs and inherited his entire estate as tenants in common. At the time of their marriage there had been no marriage settlement between them and their respective husbands, and hence, under the existing law of the State, the marital rights of their husbands attached to the estate thus inherited and it became the property of the latter. However, Middleton and Gray had no inclination to assert their **rights** to the property, and promptly proposed to relinquish the same and settle the property on their wives. To this the latter objected and, in that spirit of conjugal love and loyalty that characterized the Southern ladies of their class in those days, insisted that nothing be done that was suggestive of a separate existence of husband and wife. Their husbands yielded to their wishes in

17

the matter and, as it was desirable that the large and valuable plantation left by Mr. Ansley should not be divided, it
was arranged between Middleton and Gray that they
would jointly cultivate it as tenants in common. In accordance with this arrangement, they employed an active
and intelligent farmer to take charge of the plantation and
the numerous slaves thereon, and conduct all of the farming operations, Gray and his wife taking up their residence
at "The Oaks," and Middleton and his wife remaining
in B——.

This arrangement was harmoniously and profitably
carried out for many years and indeed until the death of
the parties to it, which occurred about three years before
the opening of our story. Middleton and Gray died the
same year, and by their deaths their only children, Ruth
Middleton and Bertha Gray, were doubly orphaned, as
their mothers had died several years before. At this time
Ruth and Bertha were about fifteen years of age, and
shortly after their fathers died Mrs. Martha Foster came
to live with them in B——, as we have before stated, and
had ever since remained in charge of their household
affairs.

The guardian who was appointed for Ruth and Bertha
continued the management of their property just as it had
been managed by their fathers, and it was still undivided
at the time of their return from Richmond. This guardian
was the elderly lawyer to whom Ashton had sold his law
library on leaving B—— for the army and who, as we
stated, was exempt from military duty on account of
physical infirmity. He had been faithful to his trust and
managed the property of his wards as well as could have
been expected under the disadvantageous circumstances incident to the war. Believing in the ultimate triumph of
the Confederate arms and acting in a spirit of loyalty to
the Government, he had each year invested the net income
of his wards' property in Confederate bonds. The invest-
ments thus made proved to be unfortunate, as the result of
the war rendered the bonds entirely worthless, but neither
of his wards blamed him for what he had done, as they
honored the motives that had controlled his conduct, and

knew that he had acted in perfectly good faith toward themselves.

As their slaves had been emancipated and the troops of Sherman, in their march through Georgia the preceding year, had stolen most of the stock and cattle on the plantation, and destroyed all of the farm products on the place, Ruth and Bertha, on arriving at home, found that they had suddenly been reduced from a condition of affluence to a state of comparative poverty; for although their land remained, they had been deprived of the means of cultivating it. However, their condition was much better than that of many other Georgians whose homes lay in the devastating lines of march of General Sherman and his merciless and marauding army, and whose property was entirely destroyed, for some of their faithful and affectionate slaves had, by carrying off and concealing the same, managed to save some of the stock and cattle on the place and sufficient forage to sustain the animals for several months. The family residence at "The Oaks" had also been saved by the forethought of their faithful servants and the deception practiced by the latter on the Federal soldiers, for, on the approach of the Federal army, these negroes induced the white man in charge of the plantation to vacate "the big house," as they called the family residence, and at once took possession of the same, apparently as a place of permanent abode. When the Federal soldiers arrived they found the negroes in possession of the house, and were at once informed by the latter that they intended making it their permanent residence until the return of its owners, who were, as they said, "two secesh gals what jined de Confedrick army, er ruther went ter Richmon' ter nuss rebel sogers." They had carried into the house their bedding, furniture, etc., and begged the soldiers not to turn them out or injure the building, as they wished to live in it. More, perhaps, for the purpose of aiding in the anticipated humiliation of the absent owners on their return, than from any real interest in or regard for the negroes, the Federal soldiers granted their request and refrained from burning the house.

The guardian of Ruth and Bertha had also managed to
preserve a part of their property, which proved of great
value to them on their return. As soon as he ascertained
the routes by which Sherman was marching through Georgia, he had the few bales of cotton then on the plantation
shipped to a point entirely out of the line of Sherman's
march, and it was thus saved from capture.

Immediately after the return of Ruth and Bertha their
guardian had a settlement with them and turned over all
that was left of their estate, as they were now of age and
entitled to the possession of the property. This action
necessitated the making of some arrangement for the management of the property, and Ruth suggested to Bertha
that they should request Carrington to take charge of it.
To this Bertha assented, and when Carrington was informed of their wishes in regard to the matter he promptly
decided to comply with the same. And this is why he
changed his plans and did not proceed to his former home,
to resume the practice of medicine.

Having consented to undertake the management of the
plantation, Carrington at once began to make preparations
for entering upon his new field of labor and, as he had
never had any experience in farming, his first step was to
secure the services of a practical farmer to aid him in his
work. Owing to the great scarcity of cotton in the country, he obtained an unprecedentedly and almost fabulously
high price for the few bales before mentioned, and realized
from their sale about twenty-five hundred dollars. He was
thus enabled to purchase stock, farming implements, etc.,
sufficient to cultivate a considerable part of the plantation,
and also to meet the current expenses of the farm for
awhile. He had no difficulty in securing as many laborers as
he wished, for nearly all of the former slaves on the place
were so much attached to Ruth and Bertha that they were
anxious to remain with and work for them on almost any
terms.

Having made contracts with as many of the negroes as
existing circumstances would authorize him to employ, Carrington immediately began his farming operations. Although it was rather late for the planting of cotton, he

determined to plant as much as could be cultivated with the force at his command, as he was satisfied that the price of cotton would be very high the next winter.

As soon as Carrington had completed his farming arrangements, he and his wife and Ruth Middleton moved out to "The Oaks," the dwelling-house there having been put in proper condition for their reception. Mrs. Foster accompanied them and continued to discharge her accustomed duties as housekeeper.

Although deprived of the luxuries and some of the comforts of life to which they had previously been accustomed, Ruth and Bertha were not only contented but also happy in their country home, and cheerfully practiced such economy as was required by their circumstances and surroundings. As Carrington had the assistance of an experienced farmer in the management of the farm, he was enabled to secure some leisure time nearly every day, and this was spent in reviewing and prosecuting his medical studies, and also in the occasional practice of his profession, to which he was thoroughly devoted.

Being a skillful physician, the success which marked his practice soon gave him an excellent reputation, and in a few months his practice became so extensive that it occupied the greater part of his time and attention.

Ruth and Bertha were greatly interested in everything about the farm, and took an active part in looking after the poultry-yard and dairy department, and by their skillful management of the affairs therein, materially aided in meeting the current expenses of the household. Thus, in a quiet but industrious manner the occupants of "The Oaks" passed the ensuing summer and autumn, the time beng enlivened by frequent visits from their numerous friends in B——. Of this number Ashton was, of course, the most frequent visitor, and the hours which he was thus enabled to spend with Ruth had been to the lovers the happiest of their lives.

He had applied himself closely to the study and practice of his profession and, so far as the number of his clients was concerned, had no cause to complain of his business, but, owing to their impoverished condition and the general scarcity of money, his compensation thus far had been by

no means proportionate to the work he had done. Several
of his cases had been such as required **extensive research**
and the exercise of great skill and judgment in their preparation, and the thorough manner in which **they had been**
prepared, and his skillful and successful conduct of them in
the court-room at once established his reputation as a profound lawyer and an able advocate. Having **thus** rapidly
risen to a high rank in his profession, he felt satisfied that
with the return of prosperous times his practice **would
become lucrative, and he** would have contentedly **awaited**
the arrival of this period but for his earnest longing to **con-**
summate his engagement with Ruth Middleton.

We have seen how his unselfish love had enabled him to
**conquer the promptings of this longing and refrain from
asking Ruth to marry him during the war, and this same
love had now sealed his lips on the subject that was nearest
and dearest to his heart, and caused him to refrain from**
requesting a consummation of their engagement on account
of his comparatively impoverished condition. **He knew**
that Ruth's love for him **was such** that she would **unhesi-**
tatingly marry him even if he were indeed **poverty-stricken,
but he** was unwilling to take advantage of this love, **and
felt that** he had no right to ask her to share his lot until **he
was able to make her** condition in life at least approxi-
mately as comfortable as that to which she had previously
been **accustomed. For a** long time he persistently entertained **this one-sided** view of **the matter, without for a**
moment **considering that, in thus acting, he** was uninten-
tionally doing injustice to Ruth and her unselfish love for
him, and that **to this love belonged the divine right of self-
abnegation and sacrifice.** He would doubtless **have** indefi-
nitely continued thus to view the matter but for the **fact
that** Carrington, who understood his views on the subject,
determined to correct what he conceived to be Ashton's
misconception of his duty toward Ruth in view **of** his unfavorable financial condition.

In pursuance of this purpose, and in the exercise of the
privilege which their intimacy gave him, Carrington soon
spoke to Ashton in regard to his relation to Ruth, expressed
surprise at their long engagement, and asked him why no

steps were being taken to consummate it. Ashton frankly answered his question, and in so doing gave the reasons already mentioned for his conduct in refraining from asking Ruth for a consummation of the engagement. Carrington told him that these reasons, although unselfish in their origin and character, were entirely one-sided, and by no means sufficient to justify his conduct, that Ruth's views on the subject ought to be consulted, and that she should at least have an opportunity for expressing her ideas and wishes in regard to the matter. Not having considered this view of the subject, Ashton was almost startled by Carrington's confident presentation of it, and, of course, did not at first accept its correctness.

Subsequently, however, he realized the reasonableness and correctness of Carrington's views, and determined that he would at least fully explain to Ruth why he had not requested a consummation of their engagement, and let the manner in which she received his explanation decide his future conduct in regard to the matter. Having formed this determination, Ashton promptly proceeded to carry it out, and visited Ruth the following day for that purpose.

On arriving at "The Oaks" he found that Bertha had accompanied Carrington on a visit to one of his patients, and that he would, therefore, have an opportunity for a private and uninterrupted conversation with Ruth without appearing to have sought it. Ruth's welcome was as warm as the most exacting lover could have wished, and the bright and happy smile that illumined her face on meeting Ashton was a renewed assurance of the fact that she loved him with her whole soul, and naturally tended to hasten the explanation which he had come to make. Hence, their happy greetings had scarcely ended before he began to unbosom himself in regard to the object of his visit. After reminding her of his all-absorbing love for her, and reiterating his often repeated assurance as to the unspeakable happiness which her love had brought to him, he told her how, for her sake, he had refrained from asking her to marry him during the war, as he could then offer her nothing but his love, and how, for similar reasons, he had for months past been daily battling with the intense longing to make her his wife, as his circumstances were such that he was unwilling to ask her to share his lot, which was so much less favorable than that to which she had always been accustomed. He then stated that although he was satisfied that she understood his past conduct and the motives which prompted it, he felt that in justice to her and to himself he ought to frankly converse with her in regard to the matter and fully explain, as he was then doing, why he had refrained from asking for a consummation of their engagement, and assure her that in thus acting he had been postponing his own happiness in order that he might become the better fitted to secure her own.

With quiet mien and downcast eyes Ruth had listened to Ashton's words, and when he finished she modestly looked up her eyes beaming with the unmistakable and yet indescribable light of love, and her cheeks roseate with blushes, and said:

"Yes, darling, I have all the while understood why you refrained from asking for a consummation of our engagement, and I appreciate and honor the motive that has prompted you in so doing; but if you had fully comprehended the workings of a woman's heart, the vicarious character of her love, and the delight which she experiences in making sacrifices for the object of her affections, you would not have so long delayed your explanation and the opportunity now afforded me for assuring you that I will gladly share your lot in life as soon as you may wish, and would willingly do this were you so poor that our future home should be but a hovel."

"Then, my noble and generous darling," joyously said Ashton, "as the sacrifice which you are ready to make will be one that love not only prompts, but delights in making, I will for once be selfish in my love and ask you to complete my happiness by becoming my wife at an early date."

Ruth willingly promised compliance with his request, and before Ashton left the wedding day way fixed for the latter part of December.

Ashton had long been happy in the possession of Ruth's love, but, as he rode back to B—— at sunset on that November afternoon, his heart was filled with inexpressible joy at the thought that he would so soon be blessed with the constant companionship and daily caresses of the woman who was dearer to him than life itself. **Although he still regretted,** for Ruth's sake, that **his financial condition was** not more favorable, Ashton no longer allowed thoughts of it to trouble him as they had previously done; for **Ruth's** words had revealed to him that such love as **hers neither** considered nor valued conditions of life except in so far as they gave to **the** person who cherished such affection opportunities for companionship with and devotion to the being on whom **it** had been bestowed. Hence, from this time forward **it** was with a light and **happy heart that he** prosecuted his professional work, **which thereby became all the easier** and pleasanter to him.

Ruth had also been rendered **very happy by the result of** her interview with Ashton, **and was almost glad that he** was comparatively poor, as that fact had enabled her to **manifest the** perfect unselfishness of her love by expressing **her** readiness to share his lot, and would still farther enable her to prove her thorough devotion to him in acts of sacrifice after their marriage.

When Carrington and Bertha returned that evening, Ruth informed **them that the day for her marriage to Ashton** had been fixed, and **the former joyously declared** that for once during the year he would eschew economy and spare no expense in making it **"a royal** wedding" and worthy of the parties to it. **To this** Ruth demurred, stating that she did **not** wish any unnecessary expense incurred in preparations for the event, and preferred that there should be no unusual display on the occasion; but Carrington **good-naturedly,** yet firmly told her that, **although** it was to be her wedding, he proposed to "boss it," and was bent on having **his** way in regard **to the** affair, and she finally yielded to **his** wishes. **As the intervening time** was short, preparations for the approaching marriage were at once begun, and among the first of these was the arrangement **by** Ruth and Bertha of a list of those to whom invitations should be sent. Heading this list were the names of **their** Virginia friends, **Mrs.** Slaughter's family, Belle Preston, **and** Lieutenants **Preston** and Harris. Immediately following these was the name of Miss Annie R——, of New Castle, Delaware, whose presence Ruth knew would give great pleasure to Ashton, and for whom she had, on his account, formed a strong attachment, although she had never seen her. This allusion to Miss R—— reminds us to state that, by practice of great economy, Ashton had saved enough money to refund the amount borrowed by him from her father, and this had been done the month before. Shortly after his return to B——, he had written to Miss R—— renewing his grateful acknowledgment of the inestimable kindness that she had shown him, and this letter led to a correspondence between them which was still in progress.

About the first of December Ashton received from the gentleman in Richmond, to whom he had sold his horse, a letter in which the gentleman informed him that he had decided to dispose of the animal and, in accordance with his promise, would give Ashton the privilege of repurchasing him. Unfortunately Ashton could not spare the money for this purpose and, with a feeling of disappointment and sadness, wrote the gentleman that he was not at that time prepared to purchase the animal. His disappointment was great and he naturally mentioned the matter to his friend Carrington, telling him how anxious he had been to recover his horse. Carrington promptly offered to loan him the money for the purpose of repurchasing the animal; but Ashton declined his offer, stating that he was unwilling to incur any debt except in a case of absolute necessity, especially in view of his approaching marriage and the increased responsibilities that he would thereby assume. In a conversation with Bertha and Ruth the following day Carrington mentioned this matter, and told them how sorry he was that Ashton had been disappointed in failing to recover his horse, and expressed regret that he would not accept a loan of the money necessary to purchase the animal. At the time Ruth did no more than express her sympathy for Ashton in his disappointment; but as soon as she could speak with Carrington privately, she requested him to write at once and purchase the horse for her, stating that she intended that Ashton should have the animal, and wished to give it to him as a Christmas present. In com-

pliance with Ruth's request, Carrington immediately wrote
to the owner of the horse, inclosing a check for the price of
the animal and explaining that he was purchasing the horse
for Ashton and wished him shipped so that he would arrive
at B—— the day before Christmas. In a few days Carrington received a letter from the owner of the horse, acknowledging the receipt of the purchase money for the animal
and stating that he would be shipped in accordance with
the instructions given. On receiving information of this
fact, Ruth was greatly pleased, and, in anticipation, re-
joiced over the agreeable surprise which she would thus be
enabled to provide for Ashton.

CHAPTER XIX.

Christmas had been fixed as the time for Ruth's marriage,
and the wedding guests from a distance arrived three days
before that time. Mrs. Slaughter and Randolph could not
come and sent their regrets by Kate. The latter came in
company with Belle Preston, Lieutenants Preston and Harris, and Miss Annie R——, who had joined the other members of the party in Richmond by an arrangement previously made at Ruth's suggestion. The two gentlemen
stopped with Ashton in B——, and the ladies of the party
became the guests of Ruth and Bertha at "The Oaks." The
meeting between the latter and their guests was a joyous
one, and the greeting which Ruth extended to Miss R——
was no less cordial than that given to the other girls. As
before stated, she had already formed a strong attachment
for this girl whom she had never seen, and now, on looking
into her pure and noble face, she felt assured that this attachment would become still stronger with an increased
knowledge of her character.

The preparations for Ruth's marriage had been vigorously
prosecuted, and at the time at which the guests arrived
there was but little to do outside of finishing the house
decorations, and in the completion of those the visitors
took an active and efficient part. While engaged in this
work the following day the ladies were interrupted by the
arrival of visitors from B——, who proved to be Lieutenants Preston and Harris and Doctor George Hardy, a
young physician with whom Carrington had recently
formed a partnership on account of the fact that his practice had so greatly increased he needed an assistant. On
discovering in what work the ladies were engaged, the gentlemen expressed regret that their visit had been made at an
inopportune time, and, suggesting that they would call
again, were about to retire, when Kate Slaughter informed
them that they could not possibly have come at a more op-
portune moment, as their assistance was just then greatly
needed, and immediately pressed them into service. They
readily and gracefully yielded obedience to her command,

and were soon busily engaged in assisting their fair companions in the work of decorating the **house**. As Kate Slaughter naturally appropriated Preston as the person to whom she had the best right to "issue orders," **and Harris,** following the promptings of his heart, having offered his services to Belle Preston, it fell to Hardy's lot to assist the other ladies. He was too gallant to discriminate between them in the offers of his services, but Ruth and Bertha soon managed to make themselves so indispensable to each other that he was left free to render constant assistance to Miss R——. In speaking to Hardy of Miss R——'s expected presence **at** Ruth's marriage, Carrington had told him of the circumstances under which Ashton had formed her **acqu**aintance, and the services which she had rendered the latter and other Confederate soldiers in the hospital at Washington, and Hardy had naturally become greatly interested in her, and formed a strong desire to meet her. In the course of the conversation that occurred between them while he was assisting Miss R—— with the decorations, Hardy alluded to what Carrington had told him of her services at the hospital in Washington, **and** manifested so much interest in the matter that she was led to speak freely and at length concerning her experience in nursing the sick and wounded Confederate soldiers who came under her **care.** This experience in some instances had been inexpressibly sad, and the recollection of the same was even then harrowing to her heart. Indeed, she could scarcely refrain **from** weeping as she told of the intense physical suffering of some stalwart soldier who had been stricken down in the full strength of manhood, and of the still greater mental anguish **of** some beardless boy who had been dangerously wounded in battle, and, having lost all hope of recovery, daily longed for the presence of his parents and lamented the heartrending grief which they would experience when they learned that he had died in a strange land, without having had their loving presence and sympathy to sustain him in his last moments. Hardy was deeply affected by the recital of such incidents in the experience of Miss R——, and, being a physician and accustomed to death-bed scenes, he was fully capacitated to understand and appreciate the

ordeals through which she had passed, and his heart was
filled with admiration akin to homage for this pure and
noble Northern girl who had thus endured the severest
trials, and devoted herself to the service of Southern
soldiers because she believed that they were **suffering in**
a just cause. By both word and look he **showed how**
much he appreciated her noble deeds, and how highly
he honored her for what she had done, and indeed **was so**
enthusiastic in his manifestation of this appreciation that
his expression of the same was only stopped by the **discov-**
ery that her cheeks were suffused with blushes. He **imme-**
diately apologized for his seeming lack of consideration **in**
thus embarrassing her, and explained his conduct by stating
that his admiration for her singularly unselfish devotion to
a cause that was inexpressibly dear to his heart, had so en-
thused him that for the moment **he** had forgotten that
praises due to modesty's achievements should always be
paid by proxy. **The explanation was, of course, satis-**
factory to Miss R,——and she soon **recovered** from her temporary embarrassment and continued her conversation with
Hardy in an easy and unconstrained manner.

Under the deft handiwork of the ladies and the less skillful
but efficient labors of the gentlemen, the task of decorating
the house rapidly progressed; but as the decorations were
to be quite elaborate, and extensive, they could not be finished **during the forenoon, and the gentlemen** were
informed **that they must remain to** dinner and aid in com-
pleting the work that afternoon. To this they readily assented, and in the course of the afternoon the work of
decorating the house was fully finished. It had been done
in such a manner as to amply repay those participating in
the same for the time and labor expended in the work; for
the wreaths and festoons of cedar, the beautiful branches
of holly with their bright red berries, and the fresh green
sprigs of mistletoe, which graced the walls of the parlors,
dining-room, and spacious hall, and the luxuriant exotic
plants and beautiful native flowers that were scattered in
graceful profusion throughout the house, presented a sight
that would have satisfied the most critical eye, and delighted the heart of a veritable *connoisseur* of the beautiful.

On taking leave of the ladies that afternoon the gentlemen told them that, although they had been in their company all day, the service into which they had been pressed had really prevented them from making their contemplated visit, and for this reason, and also as a reward for their labors, they would claim the privilege of calling after tea, but for the fact that the ladies would doubtless need a full night's rest after the fatiguing labors of the day. Kate Slaughter, in her frank and straightforward way, promptly informed them that she was glad to see that they had been so considerate of the comfort of her companions and herself; "for," said she, "you have thereby saved us from the embarrassment of having to decline such a visit, as I assure you we would not in our tiredcondition see any one to-night—— not even our sweethearts."

Ruth's wedding morn dawned bright and clear, and, although it was Christmas day, it was busily spent at "The Oaks' in final preparations for the marriage that evening, and the wedding feast that was to follow the same. However, the occupants of "The Oaks" did not, in the midst of the bustle and activity incident to the approaching event, either forget or forego the accustomed Christmas dinner, which was enlivened by the presence of their friends from B——, and was all that could be desired, both as to the quantity and quality of the viands and the excellency of the *cuisine.*

The hour appointed for the marriage was 8 o'clock that evening, and by 7 o'clock the guests began to arrive. On approaching the house they were greeted by a beautiful and attractive sight, as the magnificent grove surrounding the building was lighted up with Chinese lanterns, and every room in the mansion was brilliantly illuminated. We have alluded to the beauty of the interior decorations at the time they were completed, and they were now rendered far more beautiful by the bright lamplight falling upon them; and hence the interior of the building presented a vision of beauty that was almost bewildering in its brilliancy and loveliness. The spacious double parlors had been converted into one large room by drawing back the sliding doors that divided them, and soon the room was thronged with joy-

ous and expectant guests, as it was there that the ceremony
was to be performed. At one end of the room a beautiful
bower had been constructed of vines and **branches of vari-**
ous evergreens, and from its center hung the marriage bell,
composed of **bride roses.** At the appointed **hour, Ruth en-**
tered the room leaning on the arm of Ashton, and they
immediately took their positions under the marriage bell,
where the ceremony that united their future lives and per-
fected their happiness was impressively performed by Dr.
Robert Hastings, a distinguished divine, and a **personal**
friend of Ashton's, who resided in B——. As soon as **the**
ceremony was over, there was a hasty gathering of **the**
guests around the bride and groom to extend to the latter
their cordial congratulations on the priceless prize which he
had won, and to wish the former a happy and cloudless life.
Shortly after the last of the numerous guests had participated in this pleasant duty, supper was announced, and the
company repaired to **the spacious dining-room, where** they
found awaiting them such an abundance and variety of the
choicest and most delicious viands as would have furnished
an appropriate feast for royalty itself; for in this, **as in**
other arrangements for Ruth's marriage, Carrington had
carried out his determination to spare no expense in making it a royal wedding. Ample justice was done to the wedding feast by those for whom it had been prepared, and at
its close they returned to the parlors in a happy state of
mind, that fully fitted them for entering with zest into the
enjoyment of the farther pleasures of the evening. Although the company was a large one, its members were
perfectly congenial, and were soon freely and familiarly
chatting with each other in groups or in pairs, according
as accident or inclination had drawn them together. **Thus**
the time was spent in friendly chat, and merry jest, varied
by music, and an occasional dance. At the suggestion of
Kate Slaughter, the festivities of the evening were closed
with "the Virginia Reel," and the dance was executed with
such vivacity and *abandon* that the rapidly whirling forms
of the dancers presented a sight that was really bewildering
to those who were looking on. At its close the company
began to disperse, and soon the last of the guests had
departed.

A few hundred yards in the rear of the mansion there was a large group of cabins called "The Negro Quarter," and from that direction the sound of music and dancing could be distinctly heard, for early in the evening their occupants had assembled at several of the larger cabins to celebrate "Miss Ruth's weddin'" and the arrival of Christmas, and were still making merry the passing hours in honor of these important events.

Shortly after the guests had retired from the mansion, the music and dancing at "the quarter" ceased, and soon the heads of families among the occupants of the cabins silently repaired to "the big house" to hang up their stockings in anticipation of the accustomed visit of "Sandy Claws," as they called the patron saint of Christmas-tide. Their reason for not having done this the preceding night was the fact that it was Sunday night, and Carrington told them to defer the matter on that account, and also on account of the approaching marriage, laughingly suggesting that when "Sandy" came and found that there had been a wedding in the house he would thereby be rendered unusually jolly and good-humored, and, consequently, they might expect him to be more liberal with his gifts. Hence it was that "the darkies" had not hung up their stockings as usual on Christmas eve, and were now about to engage in that, to them, delightful and momentous occupation. These "stockings" were not stockings at all, but capacious bags, and they were soon dangling from every door-knob, and other projection at the rear of the house, or deposited on the floor of the back veranda. Having thus disposed of them, their owners promptly departed and, in a spirit of loyal trust in the "Massa" and "Missus" of the mansion, resisted a natural curiosity to watch for "Sandy's" appearance, and at once repaired to their homes. Their confidence was by no means misplaced, for in a few moments after their departure, Carrington and Bertha had with lavish hands performed the part of Santa Claus and deposited in the various bags, presents that would delight the hearts of both young and old on the morrow.

In the murky gray of the early dawn numerous figures could be seen issuing from the cabins at the negro quarter and swiftly moving toward the mansion house. The reader will readily understand that they were "the darkies" who had "hung up their stockings" the night before, and were now, as they expressed it, "gwine ter see what Sandy Claws hed fotched 'em." The eagerness with which they plunged their hands into their respective bags, feeling of and peering at the contents, and the grins of satisfaction and exclamations of delight with which they drew forth and held up to view some article that was especially acceptable to them, formed a picture of simple but perfect happiness that was both refreshing to the sight, and suggestive of the fact that, although the result of the war had destroyed the relation of master and slave in the South, it had not severed the ties of sympathy and affection which had long existed between them.

The occupants of "The Oaks" rose with the sun that morning and, after partaking of an early breakfast, began to discuss the question as to how they should spend the day, or at least the forenoon. Carrington told them that he regretted that the absence of snow would prevent the formation of a sleighing party, such as they had on the day after his and Bertha's marriage, and proposed in lieu thereof, that they form a riding party, suggesting that a gallop of ten or twelve miles in the crisp morning air would be delightful exercise, and also afford the visitors an opportunity for seeing a part of the country with which they were not familiar. His proposition was promptly accepted, and the execution of the plan suggested was only delayed to await the arrival of Preston, Harris, and Hardy, who had told the ladies, on leaving the night before, that they would ride out that morning to ascertain whether they had survived the effects of the evening's dissipation. The ladies at once retired to their rooms to don their riding habits, and Carrington gave orders to his groom to saddle the horses. Ashton's horse, which, as before stated, Ruth had repurchased for him, had safely arrived at B—— and been brought out to "The Oaks" without Ashton's knowledge, and when Carrington proposed the riding party that morning, he had in view the opportunity which it would afford Ruth for giving her husband the pleasant surprise she had prepared for him, and also the

fact that he would thus be enabled to immediately enjoy
her present. About the time at which the ladies reappeared
in their riding suits, Preston, **Harris,** and Hardy rode up,
and in a few moments the horses ordered by Carrington
were brought around in front of the house. The ladies of
the party, together with Carrington **and Ashton, were**
standing in a group on the veranda, and after hearty greetings had been exchanged between them and the gentlemen
who had just arrived, Carrington said:

"Everything is now ready for our jaunt, and in order to
save the gentlemen from the embarrassment of selecting
their partners, I will make the selections for them. Doctor
Hardy will escort Miss **R——,** Lieutenant Harris shall be
Miss Preston's companion, and Lieutenant Preston will
act as Miss Slaughter's escort. **As for Ashton and** myself,
fate has already selected our partners, and neither of us is
as yet inclined to 'fly in the face of fortune' with a view to
changing them. 'The troop'— excuse the military phrase,—
will now mount and ride off in the order named."

The horses selected for Miss R——, Belle Preston, **and**
Kate Slaughter were then in turn **led up to the horse-block,**
and the respective escorts of **those ladies assisted them to**
mount and rode off in their company. **After assisting his**
wife to mount, **Ashton stepped back to receive from the**
groom the horse intended for him. On his approach **the**
horse pricked up his ears, began to sniff excitedly and **in a**
moment was whinnying with delight. Surprised by **these**
manifestations of pleasure, and startled by something
strangely familiar in the neigh of the horse, Ashton looked
up quickly, took a hasty but critical survey of the animal,
and **almost instantly felt that the** faithful friend with
whom **he had so reluctantly parted, stood before him. In**
order to be perfectly sure of this, he approached the animal,
placed his hand on his neck **and in a low** tone of voice said:
"Mosby." **On** hearing the **name the** horse renewed his
joyous neighing and gave other **manifestations of** recognition and delight. Turning to Carrington, Ashton said:

"I have long known, Phil, that you were one of the best
friends I have ever had, but this act of generous thought
fulness in securing for me my dear and faithful horse sur-

passes any of your many deeds of kindness, and I shall never cease to be grateful for the same."

"I am really sorry and ashamed, too, John," said Carrington, "that I do not deserve your thanks and gratitude; for while I might say, without flattering myself, that I would gladly have thus befriended you, the truth of the matter is that I never thought of so doing, and you will have to repeat your thanks and expressions of gratitude to one who is far more thoughtful and considerate of your happiness than even 'one of your best friends', as you have called me."

As he finished this remark Carrington glanced toward Ruth and, hastily mounting his horse, rode off with his wife, whom he had assisted to mount while Ashton was examining his horse. Ashton immediately rushed forward to Ruth and, seizing her hand, overwhelmed her with thanks and expressions of gratitude for the generous kindness and loving thoughtfulness which she had manifested in his behalf, and concluded by whispering to her:

"But for the fact that your mouth is at present beyond my reach, you doubtless would incur the danger of being smothered with kisses."

Ruth simply said:

"I am inexpressibly happy that it was in my power thus to please my precious husband and prove my devotion to him on this gladsome day."

Ashton made no reply, except by an adoring look into Ruth's eyes, and, having mounted his horse, he and Ruth, awed into silence by the great gladness that filled their souls, rode off and soon joined the other members of the party. Although Hardy had, "under orders," ridden away from "The Oaks" at the head of the party, he had even thus early, in some way, managed to drop behind, and was now riding with Miss R——in the rear of the other couples. Appreciating the situation, Ashton and Ruth promptly passed the laggards and left them to enjoy the advantageous position which Hardy had chosen. That he constantly maintained it during the remainder of the ride, and made full use of the opportunity thus afforded him for private communion with his companion, our readers will

readily infer, and we suppose that none of them will blame
the infatuated fellow, for, similarly situated, they would
doubtless have done the same.   There was never a merrier
or more congenial riding party, and, joyously unconscious
of the flight of time or the **distance traveled, they covered**
many miles in their exhilarating gallop before turning **their**
faces homeward. In their jaunt they passed the place **of**
Ruth's dangerous adventure with **her** runaway horse, **and,**
while crossing the bridge that had replaced the one washed
away by **the** freshet and which now spanned the chasm
toward which Ruth was being rapidly borne when rescued
by Ashton, both Ruth and Ashton were vividly reminded,
not **only** of that fearful adventure, but also of the subsequent
results of the same, which had served **to bridge the chasm**
of grief and gloom separating Ashton **from society, and**
eventually united their hearts and lives in bonds **of perfect**
love, and they almost blessed the memory of the angry flood
whose raging waters had thus indirectly contributed to the
crowning of their lives with happiness.

On returning to "The Oaks," **the** riding party became
aware of the fact that the morning's **jaunt** had sharpened
their appetites, **and even** Hardy did **not** slight the sumptuous dinner that was served.

The lady visitors **had** promised to spend two or three
weeks with Ruth and Bertha, and as Ashton and Ruth had decided to remain at "The Oaks," during their stay he insisted
that Preston and Harris should also make it their home
during that time. A similar invitation was extended **by**
Carrington to Hardy and, the invitations having been accepted, the luggage of the three young men was sent for
that afternoon and they were duly installed as guests at
"The Oaks." The house-party thus formed naturally and
readily planned numerous and pleasant festivities for the
holidays, but we will not weary the reader with **an account**
of them. While the arrangement that had **been made**
proved a source **of** pleasure to **all** concerned, **it** was
especially delightful to George Hardy, as it gave him ample
opportunities for cultivating the acquaintance of Miss
R——, in whom he felt the deepest interest and for whom
his admiration was daily increasing. Owing to Hardy's

profession and its similarity to the occupation in which
Miss R—— had been engaged when at the hospital in Washington, there was a bond of sympathy between them that
was naturally conducive to mutual interest in each other;
and this fact, together with Hardy's frank manner, ingenu-
ous disposition, generous nature and bright intellect, had
rendered his society exceedingly agreeable to Miss R—— and
awakened in her mind the highest admiration for him.
Moreover, while she was in many respects an exceptional
woman, she was not an exception to the majority of her
sex as to the sense of gratification that they experience in
receiving the sincere and unselfish admiration of true and
noble men, and the reciprocal emotions which are usually
thereby awakened. Hence the admiration which Hardy
felt for Miss R——, and made no effort to conceal, was by
no means an unimportant factor in the forces which were
operating for the winning of her favor. Hardy made full
use of the opportunities which his stay at "The Oaks"
afforded him for companionship with Miss R——, and
managed to secure many hours of private communion with
her through the medium of morning walks in the adjacent
woodlands and horseback rides over the surrounding country. He soon realized beyond all doubt that which, since
the day of the riding party, he had felt to be true, viz.:
That he deeply and devotedly loved this beautiful and noble Northern girl whose life had so unexpectedly touched his
own, and he determined that, if it were possible so to do,
he would win her heart and hand. Acting purely in accordance with the promptings of his heart, and the inclinations
of his warm and impulsive nature, Hardy, without knowing it, adopted the best possible plan for the accomplishment of his object by casting caution to the winds and
unreservedly manifesting his ardent admiration for Miss
R——, without a thought as to what would be the consequences of his conduct; for he thus plainly showed the perfect purity and unselfish *abandon* of his love, which was
being freely and lavishly bestowed without any calculation
as to the chances of its return. To that extent, although a
modest man, he became a bold wooer, and most flesh-and-
blood women like such. Indeed, as some one has said:

"**That** which women most love is **love**," and, therefore, the undemonstrative, cautious, and calculating lover woos in vain the woman who is worth winning; for he really does not know *how to love*, and fails to give spontaneously and unreservedly that which she most desires. Hence it was that George Hardy, by the ardor of his wooing, showed Miss R—— that he knew how to love, and thus increased his chances for winning her heart. His wooing was prosecuted with unabated ardor and when, a few days before the end of her visit, he declared his love in burning words, telling her that it had become a part of his life, and asked her if she could give him her heart in return, and become his wife, he did not receive "nay" for his answer.

A few days thereafter the house-party at "The Oaks" was broken up by the departure of the guests, and Ashton and his wife took up their residence in B——.

We have almost reached the end of our story and there remains but little more to be told. In view of what has been said respecting the relations existing between Lieutenant Preston and Kate Slaughter and Lieutenant Harris and Belle Preston, the reader has long since naturally and correctly surmised that a yet closer relation would eventually be formed between them; and hence it is only necessary to state that the respective couples were happily married shortly after their return to Virginia.

A few months later George Hardy claimed the fulfilment of the promise which he had obtained from Miss R——, and brought her to B—— as his bride.

Carrington's farming operations were successfully continued for the benefit of Ruth and Bertha through the medium of an efficient and faithful agent, and, as the country gradually recuperated from the disastrous results of the war, his and Hardy's practice increased in extent and lucrativeness.

The same was true as to Ashton's practice, and it was only a few years before his accumulation of wealth deprived Ruth of the pleasure which she had often enjoyed in making personal sacrifices for his sake and thereby assisting him to recover from the injurious consequences of the Civil War.

THE END.